OXFORD WORLD'S CLASSICS

CATHARINE
AND OTHER WRITINGS

JANE AUSTEN was born at Steventon, Hampshire, in 1775, the daughter of a clergyman. At the age of nine she was sent to school at Reading with her elder sister Cassandra, who was her lifelong friend and confidante, but she was largely taught by her father. She began to write for recreation while still in her teens. In 1801 the family moved to Bath, the scene of so many episodes in her books and, after the death of her father in 1805, to Southampton and then to the village of Chawton, near Alton in Hampshire. Here she lived uneventfully until May 1817, when the family moved to Winchester seeking skilled medical attention for her ill-health, but she died two months later. She is buried in Winchester Cathedral.

Her best-known novels are *Sense and Sensibility* (1811), *Pride and Prejudice* (1813), *Mansfield Park* (1814), *Emma* (1816), and *Northanger Abbey* and *Persuasion*, both published posthumously in 1818.

MARGARET ANNE DOODY is Andrew W. Mellon Professor in the Humanities and Professor of English at Vanderbilt University. Her publications include *A Natural Passion: A Study of the Novels of Samuel Richardson*, *The Daring Muse: Augustan Poetry Reconsidered*, *Frances Burney: The Life in the Works*, as well as two novels, *Aristotle Detective* and *The Alchemists*. Her most recent work is *The True Story of the Novel* (1996). She has co-edited Oxford World's Classics editions of Fanny Burney's *Cecilia* and *The Wanderer*.

DOUGLAS MURRAY, Associate Professor of English at Belmont University, is the author of essays on Dryden, Richardson, Pope, and other authors of the eighteenth century as well as on English vocal music.

OXFORD WORLD'S CLASSICS

*For almost 100 years Oxford World's Classics have brought
readers closer to the world's great literature. Now with over 700
titles—from the 4,000-year-old myths of Mesopotamia to the
twentieth century's greatest novels—the series makes available
lesser-known as well as celebrated writing.*

*The pocket-sized hardbacks of the early years contained
introductions by Virginia Woolf, T. S. Eliot, Graham Greene,
and other literary figures which enriched the experience of reading.
Today the series is recognized for its fine scholarship and
reliability in texts that span world literature, drama and poetry,
religion, philosophy and politics. Each edition includes perceptive
commentary and essential background information to meet the
changing needs of readers.*

JANE AUSTEN

Catharine
and Other Writings

Edited by
MARGARET ANNE DOODY

and

DOUGLAS MURRAY

With an Introduction by
MARGARET ANNE DOODY

Oxford   New York
OXFORD UNIVERSITY PRESS

Oxford University Press, Great Clarendon Street, Oxford OX2 6DP

Oxford New York

Athens Auckland Bangkok Bogotá Buenos Aires Calcutta
Cape Town Chennai Dar es Salaam Delhi Florence Hong Kong Istanbul
Karachi Kuala Lumpur Madrid Melbourne Mexico City Mumbai
Nairobi Paris São Paulo Singapore Taipei Tokyo Toronto Warsaw
and associated companies in Berlin Ibadan

Oxford is a registered trade mark of Oxford University Press

Editorial material © Margaret Anne Doody and Douglas Murray 1993
Introduction © Margaret Anne Doody 1993

This edition first published as a World's Classics paperback 1993
Reissued as an Oxford World's Classics paperback 1998

British Library Cataloguing in Publication Data
Data available

Library of Congress Cataloging in Publication Data
Austen, Jane, 1775–1817.
Catharine and other writings / Jane Austen: edited by Margaret
Anne Doody and Douglas Murray: with an introduction by Margaret
Anne Doody
p. cm.—(Oxford World's classics)
Includes bibliographical references.
I. Doody, Margaret Anne. II. Murray, Douglas, 1951–
III. Title. IV. Series.
PR4032.D66 1993 823'.7—dc20 92-12787
ISBN 0-19-283521-1

1 3 5 7 9 10 8 6 4 2

Printed in Great Britain by
Caledonian International Book Manufacturing Ltd.
Glasgow

ACKNOWLEDGEMENTS

We wish to express our gratitude to the British Library for allowing us to inspect and transcribe the material in *Volume the Second* and *Volume the Third*, and to the Bodleian Library for allowing us access to the material in *Volume the First*. For other manuscript material we are indebted to the Pierpont Morgan Library, and to the Jane Austen Memorial Trust. We must thank the Henry W. and Albert A. Berg Collection, The New York Public Library, Astor, Lenox, and Tilden Foundations for allowing us to transcribe their copy of the verses 'When Winchester races'. We have good reason to be grateful to the librarians of these institutions, and to the Special Collections Librarian of Mills College. We wish to express particular thanks to Jean Bowden, Curator of the Jane Austen Memorial Trust at Chawton, and to Sally Brown, Curator of Modern Literary Manuscripts at the British Library.

It seems fitting to express here our gratitude to the libraries at our own universities: the Jean and Alexander Heard Library at Vanderbilt University, and the Williams Library at Belmont University, both of Nashville. We are grateful to the librarians at those institutions, especially Jane Thomas at Belmont.

Deirdre Le Faye, Jane Austen's latest biographer, has put herself out to give us assistance and advice, and we want to thank her here. We should like to give personal thanks to the following individuals for their interest in and help with the project: Paula Backscheider, Marilyn Butler, David Gilson, Jocelyn Harris, Richard Harrison, Robert Mack, Peter Sabor, and Florian Stuber.

CONTENTS

INTRODUCTION

EXCEPT for 'Plan of a Novel' and the Prayers, the prose works included in this collection were written by Jane Austen during her adolescence. They represent her earliest surviving works, written for an audience composed of her family and a few close friends. The surviving verses (with one exception, all are 'light verse') were occasional pieces, some of which enjoyed a wider circulation than the prose contents of the notebooks. Most of the surviving verses are of a later date than the notebooks' mock-novels. Jane Austen never, it appears, truly aspired to be a poet, and prose fiction always had first lien on her literary energies.

The author was born in 1775, on 16 December, a 'natal day' later to be sorrowfully commemorated in one of her poems as the anniversary of the death of her close friend Anne Lefroy (see pp. 238–9). Jane Austen's early years were spent in Steventon in Hampshire, where her father, the Revd George Austen, was Rector. The Austens lived unostentatiously in the old-fashioned Rectory; they had not much of the world's wealth, but they had enough to live like gentlefolk. They were not themselves, however, landed gentry, although they were related to members of that important class. Jane Austen's father and all but one of her brothers were men who had to make a living in one of the professions. They had no estate, no rent-roll or tenants. Through her mother's family, the Leighs, Jane Austen had gentle and even aristocratic connections, but the immediate Austen family had to depend on education and industry (as well as upon all possible connections) for advancement.

The great exception was Jane Austen's older brother Edward, who was adopted by relatives of the Revd George Austen. A distant cousin, Mr Thomas Knight, had been sufficiently rich and influential to help his kinsman to the living of Steventon, but his son was to do even more for the family. In the 1780s Thomas Knight's son (another Thomas) and daughter-in-law succeeded to the ownership

of Godmersham Park in Kent. This wealthy couple
eventually adopted Edward; the date of formal adoption is
not certain but it could not have been before 1783. Little
Edward had, however, been a welcome visitor in their
house in his earlier childhood, as his brother Henry
recollected in response to Caroline Austen's questioning:

... they received a letter from Godmersham, begging that little
Edward might spend his Holidays there ... and so he went, and at
the end of the Holidays he came back, as much Edward Austen as
before. But after this, the Summer Holidays, at the least were
spent with the Knights, he being still left to his father's tuition.
Uncle Henry could not say when it was announced in the family
that *one* son was adopted elsewhere—it was, in time, understood to
be. ...[1]

The Thomas Knights in adopting Edward changed his
name to Edward Knight, or Edward Austen Knight.
Edward himself added to the Knight family fortunes by
marrying (in 1791) Elizabeth Bridges, daughter of Sir
Brook Bridges, a wealthy country gentleman. The Knights
were able to give Edward and his bride an estate called
'Rowling' to live upon; upon the death of Mr Thomas
Knight (the younger) his widow, behaving as became a
dowager with a son, moved out of Godmersham. In 1797
Edward came into full possession of the estate. Godmersham
Park was the abode of wealth and elegance, of true gentility
combined with some luxury. Cassandra and Jane visited
Edward and Elizabeth at Godmersham, usually alternately,
as one or the other had to act as companion and caretaker
in the parental home. It is of course fortunate for us that
they did not visit together, for the letters written by Jane
Austen to or from Godmersham give us very clear ideas of
the daily patterns of life at home, and on Edward's estate,
and the differences between them.

[1] This account of Caroline's conversation with Uncle Henry and his
recollection of the process of Edward's absorption into the Godmersham
household is given by William Austen-Leigh and Montagu George Knight,
Chawton Manor and its Owners (London: Smith, Elder & Co., 1911), 157–8,
and quoted by George Holbert Tucker in *A Goodly Heritage: A History of Jane
Austen's Family* (Manchester: Carcanet New Press, 1983), 120.

The story of Edward offered to the young Jane Austen a striking example of the caprices of fortune. There is something fairy-tale-like in the way one child among the eight Austen children was exalted into wealth and status, like a princeling in disguise reclaimed by his true parents. Edward was not even the oldest son. His sober, responsible brother James, the oldest child, was to be educated at Oxford for the clerical life he was expected to follow. James's life was virtuous but not magical. At the other end of the family scale of luck was poor young George Austen, the unknown child, who appears to have been mentally deficient or physically handicapped in some fashion; his life is still a mystery, but we know that he was boarded out and did not live with the family.[2] Francis Austen and Charles Austen were sent away at the very young age customary at the time. They were not sent to a boarding-school, but to the rigours of life as a midshipman. They had to seek their fortunes on literally dangerous waters, during the wars with France, which continued through the later 1790s until the final defeat of Napoleon in 1815. When in 'The History of England' Jane Austen compliments her brother by comparing him with Sir Francis Drake, who 'will be equalled in this or the next Century by one who tho' now but young, already promises to answer all the ardent and sanguine expectations of his Relations and Freinds' (p. 141), she of course knew that this young brother (only one year older than herself) had a long and hazardous way to go before he reached the eminence she jokingly sketches. The compliment on his condition and prospects serves as an encouragement, but she must have guessed that he was sometimes miserably homesick.[3]

We have glimpses of the tastes and manners of various Austen children through Jane Austen's dedication of these

[2] Tucker, who has investigated every member of the family, gives the clearest account of what is still a puzzling matter; see *A Goodly Heritage*, 115–17. George Austen died in 1838 at the age of 72.

[3] See 'Prelude: Frank Austen's Ride', the beginning of Park Honan's *Jane Austen: Her Life* (London: Weidenfeld & Nicolson, 1987), 1–7.

early prose pieces to members of her family. Frank gets not
only 'The Adventures of Mr. Harley' (about another hero
who goes to sea) but also the highly literary 'Jack and
Alice'. The oldest son, James, who is interested in drama
and tries to write plays himself, is the dedicatee of 'The
Visit', the extremely short 'comedy in 2 acts'. The elder
sister Cassandra is the recipient not only of 'The Beautifull
Cassandra' but also of 'The History of England' in which
she was a joint labourer, supplying the illustrations.

Jane Austen was living at home during the time she wrote
the material in the notebooks, entitled by her *Volume the
First, Volume the Second, Volume the Third.* She was to remain at
home, save for brief visits, for the rest of her life, although
'home' was to change. Home ceased to be at Steventon, and
became Bath (to Jane Austen's dismay) upon her father's
retirement in 1801. After her father's death in 1805, when
she and her mother were in straitened circumstances, home
became lodgings in Southampton, and then a little house in
Chawton, in Hampshire, supplied by the now wealthy
Edward. Jane Austen did not, however, remain at home
quite all of her existence, although her only excursions 'into
the world' and away from her family were early ventures
into school life. In 1783, about the time when Edward's
adoption was becoming formalized, as we know from the
group silhouette made at the time (depicting Edward's
father presenting Edward to Mr and Mrs Knight), Jane
Austen was 8 years old. She and her elder (and only) sister
Cassandra were sent to Oxford, to the governance of Mrs
Cawley, widow of a former principal of Brasenose College.
It is strange to think of the child Jane Austen among the
silver-grey pinnacles and dreaming spires (and hard-
drinking undergraduates) of Oxford of that time. Mrs
Cawley was a connection of the Austen parents (who
certainly seem, even for the time, remarkably reluctant to
venture outside the ties of family). She was the sister-in-law
of Mrs Austen's own sister; presumably the family were
trying to help this newly impoverished gentlewoman to
support herself in something like the manner to which she
had been accustomed. Mrs Austen's sister Mrs Cooper, née

Leigh, sent her own daughter, another little Jane, to be cared for and educated by Mrs Cawley.

Mrs Cawley, a very formal and old-fashioned lady, was not loved by any of the children. Perhaps the stiff, fussy, and old-fashioned Mrs Percival of 'Catharine, or the Bower' (pp. 186–229) is in part a portrait of her. Probably because Oxford was expensive, Mrs Cawley removed to Southampton a few months after Jane's arrival in Oxford. This was a most disastrous move. Jane and Cassandra caught what was called 'putrid fever' (probably typhoid). Mrs Cawley did not inform their parents—obviously because she did not want to lose her means of livelihood. Young Jane Cooper had better sense, and informed her mother. Mrs Cooper came in haste with Mrs Austen and removed the girls. Jane Austen nearly died of this 'putrid fever'—and her unfortunate aunt, Mrs Cooper, *did* die of it. This sad and frightening experience lurks behind the comical warning of Isabel to Laura in 'Love and Freindship': 'Beware of the unmeaning Luxuries of Bath and of the Stinking fish of Southampton' (p. 77). Jane may have remembered the terrible illness being laid at the door of Southampton's 'Stinking fish' and bad air.

In 1784 the Austens sent their daughters to school again, to the Abbey School, near Reading. If the 8-year-old Jane Austen, like Catherine Morland at 17, nourished a desire to see a real abbey, that was partly gratified by her school, which was built on the ruins of a medieval priory. The woman who ran the school, the imposingly named Mrs Latournelle, was not in fact qualified to teach French (a major feature of a young gentlewoman's curriculum) as she could not speak it herself—despite her (false) name. This lady was chiefly remarkable for possessing an artificial leg made of cork. The Abbey School has generally been thought to conform to Austen's dry description of a typical girls' school offered in the quick sketch of Mrs Goddard's school in *Emma*:

Mrs. Goddard was the mistress of a School—not of a seminary, or an establishment, or any thing which professed, in long sentences of refined nonsense, to combine liberal acquirements with elegant morality upon new principles and new systems—and where young ladies for enormous pay might be screwed out of health and into vanity—but a real, honest, old-fashioned Boarding-school, where a reasonable quantity of accomplishments were sold at a reasonable price, and where girls might be sent to be out of the way and scramble themselves into a little education, without any danger of coming back prodigies. (I. 18)[4]

Harriet Smith, however, is no very great advertisement for such a school, and if Jane had been required to rely for information and intellectual stimulus on such an uninspired if unpretending place she would have fared badly. The Austens apparently did not think school-education of much importance for their daughters (and perhaps it was too expensive); they brought Jane and Cassandra home the next year.

Most of Jane Austen's education took place at home. Yet there are no signs that Mrs Austen, though of a more cultivated mind and a much higher rank by birth than Mrs Bennet, made any more effort than that excellent mother to form her girls' minds. Jane Austen's education was basically self-education, although extensive self-education would not have been possible without the companionship of a father and elder brother who were lively and educated and liked books. Jane Austen was fortunate in that her father possessed a library. Perhaps she was even more fortunate in the presence of novel-reading neighbours and the occasional lending library. Austen notes the advent of one such source of books, with the opening of a new subscription-library:

As an inducement to subscribe Mrs. Martin tells us that her Collection is not to consist only of Novels, but of every kind of Literature, &c.&c.—She might have spared this pretension to *our* family, who are great Novel-readers and not ashamed of being so. . . . (Letter to Cassandra, 18 Dec. 1798)[5]

We know from Frances Burney's Journals of the lists of books that the young Frances Burney set herself to read.

---

[4] *Emma*, ed. James Kinsley (Oxford, 1989), 32. This, and every other reference to Jane Austen's novels, cites the World's Classics editions.

[5] *Jane Austen's Letters*, ed. R. W. Chapman, 2nd edn. (Oxford, 1979), 38.

Doubtless Jane Austen made such lists too—and felt guilty over not completing them, after the manner of Emma. But there is no reason to doubt Austen's extensive and even encylopaedic knowledge of the modern English novel. Jean-Jacques Rousseau claimed he had read all the major modern novels (at least, all those in French) by the time he was 7;[6] we may believe he was stretching a point or two, and nobody would make an equally hyperbolical claim for Jane Austen. Yet it is evident from her surviving writings that by the end of the decade of the 1780s she was deeply familiar with most of the English fiction of the eighteenth century. She was as fortunate in belonging to a family of 'great Novel-readers' as Mozart was in belonging to a family of musicians. What is even more striking is the young Austen's evident command of the sheer *idea* of fiction in itself. By the time she writes the earliest works of *Volume the First*, pieces such as 'Frederic and Elfrida', 'Jack and Alice', or 'Henry and Eliza', she is entirely aware of thematic patterns and plot structures, or paradigms that could be familiar only to a reader of a multitude of books—and of a *re*-reader, at that. By the time she was 15 (or even 13 or 14—the earliest date suggested for any of the early pieces is 1787), she was as familiar with the workings of fiction as a watchmaker with the interior movements and structures of a clock.

These Juvenilia of Jane Austen exist in three manuscripts, which are three separate notebooks. The titles were given to these 'Volumes' by Jane Austen. *Volume the First*, bound in calf, is sadly worn. Several pages are dated, the most significant date being that at the end: 'End of the first Volume June 3d 1793.' There are no dates attached to the very first pieces in the volume. We also know that Austen went back and used some of the pages remaining in this notebook for later work after the summer of 1793. *Volume the Second* is a finer notebook, bound in white vellum. Jane Austen writes on the contents page, 'Ex dono mei Patris'—

---

[6] Jean-Jacques Rousseau, *Les Confessions*, in *Œuvres complètes* (Paris: Bibliothèque de la Pléiade, 1959), i. 8.

her only recorded utterance in Latin except for the '*in propria persona*' of *Mansfield Park*.[7] Had her father taught her a little Latin? We cannot know. We are on firmer ground in supposing that her father had been so pleased and entertained with the material already appearing in *Volume the First* that he supplied the finer notebook as an encouragement to further productions. Many of the pieces in *Volume the Second* are dated by Jane Austen. 'Love and Freindship' is dated 13 June 1790, and 'The History of England' is dated November 1791. Some twelve pages were removed from this book at some point; the excision took place before the contents page was written out by the author. Jane Austen also numbered her pages continuously through the volume. *Volume the Third* is another vellum notebook; on the first leaf the author wrote, 'Jane Austen— May 6th 1792.' This notebook contains only 'Evelyn' and the ambitious unfinished novel entitled 'Catharine, or the Bower' (originally 'Kitty, or the Bower'). The 'Dedication' of 'Catharine' is dated August 1792. In 1792 Jane Austen was only 17.

The author was truly 'Very Young', as noted by her father. The Revd George Austen wrote on the inside front cover of *Volume the Third*, 'Effusions of Fancy by a very Young Lady Consisting of Tales in a Style entirely new'. Austen's tales are certainly 'in a Style entirely new', but they are not to be described as 'Effusions of Fancy'. They bear all the signs of careful workmanship, and of reworking. It seems most likely that Austen wrote some first version(s) of these works somewhere else, perhaps on scrap paper, and then copied them in a (reasonably) fair hand into the notebooks. This process of writing down itself involved constant revision and rewording, even while a sentence was in progress. The 'Textual Notes' we have supplied in this present edition give the reader an idea of the young Jane Austen's engagement in the process of writing. We wished to give the reader not only a readable printed text, but the

---

[7] *Mansfield Park*, ed. James Kinsley, with an Introduction by Marilyn Butler (Oxford, 1990), 363.

closest possible indication of the nature of the manuscripts. Fortunately the notebooks are now all available to scholars; *Volume the First* is in the Bodleian Library, Oxford; *Volumes the Second* and *Third* in the British Museum.

On looking at the manuscripts we can see that many changes seem to have been executed at the time of writing (or copying-rewriting); some alterations are merely the correction of errors (the equivalent of typos). But one wonders about the purport of some marked differences between an earlier and a later version of the text. The very first 'Tale' in *Volume the First*, for instance, 'Frederic and Elfrida', begins, 'The Uncle of Elfrida was the Mother of Frederic.' Did Austen merely miswrite, and then quickly correct? Or did she commit an outrageous joke and then have second thoughts?

Some changes in the manuscript of a tale refine the comedy, as at the end of the second paragraph of 'Frederic and Elfrida'. Originally, the sentence reads, 'They . . . were both determined not to transgress the rules of Propriety by owning their attachment to any one else' (see Textual Note to p. 3). This has been changed so that the ending reads 'by owning their attachment, either to the object beloved, or to any one else'—a considerable heightening of the humour, partly through a pointed refinement of literary parody, with novels such as Samuel Richardson's *Sir Charles Grandison* (1753–4) and Frances Sheridan's *Memoirs of Miss Sidney Bidulph* (1761–7) in mind.

Austen's revisions sometimes trim down an elaborated effect, as is the case near the beginning of 'Love and Freindship': 'we were on a sudden, greatly astonished, considerably amazed and somewhat surprized' (see Textual Note to p. 78). Austen evidently felt—or came to feel—that this deliberate diminuendo detracted from the general comic effect of the conversation about rapping on the door which follows, and so struck it out.

Many of the deletions and revisions reveal the high-spirited comic sense of the very young woman who wrote this material. In 'The History of England' Jane Austen has the following comment about Lady Jane Grey's reading

Greek: 'Whether she really understood that language or whether such a Study proceeded only from an excess of vanity for which I beleive she was always rather remarkable, is uncertain' (p. 139). But the original sentence did not contain the standard moralizing word 'vanity'—it went thus: 'Whether she really understood that language or whether such a Study proceeded only from an excess of *Cockylorum* . . . is uncertain' (italics by JA). The formula of judgement, of restrained objective speculation ('Whether . . . is uncertain'), is shafted by the impudent presence of the impudently colloquial word. The *OED* defines 'cockalorum' in terms of a person: 'Little cock, bantam; self-important little man.' But the quality of *cockalorum* (or 'cockylorum') is over-confidence, the source of boastful high spirits. In this case, Austen's revision tames her sentence, partly perhaps in order not to let this mock-historian persona deviate from the kind of vocabulary historians will use.

There are some puzzles hidden in these manuscripts. Particular problems are posed by *Volume the Third* in which there are substantial passages in hands other than Austen's. One piece we have eliminated from the present volume; in the original it is several pages inserted into the notebook, rather than forming part of the *Volume* proper. This piece can be found in R. W. Chapman's edition of the *Minor Works* (pp. 240–2), just after the end of the unfinished 'Catharine', with Chapman's heading: '*Here follows a contribution to* Evelyn *by Jane Austen's niece Anna Lefroy.*' But the last part of 'Evelyn' as we have printed it, and the last part of 'Catharine' seem also to be written—or written down at the very least—by someone other than Jane Austen. The most likely candidates as authors, or at least, scribes, of these additions are two children of Jane Austen's brother James: Anna Austen (later to be Mrs Lefroy) and James Edward (later to be known as James Edward Austen-Leigh, Austen's biographer). For information, and for discussions of the Austen family's handwriting, we are grateful to Sally Brown, Curator of Modern Literary Manuscripts at the British Museum, and Deirdre Le Faye, the latest editor of Jane Austen's letters.[8] (For further comment on the paragraphs of *Volume the Third* not written down by Jane Austen, see Textual Notes to pp. 183 and 228–9.)

Deirdre Le Faye has suggested that Jane Austen redis-covered her earlier manuscript notebooks when she un-packed the family belongings at Chawton in July 1809.[9] Revisions and new material in 'Evelyn' and 'Catharine' indicate renewed work on these writings between 1809 and 1811. For instance, the date of a letter at the end of 'Evelyn' is 'Aug^{st} 19th 1809'. In 'Catharine' the heroine's friend Camilla refers to a 'new Regency walking dress' in a sentence that has been altered, presumably in order to make the fashion reference fit in with the new excitements over the Prince of Wales's accession to power as Regent, with the Regency Act of 5 February 1811. (The Regency was indeed quickly reflected in the fashion pages of ladies' magazines.) Anna Austen would have been 16 in 1809, and James Edward, 11; by the time 'Catharine' was finished— and for that time we must posit a date of at least 1811, possibly 1812—he would have been 13 or 14, quite old enough to engage in the writing game of participating in his aunt's stories, and trying to finish them.

Did Jane Austen give this nephew and niece their own heads—and let them make what they liked of the stories in the notebooks? Or did they write partly or wholly under her guidance? There are no signs of dictation. There are some stylistic differences from Jane Austen's own Juvenilia. Yet Jane Austen does not seem altogether absent—there is, for instance, the undersong of Cowper in the reference to Mrs Percival's view of London as 'the hot house of Vice' (see note to p. 228), stylistic depths certainly beyond the power

---

[8] Sally Brown was in the process of writing the British Library catalogue entry for the recently acquired *Volume the Third* when we were completing the textual work for this volume. This catalogue entry can now be consulted. We are particularly indebted to Mrs Brown for giving us the chance to talk with her and discuss the various hands and their significance in a vital telephone call of 22 May 1991. Deirdre Le Faye also touched upon the matter of the hands of *Volume the Third* in a letter of 4 May 1991 kindly responding to our queries as to MSS of the verses.

[9] See Deirdre Le Faye, *Jane Austen: A Family Record* (London, 1989), 164.

of the Anna who wrote the inserted pages. It is possible that Austen was conducting something a little like a very informal writing class, and that the contribution of the young writers received her attention and discussion before they entered it in the valued *Volume*.

One of the interesting points that emerges from this discovery is the part these notebooks played in Austen's life. We can see that she was re-reading and revising the material of her teens, as well as enjoying the fresh access of a new and pleased audience between 1809 and 1811 (and possibly after that). The year 1811 is important to us for something other than the advent of the Regency; that was the year *Sense and Sensibility* was published. At last, Jane Austen was a published—and publishing—novelist. But in the years at the beginning of the century her career as a novelist had been perpetually frustrated. She failed to interest publishers in her work. She had sold a novel entitled *Susan* to Crosby in 1807 (or rather, her brother Henry sold it for her, for ten pounds), but Crosby never actually printed the work, and in 1809 she had to buy it back. We forget how much of failure there was in Jane Austen's middle period, when she tried to write works that would appeal beyond the family circle, and to meet a public which was apparently indifferent. The advent of Anna and James Edward as interested readers and would-be writers may have been much more important for her confidence than we can imagine. Perhaps a little group of collaborators working on (and laughing at) 'Evelyn' in 1809 gave Jane Austen heart to continue in her life's work. Certainly these early works were important companions to her during the rest of her writing career.

The manuscripts of the verses are not usually as interesting, and pose fewer problems—or at least fewer problems in relation to Jane Austen's central career. The verses themselves are problematic enough simply because some manuscripts have disappeared, so we have had to rely on printed versions. Some manuscripts were not available to us. The central fact about the 'Verses' is that a verse that met the approval of family and friends could have several versions (of some sort) in circulation in Jane Austen's own lifetime and later. Her family also contributed to editing and 'polishing' these works, most particularly her eldest brother James. (See 'Maria, good-humoured, and handsome, and tall', p. 244 and Textual Note on pp. 275–6). The most interesting manuscript is that of Jane Austen's very last literary work, the set of verses beginning 'When Winchester races'. There are two manuscripts of that piece extant. One, regularized, is very obviously the work of the revising James, and it is this one which appears in Chapman's *Minor Works*. The other manuscript was spoken of so disparagingly by Chapman and by Park Honan that it seemed scarcely worth looking at. This manuscript (in the Henry W. and Albert A. Berg Collection in the New York Public Library) is, however, a revelation. It is the most moving of all of the Austen documents we have encountered in preparing this volume.

This manuscript of 'When Winchester races' is in the hand of Cassandra Austen. This is what she wrote at the dictation of her sister, the dying Jane Austen, three days before her death. It is neatly and clearly written, save for a few mistakes and irregularities of the sort that are very likely to happen in any dictation. Perhaps Jane Austen's voice was failing her a little; it is hard to believe that Cassandra was not agitated. Yet Jane Austen composed the comic verses about the Winchester races being rained out by an annoyed St Swithin, and Cassandra wrote them down, and probably both sisters laughed, sharing a little last happiness together. It was perhaps later and not on that day itself that Cassandra underlined in her sister's poem the lines 'When once we are buried you think we are gone/But behold me immortal!' (see p. 246). We may wonder why the line ends with the word 'gone' when the forthcoming rhyme word is to be 'said'. Is not the obvious phrasing 'when once we are dead'? (That is the phrasing supplied by James in his edited version.) Did Jane Austen perhaps actually say the word 'dead'—and did her sister find herself unable to write the word? It is truly moving to see this manuscript, the very piece of paper that was in the room with the two sisters, that quiet and somewhat poky room in Winchester in a rainy July.

Jane Austen wrote these verses on 15 July 1817 and died early in the morning of 18 July. Her immediate family admired the gallant spirit which allowed her to compose verses and leave evidence of a mind functioning to the end; her brother Henry, in the 'Biographical Notice' prefaced to the posthumously published *Northanger Abbey* and *Persuasion* (December 1817) mentioned the verses, even exaggerating their proximity to the very hour of death: 'The day preceding her death she composed some stanzas replete with fancy and vigour'[10]. But, as Deirdre Le Faye and Jo Modert have shown, the younger Austens in the nineteenth century did not approve of Austen's composing these last verses.[11] The reference was deleted from the 'Biographical Notice' after 1833, and James Edward Austen-Leigh refused the request of the fifth Earl Stanhope to print the interesting verses in the second edition of the *Memoir* (first published in 1870). Jane Austen's niece Caroline was vexed at 'Uncle Henry' for having referred to the lines. She and James Edward found them an embarrassment, too 'light and playful' as James Edward told the Earl. Caroline was afraid of these lines being 'introduced as the latest working of her mind . . . the joke about the dead Saint, & the Winchester races, all jumbled up together, would read badly as amongst the few details given, of the closing scene'.[12] Caroline's letter of June 1871 shows us a sharp

[10] *Persuasion*, ed. John Davie, with an Introduction by Claude Rawson (Oxford, 1990), 2–3.

[11] See Deirdre Le Faye, 'Jane Austen's Verses and Lord Stanhope's Disappointment', *Book Collector*, 37:1 (Spring 1988), 86–91, and discussion of the matter by Jo Modert in the 'Introduction' to *Jane Austen's Manuscript Letters in Facsimile* (Carbondale, Ill.: Southern Illinois University Press, 1990), pp. xxiii–xxiv. Jo Modert wishes to make the point that the younger generation of Austens cannot be treated as entirely reliable in what they say about Jane Austen's manuscripts.

[12] Letter of Caroline Austen (daugher of James Austen and Mary Lloyd, his second wife) to her brother, James Edward Austen-Leigh, written in July 1871; first published by Deirdre Le Faye in *Book Collector* (1988) (see note above), 89–90, and extensively quoted by Jo Modert, Introduction to *Jane Austen's Manuscript Letters in Facsimile*, p. xxiv.

difference between the eighteenth century and the High Victorian age. Jane Austen was an eighteenth-century woman and valued the courage of wit, as well as the endeavour to take some pleasure in the circumstances life offered. Jane herself—and the sorrowing Cassandra and Henry—could esteem the merry heart that has fortitude and flexibility enough to maintain cheerfulness (and 'fancy and vigour') even in the Valley of the Shadow.

When the young Jane Austen was writing in her notebooks, however, the Valley of the Shadow was a long way off. The young Jane Austen wrote and wrote. And yet she never wrote verbosely, or lachrymosely (common faults of adolescent writers). Even more surprising, she is not autobiographical, nor does she plunge into some form of fiction that allows easy egress to the wishes of the dreamy self. Her writing is always awake, always witty. And what she wrote are (at least in some sense) shrewd and laughing parodies of contemporary fiction. Thus far everyone is in agreement.

But as to what to make of these first works, opinion may differ widely. The easiest and most comfortable opinion is that these juvenile works are, as Lord David Cecil puts it, 'trifling enough . . . squibs and skits of the light literature of the day'.[13] According to such a view, these slight pieces have a comic charm which is the more engaging because in them we can glimpse early symptoms of the voice and interests of Austen's maturity. This opinion is certainly not utterly wrong. Undeniably, we do see in these early pieces hints of the novels that we (rather than Jane Austen) cannot help knowing are to come. The silly Camilla Stanley in 'Catharine, or the Bower' does seem the prototype of Isabella Thorpe in *Northanger Abbey*. (It is always possible that some very early form of 'Susan'/*Northanger Abbey* pre-dated 'Catharine'.) The pompous and overbearing Lady

---

[13] David Cecil, *A Portrait of Jane Austen* (London: Constable, 1978), 59. In the index, Cecil allots the heading 'first creative period' to the period of writing *Pride and Prejudice*, and alludes to these pieces only as 'youthful writings' (206), unconsciously equating 'creative' work with publishing success.

Greville in a 'Collection of Letters' in *Volume the Second* misuses her rank to browbeat a poor young woman:

It is not my way to find fault with people because they are poor, for I always think that they are more to be despised and pitied than blamed for it, especially if they cannot help it, but at the same time I must say that in my opinion your old striped Gown would have been quite fine enough for its Wearer. . . . (p. 151)

Here certainly is a preliminary sketch of Lady Catherine De Bourgh; as Mr Collins says to his female guests, 'Lady Catherine will not think the worse of you for being simply dressed. She likes to have the distinction of rank preserved.'[14] Lady Greville also summons the poor young lady, Maria, to speak with her at her coach door, so she is 'obliged to stand there at her Ladyship's pleasure though the Wind was extremely high and very cold' (p. 154). As Elizabeth Bennet, summoned by another Maria to see Charlotte Collins held in converse by Lady Catherine's daughter, exclaims bluntly, 'She is abominably rude to keep Charlotte out of doors in all this wind' (*Pride and Prejudice*, 142). Authors tend to be frugal, to recycle their own material. We know that soon after (perhaps even before) the last work of the 1790s had been done on the stories in the three manuscript *Volumes*, Jane Austen wrote the first version of *Sense and Sensibility*, presumably as *Elinor and Marianne* (*c*.1795). The first version of *Pride and Prejudice* was written also in the mid-1790s, a novel called 'First Impressions', a work completed in August 1797 and offered to a publisher shortly afterwards.

Yet there are some drawbacks to analysing these works solely in terms of what is to come. Having made our list of resemblances and echoes, we may lay the first writings down—perhaps having missed their important effects. Another mode of approach, also useful, is similarly limited. This is the 'biographical approach'. Biographers especially are likely to trace in these works some of the personal reactions of the youthful Jane Austen to the life around her.

[14] *Pride and Prejudice*, ed. James Kinsley with an Introduction by Isobel Armstrong (Oxford, 1990), 143.

The 'biographical approach' readily develops into what might be called the 'moral approach'. We see—or think we see—what Jane Austen thought of certain types of behaviour, what her moral responses are. The difficulty there is that conclusions are likely to be based on pre-existing perceptions and opinions. Earlier in this century, commentators on these earlier works (and there are not many commentators on them) leaped to the conclusion that Jane Austen is concerned with satirizing the worst excesses of the French Revolution and of sentimental romanticism. She takes it upon herself joyfully to 'send up', as we say, the revolutionary spirit of the late 1780s and the 1790s, in mocking characters (such as the 'hero' of 'Love and Freindship') who revolt against customary obligations and find it necessary on principle to disoblige their fathers. According to a prevailing view, Jane Austen is a sensible conservative, maintaining the value of home, order, and the status quo, seeing what is ridiculous and antipathetic in the new literature of the end of the century. Most of the critics of the mid-twentieth century tended not to take into account the sharply subversive moments in Jane Austen's early writing. Commentators of the early and mid-twentieth century tended not to be able to see when Austen is attacking truisms of what we may call 'the Right'—particularly the Whiggish Right. Claudia Johnson, who takes an altogether different view of Austen's political stance from that espoused by Lord David Cecil, Marilyn Butler, and some others, is able to illuminate the nuanced relations of Austen's own works to their immediate literary context.[15] She has, for

---

[15] See Claudia L. Johnson, *Jane Austen: Women, Politics and the Novel* (Chicago and London: Chicago University Press, 1988). Marilyn Butler, in *Jane Austen and the War of Ideas* (Oxford: Clarendon Press, 1975), made a very valuable contribution, as Johnson acknowledges, in demonstrating Austen's active engagement with political ideas. Butler assumed, however, that Austen fully participated in a conservative view—a conservatism with which Butler herself is not at all in accord. This notion of Austen's conservatism was supplied by earlier commentators, including editors such as R. W. Chapman and B. C. Southam. This earlier version of Austen did not permit her to be engaged in any conscious or knowledgeable way in issues or dissension.

instance, pointed out that the aunt of the heroine of 'Catharine', the censorious Mrs Percival, absurdly poses a serious argument of her day—an argument put forward by conservative novelists such as Jane West and Hannah More. Mrs Percival roundly states this position:

the welfare of every Nation depends upon the virtue of it's individuals, and any one who offends in so gross a manner against decorum and propriety is certainly hastening it's ruin. You have been giving a bad example to the World . . . (p. 222)

Many English writers of the 1790s or early 1800s, especially those writing for women, held Mrs Percival's view—that keeping the women tremblingly guarded by an inordinate sense of decorum and a frantic delicacy is the only means of preventing the structure of English society from toppling under the pressure of new revolutionary ideas about the Rights of Man—and of Woman. Mrs Percival harks back to Queen Elizabeth, and an implicit view of a Protestant and strongly governed England—a view which Catharine repudiates, as does Jane Austen herself, who throughout these early works consistently attacks all Whig views of history, and self-congratulatory Protestantism. '. . . I am myself partial to the roman catholic religion,' she remarks daringly as the historian of 'The History of England' (p. 142), flying in the face of all approved histories.[16]

Austen certainly subjects Mrs Percival's view to scrutiny and ridicule, a ridicule made the more pointed by Mrs Percival's administration to her ward of that worthy prophylactic, Hannah More's *Coelebs in Search of a Wife* (1808). More's novel, intended to support the conservative cause that Mrs Percival so parodically espouses, is the story of a good young man, a bachelor who sets out on a quest for a perfect wife. He examines every young woman attentively,

[16] See the interesting essay by Christopher Kent, 'Learning History with, and from, Jane Austen', in *Jane Austen's Beginnings*, ed. J. David Grey (Ann Arbor, Mich., and London: UMI Research Press, 1989), 59–72. A useful attempt is now being made to inspect the High Toryism in Austen's work (her pro-Stuart stance, for instance); such gestures are not necessarily 'conservative' in the sense most often attributed, and may stand as signals of dissent from prevailing law-and-order Whiggism.

but each has a fault or flaw which causes him gravely to cross her off his list of possibilities and move on. At length he finds the perfect woman, who is a slightly more alarming piece of pattern submissiveness than even the Sophie of Rousseau's *Émile* (1760). Austen in the first pieces of *Volume the First* had already ridiculed the idea that women are to be models of perfection in the hope that a most beautiful and moral young man may come to claim them. 'Jack and Alice' in its own way analyses the problems at the heart of Richardson's *Sir Charles Grandison*; the hero of Richardson's novel, who is looking for a wife worthy of him (and who has two young ladies, at least, pining away for him), has been made too perfect by his author. Sir Charles's glimpses of his own perfection make us uneasy, as at the presence of a monstrous egotist. The Grandisonian type of highly moral exemplary strong man had been borrowed by both conservative and liberal novelists for their own differing purposes. But we can see that Austen thinks that too many novelists have set up these pattern heroes in order to keep women in their places. Austen even has a running quarrel with Charlotte Smith, a writer whose works she (like the young heroine of 'Catharine') evidently enjoys, because in Smith's *Emmeline* (1788) the heroine breaks off her engagement with the impulsive and imperfect Frederic Delamere and ultimately marries a Grandisonian worthy with the Whiggish name of Godolphin. The quest of a heroine for an ideally moral lover is a quest Austen finds as suspect as the portrayed quests of heroes for the perfect young lady. Both stories are coercive and restrictive. In 'Jack and Alice' Austen breaks out of the spell of *Sir Charles Grandison*, denies its authority through impish play with it. The perfect hero outdoes even Sir Charles in sun-like qualities, so refulgent in his glory that 'none but Eagles could look him in the Face' (p. 11)—as only St John, the eagle, has traditionally been able to see the divine glory in Revelation. This shining hero is indeed unmasked in his barefaced sublimity, a sublimity of self-centredness; he is terrifying in his totally committed narcissism: 'My temper is even, my virtues innumerable, my self unparalelled. Since such, Sir, is my character, what do you mean by wishing me to marry your Daughter?' (p. 23)

Behind this Charles Adams—a most un-fallen son of Adam (in his own opinion)—we can see not only Richardson's Sir Charles, but whole sets of Enlightenment concepts of self-improvement and self-approval, concepts embraced by divines and promulgated by philosophers such as Shaftesbury and by poets of the stature of Pope. The Enlightenment wanted to think that we are naturally moral, and that self-cultivation and self-consciousness will lead to a more moral society. Equally, the new Enlightened capitalism wanted to believe that the pursuit of its own interest by each group and individual would or could lead to the good of the whole. Austen is engaged at the philosophic centre of the eighteenth century. To treat her early works as the slight works of a playful child is partly to mistreat their philosophic depths.

Austen in these early works presents a social world which is very greedy and very violent. Her satire is not directed only against those who follow their own will in the name of the newly articulated romantic values—though that can look like the case if the critic chooses to examine only Laura of 'Love and Freindship'. If we think that Austen ignores the naked selfishness of those who already have power and possessions, we have not been reading attentively. With every word a reputation dies—no rank, no order, no established conduct is safe from her:

As Sir George and Lady Harcourt were superintending the Labours of their Haymakers, rewarding the industry of some by smiles of approbation, and punishing the idleness of others, by a cudgel . . . (p. 31)

It is that throw-away phrase 'by a cudgel' that does the mischief. The sentence structure smoothly assumes the right of Sir George and Lady Harcourt to superintend, to reward, and to punish, and our expectations are controlled and soothed by the harmonious balance, so that we idly expect the punishment to parallel 'smiles' will be 'frowns' or the like—but the *cudgel* reminds us of coercive power, in its cartoon-like burlesque; the sentence, like a visual caricature, elicits through an emblem the internal nature of the matter. The Harcourts' smiles are immaterial, but they have real material power over 'their Haymakers'. The balance that tries to represent this world of ownership as a world of harmony is a false colluding balance. That this is the case is borne out by the rest of the 'novel' of 'Henry and Eliza' in which violence is done to the body of others by anyone who can claim a need, an urge, or a right. The 'Duchess' locks the heroine up; the babies eat two of Eliza's fingers. Everyone feeds off someone else—as Eliza does too, self-approvingly stealing money from her benefactors.

All of these early novels are immensely conscious of money, as are Jane Austen's later novels, but here in the early works in the notebooks illegal and even criminal appropriations or uses of money can be represented—although perhaps in *Sanditon*, that last unfinished novel about development and developers, Jane Austen was going to recover that subject. 'Henry and Eliza' disturbs the equilibrium achieved by earlier eighteenth-century novels in their attempt to come to grips with the realities of property and the demands of the social order. Fielding, for instance, arrives at harmonizing conclusions (or shows what he wants the reader to conclude) in *Joseph Andrews* (1742) and *Tom Jones* (1749). Both of these novels are in an immediate relation to 'Henry and Eliza', which picks up a number of plot points and thematic developments from them (not excluding Fielding's own brand of irony). Yet Fielding's moral balances and conclusions are distorted, disturbed, even done away with, in 'Henry and Eliza'. There are no moral equations, and highly balanced prose does *not* equal a highly balanced and harmonized civilized society.

As well as representing aspects of the biography and possessing moral (or even political) qualities, these early works possess many striking formal properties. Personal experience, political or moral views, and formal techniques and structures of course do not emanate from separate or even entirely separable facets of the writer, and it is somewhat disingenuous to pretend otherwise. Yet if we do not pay sufficient attention to the formal properties of these early works, we may miss an enormous amount that is of interest, rendering our moral or biographical commentary thin and pale. Some damage has been done to these early works by the determined tendency to consider them only or chiefly in the light of the great works to come. The Jane Austen who first wrote these early pieces did not know that she was going to be the author of *Pride and Prejudice*—still less of *Mansfield Park* and *Emma*. It is we who know that. And we are so justly taken with the beauties of these works that we cannot imagine them not being written. Nay, further, we cannot imagine Jane Austen writing without writing *towards* those works. We should, however, try to imagine that the world is not composed of inevitabilities. It was not utterly inevitable that Jane Austen should have written *Pride and Prejudice* or *Emma*. She could, of course, have written no long novels at all. It was not inevitable that she should get published—and the publication of *Sense and Sensibility* and *Pride and Prejudice* enabled and conditioned the writing of the Chawton novels. For a long while it must have seemed to Jane Austen the decree of fate that she should never publish. A lot of ink has been spilt on considering how she felt about marrying or not marrying, and how she was grieved by the loss of the mysterious lover met at the seaside. But very little attention has been paid to what may have been the most serious cause of alarm and frustration in her life—the recognition, as the new century wore on, that apparently nobody wanted her fiction. Hers was a life dedicated from childhood to an art—but she was destined in her late twenties and early thirties to experience such prolonged rejection that she must have wondered if her art were worth anything at all. By the time she did achieve publication, she had had to realize that what she wanted and what the world wanted might be different things. Being a practical person and a craftsman as well as an artist, she accommodated herself to what the world wanted, without compromising the integrity of her spirit and of wit, to be sure—and yet, did she not lose something? These early works show us what we have a hard time accepting, that Jane Austen *could* have written very differently from the mature Austen whose works we have known for so long. Of course her six novels had been known for over one hundred years before these early pieces came upon the scene to trouble our vision. It is natural that our first impulse should be to fit them neatly in with the Austen that we know.

But do they fit in neatly? And are these early prose works to be taken (as they have been taken by Cecil and others) as light 'trifles' in relation to the 'real novels'? We notice that, until 'Catharine, or the Bower', these early works (although often comically entitled 'novels' by the author) are not 'real novels' at all, nor are they 'realistic'. Austen in her youth did not yet have to try to compromise with the desires of publishers. Then—'First Impressions' did not meet the views of Cadell. It was rejected. Austen's first attempt to reach a public with her brand of fiction was a failure. So, indeed, was her second major attempt with 'Susan'. These rejections were hard lessons which taught her that her kind of writing was not yet suited to the contemporary public—or, more important, to what the publishers felt were the tastes of the contemporary public. If we think of it, we are forced to realize that in writing her comic novels of courtship Austen chose a genre which would have a certain appeal to an audience, a form of book which looked like just another story of a nice girl getting engaged. Within this acceptable and apparently unalarming genre Austen could hope to work some changes without the style and depth of what she was doing being overmuch noticed. She succeeded brilliantly in an attempt which has about it a certain element of disguise. To most reviewers, *Sense and Sensibility* when it came out was just another good moral novel about courtship, a novel, as the *Critical Review* said, that was 'just long enough to interest without fatiguing'.[17]

But the Austen who was writing in the early 1790s was not yet disciplined—or fenced in—by the necessities of the market-place. She had not yet experienced the pressures

[17] *The Critical Review* (1812), quoted by Park Honan in *Jane Austen: Her Life*, 287.

that the middlemen of that market exerted on women writers, although she knew about the pressures of the marital market-place. The young Jane Austen could write what she pleased—or at least (for families also provide some censorship) she could write largely what she pleased, and walk unrestricted in formal matters. These early works are not only parodic but also highly non-realistic variations on themes and scenes supplied by the contemporary novel, but these exquisite, aggressive, and intellectual variations have a force all their own. These are expressionistic works. Until recently we have had trouble accommodating any such writing into the theories of fiction that were being developed in Austen's own lifetime and in the century to follow. Such theories often look to Austen's own work for a touchstone. She exemplifies, to Henry James, E. M. Forster, F. R. Leavis, and others, the essential (and satisfactorily English) qualities of historical realism and psychological 'roundness'. But in the Early Works we see a Jane Austen who cared for none of these things—an impish and formally daring Austen who is most fascinated by the formal qualities of fiction itself, and by the fictionality of fiction.

When her early works came at last into print in the twentieth century, one of the few critics to write anything at all interesting about them was G. K. Chesterton, who wrote a 'Preface' to *Love and Freindship and Other Early Works* in 1922. (This was the first publication of *Volume the Second*.) Chesterton himself is not a realistic writer but an expressionistic one. He had early recognized that Christianity is not 'realistic' and that defences cannot be made of it in the old Protestant manner, in confidence that history will exhibit religion as factually true, and morality will make it prudently necessary. Chesterton's best vein is extravagant, playful, and paradoxical. His best vein is so good that it has attracted the admiration and quotation of many writers, including even those who (like myself) find some of his positions and opinions markedly distasteful. Chesterton in 1922 had more of an eye for what is going on in Austen's earlier writing than most critics have had. He ends his essay, it is true, with a little of the usual twaddle about her

being quite happy with her domestic role, making puddings
and pies quietly at home and not noticing the French
Revolution. But before that point (and he too had an
audience to placate, including hordes of 'Janeites') he is
very bold in dealing with the boldness he sees in the young
Austen:

It might seem a very wild use of the wrong word to say that Jane
Austen was elemental. It might seem even a little wanton to insist
that she was original. Yet this objection would come from the critic
not really considering what is meant by an element or an origin.

. . . .

If it seemed odd to call her elemental, it may seem equally odd
to call her exuberant. These pages betray her secret; which is that
she was naturally exuberant. And her power came, as all power
comes, from the control and direction of exuberance. But there is
the presence and pressure of that vitality behind her thousand
trivialities; she could have been extravagant if she liked. She was
the very reverse of a starched or a starved spinster; she could have
been a buffoon like the Wife of Bath if she chose. This is what gives
an infallible force to her irony. This is what gives a stunning
weight to her understatements.[18]

Chesterton obviously senses a sexual energy in Austen's
'elemental' vitality—senses it and is not repelled by it. He
uses, in describing her, the words 'force' and 'power' to
reflect the sheer 'exuberance' in these pages of Austen's
work. Chesterton might think her early pieces at times
crude, but, unlike Lord David Cecil, he does not see them
as trifling or silly. They give an impression of a vital energy
that Chesterton could see and feel all the more tellingly
because he himself was not interested in realism for its own
sake, and not particularly put out or disconcerted by its
absence. Chesterton refreshingly makes some unusual
comparisons. Jane Austen's inspiration 'was the inspiration
of Gargantua and of Pickwick; it was the gigantic inspiration
of laughter' (pp. xiv–xv). He thus sets Austen—in particular,
this Austen revealed in, for example, *Volume the Second*—
between Rabelais and Dickens.

[18] G. K. Chesterton, 'Preface' to *Love and Freindship and Other Early Works
. . By Jane Austen* (New York: Frederick A. Stokes Co., 1922), pp. xiii–xv.

That Austen can—and should—be placed on a line which runs from Rabelais to Dickens seems to me right. Or at least, Chesterton's statement points to the line to which Austen *could* have belonged—had the world and the publishers allowed such a thing. Female exuberance, a female 'buffoon' convulsed with laughter like the Wife of Bath—but the Wife of Bath as her own Chaucer, not as a character—this is a disturbing idea indeed. The public is not ready for the 'female buffoon' inspired by gigantic and seemingly heartless laughter—not in the 1790s. Perhaps the public may hardly be ready for it in the 1990s. Perhaps even Fay Weldon sometimes tames her typewriter. The laughter in Austen's early work is a disconcerting, uncompromising laughter, which cannot truly be tamed into gentle satire against approved objects (such as the sentimental novel, or Jacobin ideas). Austen's heartlessly witty laughter displays a world full of movement, where, against the regular patterns of action and the fictiveness of plot prescribed by fiction, the conventionally situated characters engage in an orgy of greed, lust, and violence. These characters prettify their universal and horrific self-interest by variants of cliché. The narrators (or mock-narrators) also can wield a mean cliché—and these clichés slip and split asunder to reveal comically shocking truths. Apparent exceptions turn out on inspection to be fulfilments of the same patern. There are perhaps happy marriages? But almost all of the marriages in Austen's Early Works turn out, on inspection, to be illicit unions: 'We were immediately united by my Father, who tho' he had never taken orders had been bred to the Church' (p. 80). The amiable Laura gives away the fact that she is not truly married with terrific unconcern, for the structure of her sentence suffices to assure her that all is as it should be. But the heroine of 'Love and Freindship' is merely typical in enjoying an illicit liaison that seems to do just as well as marriage. In 'A Collection of Letters' in *Volume the Second* the curious Sophia pesters the visiting Miss Jane to know why she is called 'Miss Jane'. The secrecy and consequent illegality of Miss Jane's marriage to Captain Dashwood would seem to supply sufficient reason, but

'Miss Jane' attributes her repudiation of her husband's surname to a piece of delicate sentiment; she could not bear to take 'a name which after my Henry's death I could never hear without emotion' (p. 150).

In the world of these early Volumes, the characters repudiate what they don't want and take what they want—and they don't have to pay for it. The world after all does belong to the forward and the bold. The good—as not in sentimental fiction—have a thin time of it, and the heartless but energetic have chosen the better part. Those who claim to be good and benevolent, like Charles Adams or Lady Williams in 'Jack and Alice', are highly successful egotists in their own right. The morals of eighteenth-century fiction are set aside.

Jane Austen was not a child as a writer when she wrote these early pieces. She possessed a sophistication rarely matched in viewing and using her own medium. She not only understood the Novel, she took the Novel apart, as one might take apart a clock, to see how it works—and she put it back together, but it was no longer the same clock. Her genius at an early age is as awe-inspiring as Mozart's. Austen's genius here is not yet tamed by young-ladyhood, and we can see how much she lost as well as gained in writing her later publishable novels. She is not a child in writing the Early Works, but she had not yet lost that child's vision, so valuable to the humorist—a vision which is not sweet at all, but encompasses the absurd and the terrifying. As a child, Jane Austen had undergone real experiences, including some experiences of violence and suffering. There was the frightening illness at Mrs Cawley's, and the death of Mrs Cooper. Good Mrs Cooper died *because* she tried to take care of her daughter. The world does not reward virtue, does not operate according to the logic of eighteenth-century fiction. An equally arbitrary event was the exaltation of the child Edward, suddenly, magically, taken up in the world, well above Jane and his other sister and his brothers. Yet other brothers were spirited away into the power of a frightening and dangerous and distant Navy. The world is irrational; fortune is

capricious. The truisms fostered in exemplary fiction are
not true. Religion is another matter—that can be true
without being cosy, and it helps one to face the hard
experience of life. We have included Austen's 'Prayers' in
this volume so as not to leave out that aspect of her life and
personality. But Christianity itself offers a consolation
entirely different from the comfort and optimism afforded
by the plot patterns and endings of the eighteenth-century
novels—and Jane Austen knew the difference. Certainly she
could not believe in fiction's truisms, its patterns of
exemplary rewards and punishments. Later, Jane Austen
would have to pretend to some extent to believe that the
truisms are true—that the world is orderly, that Virtue is
Rewarded, that time wounds all heels. But she really always
knew that it is not so, and only in the pages of fiction can it
be made so. The pages of fiction include the pages of
History—which is only Story with pretensions (as Catherine
Morland, like Jonathan Swift and others, knew too).
History is narrated by partial, prejudiced, and ignorant
historians, each with an axe to grind—and each striving too
(perhaps vainly) to offer entertainment. Entertainment
comes only with form—form fulfilled or form played with.

G. K. Chesterton read and approved this youthful
expressionistic Austen, who shows us that form itself is an
arbitrary but delicious play, depending on rules that can be
amazingly broken from moment to moment, if the writer is
daring and deeply knowing. This young Austen may
remind us of writers more recent even than Chesterton,
writers who have had more success than Austen did in
making their expressionistic fiction known to the public. If
her colleagues in this game are Rabelais and Dickens, they
are also Calvino and Borges. Except for Dickens (who also
had to pretend to be realistic), the names in this list are not
English. Europe and South America have been more
hospitable than England and North America to literature
that is not realistic-historical, perhaps because Europe
never really fell fully under the sway of Whig hegemony and
Whig philosophy—and certainly South America did not.
Calvino plays with and parodies the many crossed paths of

fiction, and the many roles that Fiction designs—such as Hero, or Reader. The fiction of Borges is like Austen's juvenile pieces, short, witty, and full of matter—and it can be fully understood only in the light of a great deal of precedent literature, and formal suppositions expressed in the precedent literature. For Borges, too, the literary game is dangerous and the characters within literature are frightening, as much wild Minotaur as brave Theseus. Borges (himself influenced a little by Chesterton) is full of play, and has a parodic—a seriously parodic—sense of the traps within all heroic roles. In one of his lightest collections, *Six Problems for Don Isidro Parodi* (a complex parody of heroes and structures of detective fiction, written with Adolfo Bioy-Casares), Borges presents a perfectly absurd and banal narrator, whose artistic pretensions and literary knowledge lead him to a style as wonderfully self-deconstructive as that of Laura in 'Love and Freindship':

There, on the outskirts of Buenos Aires, the poet was born. His first teacher was nature—on the one hand, the bean patch of his paternal half-acre; on the other, the neighbouring hen-coops that the boy visited more than once on moonless nights, armed with a long rod for angling poultry. . . .[19]

So Gervasio Montenegro (Member, Argentine Academy of Letters) tries to describe another poet. And so he attempts poetic flight himself, knowing how these things are done: 'Beneath the lavish blessing of life-giving sunshine, the fence posts, the wires, the thistles wept with joy' (p. 48). Compare Austen's Laura:

A Grove of full-grown Elms sheltered us from the East—. A Bed of full-grown Nettles from the West—. Before us ran the murmuring brook and behind us ran the turn-pike road. (p. 95)

Jane Austen, I believe, would have known what Borges was doing, not only in light moments but in the more dense and puzzling—and frightening—plays upon the fearful inevitability of fiction's fictional nature. It is not enough to guy or

[19] Jorge Luis Borges and Adolfo Bioy-Casares, *Six Problems for Don Isidro Parodi*, trans. Norman Thomas Di Giovanni (New York: E. P. Dutton, 1981), 43; translation of *Seis problemas para don Isidro Parodi*, 1942.

send up clichés, because our minds cannot function without structure, without repeated patterns. By turning these structures and patterns round and about, displaying their artificial nature, Jane Austen achieved the relief of laughter, and could allow her own 'exuberance' some room. The exuberance of these Early Works is an exuberance that reassures, once we ourselves have gazed on the deadly necessity of pattern, and asked ourselves if the lies we tell—the cultural lies, not the single lie—in the name of stability are worth it.

Jane Austen in maturity made a choice and went in another direction. At the crossroads, she had to choose, and she then wrote the realistic novel of courtship, closely and apparently even modestly related to the style of novel that had frightened her, stimulated her, and made her laugh. She could not laugh so loudly in the later works. She could not be wild as she had been in the notebook Volumes. She had to become genteel, and act like a lady. She could draw characters like the Steeles and the Crawfords (very different from each other) without sending them to the poorhouse or the guillotine for their wickedness, but she had to pretend that the world was better and its general fictions more reliable than she knew them to be.

Margaret Anne Doody

NOTE ON THE TEXT

In this edition, the texts of *Volumes the First, Second, and Third* have been prepared after consultation with the original manuscripts: the MS of *Volume the First* is in the Bodleian Library, Oxford; the MSS of *Volume the Second* and *Volume the Third* are in the British Library. We are thus offering a completely new text of these early prose works. In reprinting the contents of the three notebooks, we wished to include for the interested reader all the variants in the MSS; these are found in the ample Textual Notes. The text of 'Plan of a Novel' and the texts of many of the verses have also been freshly prepared with reference to authoritative manuscripts. It has not, however, been possible to find manuscript sources for each example of Jane Austen's light verse. The Textual Notes relating to each piece will explain the source. Again, when manuscript material has been used, the reader will be informed of variations and changes.

In presenting manuscript material, we have made some changes. In very rare cases we have supplied missing words for the sake of syntax or have changed a word that simply seems miswritten in haste; textual notes will clearly indicate the original state. Jane Austen's spellings, however, have been retained throughout (e.g. in 'freindship'), save in the case of personal names, which we have regularized so that the same character's name is spelled the same way on all occasions. We have also supplied capital letters for words such as 'Roman', 'Scotch', 'Italian' (with the exception of 'roman catholic' and 'protestant' in 'The History of England', where the lower case may indicate an editorial decision on Jane Austen's part); and have kept the regular form of contractions such as 'don't' and 'won't'. We have replaced ampersand (&) with 'and'. Abbreviations such as 'Compts' for 'Compliments' have been enlarged into the whole word for the reader's convenience, except when they appear in salutations and conclusions of letters, where the short form sustains an engaging naturalism.

A major change has been made in punctuation. We have
supplied a regular system of quotation marks, whereas
Austen sometimes uses the conventional system and sometimes does not insert all marks; we have also supplied
commas where these were demanded (e.g. after quotations)
although we have tried to refrain from adding punctuation
in cases where it could be avoided without bewildering the
reader. On the whole, we have tried to refrain from
intervening as much as possible. Our object has been to
supply the reader with a readily readable text that would, at
the same time, give a very clear idea of the manuscript
stories and verses that Jane Austen left.

SELECT BIBLIOGRAPHY

MANUSCRIPT STUDIES

CHAPMAN, R. W., *Plan of a Novel* (Oxford, 1926).
—— *Volume the First* (Oxford, 1933).
—— *Volume the Third* (Oxford, 1951).
—— *Minor Works*, in The Oxford Illustrated Jane Austen (Oxford, 1954; further rev. by B. C. Southam, 1969).
GILSON, DAVID, 'Jane Austen's Verses', *Book Collector*, 33 (Spring 1984), 25–37.
—— 'Jane Austen's Verses: Additions and a Correction', *Book Collector*, 34 (Autumn 1985), 384–5.
—— and GREY, J. DAVID, 'Jane Austen's Juvenilia and *Lady Susan*: An Annotated Bibliography', *Jane Austen's Beginnings: The Juvenilia and Lady Susan*, ed. J. David Grey (Ann Arbor, Mich., and London, 1989).
GREENE, DONALD, 'New Verses by Jane Austen', *Nineteenth-Century Fiction*, 30 (1975), 257–60.
LE FAYE, DEIRDRE, 'Jane Austen Verses', letter to *TLS*, 20 Feb. 1987, 85.
MARSHALL, MARY GAITHER, 'Jane Austen's Manuscripts of the Juvenilia and *Lady Susan*: A History and Description', *Jane Austen's Beginnings*, 107–21.
MODERT, JO, *Jane Austen's Manuscript Letters in Facsimile* (Carbondale and Edwardsville, Ill., 1990).
SOUTHAM, B. C., *Volume the Second* (Oxford, 1963).
—— *Jane Austen's Literary Manuscripts: A Study of the Novelist's Development through the Surviving Papers* (London, 1964).

BIOGRAPHY

AUSTEN, CAROLINE MARY CRAVEN, *My Aunt Jane Austen: A Memoir* (Alton, Jane Austen Society, 1952).
AUSTEN, JANE, *Jane Austen's Letters to her Sister Cassandra and Others*, ed. R. W. Chapman (2nd edn., London, 1952; repr. 1979).
AUSTEN-LEIGH, JAMES EDWARD, *A Memoir of Jane Austen* [1870; rev. 1871]; ed. R. W. Chapman (Oxford, 1926; repr. 1951).
AUSTEN-LEIGH, MARY AUGUSTA, *Personal Aspects of Jane Austen* (London, 1920).
AUSTEN-LEIGH, WILLIAM and AUSTEN-LEIGH, RICHARD ARTHUR,

Jane Austen: Her Life and Letters. A Family Record [1913] (New York, 1965).

BRABOURNE, LORD (EDWARD KNATCHBULL-HUGESSON), *The Letters of Jane Austen*, 2 vols. (London, 1884).

CHAPMAN, R. W., *Jane Austen: Facts and Problems* (Oxford, 1948; repr. 1961, 1963, 1970).

GREY, J. DAVID, LITZ, A. WALTON, and SOUTHAM, BRIAN (eds.), *The Jane Austen Companion* (New York, 1986); in UK, as *The Jane Austen Handbook* (London, 1986).

HONAN, PARK, *Jane Austen: Her Life* (London, 1987; New York, 1988).

JENKINS, ELIZABETH, *Jane Austen, a Biography* (1938; rev. edn., 1948).

LASKI, MARGHANITA, *Jane Austen and her World* (London and New York, 1969).

LE FAYE, DEIRDRE, 'Jane Austen and her Hancock Relatives', *Review of English Studies*, NS 30 (1979), 12–27.

—— *Jane Austen. A Family Record* (London, 1989).

McALEER, JOHN, 'What a Biographer Can Learn about Jane Austen from Her Juvenilia', *Jane Austen's Beginnings*, ed. J. David Grey (Ann Arbor, Mich., and London, 1989), 7–27.

TUCKER, GEORGE HOLBERT, *A Goodly Heritage: A History of Jane Austen's Family* (Manchester, 1983).

CRITICISM

BAILEY, JOHN CANN, *Introductions to Jane Austen* (London, 1931).

BARKER, GERARD A., *Grandison's Heirs: The Paragon's Progress in the Late Eighteenth-Century English Novel* (Newark, Del., 1985).

BEER, FRANCES, *The Juvenilia of Jane Austen and Charlotte Brontë* (Harmondsworth, 1986).

BROPHY, BRIGID, 'Jane Austen and the Stuarts', *Critical Essays on Jane Austen*, ed. B. C. Southam (London, 1968).

BUTLER, MARILYN, *Jane Austen and the War of Ideas* (Oxford, 1972).

CHAPMAN, R. W., 'Preface' to *Volume the First* (Oxford, 1933), pp. v–ix.

—— 'Preface' to *Volume the Third* (Oxford, 1951), pp. v–ix.

CHESTERTON, G. K., 'Preface' to *'Love and Freindship' and Other Early Works* (London, 1922), pp. ix–xv.

DOODY, MARGARET ANNE, 'Jane Austen's Reading', in *The Jane Austen Companion*, ed. J. David Grey, A. Walton Litz, and Brian Southam (London, 1986), 347–63.

EPSTEIN, JULIA, 'Jane Austen's Juvenilia and the Female Epistolary Tradition', *Papers on Language and Literature*, 21 (1985), 399–416.

GILBERT, SANDRA M. and GUBAR, SUSAN, 'Shut Up in Prose: Gender and Genre in Austen's Juvenilia', *The Madwoman in the Attic: The Woman Writer and the Nineteenth-Century Literary Imagination* (New Haven, Conn., and London, 1979), 107–45.

HARRIS, JOCELYN, *Jane Austen's Art of Memory* (Cambridge, 1989).

JOHNSON, CLAUDIA L., *Jane Austen: Women, Politics and the Novel* (Chicago, 1988).

LITZ, A. WALTON, *Jane Austen: A Study of Her Artistic Development* (London, 1965).

MUDRICK, MARVIN, *Jane Austen: Irony as Defense and Discovery* (Princeton, NJ, 1952).

RHYDDERCH, DAVID, 'Jane Austen's Reading', *TLS*, 17 Apr. 1930, 336.

TODD, JANET (ed.), *Jane Austen: New Perspectives*, in *Women and Literature*, NS 3 (New York, 1983).

WOOLF, VIRGINIA, 'Jane Austen', in *The Common Reader*, First Series (London, 1925; New York, 1953), 137–49 [based on Woolf's original review, 'Jane Austen at Sixty', in *The Nation and Athenaeum*, 34 (1923), 433–4].

WRIGHT, ANDREW, 'Jane Austen Adapted', *Nineteenth-Century Fiction* 30:3 (Dec. 1975), 421–53.

A CHRONOLOGY OF JANE AUSTEN

1775	(16 Dec.) Jane Austen born at Steventon, Hampshire, seventh child of the Revd George Austen (1731–1805) and Cassandra Austen, née Leigh (1739–1827).
1779	JA's oldest brother James goes to St John's College, Oxford, aged 14.
1782/3	JA and sister Cassandra at Mrs Cawley's boarding-school in Oxford.
1783	By this year JA's brother Edward is adopted by Thomas Knight the younger and his wife, of Godmersham in Kent, as evidenced by formal silhouette of his presentation to the Knights. Mrs Cawley's boarding-school moves to Southampton (Oct.). JA, Cassandra, and cousin Jane Cooper seriously ill of typhoid fever; aunt Jane Cooper, after nursing her daughter, dies of typhoid.
1784/5	JA and Cassandra at Abbey School, Reading.
1786	(Apr.) JA's brother Francis enters Royal Naval Academy at Portsmouth.
1786/8	Edward on Grand Tour.
1787/90	JA works on *Volume the First*.
1787	(Dec.) Eliza de Feuillide visits Steventon; family participate in amateur theatricals.
1788	Francis Austen sails as a volunteer aboard the *Perseverance*.
1790	(13 June) JA completes 'Love and Freindship'.
1791	JA's brother Charles goes to Royal Naval Academy, Portsmouth; (26 Nov.) JA completes 'The History of England'; Edward marries (27 Dec.) Elizabeth Bridges, and goes to live at Rowling.
1792	Earliest extant of verses dated Jan. 1792. JA writes 'Lesley Castle'. (May) JA writes 'Volume the Third' on title-page and gives date 'May 6th 1792'. JA writes 'Evelyn' and begins 'Catharine, or the Bower', Aug. 1792.

1793 (June) JA writes 'End of the volume' and gives date 'June 3, 1793'.

1795 JA working on 'Elinor and Marianne'. *Lady Susan* probably written in this period.

1796 (Oct.) 'First Impressions' begun, finished Aug. 1797.

1797 (Aug.) JA completes 'First Impressions'. *Sense and Sensibility* begun (Nov.). 'First Impressions' unsuccessfully offered to Cadell. Edward comes into possession of Godmersham.

1797/8 JA working on 'Susan' (later *Northanger Abbey*).

1801 Revd George Austen retires; Austens settle in Bath.

1802 (2 Dec.) JA engaged for one night to Harris Bigg-Wither.

1803 'Susan' sold to Crosby & Co. for £10.

1805 Revd George Austen dies; JA ceases to work on *The Watsons*.

1806 Mrs Austen, Cassandra, and JA leave Bath for Clifton near Bristol, visiting Adlestrop and Stoneleigh.

1807 JA with Mrs Austen and Cassandra takes lodgings in Southampton.

1809 (5 Apr.) Under the pseudonym of 'Mrs Ashton Dennis' with the signed initials 'M.A.D.' JA writes to Crosby to reclaim MS of 'Susan'. (9 July) JA with Mrs Austen and Cassandra moves to house in Chawton, Hampshire, owned by Edward (now Edward Knight).

1811 *Mansfield Park* begun (Feb.). *Sense and Sensibility* published (Nov.).

1812 (Nov.) *Pride and Prejudice* sold to Egerton.

1813 (Jan.) *Pride and Prejudice* published. (Nov.) Second editions of this and *Sense and Sensibility*.

1814 (21 Jan.) *Emma* begun (finished 29 Mar. 1815). (May) *Mansfield Park* published by Egerton.

1815 (?Summer) *Persuasion* begun (finished Aug. 1816). (Dec.) *Emma* published by John Murray. *Raison et Sensibilité . . . traduit librement . . . par Mme Isabelle de Montolieu* (Paris; repr. 1828). James Stanier Clarke writes to JA to tell her she may dedicate *Emma* to the Prince Regent. Correspondence with Clarke, Nov. 1815–Apr. 1816.

1816   *Emma* published, with dedication to Prince Regent. *Mansfield Park*, second edition. Translations, *Le Parc de Mansfield* and *La Nouvelle Emma* (Paris). JA writes 'Plan of a Novel' after correspondence with Clarke.

1817   (Jan.–Mar.) JA works on *Sanditon*. (24 May) JA moves to lodgings in Winchester. (15 July) JA composes 'When Winchester races'. 18 July, JA dies; buried in Winchester Cathedral. (Dec.) *Northanger Abbey* and *Persuasion* published together (dated 1818).

VOLUME THE FIRST

CONTENTS

To Miss Lloyd

My dear Martha

    As a small testimony of the gratitude I feel for your late generosity to me in finishing my muslin Cloak, I beg leave to offer you this little production of your sincere Freind

                              The Author

Frederic and Elfrida

a novel

Chapter the First

The Uncle of Elfrida was the Father of Frederic; in other words, they were first cousins by the Father's side.

Being both born in one day and both brought up at one school, it was not wonderfull that they should look on each other with something more than bare politeness. They loved with mutual sincerity but were both determined not to transgress the rules of Propriety* by owning their attachment, either to the object beloved, or to any one else.

They were exceedingly handsome and so much alike,* that it was not every one who knew them apart. Nay even their most intimate freinds had nothing to distinguish them by, but the shape of the face, the colour of the Eye, the length of the Nose and the difference of the complexion.

Elfrida had an intimate freind to whom, being on a visit to an Aunt, she wrote the following Letter.

To Miss Drummond

Dear Charlotte

I should be obliged to you, if you would buy me, during your stay with Mrs Williamson, a new and fashionable Bonnet,* to suit the complexion of your

E. Falknor

Charlotte, whose character was a willingness to oblige every one, when she returned into the Country, brought her Freind the wished-for Bonnet, and so ended this little adventure, much to the satisfaction of all parties.

On her return to Crankhumdunberry (of which sweet village* her father was Rector) Charlotte was received with the greatest Joy by Frederic and Elfrida, who, after pressing her alternately to their Bosoms, proposed to her to take a walk in a Grove of Poplars which led from the Parsonage to a verdant Lawn enamelled with a variety of variegated flowers and watered by a purling Stream,* brought from the Valley of Tempé* by a passage under ground.

In this Grove they had scarcely remained above 9 hours, when they were suddenly agreably surprized by hearing a most delightfull voice warble the following stanza.

Song

That Damon* was in love with me
I once thought and beleiv'd
But now that he is not I see,
I fear I was deceiv'd

No sooner were the lines finished than they beheld by a turning in the Grove 2 elegant young women leaning on each other's arm, who immediately on perceiving them, took a different path and disappeared from their sight.

Chapter the Second

As Elfrida and her companions, had seen enough of them to know that they were neither the 2 Miss Greens, nor Mrs Jackson and her Daughter, they could not help expressing their surprise at their appearance; till at length recollecting, that a new family had lately taken a House not far from the Grove, they hastened home, determined to lose no time in forming an acquaintance with 2 such amiable and worthy Girls, of which family they rightly imagined them to be a part.

Agreable to such a determination, they went that very evening to pay their respects to Mrs Fitzroy and her two Daughters. On being shewn into an elegant dressing room, ornamented with festoons of artificial flowers,* they were struck with the engaging Exterior and beautifull outside of Jezalinda the eldest of the young Ladies; but e'er they had been many minutes seated, the Wit and Charms which shone resplendent in the conversation of the amiable Rebecca, enchanted them so much that they all with one accord jumped up and exclaimed.

'Lovely and too charming Fair one, notwithstanding your forbidding Squint, your greazy tresses and your swelling Back, which are more frightfull than imagination can paint or pen describe, I cannot refrain from expressing my raptures, at the engaging Qualities of your Mind, which so amply atone for the Horror, with which your first appearance must ever inspire the unwary visitor.

'Your sentiments so nobly expressed on the different excellencies of Indian and English Muslins,* and the judicious preference you give the former, have excited in me an admiration of which I can alone give an adequate idea, by assuring you it is nearly equal to what I feel for myself.'

Then making a profound Curtesy to the amiable and abashed Rebecca, they left the room and hurried home.

From this period, the intimacy between the Families of Fitzroy, Drummond, and Falknor, daily increased till at length it grew to such a pitch, that they did not scruple to kick one another out of the window on the slightest provocation.

During this happy state of Harmony, the eldest Miss Fitzroy ran off with the Coachman and the amiable Rebecca was asked in marriage by Captain Roger of Buckinghamshire.

Mrs Fitzroy did not approve of the match on account of the tender years of the young couple, Rebecca being but 36 and Captain Roger little more than 63. To remedy this objection, it was agreed that they should wait a little while till they were a good deal older.

Chapter the Third

In the mean time the parents of Frederic proposed* to those of Elfrida, an union between them, which being accepted with pleasure, the wedding cloathes were brought and nothing remained to be settled but the naming of the Day.

As to the lovely Charlotte, being importuned with eagerness to pay another visit to her Aunt, she determined to accept the invitation and in consequence of it walked to Mrs Fitzroys to take leave of the amiable Rebecca, whom she found surrounded by Patches, Powder,* Pomatum* and Paint* with which she was vainly endeavouring to remedy the natural plainness of her face.

'I am come my amiable Rebecca, to take my leave of you for the fortnight I am destined to spend with my aunt. Beleive me this separation is painfull to me, but it is as necessary as the labour which now engages you.'

'Why to tell you the truth my Love,' replied Rebecca, 'I have lately taken it into my head to think (perhaps with little reason) that my complexion is by no means equal to the rest of my face and have therefore taken, as you see, to white and red paint which I would scorn to use on any other occasion as I hate art.'

Charlotte, who perfectly understood the meaning of her freind's speech, was too good-tempered and obliging to refuse her, what she knew she wished,—a compliment; and they parted the best freinds in the world.

With a heavy heart and streaming Eyes did she ascend the lovely vehicle[1] which bore her from her freinds and home; but greived as she was, she little thought in what a strange and different manner she should return to it.

On her entrance into the city of London which was the place of Mrs Williamson's abode, the postilion,* whose stupidity was amazing, declared and declared even without the least shame or Compunction, that having never been

[1] a post-chaise*

informed he was totally ignorant of what part of the Town, he was to drive to.

Charlotte, whose nature we have before intimated, was an earnest desire to oblige every one, with the greatest Condescension and Good humour informed him that he was to drive to Portland Place,* which he accordingly did and Charlotte soon found herself in the arms of a fond Aunt.

Scarcely were they seated as usual, in the most affectionate manner in one chair, than the Door suddenly opened and an aged gentleman with a sallow face and old pink Coat,* partly by intention and partly thro' weakness was at the feet of the lovely Charlotte, declaring his attachment to her and beseeching her pity in the most moving manner.

Not being able to resolve to make any one miserable, she consented to become his wife; where upon the Gentleman left the room and all was quiet.

Their quiet however continued but a short time, for on a second opening of the door a young and Handsome Gentleman with a new blue coat,* entered and intreated from the lovely Charlotte, permission to pay to her, his addresses.

There was a something in the appearance of the second Stranger, that influenced Charlotte in his favour, to the full as much as the appearance of the first: she could not account for it, but so it was.

Having therefore, agreable to that and the natural turn of her mind to make every one happy, promised to become his Wife the next morning, he took his leave and the two Ladies sat down to Supper on a young Leveret,* a brace of Partridges, a leash* of Pheasants and a Dozen of Pigeons.

Chapter the Fourth

It was not till the next morning that Charlotte recollected the double engagement she had entered into; but when she did, the reflection of her past folly, operated so strongly on her mind, that she resolved to be guilty of a greater, and to that end threw herself into a deep stream which ran thro' her Aunt's pleasure Grounds in Portland Place.*

She floated to Crankhumdunberry where she was picked up and buried; the following epitaph, composed by Frederic, Elfrida and Rebecca, was placed on her tomb.

Epitaph

Here lies our friend who having promis-ed
That unto two she would be marri-ed
Threw her sweet Body and her lovely face
Into the Stream that runs thro' Portland Place.

These sweet lines, as pathetic as beautifull were never read by any one who passed that way, without a shower of tears, which if they should fail of exciting in you, Reader, your mind must be unworthy to peruse them.

Having performed the last sad office to their departed freind, Frederic and Elfrida together with Captain Roger and Rebecca returned to Mrs Fitzroy's at whose feet they threw themselves with one accord and addressed her in the following Manner.

'Madam

'When the sweet Captain Roger first addressed the amiable Rebecca, you alone objected to their union on account of the tender years of the Parties. That plea can be no more, seven days being now expired, together with the lovely Charlotte, since the Captain first spoke to you on the subject.

'Consent then Madam to their union and as a reward, this smelling Bottle* which I enclose in my right hand, shall be yours and yours forever; I never will claim it again. But if you refuse to join their hands in 3 days time, this dagger* which I enclose in my left shall be steeped in your hearts blood.

'Speak then Madam and decide their fate and yours.'

Such gentle and sweet persuasion could not fail of having the desired effect. The answer they received, was this.

'My dear young freinds

'The arguments you have used are too just and too eloquent to be withstood; Rebecca in 3 days time, you shall be united to the Captain.'

This speech, than which nothing could be more satisfactory, was received with Joy by all; and peace being once more restored on all sides, Captain Roger intreated Rebecca to favour them with a Song, in compliance with which request having first assured them that she had a terrible cold, she sung as follows.

Song

When Corydon* went to the fair
He bought a red ribbon for Bess,
With which she encircled her hair
And made herself look very fess.*

Chapter the Fifth

At the end of 3 days Captain Roger and Rebecca were united and immediately after the Ceremony set off in the Stage Waggon* for the Captain's seat* in Buckinghamshire.*

The parents of Elfrida, alltho' they earnestly wished to see her married to Frederic before they died, yet knowing the delicate frame of her mind could ill bear the least exertion and rightly judging that naming her wedding day would be too great a one, forebore to press her on the subject.

Weeks and Fortnights flew away without gaining the least ground; the Cloathes grew out of fashion and at length Captain Roger and his Lady arrived, to pay a visit to their

Mother and introduce to her their beautifull Daughter of eighteen.

Elfrida, who had found her former acquaintance were growing too old and too ugly to be any longer agreable, was rejoiced to hear of the arrival of so pretty a girl as Eleanor with whom she determined to form the strictest freindship.

But the Happiness she had expected from an acquaintance with Eleanor, she soon found was not to be received, for she had not only the mortification of finding herself treated by her as little less than an old woman, but had actually the horror of perceiving a growing passion in the Bosom of Frederic for the Daughter of the amiable Rebecca.

The instant she had the first idea of such an attachment, she flew to Frederic and in a manner truly heroick, spluttered* out to him her intention of being married the next Day.

To one in his predicament who possessed less personal Courage than Frederic was master of, such a speech would have been Death; but he not being the least terrified boldly replied.

'Damme Elfrida *you* may be married tomorrow but *I* won't.'

This answer distressed her too much for her delicate Constitution. She accordingly fainted and was in such a hurry to have a succession of fainting fits, that she had scarcely patience enough to recover from one before she fell into another.

Tho', in any threatening Danger to his Life or Liberty, Frederic was as bold as brass yet in other respects his heart was as soft as cotton and immediately on hearing of the dangerous way Elfrida was in, he flew to her and finding her better than he had been taught to expect, was united to her Forever—.

Finis

Jack and Alice

a novel

Is respectfully inscribed to Francis William Austen Esqr* Midshipman on board his Majesty's Ship the Perseverance by his obedient humble Servant The Author

Chapter the First

Mr Johnson* was once upon a time about 53; in a twelvemonth afterwards he was 54, which so much delighted him that he was determined to celebrate his next Birth day by giving a Masquerade* to his Children and Freinds. Accordingly on the Day he attained his 55th year* tickets* were dispatched to all his Neighbours to that purpose. His acquaintance indeed in that part of the World were not very numerous as they consisted only of Lady Williams, Mr and Mrs Jones, Charles Adams and the 3 Miss Simpsons, who composed the neighbourhood of Pammydiddle* and formed the Masquerade.

Before I proceed to give an account of the Evening, it will be proper to describe to my reader, the persons and Characters of the party introduced to his acquaintance. Mr and Mrs Jones were both rather tall and very passionate, but were in other respects, good tempered, well behaved People. Charles Adams was an amiable, accomplished and bewitching young Man; of so dazzling a Beauty that none but Eagles could look him in the Face.*

Miss Simpson was pleasing in her person, in her Manners and in her Disposition; an unbounded ambition was her only fault. Her second sister Sukey* was Envious, Spitefull and Malicious. Her person was short, fat and disagreable. Cecilia* (the youngest) was perfectly handsome but too affected to be pleasing.

In Lady Williams* every virtue met. She was a widow with a handsome Jointure* and the remains of a very handsome face. Tho' Benevolent and Candid, she was Generous and sincere; Tho' Pious and Good, she was Religious and amiable, and Tho' Elegant and Agreable, she was Polished and Entertaining.*

The Johnsons were a family of Love,* and though a little addicted to the Bottle and the Dice, had many good Qualities.

Such was the party assembled in the elegant Drawing Room of Johnson Court, amongst which the pleasing figure of a Sultana* was the most remarkable of the female Masks.* Of the Males a Mask representing the Sun,* was the most universally admired. The Beams that darted from his Eyes were like those of that glorious Luminary tho' infinitely superior. So strong were they that no one dared venture within half a mile of them; he had therefore the best part of the Room to himself, its size not amounting to more than 3 quarters of a mile in length and half a one in breadth. The Gentleman at last finding the feirceness of his beams to be very inconvenient to the concourse by obliging them to croud together in one corner of the room, half shut his eyes by which means, the Company discovered him to be Charles Adams in his plain green Coat, without any mask at all.

When their astonishment was a little subsided their attention was attracted by 2 Dominos* who advanced in a horrible Passion; they were both very tall, but seemed in other respects to have many good qualities. 'These,' said the witty Charles, 'these are Mr and Mrs Jones,' and so indeed they were.

No one could imagine who was the Sultana! Till at length on her addressing a beautifull Flora* who was reclining in a studied attitude on a couch, with 'Oh Cecilia, I wish I was really what I pretend to be', she was discovered by the never failing genius of Charles Adams, to be the elegant but ambitious Caroline Simpson, and the person to whom she addressed herself, he rightly imagined to be her lovely but affected sister Cecilia.

The Company now advanced to a Gaming Table where sat 3 Dominos (each with a bottle in their hand) deeply engaged; but a female in the character of Virtue fled with hasty footsteps from the shocking scene, whilst a little fat woman representing Envy, sate alternately on the foreheads of the 3 Gamesters. Charles Adams was still as bright as ever; he soon discovered the party at play to be the 3 Johnsons, Envy to be Sukey Simpson and Virtue to be Lady Williams.

The Masks were then all removed and the Company retired to another room, to partake of an elegant and well managed Entertainment, after which the Bottle being pretty briskly pushed about by the 3 Johnsons, the whole party not excepting even Virtue were carried home, Dead Drunk.

Chapter the Second

For three months did the Masquerade afford ample subject for conversation to the inhabitants of Pammydiddle; but no character at it was so fully expatiated on as Charles Adams. The singularity of his appearance, the beams which darted from his eyes, the brightness of his Wit, and the whole *tout ensemble** of his person had subdued the hearts of so many of the young Ladies, that of the six present at the Masquerade but five had returned uncaptivated. Alice Johnson was the unhappy sixth whose heart had not been able to withstand the power of his Charms. But as it may appear strange to my Readers, that so much worth and Excellence as he possessed should have conquered only hers, it will be necessary to inform them that the Miss Simpsons were defended from his Power by Ambition, Envy, and Self-admiration.

Every wish of Caroline was centered in a titled Husband;

whilst in Sukey such superior excellence could only raise her Envy not her Love, and Cecilia was too tenderly attached to herself to be pleased with any one besides. As for Lady Williams and Mrs Jones, the former of them was too sensible, to fall in love with one so much her Junior and the latter, tho' very tall and very passionate was too fond of her Husband to think of such a thing.

Yet in spite of every endeavour on the part of Miss Johnson to discover any attachment to her in him; the cold and indifferent heart of Charles Adams still to all appearance, preserved its native freedom; polite to all but partial to none, he still remained the lovely, the lively, but insensible Charles Adams.

One evening, Alice finding herself somewhat heated by wine (no very uncommon case) determined to seek a relief for her disordered Head and Love-sick Heart in the Conversation of the intelligent Lady Williams.

She found her Ladyship at home as was in general the Case, for she was not fond of going out, and like the great Sir Charles Grandison scorned to deny herself when at Home,* as she looked on that fashionable method of shutting out disagreable Visitors, as little less than downright Bigamy.*

In spite of the wine she had been drinking, poor Alice was uncommonly out of spirits;* she could think of nothing but Charles Adams, she could talk of nothing but him, and in short spoke so openly that Lady Williams soon discovered the unreturned affection she bore him, which excited her Pity and Compassion so strongly that she addressed her in the following Manner.

'I perceive but too plainly my dear Miss Johnson, that your Heart has not been able to withstand the fascinating Charms of this Young Man and I pity you sincerely. Is it a first Love?'

'It is.'

'I am still more greived to hear *that*; I am myself a sad example of the Miseries, in general attendant on a first Love and I am determined for the future to avoid the like Misfortune. I wish it may not be too late for you to do the same; if it is not endeavour my dear Girl to secure yourself from so great a Danger. A second attachment* is seldom attended with any serious consequences; against *that* therefore I have nothing to say. Preserve yourself from a first Love and you need not fear a second.'

'You mentioned Madam something of your having yourself been a sufferer by the misfortune you are so good as to wish me to avoid. Will you favour me with your Life and Adventures?'*

'Willingly my Love.'

Chapter the Third

'My Father was a gentleman of considerable Fortune in Berkshire;* myself and a few more his only Children. I was but six years old when I had the misfortune of losing my Mother and being at that time young and Tender, my father instead of sending me to School, procured an able handed Governess to superintend my Education at Home. My Brothers were placed at Schools suitable to their Ages and my Sisters being all younger than myself, remained still under the Care of their Nurse.

'Miss Dickins was an excellent Governess. She instructed me in the Paths of Virtue; under her tuition I daily became more amiable, and might perhaps by this time have nearly attained perfection, had not my worthy Preceptoress been torn from my arms, e'er I had attained my seventeenth year. I never shall forget her last words. "My dear Kitty she said, Good night t'ye." I never saw here afterwards,' continued Lady Williams wiping her eyes, 'She eloped with the Butler the same night.

'I was invited the following year by a distant relation of my Father's to spend the Winter with her in town.* Mrs Watkins was a Lady of Fashion, Family and fortune; she was in general esteemed a pretty Woman, but I never thought her very handsome, for my part. She had too high a forehead, Her eyes were too small and she had too much colour.'*

'How can *that* be?' interrupted Miss Johnson reddening with anger; 'Do you think that any one can have too much colour?'

'Indeed I do, and I'll tell you why I do my dear Alice; when a person has too great a degree of red in their Complexion, it gives their face in my opinion, too red a look.'

'But can a face my Lady have too red a look?'

'Certainly my dear Miss Johnson and I'll tell you why. When a face has too red a look it does not appear to so much advantage as it would were it paler.'

'Pray Ma'am proceed in your story.'

'Well, as I said before, I was invited by this Lady to spend some weeks with her in town. Many Gentlemen thought her Handsome but in my opinion, Her forehead was too high, her eyes too small and she had too much colour.'

'In that Madam as I said before your Ladyship must have been mistaken. Mrs Watkins could not have too much colour since no one can have too much.'

'Excuse me my Love if I do not agree with you in that particular. Let me explain myself clearly; my idea of the case is this. When a Woman has too great a proportion of red in her Cheeks, she must have too much colour.'

'But Madam I deny that it is possible for any one to have too great a proportion of red in their Cheeks.'

'What my Love not if they have too much colour?'

Miss Johnson was now out of all patience, the more so perhaps as Lady Williams still remained so inflexibly cool. It must be remembered however that her Ladyship had in one respect by far the advantage of Alice; I mean in not being drunk, for heated with wine and raised by Passion, she could have little command of her Temper.

The Dispute at length grew so hot on the part of Alice that, 'From Words she almost came to Blows'* When Mr Johnson luckily entered and with some difficulty forced her away from Lady Williams, Mrs Watkins and her red cheeks.

Chapter the Fourth

My Readers may perhaps imagine that after such a fracas, no intimacy could longer subsist between the Johnsons and Lady Williams, but in that they are mistaken for her Ladyship was too sensible to be angry at a conduct which she could not help perceiving to be the natural consequence of inebriety and Alice had too sincere a respect for Lady Williams and too great a relish for her Claret,* not to make every concession in her power.

A few days after their reconciliation Lady Williams called on Miss Johnson to propose a walk in a Citron Grove* which led from her Ladyship's pigstye to Charles Adams's Horsepond.* Alice was too sensible of Lady Williams's kindness in proposing such a walk and too much pleased with the prospect of seeing at the end of it, a Horsepond of Charles's, not to accept it with visible delight. They had not proceeded far before she was roused from the reflection of the happiness she was going to enjoy, by Lady Williams's thus addressing her.

'I have as yet forborn my dear Alice to continue the narrative of my Life from an unwillingness of recalling to your Memory a scene which (since it reflects on you rather disgrace than credit) had better be forgot than remembered.'

Alice had already begun to colour up and was beginning to speak, when her Ladyship perceiving her displeasure, continued thus.

'I am afraid my dear Girl that I have offended you by what I have just said; I assure you I do not mean to distress you by a retrospection of what cannot now be helped; considering all things I do not think you so much to blame as many People do; for when a person is in Liquor, there is no answering for what they may do.'

'Madam, this is not to be borne; I insist—'

'My dear Girl don't vex yourself about the matter; I assure you I have entirely forgiven every thing respecting it;

indeed I was not angry at the time, because as I saw all along, you were nearly dead drunk. I knew you could not help saying the strange things you did. But I see I distress you; so I will change the subject and desire it may never again be mentioned; remember it is all forgot—I will now pursue my story; but I must insist upon not giving you any description of Mrs Watkins; it would only be reviving old stories and as you never saw her, it can be nothing to you, if her forehead *was* too high, her eyes *were* too small, or if she *had* too much colour.'

'Again! Lady Williams: this is too much'——

So provoked was poor Alice at this renewal of the old story, that I know not what might have been the consequence of it, had not their attention been engaged by another object. A lovely young Woman lying apparently in great pain beneath a Citron-tree, was an object too interesting not to attract their notice. Forgetting their own dispute they both with simpathizing Tenderness advanced towards her and accosted her in these terms.

'You seem fair Nymph to be labouring under some misfortune which we shall be happy to relieve if you will inform us what it is. Will you favour us with your Life and adventures?'*

'Willingly Ladies, if you will be so kind as to be seated.' They took their places and she thus began.

Chapter the Fifth

'I am a native of North Wales* and my Father is one of the most capital Taylors in it. Having a numerous family, he was easily prevailed on by a sister of my Mother's who is a widow in good circumstances and keeps an alehouse in the next Village to ours, to let her take me and breed me up at her own expence. Accordingly I have lived with her for the last 8 years of my Life, during which time she provided me with some of the first rate Masters, who taught me all the

accomplishments requisite for one of my sex and rank.*
Under their instructions I learned Dancing, Music, Drawing
and various Languages, by which means I became more
accomplished than any other Taylor's Daughter in Wales.
Never was there a happier Creature than I was, till within
the last half year—but I should have told you before that
the principal Estate in our Neighbourhood belongs to
Charles Adams, the owner of the brick House, you see
yonder.'

'Charles Adams!' exclaimed the astonished Alice; 'are
you acquainted with Charles Adams?'

'To my sorrow madam I am. He came about half a year
ago to receive the rents of the Estate* I have just
mentioned. At that time I first saw him; as you seem ma'am
acquainted with him, I need not describe to you how
charming he is. I could not resist his attractions;'——

'Ah! who can,' said Alice with a deep sigh.

'My aunt being in terms of the greatest intimacy with his
cook, determined, at my request, to try whether she could
discover, by means of her freind if there were any chance of
his returning my affection. For this purpose she went one
evening to drink tea with Mrs Susan, who in the course of
Conversation mentioned the goodness of her Place* and the
Goodness of her Master; upon which my Aunt began
pumping her with so much dexterity that in a short time
Susan owned, that she did not think her Master would ever
marry, "for (said she) he has often and often declared to me
that his wife, whoever she might be, must possess, Youth,
Beauty, Birth, Wit, Merit, and Money.* I have many a
time (she continued) endeavoured to reason him out of his
resolution and to convince him of the improbability of his
ever meeting with such a Lady; but my arguments have had
no effect and he continues as firm in his determination as
ever." You may imagine Ladies my distress on hearing this;
for I was fearfull that tho' possessed of Youth, Beauty, Wit
and Merit, and tho' the probable Heiress of my Aunts
House and business, he might think me deficient in Rank,
and in being so, unworthy of his hand.

'However I was determined to make a bold push and

therefore wrote him a very kind letter, offering him with great tenderness my hand and heart.* To this I received an angry and peremptory refusal, but thinking it might be rather the effect of his modesty than any thing else, I pressed him again on the subject. But he never answered any more of my Letters and very soon afterwards left the Country. As soon as I heard of his departure I wrote to him here, informing him that I should shortly do myself the honour of waiting on him at Pammydiddle, to which I received no answer; therefore choosing to take, Silence for Consent, I left Wales, unknown to my Aunt, and arrived here after a tedious Journey this Morning. On enquiring for his House I was directed thro' this Wood, to the one you there see. With a heart elated by the expected happiness of beholding him I entered it and had proceeded thus far in my progress thro' it, when I found myself suddenly seized by the leg and on examining the cause of it, found that I was caught in one of the steel traps* so common in gentlemen's grounds.'

'Ah,' cried Lady Williams, 'how fortunate we are to meet with you; since we might otherwise perhaps have shared the like misfortune'——

'It is indeed happy for you Ladies, that I should have been a short time before you. I screamed as you may easily imagine till the woods resounded again and till one of the inhuman Wretch's servants came to my assistance and released me from my dreadfull prison, but not before one of my legs was entirely broken.'

Chapter the Sixth

At this melancholy recital the fair eyes of Lady Williams, were suffused in tears and Alice could not help exclaiming,

'Oh! cruel Charles to wound the hearts and legs of all the fair.'

Lady Williams now interposed and observed that the

young Lady's leg ought to be set without farther delay. After examining the fracture therefore, she immediately began and performed the operation with great skill which was the more wonderfull on account of her having never performed such a one before.* Lucy, then arose from the ground and finding that she could walk with the greatest ease, accompanied them to Lady Williams's House at her Ladyship's particular request.

The perfect form, the beautifull face, and elegant manners of Lucy so won on the affections of Alice that when they parted, which was not till after Supper, she assured her that except her Father, Brother, Uncles, Aunts, Cousins and other relations, Lady Williams, Charles Adams and a few dozen more of particular freinds, she loved her better than almost any other person in the world.

Such a flattering assurance of her regard would justly have given much pleasure to the object of it, had she not plainly perceived that the amiable Alice had partaken too freely of Lady Williams's claret.

Her Ladyship (whose discernment was great) read in the intelligent countenance of Lucy her thoughts on the subject and as soon as Miss Johnson had taken her leave, thus addressed her.

'When you are more intimately acquainted with my Alice you will not be surprised, Lucy, to see the dear Creature drink a little too much; for such things happen every day. She has many rare and charming qualities, but Sobriety is not one of them. The whole Family are indeed a sad drunken set. I am sorry to say too that I never knew three such thorough Gamesters as they are, more particularly Alice. But she is a charming girl. I fancy not one of the sweetest tempers in the world; to be sure I have seen her in such passions! However she is a sweet young Woman. I am sure you'll like her. I scarcely know any one so amiable.— Oh! that you could but have seen her the other Evening! How she raved! and on such a trifle too! She is indeed a most pleasing Girl! I shall always love her!'

'She appears by your ladyship's account to have many good qualities', replied Lucy. 'Oh! a thousand,' answered

Lady Williams; 'tho' I am very partial to her, and perhaps am blinded by my affection, to her real defects.'

Chapter the Seventh

The next morning brought the three Miss Simpsons to wait on Lady Williams, who received them with the utmost politeness and introduced to their acquaintance Lucy, with whom the eldest was so much pleased that at parting she declared her sole *ambition* was to have her accompany them the next morning to Bath,* whither they were going for some weeks.

'Lucy,' said Lady Williams, 'is quite at her own disposal and if she chooses to accept so kind an invitation, I hope she will not hesitate, from any motives of delicacy on my account. I know not indeed how I shall ever be able to part with her. She never was at Bath and I should think that it would be a most agreable Jaunt* to her. Speak my Love,' continued she, turning to Lucy, 'what say you to accompanying these Ladies? I shall be miserable without you—t'will be a most pleasant tour to you—I hope you'll go; if you do I am sure t'will be the Death of me—pray be persuaded'——

Lucy begged leave to decline the honour of accompanying them, with many expressions of gratitude for the extream politeness of Miss Simpson in inviting her.

Miss Simpson appeared much disappointed by her refusal. Lady Williams insisted on her going—declared that she would never forgive her if she did not, and that she should never survive it if she did, and in short used such persuasive arguments that it was at length resolved she was to go. The Miss Simpsons called for her at ten o'clock the next morning and Lady Williams had soon the satisfaction of receiving from her young freind, the pleasing intelligence of their safe arrival in Bath.

It may now be proper to return to the Hero of this Novel, the brother of Alice, of whom I beleive I have scarcely ever had occasion to speak; which may perhaps be partly oweing to his unfortunate propensity to Liquor, which so compleatly deprived him of the use of those faculties Nature had endowed him with, that he never did anything worth mentioning. His Death happened a short time after Lucy's departure and was the natural Consequence of this pernicious practice. By his decease, his sister became the sole inheritress of a very large fortune, which as it gave her fresh Hopes of rendering herself acceptable as a wife to Charles Adams could not fail of being most pleasing to her—and as the effect was Joyfull the Cause could scarcely be lamented.

Finding the violence of her attachment to him daily augment, she at length disclosed it to her Father and desired him to propose a union between them to Charles. Her father consented and set out one morning to open the affair to the young Man. Mr Johnson being a man of few words his part was soon performed and the answer he received was as follows—

'Sir, I may perhaps be expected to appear pleased at and gratefull for the offer you have made me: but let me tell you that I consider it as an affront. I look upon myself to be Sir a perfect Beauty—where would you see a finer figure or a more charming face. Then, sir I imagine my Manners and Address to be of the most polished kind; there is a certain elegance a peculiar sweetness in them that I never saw equalled and cannot describe*—. Partiality aside, I am certainly more accomplished in every Language, every Science, every Art and every thing than any other person in Europe. My temper is even, my virtues innumerable, my self unparalelled. Since such, Sir, is my character, what do you mean by wishing me to marry your Daughter? Let me give you a short sketch of yourself and of her. I look upon you Sir to be a very good sort of Man in the main; a drunken old Dog to be sure, but that's nothing to me. Your daughter sir, is neither sufficiently beautifull, sufficiently amiable, sufficiently witty, nor sufficiently rich for me—. I expect nothing more in my wife than my wife will find in me—Perfection. These sir, are my sentiments and I honour myself for having such. One freind I have and glory in having but one——. She is at present preparing my Dinner, but if you choose to see her, she shall come and she will inform you that these have ever been my sentiments.'

Mr Johnson was satisfied: and expressing himself to be much obliged to Mr Adams for the characters he had favoured him with of himself and his Daughter, took his leave.

The unfortunate Alice on receiving from her father the sad account of the ill success his visit had been attended with, could scarcely support the disappointment—She flew to her Bottle and it was soon forgot.*

Chapter the Eighth

While these affairs were transacting at Pammydiddle, Lucy was conquering every Heart at Bath. A fortnight's residence there had nearly effaced from her remembrance the captivating form of Charles—The recollection of what her Heart had formerly suffered by his charms and her Leg by his trap, enabled her to forget him with tolerable Ease, which was what she determined to do; and for that purpose dedicated five minutes in every day to the employment of driving him from her remembrance.

Her second Letter to Lady Williams contained the pleasing intelligence of her having accomplished her under-taking to her entire satisfaction; she mentioned in it also an offer of marriage she had received from the Duke of —— an elderly Man of noble fortune whose ill health was the chief inducement of his Journey to Bath. 'I am distressed (she continued) to know whether I mean to accept him or not. There are a thousand advantages to be derived from a marriage with the Duke, for besides those more inferior ones of Rank and Fortune it will procure me a home, which of all other things is what I most desire. Your Ladyship's kind wish of my always remaining with you, is noble and generous but I cannot think of becoming so great a burden on one I so much love and esteem. That one should receive obligations only from those we despise, is a sentiment instilled into my mind by my worthy aunt, in my early years, and cannot in my opinion be too strictly adhered to. The excellent woman of whom I now speak, is I hear too much incensed by my imprudent departure from Wales, to receive me again—. I most earnestly wish to leave the Ladies I am now with. Miss Simpson is indeed (setting aside ambition) very amiable, but her 2^d Sister the envious and malvolent Sukey is too disagreable to live with. I have reason to think that the admiration I have met with in the circles of the great at this Place, has raised her Hatred and Envy; for often has she threatened, and sometimes endeavoured to cut my throat.—Your Ladyship will therefore allow that I am not wrong in wishing to leave Bath, and in wishing to have a home to receive me, when I do. I shall expect with impatience your advice concerning the Duke and am your most obliged

&c. Lucy.'

Lady Williams sent her, her opinion on the subject in the following Manner.

'Why do you hesitate my dearest Lucy, a moment with respect to the Duke? I have enquired into his Character and find him to be an unprincipaled, illiterate Man. Never shall my Lucy be united to such a one! He has a princely fortune, which is every day encreasing. How nobly will you spend it!, what credit will you give him in the eyes of all! How much will he be respected on his Wife's account!* But why my dearest Lucy, why will you not at once decide this affair by returning to me and never leaving me again? Altho' I admire your noble sentiments with respect to obligations, yet, let me beg that they may not prevent your making me happy. It will to be sure be a great expence to me, to have you always with me—I shall not be able to support it—but what is that in comparison with the happiness I shall enjoy in your society?—'twill ruin me I know—you will not therefore surely, withstand these arguments, or refuse to return to yours most affectionately &c. &c.

C. Williams.'

Chapter the Ninth

What might have been the effect of her Ladyship's advice, had it ever been received by Lucy, is uncertain, as it reached Bath a few Hours after she had breathed her last. She fell a sacrifice to the Envy and Malice of Sukey who jealous of her superior charms took her by poison from an admiring World at the age of seventeen.

Thus fell the amiable and lovely Lucy whose Life had been marked by no crime, and stained by no blemish but her imprudent departure from her Aunts, and whose death was sincerely lamented by every one who knew her. Among the most afflicted of her friends were Lady Williams, Miss Johnson and the Duke; the 2 first of whom had a most sincere regard for her, more particularly Alice, who had spent a whole evening in her company and had never thought of her since. His Grace's affliction may likewise be easily accounted for, since he lost one for whom he had experienced during the last ten days, a tender affection and sincere regard. He mourned her loss with unshaken constancy for the next fortnight at the end of which time, he gratified the ambition of Caroline Simpson by raising her to the rank of a Dutchess. Thus was she at length rendered compleatly happy in the gratification of her favourite passion. Her sister the perfidious Sukey, was likewise shortly after exalted in a manner she truly deserved, and by her actions appeared to have always desired. Her barbarous Murder was discovered and in spite of every interceding freind* she was speedily raised to the Gallows*—. The beautifull but affected Cecilia was too sensible of her own superior charms. not to imagine that if Caroline could engage a Duke, she might without censure aspire to the affections of some Prince—and knowing that those of her native Country were cheifly engaged,* she left England and I have since heard is at present the favourite Sultana of the great Mogul*—.

In the mean time the inhabitants of Pammydiddle were in a state of the greatest astonishment and Wonder, a report being circulated of the intended marriage of Charles Adams. The Lady's name was still a secret. Mr and Mrs Jones imagined it to be, Miss Johnson; but *she* knew better; all *her* fears were centered in his Cook, when to the astonishment of every one, he was publicly united to Lady Williams—

Finis

Edgar and Emma

a tale

Chapter the First

'I cannot imagine,' said Sir Godfrey to his Lady,* 'why we continue in such deplorable Lodgings as these, in a paltry Market-town,* while we have 3 good Houses of our own situated in some of the finest parts of England, and perfectly ready to receive us!'

'I'm sure, Sir Godfrey,' replied Lady Marlow, 'it has been much against my inclination that we have staid here so long; or why we should ever have come at all indeed, has been to me a wonder, as none of our Houses have been in the least want of repair.'

'Nay, my dear,' answered Sir Godfrey, 'you are the last person who ought to be displeased with what was always meant as a compliment to you; for you cannot but be sensible of the very great inconvenience your Daughters and I have been put to, during the 2 years we have remained crowded in these Lodgings in order to give you pleasure.'

'My dear,' replied Lady Marlow, 'How can you stand and tell such lies, when you very well know that it was merely to oblige the Girls and you, that I left a most commodious House situated in a most delightfull Country and surrounded by a most agreable Neighbourhood, to live 2 years cramped up in Lodgings three pair of Stairs high,* in a smokey and unwholesome town, which has given me a continual fever and almost thrown me into a Consumption.'

As, after a few more speeches on both sides, they could not determine which was the most to blame, they prudently laid aside the debate, and having packed up their Cloathes and paid their rent, they set out the next morning with their 2 Daughters for their seat in Sussex.*

Sir Godfrey and Lady Marlow were indeed very sensible people and tho' (as in this instance) like many other sensible People, they sometimes did a foolish thing, yet in general their actions were guided by Prudence and regulated by discretion.

After a Journey of two Days and a half they arrived at Marlhurst* in good health and high spirits; so overjoyed were they all to inhabit again a place, they had left with mutual regret for two years, that they ordered the bells to be rung and distributed ninepence among the Ringers.*

Chapter the Second

The news of their arrival being quickly spread throughout the Country, brought them in a few Days visits of congratulation from every family in it.

Amongst the rest came the inhabitants of Willmot Lodge a beautifull Villa* not far from Marlhurst. Mr Willmot* was the representative of a very ancient Family and possessed besides his paternal Estate, a considerable share in a Lead mine* and a ticket in the Lottery.* His Lady was an agreable Woman. Their Children were too numerous to be particularly described; it is sufficient to say that in general they were virtuously inclined and not given to any wicked ways. Their family being too large to accompany them in every visit, they took nine with them alternately. When their Coach stopped at Sir Godfrey's door, the Miss Marlow's Hearts throbbed in the eager expectation of once more beholding a family so dear to them. Emma the youngest (who was more particularly interested in their arrival, being attached to their eldest Son) continued at her Dressing-room window in anxious Hopes of seeing young Edgar descend from the Carriage.

Mr and Mrs Willmot with their three eldest Daughters first appeared—Emma began to tremble. Robert, Richard, Ralph, and Rodolphus followed—Emma turned pale. Their two youngest Girls were lifted from the Coach—Emma sunk breathless on a Sopha.* A footman came to announce to her the arrival of Company; her heart was too full to contain its afflictions. A confidante* was necessary—In Thomas she hoped to experience a faithfull one—for one she must have and Thomas was the only one at Hand. To him she unbosomed herself without restraint and after owning her passion for young Willmot, requested his advice in what manner she should conduct herself in the melancholy Disappointment under which she laboured.

Thomas, who would gladly have been excused from listening to her complaint, begged leave to decline giving any advice concerning it, which much against her will, she was obliged to comply with.

Having dispatched him therefore with many injunctions of secrecy, she descended with a heavy heart into the Parlour, where she found the good Party seated in a social Manner round a blazing fire.

Chapter the Third

Emma had continued in the Parlour some time before she could summon up sufficient courage to ask Mrs Willmot after the rest of her family; and when she did, it was in so low, so faltering a voice that no one knew she spoke. Dejected by the ill success of her first attempt she made no other, till on Mrs Willmot's desiring one of the little Girls to ring the bell for their Carriage, she stepped across the room and seizing the string said in a resolute manner.

'Mrs Willmot, you do not stir from this House till you let me know how all the rest of your family do, particularly your eldest son.'

They were all greatly surprised by such an unexpected address and the more so, on account of the manner in which it was spoken; but Emma, who would not be again disappointed, requesting an answer, Mrs Willmot made the following eloquent oration.

'Our children are all extremely well but at present most of them from home. Amy is with my sister Clayton. Sam at Eton.* David with his Uncle John. Jem and Will at Winchester.* Kitty at Queen's Square.* Ned with his Grandmother. Hetty and Patty in a Convent at Brussells.* Edgar at college,* Peter at Nurse,* and all the rest (except the nine here) at home.'

It was with difficulty that Emma could refrain from tears on hearing of the absence of Edgar; she remained however tolerably composed till the Willmots were gone when having no check to the overflowings of her greif, she gave free vent to them, and retiring to her own room, continued in tears the remainder of her Life.

Finis

Henry and Eliza*

a novel

Is humbly dedicated to Miss Cooper* by her obedient Humble
Servant

The Author

As Sir George and Lady Harcourt were superintending the
Labours of their Haymakers, rewarding the industry of
some by smiles of approbation,* and punishing the idleness
of others, by a cudgel,* they perceived lying closely
concealed beneath the thick foliage of a Haycock,* a
beautifull little Girl not more than 3 months old.

Touched with the enchanting Graces of her face and
delighted with the infantine tho' sprightly answers she
returned to their many questions, they resolved to take her
home and, having no Children of their own, to educate her
with care and cost.

Being good People themselves, their first and principal
Care was to incite in her a Love of Virtue and a Hatred of
Vice, in which they so well succeeded (Eliza having a
natural turn that way herself) that when she grew up, she
was the delight of all who knew her.

Beloved by Lady Harcourt, adored by Sir George and
admired by all the World, she lived in a continued course of
uninterrupted Happiness, till she had attained her eighteenth
year, when happening one day to be detected in stealing a
banknote of 50£,* she was turned out of doors by her
inhuman Benefactors. Such a transition to one who did not
possess so noble and exalted a mind as Eliza, would have
been Death, but she, happy in the conscious knowledge of
her own Excellence, amused herself, as she sate beneath a
tree with making and singing the following Lines.

Song.

Though misfortunes my footsteps may ever attend
I hope I shall never have need of a Freind
as an innocent Heart I will ever preserve
and will never from Virtue's dear boundaries swerve.

Having amused herself some hours, with this song and her own pleasing reflections, she arose and took the road to M., a small market town of which place her most intimate freind kept the red Lion.*

To this freind she immediately went, to whom having recounted her late misfortune, she communicated her wish of getting into some family in the capacity of Humble Companion.*

Mrs Wilson, who was the most amiable creature on earth, was no sooner acquainted with her Desire, than she sate down in the Bar and wrote the following Letter to the Dutchess of F., the woman whom of all others, she most Esteemed.

'To the Dutchess of F.'

Receive into your Family, at my request a young woman of unexceptionable Character, who is so good as to choose your Society in preference to going to Service. Hasten, and take her from the arms of your

Sarah Wilson

The Dutchess, whose freindship for Mrs Wilson would have carried her any lengths, was overjoyed at such an opportunity of obliging her and accordingly sate out immediately on the receipt of her letter for the red Lion, which she reached the same Evening. The Dutchess of F. was about 45 and a half; Her passions were strong, her freindships firm and her Enmities, unconquerable. She was a widow and had only one Daughter who was on the point of marriage with a young Man of considerable fortune.

The Dutchess no sooner beheld our Heroine than throwing her arms around her neck, she declared herself so much pleased with her, that she was resolved they never more should part. Eliza was delighted with such a protestation of freindship, and after taking a most affecting leave of her dear Mrs Wilson, accompanied her grace the next morning to her seat in Surry.

With every expression of regard did the Dutchess introduce her to Lady Harriet, who was so much pleased with her appearance that she besought her, to consider her as her Sister, which Eliza with the greatest Condescension promised to do.

Mr Cecil, the Lover of Lady Harriet, being often with the family was often with Eliza. A mutual Love took place and Cecil having declared his first, prevailed on Eliza to consent to a private union,* which was easy to be effected, as the Dutchess's chaplain being very much in love with Eliza himself, would they were certain do anything to oblige her.

The Dutchess and Lady Harriet being engaged one evening to an assembly, they took the opportunity of their absence and were united by the enamoured Chaplain.

When the Ladies returned, their amazement was great at finding instead of Eliza the following Note.

'Madam

We are married and gone.

Henry & Eliza Cecil.'

Her Grace as soon as she had read the letter, which sufficiently explained the whole affair, flew into the most violent passion and after having spent an agreable half hour, in calling them by all the shocking Names her rage could suggest to her, sent out after them 300 armed Men, with orders not to return without their Bodies, dead or alive; intending that if they should be brought to her in the latter condition to have them put to Death in some torturelike manner, after a few years Confinement.

In the mean time Cecil and Eliza continued their flight to

the Continent,* which they judged to be more secure than their native Land, from the dreadfull effects of the Dutchess's vengeance, which they had so much reason to apprehend.

In France they remained 3 years, during which time they became the parents of two Boys, and at the end of it Eliza became a widow without any thing to support either her or her Children. They had lived since their Marriage at the rate of 18,000£ a year,* of which Mr Cecil's estate being rather less than the twentieth part, they had been able to save but a trifle, having lived to the utmost extent of their Income.

Eliza, being perfectly conscious of the derangement in their affairs, immediately on her Husband's death set sail for England, in a man of War of 55 Guns,* which they had built in their more prosperous Days. But no sooner had she stepped on Shore at Dover, with a Child in each hand, than she was seized by the officers of the Dutchess, and conducted by them to a snug little Newgate* of their Lady's which she had erected for the reception of her own private Prisoners.*

No sooner had Eliza entered her Dungeon than the first thought which occurred to her, was how to get out of it again.

She went to the Door; but it was locked. She looked at the Window; but it was barred with iron; disappointed in both her expectations, she dispaired of effecting her Escape, when she fortunately perceived in a Corner of her Cell, a small saw and Ladder of ropes. With the saw she instantly went to work and in a few weeks had displaced every Bar but one to which she fastened the Ladder.

A difficulty then occurred which for some time, she knew not how to obviate. Her Children were too small to get down the Ladder by themselves, nor would it be possible for her to take them in her arms, when *she* did. At last she determined to fling down all her Cloathes, of which she had a large Quantity, and then having given them strict Charge not to hurt themselves, threw her Children after them. She herself with ease discended by the Ladder, at the bottom of

which she had the pleasure of finding her little boys in
perfect Health and fast asleep.

Her wardrobe she now saw a fatal necessity of selling,
both for the preservation of her Children and herself. With
tears in her eyes, she parted with these last reliques of her
former Glory, and with the money she got for them, bought
others more usefull, some playthings for Her Boys and a
gold Watch for herself.*

But scarcely was she provided with the above-mentioned
necessaries, than she began to find herself rather hungry,
and had reason to think, by their biting off two of her
fingers,* that her Children were much in the same
situation.

To remedy these unavoidable misfortunes, she determined
to return to her old freinds, Sir George and Lady Harcourt,
whose generosity she had so often experienced and hoped to
experience as often again.

She had about 40 miles to travel before she could reach
their hospitable Mansion, of which having walked 30
without stopping, she found herself at the Entrance of a
Town, where often in happier times, she had accompanied
Sir George and Lady Harcourt to regale themselves with a
cold collation* at one of the Inns.

The reflections that her adventures since the last time she
had partaken of these happy *Junketings*,* afforded her,
occupied her mind, for some time, as she sate on the steps
at the door of a Gentleman's house. As soon as these
reflections were ended, she arose and determined to take
her station at the very inn, she remembered with so much
delight, from the Company of which, as they went in and
out, she hoped to receive some Charitable Gratuity.

She had but just taken her post at the Innyard before a
Carriage drove out of it, and on turning the Corner at which
she was stationed, stopped to give the Postilion an
opportunity of admiring the beauty of the prospect. Eliza
then advanced to the carriage and was going to request
their Charity, when on fixing her Eyes on the Lady, within
it, she exclaimed,

'Lady Harcourt!'

To which the lady replied,
'Eliza!'

'Yes Madam it is the wretched Eliza herself.'

Sir George, who was also in the Carriage, but too much amazed to speek, was proceeding to demand an explanation from Eliza of the Situation she was then in, when Lady Harcourt in transports of Joy, exclaimed.

'Sir George, Sir George, she is not only Eliza our adopted Daughter, but our real Child.'*

'Our real Child! What Lady Harcourt, do you mean? You know you never even was with child. Explain yourself, I beseech you.'

'You must remember Sir George, that when you sailed for America, you left me breeding.'

'I do, I do, go on dear Polly.'

'Four months after you were gone, I was delivered of this Girl, but dreading your just resentment at her not proving the Boy you wished, I took her to a Haycock and laid her down. A few weeks afterwards, you returned, and fortunately for me, made no enquiries on the subject. Satisfied within myself of the wellfare of my Child, I soon forgot I had one, insomuch that when, we shortly after found her in the very Haycock, I had placed her, I had no more idea of her being my own, than you had, and nothing I will venture to say would have recalled the circumstance to my remembrance, but my thus accidentally hearing her voice, which now strikes me as being the very counterpart of my own Child's.'

'The rational and convincing Account you have given of the whole affair,' said Sir George, 'leaves no doubt of her being our Daughter and as such I freely forgive the robbery she was guilty of.'

A mutual Reconciliation then took place, and Eliza, ascending the Carriage with her two Children returned to that home from which she had been absent nearly four years.

No sooner was she reinstated in her accustomed power at Harcourt Hall, than she raised an Army, with which she entirely demolished the Dutchess's Newgate, snug as it was, and by that act, gained the Blessings of thousands, and the Applause of her own Heart.*

Finis

The adventures of Mr Harley*

a short, but interesting Tale, is with all imaginable Respect inscribed to Mr Francis William Austen* Midshipman* on board his Majesty's Ship the Perseverance by his Obedient Servant

The Author.

Mr Harley was one of many Children. Destined by his father for the Church and by his Mother for the Sea, desirous of pleasing both, he prevailed on Sir John to obtain for him a Chaplaincy on board a Man of War. He accordingly, cut his Hair and sailed.

In half a year he returned and set-off in the Stage Coach for Hogsworth Green,* the seat of Emma. His fellow travellers were, A man without a Hat, Another with two, An old maid and a young Wife.

This last appeared about 17 with fine dark Eyes and an elegant Shape; in short Mr Harley soon found out, that she was his Emma and recollected he had married her a few weeks before he left England.

Finis

Sir William Mountague*

an unfinished performance
is humbly dedicated to Charles John
Austen Esqre,* by his most obedient humble
Servant
The Author

Sir William Mountague was the son of Sir Henry Mountague, who was the son of Sir John Mountague, a descendant of Sir Christopher Mountague, who was the nephew of Sir Edward Mountague, whose ancestor was Sir James Mountague a near relation of Sir Robert Mountague, who inherited the Title and Estate from Sir Frederic Mountague.

Sir William was about 17 when his Father died, and left him a handsome fortune, an ancient House and a Park well stocked with Deer.* Sir William had not been long in the possession of his Estate before he fell in Love with the 3 Miss Cliftons of Kilhoobery Park.* These young Ladies were all equally young, equally handsome, equally rich and equally amiable—Sir William was equally in Love with them all,* and knowing not which to prefer, he left the Country and took Lodgings in a small Village near Dover.

In this retreat, to which he had retired in the hope of finding a shelter from the Pangs of Love, he became enamoured of a young Widow of Quality, who came for change of air to the same Village, after the death of a Husband, whom she had always tenderly loved and now sincerely lamented.

Lady Percival was young, accomplished and lovely. Sir William adored her and she consented to become his Wife. Vehemently pressed by Sir William to name the day in which he might conduct her to the Altar, she at length fixed on the following Monday, which was the first of September.*

Sir William was a Shot and could not support the idea of losing such a Day, even for such a Cause. He begged her to delay the Wedding a short time. Lady Percival was enraged and returned to London the next Morning.

Sir William was sorry to lose her, but as he knew that he should have been much more greived by the Loss of the 1st of September, his Sorrow was not without a mixture of Happiness, and his Affliction was considerably lessened by his Joy.

After staying at the Village a few weeks longer, he left it and went to a freind's House in Surry.* Mr Brudenell was a sensible Man, and had a beautifull Neice with whom Sir William soon fell in love. But Miss Arundel was cruel; she preferred a Mr Stanhope:* Sir William shot Mr Stanhope;* the lady had then no reason to refuse him; she accepted him, and they were to be married on the 27th of October. But on the 25th Sir William received a visit from Emma Stanhope, the sister of the unfortunate Victim of his rage. She begged some recompence, some atonement for the cruel Murder of her Brother. Sir William bade her name her price. She fixed on 14*s*. Sir William offered her himself and Fortune. They went to London the next day and were there privately married.* For a fortnight Sir William was compleatly happy, but chancing one day to see a charming young Woman entering a Chariot* in Brook Street,* he became again most violently in love. On enquiring the name of this fair Unknown, he found that she was the Sister of his old freind Lady Percival, at which he was much rejoiced, as he hoped to have, by his acquaintance with her Ladyship, free access to Miss Wentworth. . . .

Finis

To Charles John Austen Esqre

Sir,

   Your generous patronage of the unfinished tale, I have already taken the Liberty of dedicating to you, encourages me to dedicate to you a second, as unfinished as the first.

I am Sir with every expression
of regard for you and yr noble
Family, your most obed^t
&c. &c. . . .
The Author

Memoirs of Mr Clifford

an unfinished tale

Mr Clifford lived at Bath; and having never seen London, set off one Monday morning determined to feast his eyes with a sight of that great Metropolis. He travelled in his Coach and Four,* for he was a very rich young Man and kept a great many Carriages of which I do not recollect half. I can only remember that he had a Coach, a Chariot, a Chaise,* a Landeau,* a Landeaulet,* a Phaeton,* a Gig,* a Whisky,* an Italian Chair,* a Buggy,* a Curricle* & a wheelbarrow.* He had likewise an amazing fine stud of Horses. To my knowledge he had six Greys, 4 Bays, eight Blacks and a poney.*

   In his Coach & 4 Bays Mr Clifford sate forward about 5 o'clock on Monday Morning the 1st of May for London. He always travelled remarkably expeditiously and contrived therefore to get to Devizes* from Bath, which is no less than nineteen miles, the first Day. To be sure he did not get in till eleven at night and pretty tight work it was as you may imagine.

   However when he was once got to Devizes he was determined to comfort himself with a good hot Supper and therefore ordered a whole Egg to be boiled for him and his Servants. The next morning he pursued his Journey and in the course of 3 days hard labour reached Overton,* where he was seized with a dangerous fever the Consequence of too violent Excercise.

Five months did our Hero remain in this celebrated City under the care of its no less celebrated Physician, who at length compleatly cured him of his troublesome Desease.

As Mr Clifford still continued very weak, his first Day's Journey carried him only to Dean Gate,* where he remained a few Days and found himself much benefited by the change of Air.

In easy Stages he proceeded to Basingstoke.* One day Carrying him to Clarkengreen,* the next to Worting,* the 3d to the bottom of Basingstoke Hill, and the fourth, to Mr Robins's.* . . .

Finis

The Beautifull Cassandra

a novel in twelve Chapters

dedicated by permission to Miss Austen.*

Dedication.

Madam

You are a Phoenix. Your taste is refined, your Sentiments are noble, and your Virtues innumerable. Your Person is lovely, your Figure, elegant, and your Form, magestic. Your Manners are polished, your Conversation is rational and your appearance singular. If therefore the following Tale will afford one moment's amusement to you, every wish will be gratified of

Your most obedient
humble servant
The Author

The Beautifull Cassandra

Chapter the First

Cassandra was the Daughter and the only Daughter of a celebrated Millener in Bond Street.* Her father was of noble Birth, being the near relation of the Dutchess of ——'s Butler.

Chapter the 2^d

When Cassandra had attained her 16th year, she was lovely and amiable and chancing to fall in love with an elegant Bonnet,* her Mother had just compleated bespoke by the Countess of —— she placed it on her gentle Head and walked from her Mother's shop to make her Fortune.

Chapter the 3^d

The first person she met, was the Viscount of —— a young Man, no less celebrated for his Accomplishments and Virtues, than for his Elegance and Beauty. She curtseyed and walked on.

Chapter the 4th

She then proceeded to a Pastry-cooks where she devoured six ices,* refused to pay for them, knocked down the Pastry Cook and walked away.

Chapter the 5th

She next ascended a Hackney Coach* and ordered it to Hampstead,* where she was no sooner arrived than she ordered the Coachman to turn round and drive her back again.

Chapter the 6th

Being returned to the same spot of the same Street she had sate out from, the Coachman demanded his Pay.

Chapter the 7th

She searched her pockets over again and again; but every search was unsuccessfull. No money could she find. The man grew peremptory. She placed her bonnet on his head and ran away.

Chapter the 8th

Thro' many a street she then proceeded and met in none the least Adventure till on turning a Corner of Bloomsbury Square,* she met Maria.

Chapter the 9th

Cassandra started and Maria seemed surprised; they trembled, blushed, turned pale and passed each other in a mutual silence.

Chapter the 10th

Cassandra was next accosted by her freind the Widow, who squeezing out her little Head thro' her less window, asked her how she did? Cassandra curtseyed and went on.

Chapter the 11th

A quarter of a mile brought her to her paternal roof in Bond Street from which she had now been absent nearly 7 hours.

Chapter the 12th

She entered it and was pressed to her Mother's bosom by that worthy Woman. Cassandra smiled and whispered to herself 'This is a day well spent.'

Finis

Amelia Webster

an interesting and well written Tale
is dedicated by Permission
to
Mrs Austen*
by
Her humble Servant

The Author

Letter the first

To Miss Webster

My dear Amelia

You will rejoice to hear of the return of my amiable
Brother from abroad. He arrived on Thursday, and never
did I see a finer form, save that of your sincere freind

Matilda Hervey

Letter the 2ᵈ

To H. Beverley* Esquire

Dear Beverley

I arrived here last Thursday and met with a hearty
reception from my Father, Mother and Sisters. The latter
are both fine Girls—particularly Maud, who I think would
suit you as a Wife well enough. What say you to this? She
will have two thousand Pounds* and as much more as you
can get. If you don't marry her you will mortally offend

George Hervey

Letter the 3ᵈ

To Miss Hervey

Dear Maud

Beleive me I'm happy to hear of your Brother's arrival. I
have a thousand things to tell you, but my paper will only
permit me to add that I am yʳ affecᵗ Freind

Amelia Webster

Letter the 4th

To Miss S. Hervey

Dear Sally

I have found a very convenient old hollow oak to put our Letters in; for you know we have long maintained a private Correspondence.* It is about a mile from my House and seven from yours. You may perhaps imagine that I might have made choice of a tree which would have divided the Distance more equally—I was sensible of this at the time, but as I considered that the walk would be of benefit to you in your weak and uncertain state of Health, I preferred it to one nearer your House, and am y^r faithfull

Benjamin Bar

Letter the 5th

To Miss Hervey

Dear Maud

I write now to inform you that I did not stop at your house in my way to Bath last Monday.—I have many things to inform you of besides; but my Paper reminds me of concluding;* and beleive me y^{rs} ever &c.

Amelia Webster

Letter the 6th

To Miss Webster

Madam   Saturday

An humble Admirer now addresses you.—I saw you lovely Fair one as you passed on Monday last, before our House in your way to Bath. I saw you thro' a telescope, and was so struck by your Charms that from that time to this I have not tasted human food.

George Hervey

Letter the 7th

To Jack

As I was this morning at Breakfast the Newspaper was brought me, and in the list of Marriages I read the following.

'George Hervey Esqre to Miss Amelia Webster.'
'Henry Beverley Esqre to Miss Hervey'
&
'Benjamin Bar Esqre to Miss Sarah Hervey'.

yours, Tom

Finis

The Visit

a comedy in 2 acts

Dedication.
To the Revd James Austen*

Sir,
   The following Drama, which I humbly recommend to your Protection and Patronage, tho' inferior to those celebrated Comedies called 'The School for Jealousy' and 'The travelled Man',* will I hope afford some amusement to so respectable a *Curate** as yourself; which was the end in veiw when it was first composed by your Humble Servant the Author.

Dramatis Personae

Sir Arthur Hampton	Lady Hampton
Lord Fitzgerald	Miss Fitzgerald
Stanly	Sophy Hampton
Willoughby, Sir Arthur's nephew	Cloe Willoughby

The scenes are laid in
Lord Fitzgerald's House.

Act the First

Scene the first, a Parlour——

enter Lord Fitzgerald and Stanly

Stanly. Cousin your servant.

Fitzgerald. Stanly, good morning to you. I hope you slept well last night.

Stanly. Remarkably well, I thank you.

Fitzgerald. I am afraid you found your Bed too short. It was bought in my Grandmother's time, who was herself a very short woman and made a point of suiting all her Beds to her own length, as she never wished to have any company in the House, on account of an unfortunate impediment in her speech, which she was sensible of being very disagreable to her inmates.

Stanly. Make no more excuses dear Fitzgerald.

Fitzgerald. I will not distress you by too much civility—I only beg you will consider yourself as much at home as in your Father's house. Remember, 'The more free, the more Wellcome.'*

(exit Fitzgerald)

Stanly. Amiable Youth!

'Your virtues could he imitate
How happy would be Stanly's fate!'

(exit Stanly)

Scene the 2ᵈ

Stanly and Miss Fitzgerald, discovered.*

Stanly. What Company is it you expect to dine with you to Day, Cousin?

Miss F. Sir Arthur and Lady Hampton; their Daughter, Nephew and Neice.

Stanly. Miss Hampton and her Cousin are both Handsome, are they not?

Miss F. Miss Willoughby is extreamly so. Miss Hampton is a fine Girl, but not equal to her.

Stanly. Is not your Brother attached to the Latter?

Miss F. He admires her I know, but I beleive nothing

more. Indeed I have heard him say that she was the most beautifull, pleasing, and amiable Girl in the world, and that of all others he should prefer her for his Wife. But it never went any farther I'm certain.

Stanly. And yet my Cousin never says a thing he does not mean.

Miss F. Never. From his Cradle he has always been a strict adherent to Truth.

(Exeunt Severally)

End of the First Act.

Act the Second

Scene the first. The Drawing Room.

Chairs set round in a row.* Lord Fitzgerald, Miss Fitzgerald and Stanly seated.

Enter a Servant.

Servant. Sir Arthur and Lady Hampton. Miss Hampton, Mr and Miss Willoughby.

(exit Servant)

Enter the Company.

Miss F. I hope I have the pleasure of seeing your Ladyship well. Sir Arthur, your servant. Yours Mr Willoughby. Dear Sophy, Dear Cloe,—

(They pay their Compliments alternately.)

Miss F. Pray be seated.

(They sit)

Bless me! there ought to be 8 Chairs and there are but 6. However, if your Ladyship will but take Sir Arthur in your Lap, and Sophy my Brother in hers, I beleive we shall do pretty well.

Lady H. Oh! with pleasure. . . .

Sophy. I beg his Lordship would be seated.

Miss F. I am really shocked at crouding you in such a manner, but my Grandmother (who bought all the

furniture of this room) as she had never a very large
Party, did not think it necessary to buy more Chairs than
were sufficient for her own family and two of her
particular freinds.

Sophy. I beg you will make no apologies. Your Brother is
very light.

Stanly, aside) What a cherub is Cloe!

Cloe, aside) What a seraph is Stanly!

Enter a Servant.

Servant. Dinner is on table.

They all rise.

Miss F. Lady Hampton, Miss Hampton, Miss Willoughby.

Stanly hands* Cloe, Lord Fitzgerald, Sophy, Willoughby
Miss Fitzgerald, and Sir Arthur, Lady Hampton.

(Exeunt.)

Scene the 2^d

The Dining Parlour.

Miss Fitzgerald at top. Lord Fitzgerald at bottom.*
Company ranged on each side. Servants waiting.

Cloe. I shall trouble Mr Stanly for a Little of the fried
Cowheel and Onion.*

Stanly. Oh Madam, there is a secret pleasure in helping so
amiable a Lady—.

Lady H. I assure you my Lord, Sir Arthur never touches
wine; but Sophy will toss off a bumper* I am sure to
oblige your Lordship.

Lord F. Elder wine* or Mead,* Miss Hampton?

Sophy. If it is equal to you Sir, I should prefer some warm
ale with a toast and nutmeg.*

Lord F. Two glasses of warmed ale with a toast and
nutmeg.

Miss F. I am afraid Mr Willoughby you take no care of
yourself. I fear you don't meet with any thing to your
liking.

Willoughby. Oh! Madam, I can want for nothing while
there are red herrings on table.

Lord F. Sir Arthur taste that Tripe.* I think you will not find it amiss.

Lady H. Sir Arthur never eats Tripe; tis too savoury for him you know my Lord.

Miss F. Take away the Liver and Crow* and bring in the suet pudding.*

(a short Pause.)

Miss F. Sir Arthur shan't I send you a bit of pudding?

Lady H. Sir Arthur never eats suet pudding Ma'am. It is too high a Dish for him.

Miss F. Will no one allow me the honour of helping them? Then John take away the Pudding, and bring the Wine.* (Servants take away the things and bring in the Bottles and Glasses.)

Lord F. I wish we had any Desert* to offer you. But my Grandmother in her Lifetime, destroyed the Hothouse* in order to build a receptacle for the Turkies with it's materials; and we have never been able to raise another tolerable one.

Lady H. I beg you will make no apologies my Lord.

Willoughby. Come Girls, let us circulate the Bottle.

Sophy. A very good motion, Cousin; and I will second it with all my Heart. Stanly, you don't drink.

Stanly. Madam, I am drinking draughts of Love from Cloe's eyes.

Sophy. That's poor nourishment truly. Come, drink to her better acquaintance.

(Miss Fitzgerald goes to a Closet* and brings out a bottle)

Miss F. This, Ladies and Gentlemen is some of my dear Grandmother's own manufacture. She excelled in Gooseberry Wine.* Pray taste it, Lady Hampton?

Lady H. How refreshing it is!

Miss F. I should think with your Ladyship's permission, that Sir Arthur might taste a little of it.

Lady H. Not for Worlds. Sir Arthur never drinks any thing so high.

Lord F. And now my amiable Sophia condescend to marry me.

(He takes her hand and leads her to the front)

Stanly. Oh! Cloe, could I but hope you would make me blessed—

Cloe. I will.

(They advance.)

Miss F. Since you, Willoughby, are the only one left, I cannot refuse your earnest solicitations—There is my Hand.

Lady H. And may you all be Happy!

―――――――

Finis

The Mystery

an unfinished Comedy

Dedication
To the Revd George Austen*

Sir,

I humbly solicit your Patronage to the following Comedy, which tho' an unfinished one, is I flatter myself as *complete* a *Mystery* as any of its kind.

I am Sir your most Hum^le
Servant
The Author

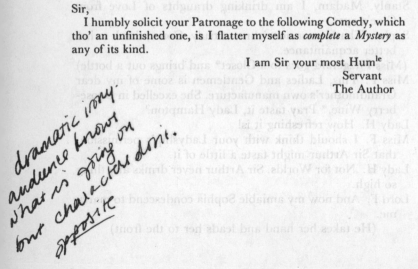

dramatic irony — audience know what is going on but characters don't. opposite

The Mystery

a comedy

Dramatis Personae

Men	Women
Colonel Elliott	Fanny Elliott
Sir Edward Spangle*	Mrs Humbug
Old Humbug*	and
Young Humbug	Daphne*
and	
Corydon	

Act the First

Scene the 1st

A Garden.

Enter Corydon.

Cory. But Hush! I am interrupted.

(Exit Corydon)

Enter Old Humbug and his Son, talking.

Old Hum. It is for that reason I wish you to follow my advice. Are you convinced of its propriety?

Young Hum. I am, Sir, and will certainly act in the manner you have pointed out to me.

Old Hum. Then let us return to the House.

(Exeunt)

Scene the 2d

A Parlour in Humbug's House.

Mrs Humbug and Fanny, discovered at work.

Mrs Hum. You understand me, my Love?

Fanny. Perfectly ma'am. Pray continue your narration.

Mrs Hum. Alas! it is nearly concluded, for I have nothing more to say on the Subject.

Fanny. Ah! here's Daphne.

Enter Daphne.

Daphne. My dear Mrs Humbug, how d'ye do? Oh! Fanny, t'is all over.

Fanny. It is indeed!

Mrs Hum. I'm very sorry to hear it.

Fanny. Then t'was to no purpose that I . . . .

Daphne. None upon Earth.

Mrs Hum. And what is to become of? . . . . .

Daphne. Oh! that's all settled.

(whispers Mrs Humbug)

Fanny. And how is it determined?

Daphne. I'll tell you.

(whispers Fanny)

Mrs Hum. And is he to? . . .

Daphne. I'll tell you all I know of the matter.

(whispers Mrs Humbug and Fanny)

Fanny. Well! now I know everything about it, I'll go away.

Mrs Hum. ⎫
Daphne. ⎬ And so will I.

(Exeunt)

Scene the 3ᵈ

The Curtain rises and discovers Sir Edward Spangle reclined in an elegant Attitude on a Sofa, fast asleep.*

Enter Colonel Elliott.

Colonel. My Daughter is not here I see . . . there lies Sir Edward . . . Shall I tell him the secret? . . . No, he'll certainly blab it. . . . But he is asleep and won't hear me. . . . So I'll e'en venture.*

(Goes up to Sir Edward, whispers him, and Exit)

End of the 1ˢᵗ Act.

Finis

To Edward Austen Esqre*

The following unfinished Novel
is respectfully inscribed
by
His obedient hum^{le} serv^t

The Author

The Three Sisters

a novel

Letter 1st

Miss Stanhope to Mrs . . .

My dear Fanny

I am the happiest creature in the World, for I have
received an offer of marriage from Mr Watts. It is the first I
have ever had and I hardly know how to value it enough.
How I will triumph over the Duttons! I do not intend to
accept it, at least I beleive not, but as I am not quite certain
I gave him an equivocal answer and left him. And now my
dear Fanny I want your Advice whether I should accept his
offer or not, but that you may be able to judge of his merits
and the situation of affairs I will give you an account of
them. He is quite an old Man, about two and thirty, very
plain *so* plain that I cannot bear to look at him. He is
extremely disagreable and I hate him more than any body
else in the world. He has a large fortune and will make great
Settlements* on me; but then he is very healthy. In short I
do not know what to do. If I refuse him he as good as told
me that he should offer himself to Sophia and if *she* refused
him to Georgiana, and I could not bear to have either of
them married before me. If I accept him I know I shall be
miserable all the rest of my Life, for he is very ill tempered

and peevish extremely jealous, and so stingy that there is no living in the house with him. He told me he should mention the affair to Mama, but I insisted upon it that he did not for very likely she would make me marry him whether I would or no; however probably he *has* before now, for he never does anything he is desired to do. I believe I shall have him. It will be such a triumph to be married before Sophy, Georgiana, and the Duttons; And he promised to have a new Carriage on the occasion, but we almost quarrelled about the colour, for I insisted upon its being blue spotted with silver, and he declared it should be a plain Chocolate;* and to provoke me more said it should be just as low as his old one.* I won't have him I declare. He said he should come again tomorrow and take my final answer, so I believe I must get him while I can. I know the Duttons will envy me and I shall be able to chaprone* Sophy and Georgiana to all the Winter Balls.* But then what will be the use of that when very likely he won't let me go myself, for I know he hates dancing and what he hates himself he has no idea of any other person's liking; and besides he talks a great deal of Women's always Staying at home and such stuff. I beleive I shan't have him; I would refuse him at once if I were certain that neither of my Sisters would accept him, and that if they did not, he would not offer to the Duttons. I cannot run such a risk, so, if he will promise to have the Carriage ordered as I like, I will have him, if not he may ride in it by himself for me. I hope you like my determination; I can think of nothing better;

And am your ever Affec^te

Mary Stanhope

From the Same to the Same

Dear Fanny

I had but just sealed my last letter to you when my Mother came up and told me she wanted to speak to me on a very particular subject.

'Ah! I know what you mean;' (said I) 'That old fool Mr Watts has told you all about it, tho' I bid him not. However you shan't force me to have him if I don't like it.'

'I am not going to force you, Child, but only want to know what your resolution is with regard to his Proposals, and to insist upon your making up your mind one way or t'other, that if *you* don't accept him *Sophy* may.'

'Indeed' (replied I hastily) 'Sophy need not trouble herself for I shall certainly marry him myself.'

'If that is your resolution' (said my Mother) 'why should you be afraid of my forcing your inclinations?'

'Why, because I have not settled whether I shall have him or not.'

'You are the strangest Girl in the World, Mary. What you say one moment, you unsay the next. Do tell me once for all, whether you intend to marry Mr Watts or not?'

'Law,* Mama, how can I tell you what I don't know myself?'

'Then I desire you will know, and quickly too, for Mr Watts says he won't be kept in suspense.'

'That depends upon me.'

'No it does not, for if you do not give him your final answer tomorrow when he drinks Tea* with us, he intends to pay his Addresses to Sophy.'

'Then I shall tell all the World that he behaved very ill to me.'

'What good will that do? Mr Watts has been too long abused by all the World to mind it now.'

'I wish I had a Father or a Brother because then they should fight him.'

'They would be cunning if they did, for Mr Watts would run away first; and therefore you must and shall resolve either to accept or refuse him before tomorrow evening.'

'But why if I don't have him, must he offer to my Sisters?'

'Why! because he wishes to be allied to the Family and because they are as pretty as you are.'

'But will Sophy marry him, Mama, if he offers to her?'

'Most likely. Why should not she? If however she does not choose it, then Georgiana must, for I am determined not to let such an opportunity escape of settling one of my Daughters so advantageously. So, make the most of your time; I leave you to settle the Matter with yourself.' And then she went away. The only thing I can think of my dear Fanny is to ask Sophy and Georgiana whether they would have him were he to make proposals to them, and if they say they would not I am resolved to refuse him too, for I hate him more than you can imagine. As for the Duttons if he marries one of *them* I shall still have the triumph of having refused him first. So, adeiu my dear Freind—

Y^{rs} ever M. S.

Miss Georgiana Stanhope to Miss XXX*

My dear Anne   Wednesday

Sophy and I have just been practising a little deceit on our eldest Sister, to which we are not perfectly reconciled, and yet the circumstances were such that if any thing will excuse it, they must. Our neighbour Mr Watts has made proposals to Mary; Proposals which she knew not how to receive,* for tho' she has a particular Dislike to him (in which she is not singular) yet she would willingly marry him sooner than risk his offering to Sophy or me which in case of a refusal from herself, he told her he should do, for you must know the poor Girl considers our marrying before her as one of the greatest misfortunes that can possibly befall her, and to prevent it would willingly ensure herself everlasting Misery by a Marriage with Mr Watts. An hour ago she came to us to sound our inclinations respecting the affair which were to determine hers. A little before she came my Mother had given us an account of it, telling us that she certainly would not let him go farther than our own family for a Wife. 'And therefore' (said she) 'If Mary won't have him Sophy must, and if Sophy won't Georgiana *shall*.' Poor Georgiana!—We neither of us attempted to alter my Mother's resolution, which I am sorry to say is generally more strictly kept than rationally formed. As soon as she was gone however I broke silence to assure Sophy that if Mary should refuse Mr Watts I should not expect her to sacrifice *her* happiness by becoming his Wife from a motive of Generosity to me, which I was afraid her Good nature and Sisterly affection might induce her to do.

'Let us flatter ourselves' (replied She) 'that Mary will not refuse him. Yet how can I hope that my Sister may accept a Man who cannot make her happy.'

'*He* cannot it is true but his Fortune, his Name, his House, his Carriage will and I have no doubt but that Mary will marry him; indeed why should she not? He is not more than two and thirty; a very proper age for a Man to marry at; He is rather plain to be sure, but then what is Beauty in a Man; if he has but a genteel figure* and a sensible looking Face it is quite sufficient.'

'This is all very true, Georgiana, but Mr Watts's figure is unfortunately extremely vulgar and his Countenance is very heavy.'

'And then as to his temper; it has been reckoned bad, but may not the World be deceived in their Judgement of it. There is an open Frankness in his Disposition which becomes a Man; They say he is stingy; We'll call that Prudence. They say he is suspicious. *That* proceeds from a warmth of Heart always excusable in Youth, and in short I see no reason why he should not make a very good Husband, or why Mary should not be very happy with him.'

Sophy laughed; I continued,

'However whether Mary accepts him or not I am resolved. My determination is made. I never would marry Mr Watts were Beggary the only alternative. So deficient in every respect! Hideous in his person and without one good Quality to make amends for it. His fortune to be sure is good. Yet not so very large! Three thousand a year*. What is three thousand a year? It is but six times as much as my Mother's income. It will not tempt me.'

'Yet it will be a noble fortune for Mary' said Sophy laughing again.

'For Mary! Yes indeed it will give *me* pleasure to see *her* in such affluence.'

Thus I ran on to the great Entertainment of my Sister till Mary came into the room to appearance in great agitation. She sate down. We made room for her at the fire. She seemed at a loss how to begin and at last said in some confusion.

'Pray, Sophy, have you any mind to be married?'

'To be married! None in the least. But why do you ask me? Are you acquainted with any one who means to make me proposals?'

'I—no, how should I? But mayn't I ask a common question?'

'Not a very *common* one, Mary, surely.' (said I). She paused and after some moments silence went on—

'How should you like to marry Mr Watts, Sophy?'

I winked at Sophy and replied for her. 'Who is there but must rejoice to marry a man of three thousand a year?'

'Very true' (she replied) 'That's very true. So you would have him if he would offer, Georgiana, and would *you* Sophy?'

Sophy did not like the idea of telling a lie and deceiving her Sister; she prevented the first and saved half her conscience by equivocation.

'I should certainly act just as Georgiana would do.'

'Well then,' said Mary with triumph in her Eyes, '*I* have had an offer from Mr Watts.'

We were of course very much surprised; 'Oh! do not accept him,' said I, 'and then perhaps he may have me.'

In short my scheme took and Mary is resolved to do *that* to prevent our supposed happiness which she would not have done to ensure it in reality. Yet after all my Heart cannot acquit me and Sophy is even more scrupulous. Quiet our Minds my dear Anne by writing and telling us you approve our conduct. Consider it well over. Mary will have real pleasure in being a married Woman, and able to chaprone us, which she certainly shall do, for I think myself bound to contribute as much as possible to her happiness in a State I have made her choose. They will probably have a new Carriage, which will be paradise to her, and if we can prevail on Mr W. to set up his Phaeton* she will be too happy. These things however would be no consolation to Sophy or me for domestic Misery. Remember all this and do not condemn us.

Friday.

Last night Mr Watts by appointment drank tea with us. As soon as his Carriage stopped at the Door, Mary went to the Window.

'Would you beleive it, Sophy' (said she) 'the old Fool wants to have his new Chaise* just the colour of the old one, and hung as low too. But it shan't—I *will* carry my point. And if he won't let it be as high as the Duttons, and blue spotted with Silver, I won't have him. Yes I will too. Here he comes. I know he'll be rude; I know he'll be ill tempered and won't say one civil thing to me! nor behave at all like a Lover.' She then sate down and Mr Watts entered.

'Ladies your most obedient.' We paid our Compliments and he seated himself.

'Fine Weather, Ladies.' Then turning to Mary, 'Well Miss Stanhope, I hope you have *at last* settled the Matter in your own mind; and will be so good as to let me know whether you will *condescend* to marry me or not.'

'I think Sir' (said Mary) 'You might have asked in a genteeler way than that. I do not know whether I *shall* have you if you behave so odd.'

'Mary!' (said my Mother). 'Well Mama, if he will be so cross . . .'

'Hush, hush, Mary, you shall not be rude to Mr Watts.'

'Pray, Madam, do not lay any restraint on Miss Stanhope by obliging her to be civil. If she does not choose to accept my hand, I can offer it else where, for as I am by no means guided by a particular preference to you above your Sisters it is equally the same to me which I marry of the three.' Was there ever such a Wretch! Sophy reddened with anger and I felt *so* spiteful!

'Well then' (said Mary in a peevish Accent) 'I *will* have you if I *must*.'

'I should have thought, Miss Stanhope, that when such Settlements are offered as I have offered to you there can be no great violence done to the inclinations in accepting of them.'

Mary mumbled out something, which I who sate close to her could just distinguish to be 'What's the use of a great Jointure* if Men live forever?' And then audibly 'Remember the pinmoney;* two hundred a year.'*

'A hundred and seventy-five Madam.'

'Two hundred indeed Sir' said my Mother.

'And Remember I am to have a new Carriage hung as high as the Duttons', and blue spotted with silver; and I shall expect a new saddle horse, a suit of fine lace, and an infinite number of the most valuable Jewels. Diamonds such as never were seen! and Pearls, Rubies, Emeralds, and Beads out of number. You must set up your Phaeton which must be cream coloured with a wreath of silver flowers round it,* You must buy 4 of the finest Bays in the Kingdom and you must drive me in it every day. This is not all; You must entirely new furnish your House after my Taste, You must hire two more Footmen to attend me, two Women to wait on me, must always let me do just as I please and make a very good husband.'

Here she stopped, I beleive rather out of breath.

'This is all very reasonable, Mr Watts, for my Daughter to expect.'

'And it is very reasonable, Mrs Stanhope, that your daughter should be disappointed.' He was going on but Mary interrupted him, 'You must build me an elegant Greenhouse and stock it with plants. You must let me spend every Winter in Bath,* every Spring in Town,* Every Summer in taking some Tour,* and every Autumn at a Watering Place,* and if we are at home the rest of the year' (Sophy and I laughed) 'You must do nothing but give Balls and Masquerades. You must build a room on purpose and a Theatre to act Plays in.* The first Play we have shall be *Which is the Man*,* and I will do Lady Bell Bloomer.'*

'And pray Miss Stanhope' (said Mr Watts) 'What am I to expect from you in return for all this?'

'Expect? why you may expect to have me pleased.'

'It would be odd if I did not. Your expectations, Madam, are too high for me, and I must apply to Miss Sophy who perhaps may not have raised her's so much.'

'You are mistaken, Sir, in supposing so,' (said Sophy) 'for tho' they may not be exactly in the same Line, yet my expectations are to the full as high as my Sister's; for I expect my Husband to be good tempered and Chearful; to consult my Happiness in all his Actions, and to love me with Constancy and Sincerity.'

Mr Watts stared. 'These are very odd Ideas truly, young Lady. You had better discard them before you marry, or you will be obliged to do it afterwards.'

My Mother in the meantime was lecturing Mary who was sensible that she had gone too far, and when Mr Watts was just turning towards me in order I beleive to address me, she spoke to him in a voice half humble, half sulky.

'You are mistaken, Mr Watts, if you think I was in earnest when I said I expected so much. However I must have a new Chaise.'

'Yes Sir, you must allow that Mary has a right to expect that.'

'Mrs Stanhope, I *mean* and have always meant to have a new one on my Marriage. But it shall be the colour of my present one.'

'I think, Mr Watts, you should pay my Girl the compliment of consulting her Taste on such Matters.'

Mr Watts would not agree to this, and for some time insisted upon its being a Chocolate colour, while Mary was as eager for having it blue with silver Spots. At length however Sophy proposed that to please Mr W. it should be a dark brown and to please Mary it should be hung rather high and have a silver Border.* This was at length agreed to, tho' reluctantly on both sides, as each had intended to carry their point entire. We then proceeded to other Matters, and it was settled that they should be married as soon as the Writings could be completed. Mary was very eager for a Special Licence* and Mr Watts talked of Banns.* A common Licence* was at last agreed on. Mary is to have all the Family Jewels which are very inconsiderable I beleive and Mr W. promised to buy her a Saddle horse;* but in return she is not to expect to go to Town or any other public place for these three Years.* She is to have neither

Greenhouse, Theatre or Phaeton; to be contented with one Maid without an additional Footman. It engrossed the whole Evening to settle these affairs; Mr W. supped with us and did not go till twelve. As soon as he was gone Mary exclaimed 'Thank Heaven! he's off at last; how I do hate him!' It was in vain that Mama represented to her the impropriety she was guilty of in disliking him who was to be her Husband, for she persisted in declaring her aversion to him and hoping she might never see him again. What a Wedding will this be! Adeiu my dear Anne. Y^r faithfully Sincere

Georgiana Stanhope

From the Same to the Same

Dear Anne   Saturday

Mary, eager to have every one know of her approaching Wedding and more particularly desirous of triumphing as she called it over the Duttons, desired us to walk with her this Morning to Stoneham.* As we had nothing else to do we readily agreed, and had as pleasant a walk as we could have with Mary whose conversation entirely consisted in abusing the Man she is soon to marry and in longing for a blue Chaise spotted with Silver. When we reached the Duttons we found the two Girls in the dressing-room with a very handsome Young Man, who was of course introduced to us. He is the son of Sir Henry Brudenell of Leicestershire.* Mr Brudenell is the handsomest Man I ever saw in my Life; we are all three very much pleased with him. Mary, who from the moment of our reaching the Dressing-room had been swelling with the knowledge of her own importance and with the Desire of making it known, could not remain long silent on the Subject after we were seated, and soon addressing herself to Kitty said,

'Don't you think it will be necessary to have all the Jewels new set?'

'Necessary for what?'

'For What! Why for my appearance.'*

'I beg your pardon but I really do not understand you.

What Jewels do you speak of, and where is your appearance to me made?'

'At the next Ball to be sure after I am married.'

You may imagine their Surprise. They were at first incredulous, but on our joining in the Story they at last beleived it. 'And who is it to' was of course the first Question. Mary pretended Bashfulness, and answered in Confusion her Eyes cast down 'to Mr Watts'. This also required Confirmation from us, for that anyone who had the Beauty and fortune (tho' small yet a provision) of Mary would willingly marry Mr Watts, could by them scarcely be credited. The subject being now fairly introduced and she found herself the object of every one's attention in company, she lost all her confusion and became perfectly unreserved and communicative.

'I wonder you should never have heard of it before for in general things of this Nature are very well known in the Neighbourhood.'

'I assure you,' said Jemima, 'I never had the least suspicion of such an affair. Has it been in agitation long?'

'Oh! Yes, ever since Wednesday.'

They all smiled particularly Mr Brudenell.

'You must know Mr Watts is very much in love with me, so that it is quite a match of Affection on his side.'

'Not on his only, I suppose' said Kitty.

'Oh! when there is so much Love on one side there is no occasion for it on the other. However I do not much dislike him tho' he is very plain to be sure.'

Mr Brudenell stared, the Miss Duttons laughed and Sophy and I were heartily ashamed of our Sister. She went on. *first time shame is mentioned*

'We are to have a new Postchaise and very likely may set up our Phaeton.'

This we knew to be false but the poor Girl was pleased at the idea of persuading the company that such a thing was to be and I would not deprive her of so harmless an Enjoyment. She continued.

'Mr Watts is to present me with the family Jewels which I fancy are very considerable.' I could not help whispering

Sophy 'I fancy not'. 'These Jewels are what I suppose must be new set before they can be worn. I shall not wear them till the first Ball I go to after my Marriage. If Mrs Dutton should not go to it, I hope you will let me chaprone you; I shall certainly take Sophy and Georgiana.'

'You are very good' (said Kitty) 'and since you are inclined to undertake the Care of young Ladies, I should advise you to prevail on Mrs Edgecumbe to let you chaprone her six Daughters which with your two Sisters and ourselves will make your Entrée very respectable.'

Kitty made us all smile except Mary who did not understand her Meaning and coolly said that she should not like to chaprone so many. Sophy and I now endeavoured to change the conversation but succeeded only for a few Minutes, for Mary took care to bring back their attention to her and her approaching Wedding. I was sorry for my Sister's sake to see that Mr Brudenell seemed to take pleasure in listening to her account of it, and even encouraged her by his Questions and Remarks, for it was evident that his only Aim was to laugh at her. I am afraid he found her very ridiculous. He kept his Countenance extremely well, yet it was easy to see that it was with difficulty he kept it. At length however he seemed fatigued and Disgusted with her ridiculous Conversation, as he turned from her to us, and spoke but little to her for about half an hour before we left Stoneham. As soon as we were out of the House we all joined in praising the Person and Manners of Mr Brudenell.

We found Mr Watts at home.

'So, Miss Stanhope' (said he) 'you see I am come a courting in a true Lover like Manner.'

'Well you need not have *told* me that. I knew why you came very well.'

Sophy and I then left the room, imagining of course that we must be in the way, if a Scene of Courtship were to begin. We were surprised at being followed almost immediately by Mary.

'And is your Courting so soon over?' said Sophy.

'Courting!' (replied Mary) 'we have been quarrelling.

Watts is such a Fool! I hope I shall never see him again.'

'I am afraid you will,' (said I) 'as he dines here today. But what has been your dispute?'

'Why only because I told him that I had seen a Man much handsomer than he was this Morning, he flew into a great Passion and called me a Vixen,* so I only stayed to tell him I thought him a Blackguard* and came away.'

'Short and sweet;' (said Sophy) 'but pray, Mary, how will this be made up?'

'He ought to ask my pardon; but if he did, I would not forgive him.'

'His Submission then would not be very useful.'

When we were dressed* we returned to the Parlour where Mama and Mr Watts were in close Conversation. It seems that he had been complaining to her of her Daughter's behaviour, and she had persuaded him to think no more of it. He therefore met Mary with all his accustomed Civility, and except one touch at the Phaeton and another at the Greenhouse, the Evening went off with a great Harmony and Cordiality. Watts is going to Town to hasten the preparations for the Wedding.

I am your affec^te Freind G. S.

[Detached pieces]

To Miss Jane Anna Elizabeth Austen*

My Dear Neice

Though you are at this period not many degrees removed from Infancy,* Yet trusting that you will in time be older, and that through the care of your excellent Parents, You will one day or another be able to read written hand, I dedicate to You the following Miscellanious Morsels, convinced that if you seriously attend to them, You will derive from them very important Instructions, with regard to your Conduct in Life.—If such my hopes should hereafter be realized, never shall I regret the Days and Nights that have been spent in composing these Treatises for your Benefit.* I am my dear Neice

Your very Affectionate

Aunt.

The Author

June 2ᵈ
. 1793

A beautiful description of the different effects of Sensibility* on different Minds

I am but just returned from Melissa's Bedside, and in my Life tho' it has been a pretty long one, and I have during the course of it been at many Bedsides, I never saw so affecting an object* as she exhibits. She lies wrapped in a book muslin* bedgown, a chambray gauze* shift,* and a French net nightcap.* Sir William is constantly at her bedside. The only repose he takes is on the Sopha in the Drawing room, where for five minutes every fortnight he remains in an imperfect Slumber, starting up every Moment and exclaiming 'Oh! Melissa, Ah! Melissa,' then sinking down again, raises his left arm and scratches his head. Poor Mrs Burnaby is beyond measure afflicted. She sighs every now and then, that is about once a week; while the melancholy Charles says every Moment 'Melissa, how are you?' The lovely Sisters are much to be pitied. Julia is ever lamenting the situation of her friend, while lying behind her pillow and supporting her head—Maria more mild in her greif talks of going to Town next week, and Anna is always recurring to the pleasures we once enjoyed when Melissa was well.—I am usually at the fire cooking some little delicacy for the unhappy invalid—Perhaps hashing up* the remains of an old Duck, toasting some cheese or making a Curry* which are the favourite Dishes of our poor friend.—In these situations we were this morning surprised by receiving a visit from Dr Dowkins; 'I am come to see Melissa,' said he. 'How is She?' 'Very weak indeed,' said the fainting Melissa—'Very weak,' replied the punning Doctor, 'aye indeed it is more than a very *week* since you have taken to your bed—How is your appetite?' 'Bad, very bad,' said Julia. 'That *is* very bad'—replied he. 'Are her spirits good, Madam?' 'So poorly, Sir, that we are obliged to strengthen her with cordials every Minute.'—'Well then she receives *Spirits* from your being with her. Does she sleep?' 'Scarcely ever.'—'And Ever Scarcely I suppose when she does. Poor thing! Does she think of dieing?' 'She has not strength to *Think* at all.' 'Nay then she cannot think to have Strength.'

The generous Curate

a moral Tale, setting forth the Advantages of being Generous and a Curate.

In a part little known of the County of Warwick,* a very worthy Clergyman lately resided. The income of his living* which amounted to about two hundred pound, and the interest of his Wife's fortune which was nothing at all, was entirely sufficient for the Wants and Wishes of a Family who neither wanted or wished for anything beyond what their income afforded them. Mr Williams had been in possession of his living above twenty Years, when this history commences, and his Marriage which had taken place soon after his presentation to it, had made him the father of six very fine Children. The eldest had been placed at the Royal Academy for Seamen at Portsmouth* when about thirteen years old, and from thence had been discharged on board of one of the Vessels of a small fleet destined for Newfoundland, where his promising and amiable disposition had procured him many friends among the Natives, and from whence he regularly sent home a large Newfoundland Dog* every Month to his family. The second, who was also a Son, had been adopted by a neighbouring Clergyman with the intention of educating him at his own expence, which would have been a very desirable Circumstance had the Gentleman's fortune been equal to his generosity, but as he had nothing to support himself and a very large family but a Curacy of fifty pound a year, Young Williams knew nothing more at the age of 18 than what a twopenny Dame's School* in the village could teach him. His Character however was perfectly amiable though his genius might be cramped, and he was addicted to no vice, or ever guilty of any fault beyond what his age and situation rendered perfectly excusable. He had indeed sometimes been detected in flinging Stones at a Duck or putting brickbats* into his Benefactor's bed; but these innocent efforts of wit were considered by that good Man rather as the effects of a lively imagination, than of anything bad in his Nature, and if any punishment were decreed for the offence it was in general no greater than that the Culprit should pick up the Stones or take the brickbats away.—

Finis

To Miss Austen,* the following Ode to Pity is dedicated, from a thorough knowledge of her pitiful Nature, by her obed^t hum^{le} Servt

The Author

Ode to Pity*

1

Ever musing I delight to tread
    The Paths of honour and the Myrtle* Grove
Whilst the pale Moon her beams doth shed
      On disappointed Love.
While Philomel* on airy hawthorn Bush
    Sings sweet and Melancholy, And the thrush
Converses with the Dove.

2

Gently brawling down the turnpike road,*
    Sweetly noisy falls the Silent Stream—
The Moon emerges from behind a Cloud
    And darts upon the Myrtle Grove her beam.
Ah! then what Lovely Scenes appear,
    The hut, the Cot,* the Grot,* and Chapel
    queer,*
And eke the Abbey* too a mouldering heap,
    Conceal'd by aged pines her head doth rear
And quite invisible doth take a peep.

End of the first volume

June 3ᵈ 1793

7

Gently brawling down the turnpike-road,*
Sweetly noisy falls the Silent Stream—
The Moon emerges from behind a Cloud
And darts upon the Myrtle Grove her beam.
Ah! then what Lovely Scenes appear,
The hut, the Cot,* the Grot,* and Chapel
    queer,
And eke the Abbey* too a mouldering heap,
Conceal'd by aged pines her head doth rear
And quite invisible doth take a peep.

End of the first volume

June 3d 1793

VOLUME THE SECOND

Ex dono mei Patris*

CONTENTS

To Madame La Comtesse De Feuillide*
This Novel is inscribed by
Her obliged Humble Servant
The Author

Love and Freindship

a novel
in a series of Letters.

'Deceived in Freindship and Betrayed in Love'*

Letter the First
From Isabel to Laura*

How often, in answer to my repeated intreaties that you would give my Daughter a regular detail of the Misfortunes and Adventures of your Life, have you said 'No, my freind, never will I comply with your request till I may be no longer in Danger of again experiencing such dreadful ones.'

Surely that time is now at hand. You are this Day 55. If a woman may ever be said to be in safety from the determined Perseverance of disagreable Lovers and the cruel Persecutions of obstinate Fathers, surely it must be at such a time of Life.

Isabel.

Letter 2nd
Laura to Isabel

Altho' I cannot agree with you in supposing that I shall never again be exposed to Misfortunes as unmerited as those I have already experienced, yet to avoid the imputation of Obstinacy or ill-nature, I will gratify the curiosity of your Daughter; and may the fortitude with which I have suffered the many Afflictions of my past Life, prove to her a useful Lesson for the support of those which may befall her in her own.

Laura

Letter 3rd
Laura to Marianne

As the Daughter of my most intimate freind I think you entitled to that knowledge of my unhappy Story, which your Mother has so often solicited me to give you.

My Father was a native of Ireland and an inhabitant of Wales; My Mother was the natural* Daughter of a Scotch Peer by an Italian Opera-girl*—I was born in Spain and received my Education at a Convent in France.

When I had reached my eighteenth Year I was recalled by my Parents to my paternal roof in Wales. Our mansion was situated in one of the most romantic* parts of the Vale of Uske.* Tho' my Charms are now considerably softened and somewhat impaired by the Misfortunes I have undergone, I was once beautiful. But lovely as I was the Graces of my Person were the least of my Perfections. Of every accomplishment accustomary* to my sex, I was Mistress. When in the Convent, my progress had always exceeded my instructions, my Acquirements had been wonderfull for my Age, and I had shortly surpassed my Masters.

In my Mind, every Virtue that could adorn it was centered; it was the Rendez-vous* of every good Quality and of every noble sentiment.

A sensibility too tremblingly alive to every affliction of my Freinds, my Acquaintance and particularly to every affliction of my own, was my only fault, if a fault it could be called. Alas! how altered now! Tho' indeed my own misfortunes do not make less impression on me than they ever did, yet now I never feel for those of an other. My accomplishments too, begin to fade—I can neither sing so well nor Dance so gracefully as I once did—and I have entirely forgot the *Minuet Dela Cour.*

Adeiu.

Laura

Letter 4th
Laura to Marianne

Our neighbourhood was small, for it consisted only of your Mother. She may probably have already told you that being left by her Parents in indigent Circumstances she had retired into Wales on eoconomical motives. There it was, our freindship first commenced. Isabel was then one and twenty—Tho' pleasing both in her Person and Manners *appearance* (between ourselves) she never possessed the hundredth part *abilities* of my Beauty or Accomplishments. Isabel had seen the World. She had passed 2 Years at one of the first Boarding schools* in London; had spent a fortnight in Bath and had supped one night in Southampton.

'Beware my Laura' (she would often say) 'Beware of the insipid Vanities and idle Dissipation of the Metropolis of England; Beware of the unmeaning Luxuries of Bath and of the Stinking fish of Southampton.'*

'Alas!' (exclaimed I) 'how am I to avoid those evils I shall never be exposed to? What probability is there of my ever tasting the Dissipation of London, the Luxuries of Bath or the stinking fish of Southampton? I who am doomed to waste my Days of Youth and Beauty in an humble Cottage in the Vale of Uske.'

Ah! little did I then think I was ordained so soon to quit that humble Cottage for the Deceitfull Pleasures of the World.

adeiu
Laura

Letter 5th
Laura to Marianne

One Evening in December as my Father, my Mother and myself, were arranged in social converse round our Fireside, we were on a sudden, greatly astonished, by hearing a violent knocking on the outward Door of our rustic Cot.*

My Father started—'What noise is that,' (said he.) 'It sounds like a loud rapping at the Door'—(replied my Mother.) 'It does indeed.' (cried I.) 'I am of your opinion;' (said my Father) 'it certainly does appear to proceed from some uncommon violence exerted against our unoffending Door.'

'Yes,' (exclaimed I) 'I cannot help thinking it must be somebody who knocks for Admittance.'

'That is another point' (replied he;) 'We must not pretend to determine on what motive the person may Knock—tho' that someone *does* rap at the Door, I am partly convinced.'

Here, a 2d tremendous rap interrupted my Father in his speech and somewhat alarmed my Mother and me.

'Had we not better go and see who it is?' (said she), 'the Servants are out.' 'I think we had.' (replied I.) 'Certainly,' (added my Father) 'by all means.' 'Shall we go now?' (said my Mother.) 'The sooner the better.' (answered he). 'Oh! let no time be lost.' (cried I.)

A third more violent Rap than ever again assaulted our ears. 'I am certain there is somebody knocking at the Door.' (said my Mother.) 'I think there must,' (replied my Father) 'I fancy the Servants are returned;' (said I) 'I think I hear Mary going to the Door.' 'I'm glad of it' (cried my Father) 'for I long to know who it is.'

I was right in my Conjecture; for Mary instantly entering the Room, informed us that a young Gentleman and his Servant were at the Door, who had lossed their way, were very cold and begged leave to warm themselves by our fire.

'Won't you admit them?' (said I) 'You have no objection, my Dear?' (said my Father.) 'None in the World.' (replied my Mother.)

Mary, without waiting for any further commands, immediately left the room and quickly returned introducing the most beauteous and amiable Youth, I had ever beheld. The servant, She kept to herself.

My natural Sensibility had already been greatly affected

by the sufferings of the unfortunate Stranger and no sooner
did I first behold him, than I felt that on him the happiness
or Misery of my future Life must depend.

adeiu.
Laura.

Letter 6th
Laura to Marianne

The noble Youth informed us that his name was Lindsay*—
for particular reasons however I shall conceal it under that
of Talbot.* He told us that he was the son of an English
Baronet,* that his Mother had been many years no more
and that he had a Sister of the middle size.* 'My Father' (he
continued) 'is a mean and mercenary wretch—it is only to
such particular freinds as this Dear Party that I would thus
betray his failings. Your Virtues my amiable Polydore'*
(addressing himself to my father) 'yours, Dear Claudia,*
and yours, my Charming Laura, call on me to repose in
you, my Confidence.' We bowed. 'My Father, seduced by
the false glare of Fortune and the Deluding Pomp of Title,
insisted on my giving my hand to Lady Dorothea. No never
exclaimed I. Lady Dorothea is lovely and Engaging; I
prefer no woman to her; but Know Sir, that I scorn to
marry her in compliance with your Wishes. No! Never shall
it be said that I obliged my Father.'*

We all admired the noble Manliness of his reply. He
continued.

'Sir Edward was surprized; he had perhaps little expected
to meet with so spirited an opposition to his will. "Where,
Edward, in the name of wonder" (said he) "did you pick up
this unmeaning Gibberish? You have been studying Novels
I suspect."* I scorned to answer: it would have been
beneath my Dignity. I mounted my Horse and followed by
my faithful William set forwards for my Aunt's.'

'My Father's house is situated in Bedfordshire, my
Aunt's in Middlesex,* and tho' I flatter myself with being a
tolerable proficient in Geography, I know not how it

happened, but I found myself entering this beautifull Vale which I find is in South Wales, when I had expected to have reached my Aunt's.

'After having wandered some time on the Banks of the Uske without knowing which way to go, I began to lament my cruel Destiny in the bitterest and most pathetic Manner. It was now perfectly Dark, not a single Star was there to direct my steps, and I know not what might have befallen me had I not at length discerned thro' the solemn Gloom that surrounded me a distant Light,* which as I approached it, I discovered to be the chearfull Blaze of your fire. Impelled by the combination of Misfortunes under which I laboured, namely Fear, Cold and Hunger I hesitated not to ask admittance which at length I have gained; and now, my Adorable Laura' (continued he taking my Hand) 'when may I hope to receive that reward of all the painfull sufferings I have undergone during the course of my Attachment to you, to which I have ever aspired? Oh! when will you reward me with Yourself?'

'This instant, Dear and Amiable Edward,' (replied I.). We were immediately united by my Father, who tho' he had never taken orders* had been bred to the Church.

adeiu
Laura.

Letter 7th
Laura to Marianne

We remained but a few Days after our Marriage, in the Vale of Uske. After taking my affecting Farewell of my Father, my Mother and my Isabel, I accompanied Edward to his Aunt's in Middlesex. Philippa received us both with every expression of affectionate Love. My arrival was indeed a most agreable surprize to her as she had not only been totally ignorant of my Marriage with her Nephew, but had never even had the slightest idea of there being such a person in the World.

Augusta, the sister of Edward was on a visit to her when

we arrived. I found her exactly what her Brother had described her to be—of the middle size. She received me with equal surprize though not with equal Cordiality, as Philippa. There was a Disagreable Coldness and Forbidding Reserve in her reception of me which was equally Distressing and Unexpected. None of that interesting Sensibility or amiable Simpathy in her Manners and Address to me which should have Distinguished our introduction to each other. Her Language was neither warm, nor affectionate, her expressions of regard were neither animated nor cordial; her arms were not opened to receive me to her Heart, tho' my own were extended to press her to mine.

A short Conversation between Augusta and her Brother, which I accidentally overheard encreased my Dislike to her, and convinced me that her Heart was no more formed for the soft ties of Love than for the endearing intercourse of Freindship.

'But do you think that my Father will ever be reconciled to this imprudent connection?' (said Augusta.)

'Augusta,' (replied the noble Youth) 'I thought you had a better opinion of me, than to imagine I would so abjectly degrade myself as to consider my Father's Concurrence in any of my Affairs, either of Consequence or concern to me. Tell me Augusta tell me with sincerity; did you ever know me consult his inclinations or follow his Advice in the least trifling Particular since the age of fifteen?'

'Edward,' (replied she) 'you are surely too diffident in your own praise. Since you were fifteen only!—My Dear Brother since you were five years old, I entirely acquit you of ever having willingly contributed to the Satisfaction of your Father. But still I am not without apprehensions of your being shortly obliged to degrade yourself in your own eyes by seeking a Support for your Wife in the Generosity of Sir Edward.'

'Never, never Augusta, will I so demean myself,' (said Edward). 'Support! What Support will Laura want which she can receive from him?'

'Only those very insignificant ones of Victuals and Drink,' (answered she.)

'Victuals and Drink!' (replied my Husband in a most nobly contemptuous Manner) 'and dost thou then imagine that there is no other support for an exalted Mind (such as is my Laura's) than the mean and indelicate employment of Eating and Drinking?'

'None that I know of, so efficacious,' (returned Augusta).

'And did you then never feel the pleasing Pangs of Love, Augusta?' (replied my Edward). 'Does it appear impossible to your vile and corrupted Palate, to exist on Love? Can you not conceive the Luxury of living in every Distress that Poverty can inflict, with the object of your tenderest Affection?'

'You are too ridiculous' (said Augusta) 'to argue with; perhaps however you may in time be convinced that . . .'

Here I was prevented from hearing the remainder of her Speech, by the Appearance of a very Handsome Young Woman, who was ushered into the Room at the Door of which I had been listening. On hearing her announced by the Name of 'Lady Dorothea', I instantly quitted my Post and followed her into the Parlour, for I well remembered that she was the Lady, proposed as a Wife for my Edward by the Cruel and Unrelenting Baronet.

Altho' Lady Dorothea's visit was nominally to Philippa and Augusta, yet I have some reason to imagine that (acquainted with the Marriage and arrival of Edward) to see me was a principal motive to it.

I soon perceived that tho' lovely and Elegant in her Person and tho' Easy and Polite in her Address, she was of that inferior order of Beings with regard to Delicate feeling, tender Sentiments, and refined Sensibility, of which Augusta was one.

She staid but half an hour and neither in the Course of her Visit, confided to me any of her Secret thoughts, nor requested me to confide in her, any of Mine. You will easily imagine therefore my Dear Marianne that I could not feel any ardent Affection or very sincere Attachment for Lady Dorothea.

Adeiu
Laura

Letter 8th
Laura to Marianne, in continuation

Lady Dorothea had not left us long before another visitor as unexpected a one as her Ladyship, was announced. It was Sir Edward, who informed by Augusta of her Brother's marriage, came doubtless to reproach him for having dared to unite himself to me without his Knowledge. But Edward, foreseeing his Design, approached him with heroic fortitude as soon as he entered the Room, and addressed him in the following Manner.

'Sir Edward, I know the motive of your Journey here— You come with the base Design of reproaching me for having entered into an indissoluble engagement with my Laura without your Consent—But Sir, I glory in the Act—. It is my greatest boast that I have incurred the Displeasure of my Father!'

So saying, he took my hand and whilst Sir Edward, Philippa, and Augusta were doubtless reflecting with Admiration on his undaunted Bravery, led me from the Parlour to his Father's Carriage, which yet remained at the Door and in which we were instantly conveyed from the pursuit of Sir Edward.

The Postilions had at first received orders only to take the London road; as soon as we had sufficiently reflected However, we ordered them to Drive to M——. the seat of Edward's most particular freind, which was but a few miles distant.

At M——. we arrived in a few hours; and on sending in our names were immediately admitted to Sophia, the Wife of Edward's freind. After having been deprived during the course of 3 weeks of a real freind (for such I term your Mother) imagine my transports at beholding one, most truly worthy of the Name. Sophia was rather above the middle size; most elegantly formed. A soft Languor spread over her lovely features, but increased their Beauty.—It was the Charectaristic of her Mind—. She was all Sensibility and Feeling. We flew into each others arms and after having exchanged vows of mutual Friendship for the rest of our Lives, instantly unfolded to each other the most inward Secrets of our Hearts—.* We were interrupted in this Delightfull Employment by the entrance of Augustus, (Edward's freind) who was just returned from a solitary ramble.

Never did I see such an affecting Scene as was the meeting of Edward and Augustus.

'My Life! my Soul!' (exclaimed the former). 'My Adorable Angel!' (replied the latter) as they flew into each other's arms. It was too pathetic for the feelings of Sophia and myself—We fainted alternately on a Sofa.*

adeiu

Laura

Letter the 9th
From the Same to the Same

Towards the close of the Day we received the following Letter from Philippa.

'Sir Edward is greatly incensed by your abrupt departure; he has taken back Augusta with him to Bedfordshire. Much as I wish to enjoy again your charming Society, I cannot determine to snatch you from that, of such dear and deserving Freinds—When your Visit to them is terminated, I trust you will return to the arms of your

Philippa.'

We returned a suitable answer to this affectionate Note and after thanking her for her kind invitation assured her that we would certainly avail ourselves of it, whenever we might have no other place to go to. Tho' certainly nothing could to any reasonable Being, have appeared more satisfactory, than so gratefull a reply to her invitation, yet I know not how it was, but she was certainly capricious enough to be displeased with our behaviour and in a few weeks after, either to revenge our Conduct, or relieve her own solitude, married a young and illiterate Fortune-hunter. This imprudent Step (tho' we were sensible that it would probably deprive us of that fortune which Philippa had ever taught us to expect) could not on our own accounts, excite from our exalted Minds a single sigh; yet fearfull lest it might prove a source of endless misery to the deluded Bride, our trembling Sensibility was greatly affected when we were first informed of the Event. The affectionate Entreaties of Augustus and Sophia that we would for ever consider their House as our Home, easily prevailed on us to determine never more to leave them—. In the Society of my Edward and this Amiable Pair, I passed the happiest moments of my Life: Our time was most delightfully spent, in mutual Protestations of Freindship, and in vows of unalterable Love, in which we were secure from being interrupted, by intruding and disagreable Visitors, as Augustus and Sophia had on their first Entrance in the Neighbourhood, taken due care to inform the surrounding Families, that as their Happiness centered wholly in themselves, they wished for no other society. But alas! my Dear Marianne such Happiness as I then enjoyed was too perfect to be lasting. A most severe and unexpected Blow at once destroyed every Sensation of Pleasure. Convinced as you must be from what I have already told you concerning Augustus and Sophia, that there never were a happier Couple, I need not I imagine inform you that their union had been contrary to the inclinations of their Cruel and Mercenary Parents; who had vainly endeavoured with obstinate Perseverance to force them into a Marriage with those whom they had ever abhorred; but with an Heroic Fortitude worthy to be related and Admired, they had both, constantly refused to submit to such despotic Power.

After having so nobly disentangled themselves from the Shackles of Parental Authority, by a Clandestine Marriage,* they were determined never to forfeit the good opinion they had gained in the World, in so doing, by accepting any proposals of reconciliation that might be offered them by their Fathers—to this farther tryal of their noble independance however they never were exposed.

They had been married but a few months when our visit to them commenced during which time they had been amply supported by a considerable sum of Money which Augustus had gracefully purloined* from his Unworthy father's Escritoire,* a few days before his union with Sophia.

By our arrival their Expences were considerably encreased tho' their means for supplying them were then nearly exhausted. But they, Exalted Creatures! scorned to reflect a moment on their pecuniary Distresses and would have blushed at the idea of paying their Debts.*—Alas! what was their Reward for such disinterested Behaviour! The beautifull Augustus was arrested* and we were all undone. Such perfidious Treachery in the merciless perpetrators of the Deed will shock your gentle nature Dearest Marianne as much as it then affected the Delicate Sensibility of Edward, Sophia, your Laura, and of Augustus himself. To compleat such unparalelled Barbarity we were informed that an Execution in the House* would shortly take place. Ah! what could we do but what we did! We sighed and fainted on the Sofa.

Adeiu
Laura

Letter 10th
Laura in continuation

When we were somewhat recovered from the overpowering Effusions of our Grief, Edward desired that we would consider what was the most prudent step to be taken in our unhappy situation while he repaired to his imprisoned freind to lament over his misfortunes. We promised that we would, and he set forwards on his Journey to Town. During his Absence we faithfully complied with his Desire and after the most mature Deliberation, at length agreed that the best thing we could do was to leave the House; of which we every moment expected the Officers of Justice* to take possession. We waited therefore with the greatest impatience, for the return of Edward in order to impart to him the result of our Deliberations—. But no Edward appeared—. In vain did we count the tedious Moments of his Absence—in vain did we weep—in vain even did we sigh—no Edward returned—. This was too cruel, too unexpected a Blow to our Gentle Sensibility—. we could not support it—we could only faint—. At length collecting all the Resolution I was Mistress of, I arose and after packing up some necessary Apparel for Sophia and myself, I dragged her to a Carriage I had ordered and we instantly set out for London. As the Habitation of Augustus was within twelve miles of Town, it was not long e'er we arrived there, and no sooner had we entered Holbourn* than letting down one of the Front Glasses I enquired of every decent-looking Person that we passed 'If they had seen my Edward'?

But as we drove too rapidly to allow them to answer my repeated Enquiries, I gained little, or indeed, no information concerning him. 'Where am I to Drive?' said the Postilion.* 'To Newgate,* Gentle Youth,' (replied I), 'to see Augustus.' 'Oh! no, no,' (exclaimed Sophia), 'I cannot go to Newgate; I shall not be able to support the sight of my Augustus in so cruel a confinement—my feelings are sufficiently shocked by the *recital*, of his Distress, but to behold it will overpower my Sensibility.' As I perfectly agreed with her in the Justice of her Sentiments the Postilion was instantly directed to return into the Country. You may perhaps have been somewhat surprised my Dearest Marianne, that in the Distress I then endured, destitute of any Support, and unprovided with any Habitation, I should never once have remembered my Father and Mother or my paternal Cottage in the Vale of Uske. To account for this seeming forgetfullness I must inform you of a trifling Circumstance concerning them which I have as yet never mentioned—. The death of my Parents a few weeks after my Departure, is the circumstance I allude to. By their decease I became the lawfull Inheritress of their House and Fortune. But alas! the House had never been their own and their Fortune had only been an Annuity* on their own Lives. Such is the Depravity of the World! To your Mother I should have returned with

Pleasure, should have been happy to have introduced to her, my Charming Sophia and should have with Chearfullness have passed the remainder of my Life in their dear Society in the Vale of Uske, had not one obstacle to the execution of so agreable a Scheme, intervened; which was the Marriage and Removal of your Mother to a Distant part of Ireland.

Adeiu.
Laura.

Letter 11th
Laura in continuation

'I have a Relation in Scotland' (said Sophia to me as we left London) 'who I am certain would not hesitate in receiving me.' 'Shall I order the Boy to drive there?' said I—but instantly recollecting myself, exclaimed 'Alas, I fear it will be too long a Journey for the Horses.' Unwilling however to act only from my own inadequate Knowledge of the Strength and Abilities of Horses, I consulted the Postilion, who was entirely of my Opinion concerning the Affair. We therefore determined to change Horses at the next Town and to travel Post* the remainder of the Journey—. When we arrived at the last Inn we were to stop at, which was but a few miles from the House of Sophia's Relation, unwilling to intrude our Society on him unexpected and unthought of, we wrote a very elegant and well-penned Note to him containing an Account of our Destitute and melancholy Situation, and of our intention to spend some months with him in Scotland. As soon as we had dispatched this letter, we immediately prepared to follow it in person and were stepping into the Carriage for that Purpose when our Attention was attracted by the Entrance of a coroneted Coach and 4 into the Inn-yard. A Gentleman considerably advanced in years, descended from it—. At his first Appearance my Sensibility was wonderfully affected and e'er I had gazed at him a 2d time, an instinctive Sympathy* whispered to my Heart, that he was my Grandfather.

Convinced that I could not be mistaken in my conjecture I instantly sprang from the Carriage I had just entered, and following the Venerable Stranger into the Room he had been shewn to, I threw myself on my knees before him and besought him to acknowledge me as his Grand-Child.—He started, and after having attentively examined my features, raised me from the Ground and throwing his Grand-fatherly arms around my neck, exclaimed, 'Acknowledge thee! Yes dear resemblance of my Laurina and my Laurina's Daughter, sweet image of my Claudia and my Claudia's Mother, I do acknowledge thee as the Daughter of the one and the Grandaughter of the other.' While he was thus tenderly embracing me, Sophia, astonished at my precipitate Departure, entered the Room in search of me—. No sooner had she caught the eye of the venerable Peer, than he exclaimed with every mark of Astonishment— 'Another Grandaughter! Yes, yes, I see you are the Daughter of my Laurina's eldest Girl; Your resemblance to the beauteous Matilda* sufficiently proclaims it.' 'Oh!' replied Sophia, 'when I first beheld you the instinct of Nature whispered me that we were in some degree related—But whether Grandfathers, or Grandmothers, I could not pretend to determine.' He folded her in his arms, and whilst they were tenderly embracing, the Door of the Apartment opened and a most beautifull Young Man appeared. On perceiving him Lord St. Clair* started and retreating back a few paces, with uplifted Hands, said 'Another Grand-Child! What an unexpected Happiness is this! to discover in the space of 3 minutes, as many of my Descendants! This, I am certain is Philander* the son of my Laurina's 3d Girl, the amiable Bertha; there wants now but the presence of Gustavus* to compleat the Union of my Laurina's Grand-Children.'

'And here he is;' (said a Gracefull Youth who that instant entered the room) 'here is the Gustavus you desire to see. I am the son of Agatha, your Laurina's 4th and Youngest Daughter.' 'I see you are indeed;' replied Lord St. Clair— 'But tell me' (continued he looking fearfully towards the Door) 'tell me, have I any other Grand-Children in the

House?"* 'None, my Lord.' 'Then I will provide for you all without further delay—Here are 4 Banknotes of 50£ each—Take them and remember I have done the Duty of a Grandfather—.' He instantly left the Room and immediately afterwards the House.

Adeiu.
Laura.

Letter the 12th
Laura in continuation

You may imagine how greatly we were surprised by the sudden departure of Lord St. Clair. 'Ignoble Grand-sire!' exclaimed Sophia. 'Unworthy Grand-father!' said I, and instantly fainted in each other's arms. How long we remained in this situation I know not; but when we recovered we found ourselves alone, without either Gustavus, Philander or the Bank-notes. As we were deploring our unhappy fate, the Door of the Apartment opened and 'Macdonald' was announced. He was Sophia's cousin. The haste with which he came to our releif so soon after the receipt of our Note, spoke so greatly in his favour that I hesitated not to pronounce him at first sight, a tender and simpathetic Freind. Alas! he little deserved the name—for though he told us that he was much concerned at our Misfortunes, yet by his own account it appeared that the perusal of them, had neither drawn from him a single sigh, nor induced him to bestow one curse on our vindictive Stars—. He told Sophia that his Daughter depended on her returning with him to Macdonald-Hall, and that as his Cousin's freind he should be happy to see me there also. To Macdonald-Hall, therefore, we went, and were received with great kindness by Janetta,* the daughter of Macdonald, and the Mistress of the Mansion. Janetta was then only fifteen; naturally well disposed, endowed with a susceptible Heart, and a simpathetic Disposition, she might, had these amiable Qualities been properly encouraged, have been an ornament to human Nature; but unfortunately her Father possessed not a soul sufficiently exalted to admire so promising a Disposition, and had endeavoured by every means in his power to prevent its encreasing with her Years. He had actually so far extinguished the natural noble Sensibility of her Heart, as to prevail on her to accept an offer from a young Man of his Recommendation. They were to be married in a few Months, and Graham,* was in the House when we arrived. *We* soon saw through his Character—. He was just such a Man as one might have expected to be the choice of Macdonald. They said he was Sensible, well-informed, and Agreable; we did not pretend to Judge of such trifles, but as we were convinced he had no soul, that he had never read the Sorrows of Werter,* and that his Hair bore not the slightest resemblance to Auburn, we were certain that Janetta could feel no affection for him, or at least that she ought to feel none. The very circumstance of his being her father's choice too, was so much in his disfavour, that had he been deserving her, in every other respect yet *that* of itself ought to have been a sufficient reason in the Eyes of Janetta for rejecting him. These considerations we were determined to represent to her in their proper light and doubted not of meeting with the desired Success from one naturally so well disposed, whose errors in the affair had only arisen from a want of proper confidence in her own opinion, and a suitable contempt of her father's. We found her indeed all that our warmest wishes could have hoped for; we had no difficulty to convince her that it was impossible she could love Graham, or that it was her Duty to disobey her Father; the only thing at which she rather seemed to hesitate was our assertion that she must be attached to some other Person. For some time, she persevered in declaring that she knew no other young Man for whom she had the smallest Affection; but upon explaining the impossibility of such a thing she said that she beleived she *did like* Captain M'Kenzie better than any one she knew besides. This confession satisfied us and after having enumerated the good Qualities of M'Kenzie and assured her that she was violently in love with him, we desired to know whether he had ever in any wise declared his Affection to her.

'So far from having ever declared it, I have no reason to imagine that he has ever felt any for me,' said Janetta. 'That he certainly adores you' (replied Sophia) 'there can be no doubt—. The Attachment must be reciprocal—. Did he never gaze on you with admiration—tenderly press your hand—drop an involuntary tear—and leave the room abruptly?' 'Never' (replied She) 'that I remember—he has always left the room indeed when his visit has been ended, but has never gone away particularly abruptly or without making a bow.'

'Indeed my Love' (said I) 'you must be mistaken—: for it is absolutely impossible that he should ever have left you but with Confusion, Despair, and Precipitation—. Consider but for a moment, Janetta, and you must be convinced how absurd it is to suppose that he could ever make a Bow, or behave like any other Person.' Having settled this Point to our satisfaction, the next we took into consideration was, to determine in what manner we should inform M'Kenzie of the favourable Opinion Janetta entertained of him—. We at length agreed to acquaint him with it by an anonymous Letter which Sophia drew up in the following Manner.

'Oh! happy Lover of the beautifull Janetta, oh! enviable Possessor of *her* Heart whose hand is destined to another, why do you thus delay a confession of your Attachment to the amiable Object of it? Oh! consider that a few weeks will at once put an end to every flattering Hope that you may now entertain, by uniting the unfortunate Victim of her father's Cruelty to the execrable and detested Graham.

'Alas! why do you thus so cruelly connive at the projected Misery of her and of yourself by delaying to communicate that scheme which has doubtless long possessed your imagination? A secret Union will at once secure the felicity of both.'

The amiable M'Kenzie, whose modesty as he afterwards assured us had been the only reason of his having so long concealed the violence of his affection for Janetta, on receiving this Billet flew on the wings of Love to Macdonald-

Hall, and so powerfully pleaded his Attachment to her who inspired it, that after a few more private interveiws, Sophia and I experienced the Satisfaction of seeing them depart for Gretna-Green,* which they chose for the celebration of their Nuptials, in preference to any other place although it was at a considerable distance from Macdonald-Hall.

Adeiu—
Laura—

Letter the 13th
Laura in Continuation

They had been gone nearly a couple of Hours, before either Macdonald or Graham had entertained any suspicion of the affair—. And they might not even then have suspected it, but for the following little Accident. Sophia happening one Day to open a private Drawer in Macdonald's Library with one of her own keys, discovered that it was the Place where he kept his Papers of consequence and amongst them some bank notes of considerable amount. This discovery she imparted to me; and having agreed together that it would be a proper treatment of so vile a Wretch as Macdonald to deprive him of Money, perhaps dishonestly gained, it was determined that the next time we should either of us happen to go that way, we would take one or more of the Bank notes from the drawer. This well-meant Plan we had often successfully put in Execution; but alas! on the very day of Janetta's Escape, as Sophia was majestically removing the 5th Bank-note from the Drawer to her own purse, she was suddenly most impertinently interrupted in her employment by the entrance of Macdonald himself, in a most abrupt and precipitate Manner. Sophia (who though naturally all winning sweetness could when occasions demanded it call forth the Dignity of her Sex) instantly put on a most forbidding look, and darting an angry frown on the undaunted Culprit, demanded in a haughty tone of voice 'Wherefore her retirement was thus insolently broken in on?'* The unblushing Macdonald, without even endeavouring to exculpate himself from the crime he was charged with, meanly endeavoured to reproach Sophia with ignobly defrauding him of his Money . . . The dignity of Sophia was wounded; 'Wretch' (exclaimed she, hastily replacing the Bank-note in the Drawer) 'how darest thou to accuse me of an Act, of which the bare idea makes me blush?' The base wretch was still unconvinced and continued to upbraid the justly-offended Sophia in such opprobrious Language, that at length he so greatly provoked the gentle sweetness of her Nature, as to induce her to revenge herself on him by informing him of Janetta's Elopement, and of the active Part we had both taken in the Affair. At this period of their Quarrel I entered the Library and was as you may imagine equally offended as Sophia at the ill-grounded Accusations of the malevolent and contemptible Macdonald. 'Base Miscreant' (cried I) 'how canst thou thus undauntedly endeavour to sully the spotless reputation of such bright Excellence? Why dost thou not suspect *my* innocence as soon?'

'Be satisfied, Madam' (replied he) 'I *do* suspect it, and therefore must desire that you will both leave this House in less than half an hour.'

'We shall go willingly;' (answered Sophia) 'our hearts have long detested thee, and nothing but our freindship for thy Daughter could have induced us to remain so long beneath thy roof.'

'Your Freindship for my Daughter has indeed been most powerfully exerted by throwing her into the arms of an unprincipled Fortune-hunter,' (replied he).

'Yes,' (exclaimed I) 'amidst every misfortune, it will afford us some consolation to reflect that by this one act of Freindship to Janetta, we have amply discharged every obligation that we have received from her father.'

'It must indeed be a most gratefull reflection, to your exalted minds' (said he).

As soon as we had packed up our wardrobe and valuables, we left Macdonald Hall, and after having walked about a mile and a half we sate down by the side of a clear limpid stream* to refresh our exhausted limbs. The place was suited to meditation—. A Grove of full-grown Elms sheltered us from the East—. A Bed of full-grown Nettles from the West—. Before us ran the murmuring brook and behind us ran the turn-pike road.* We were in a mood for contemplation and in a Disposition to enjoy so beautifull a spot. A mutual Silence which had for some time reigned between us, was at length broke by my exclaiming—'What a lovely Scene! Alas, why are not Edward and Augustus here to enjoy its Beauties with us?'

'Ah! my beloved Laura' (cried Sophia) 'for pity's sake forbear recalling to my remembrance the unhappy situation of my imprisoned Husband. Alas, what would I not give to learn the fate of my Augustus!—to know if he is still in Newgate, or if he is yet hung.—But never shall I be able so far to conquer my tender sensibility as to enquire after him. Oh! do not I beseech you ever let me again hear you repeat his beloved Name—. It affects me too deeply—. I cannot bear to hear him mentioned, it wounds my feelings.'

'Excuse me my Sophia for having thus unwillingly offended you—' replied I—and then changing the conversation, desired her to admire the Noble Grandeur of the Elms which Sheltered us from the Eastern Zephyr.* 'Alas! my Laura' (returned she) 'avoid so melancholy a subject, I intreat you.— Do not again wound my Sensibility by Observations on those elms. They remind me of Augustus—. He was like them, tall, magestic—he possessed that noble grandeur which you admire in them.'

I was silent, fearfull lest I might any more unwillingly distress her by fixing on any other subject of conversation which might again remind her of Augustus.

'Why do you not speak, my Laura?' (said she after a short pause) 'I cannot support this silence—you must not leave me to my own reflections; they ever recur to Augustus.'

'What a beautifull Sky!' (said I) 'How charmingly is the azure varied by those delicate streaks of white!'

'Oh! my Laura' (replied she hastily withdrawing her Eyes from a momentary glance at the sky) 'do not thus distress me by calling my Attention to an object which so cruelly reminds me of my Augustus's blue sattin Waistcoat striped with white!* In pity to your unhappy freind avoid a subject so distressing.' What could I do? The feelings of Sophia were at that time so exquisite, and the tenderness she felt for Augustus so poignant that I had not the power to start any other topic, justly fearing that it might in some unforseen manner again awaken all her sensibility by directing her thoughts to her Husband.—Yet to be silent would be cruel; She had intreated me to talk.

From this Dilemma I was most fortunately releived by an accident truly apropos;* it was the lucky overturning of a Gentleman's Phaeton, on the road which ran murmuring behind us. It was a most fortunate Accident as it diverted the Attention of Sophia from the melancholy reflections which she had been before indulging.

We instantly quitted our seats and ran to the rescue of those who but a few moments before had been in so elevated a situation as a fashionably high Phaeton, but who were now laid low and sprawling in the Dust—. 'What an ample subject for reflection on the uncertain Enjoyments of this World, would not that Phaeton and the Life of Cardinal Wolsey afford a thinking Mind!'* said I to Sophia as we were hastening to the field of Action.

She had not time to answer me, for every thought was now engaged by the horrid Spectacle before us. Two Gentlemen most elegantly attired but weltering in their blood was what first struck our Eyes—we approached—they were Edward and Augustus—Yes, dearest Marianne, they were our Husbands. Sophia shreiked and fainted on the Ground—I screamed and instantly ran mad—. We remained thus mutually deprived of our Senses some minutes, and on regaining them were deprived of them again—. For an Hour and a Quarter did we continue in this unfortunate Situation—Sophia fainting every moment and I running Mad as often. At length a Groan from the hapless Edward (who alone retained any share of Life) restored us to ourselves—. Had we indeed before imagined that either of them lived, we should have been more sparing of our Greif—but as we had supposed when we first beheld them that they were no more, we knew that nothing could remain to be done but what we were about—. No sooner therefore did we hear my Edward's groan than postponing our Lamentations for the present, we hastily ran to the Dear Youth and kneeling on each side of him implored him not to die—. 'Laura' (said He fixing his now languid Eyes on me) 'I fear I have been overturned.'

I was overjoyed to find him yet sensible*—.

'Oh! tell me Edward' (said I) 'tell me I beseech you before you die, what has befallen you since that unhappy Day in which Augustus was arrested and we were separated—'

'I will' (said he) and instantly fetching a Deep sigh, Expired—. Sophia immediately sunk again into a swoon—. *My* Greif was more audible, My voice faltered, My Eyes assumed a vacant Stare, My face became as pale as Death, and my Senses were considerably impaired—.

'Talk not to me of Phaetons' (said I, raving in a frantic, incoherent manner)—'Give me a violin—. I'll play to him and sooth him in his melancholy Hours—Beware ye gentle Nymphs of Cupid's Thunderbolts, avoid the piercing Shafts of Jupiter—Look at that Grove of Firs—I see a Leg of Mutton—They told me Edward was not Dead; but they deceived me—they took him for a Cucumber*—' Thus I continued wildly exclaiming on my Edward's Death—. For two Hours did I rave thus madly and should not then have left off, as I was not in the least fatigued, had not Sophia who was just recovered from her swoon, intreated me to consider that Night was now approaching and that the Damps began to fall. 'And whither shall we go' (said I) 'to shelter us from either?' 'To that white Cottage.' (replied she, pointing to a neat Building which rose up amidst the Grove of Elms and which I had not before observed—). I agreed and we instantly walked to it—we knocked at the door—it was opened by an old Woman; on being requested to afford us a Night's Lodging, she informed us that her House was but small, that she had only two Bed-rooms, but that However we should be wellcome to one of them. We were satisfied and followed the good Woman into the House where we were greatly cheered by the sight of a comfortable

fire——. She was a Widow and had only one Daughter, who
was then just Seventeen*——One of the best of ages; but alas!
she was very plain and her name was Bridget*. . . .
Nothing therefore could be expected from her——she could
not be supposed to possess either exalted Ideas, Delicate
Feelings or refined Sensibilities——She was nothing more
than a mere good-tempered, civil and obliging Young
Woman; as such we could scarcely dislike her——she was
only an Object of Contempt——.

Adeiu
Laura——

Letter the 14th
Laura in continuation

Arm yourself, my amiable Young Freind, with all the
philosophy you are Mistress of; summon up all the fortitude
you possess, for Alas! in the perusal of the following Pages
your sensibility will be most severely tried. Ah! what were
the Misfortunes I had before experienced and which I have
already related to you, to the one I am now going to inform
you of. The Death of my Father, my Mother, and my
Husband, though almost more than my gentle Nature could
support, were trifles in comparison to the misfortune I am
now proceeding to relate. The morning after our arrival at
the Cottage, Sophia complained of a violent pain in her
delicate limbs, accompanied with a disagreable Head-ake.
She attributed it to a cold caught by her continued faintings
in the open Air as the Dew was falling the Evening before.
This I feared was but too probably the case; since how
could it be otherwise accounted for that I should have
escaped the same indisposition, but by supposing that the
bodily Exertions I had undergone in my repeated fits of
frenzy, had so effectually circulated and warmed my Blood
as to make me proof against the chilling Damps of Night,
whereas, Sophia lying totally inactive on the Ground must
have been exposed to all their Severity. I was most seriously
alarmed by her illness which trifling as it may appear to

you, a certain instinctive Sensibility whispered me, would in the End be fatal to her.

Alas! my fears were but too fully justified; she grew gradually worse—and I daily became more alarmed for her.—At length she was obliged to confine herself solely to the Bed allotted us by our worthy Landlady—. Her disorder turned to a galloping Consumption* and in a few Days carried her off. Amidst all my Lamentations for her (and violent you may suppose they were) I yet received some consolation in the reflection of my having paid every Attention to her, that could be offered, in her illness. I had wept over her every Day—had bathed her sweet face with my tears and had pressed her fair Hands continually in mine—. 'My beloved Laura' (said she to me a few Hours before she died) 'take warning from my unhappy End and avoid the imprudent conduct which has occasioned it. . . . Beware of fainting-fits. . . . Though at the time they may be refreshing and Agreable yet beleive me they will in the end, if too often repeated and at improper seasons, prove destructive to your Constitution . . . My fate will teach you this . . . I die a Martyr to my greif for the loss of Augustus . . . One fatal swoon has cost me my Life . . . Beware of swoons, Dear Laura. . . . A frenzy fit is not one quarter so pernicious; it is an exercise to the Body and if not too violent, is I dare say conducive to Health in its con-sequences—Run mad as often as you chuse; but do not faint—'

These were the last words she ever adressed to me . . . It was her dieing Advice to her afflicted Laura, who has ever most faithfully adhered to it.

After having attended my lamented freind to her Early Grave, I immediately (tho' late at night) left the detested Village in which she died, and near which had expired my Husband and Augustus. I had not walked many yards from it before I was overtaken by a Stage-Coach, in which I instantly took a place, determined to proceed in it to Edinburgh, where I hoped to find some kind pitying Freind who would receive and comfort me in my Afflictions.

It was so dark when I entered the Coach that I could not

distinguish the Number of my Fellow-travellers; I could only perceive that they were Many. Regardless however of any thing concerning them, I gave myself up to my own sad Reflections. A general Silence prevailed—A Silence, which was by nothing interrupted but by the loud and repeated snores of one of the Party.

'What an illiterate villain must that Man be!' (thought I to myself). 'What a total Want of delicate refinement must he have who can thus shock our senses by such a brutal Noise! He must I am certain be capable of every bad Action! There is no crime too black for such a Character!' Thus reasoned I within myself, and doubtless such were the reflections of my fellow travellers.

At length, returning Day enabled me to behold the unprincipled Scoundrel who had so violently disturbed my feelings. It was Sir Edward, the father of my Deceased Husband. By his side, sate Augusta, and on the same seat with me were your Mother and Lady Dorothea. Imagine my Surprise at finding myself thus seated amongst my old Acquaintance. Great as was my astonishment, it was yet increased, when on looking out of Windows, I beheld the Husband of Philippa, with Philippa by his side, on the Coach-box,* and when on looking behind, I beheld, Philander and Gustavus in the Basket.* 'Oh! Heavens,' (exclaimed I)' is it possible that I should so unexpectedly be surrounded by my nearest Relations and Connections?'* These words roused the rest of the Party, and every eye was directed to the corner in which I sat. 'Oh! my Isabel' (continued I, throwing myself, across Lady Dorothea into her arms) 'receive once more to your Bosom the unfortunate Laura. Alas! when we last parted in the Vale of Usk, I was happy in being united to the best of Edwards; I had then a Father and a Mother, and had never known misfortunes— But now deprived of every freind but you—'.

'What!' (interrupted Augusta) 'is my Brother dead then? Tell us, I intreat you, what is become of him?'

'Yes, cold and insensible Nymph,' (replied I) 'that luckless Swain your Brother, is no more, and you may now glory in being the Heiress of Sir Edward's fortune.'

Although I had always despised her from the Day I had overheard her conversation with my Edward, yet in civility I complied with hers and Sir Edward's intreaties that I would inform them of the whole melancholy Affair. They were greatly shocked—Even the obdurate Heart of Sir Edward and the insensible one of Augusta, were touched with Sorrow, by the unhappy tale. At the request of your Mother I related to them every other misfortune which had befallen me since we parted. Of the imprisonment of Augustus and the absence of Edward—of our arrival in Scotland—of our unexpected Meeting with our Grandfather and our cousins—of our visit to Macdonald-Hall—of the singular Service we there performed towards Janetta—of her Father's ingratitude for it. . . . of his inhuman Behaviour, unaccountable suspicions, and barbarous treatment of us, in obliging us to leave the House. . . . of our Lamentations on the loss of Edward and Augustus and finally of the melancholy Death of my beloved Companion.

Pity and Surprise were strongly depictured in your Mother's Countenance, during the whole of my narration, but I am sorry to say, that to the eternal reproach of her Sensibility, the latter infinitely predominated. Nay, faultless as my Conduct had certainly been during the whole Course of my late Misfortunes and Adventures, she pretended to find fault with my Behaviour in many of the situations in which I had been placed. As I was sensible myself, that I had always behaved in a manner which reflected Honour on my Feelings and Refinement, I paid little attention to what she said, and desired her to satisfy my Curiosity by informing me how she came there, instead of wounding my spotless reputation with unjustifiable Reproaches. As soon as she had complyed with my wishes in this particular and had given me an accurate detail of every thing that had befallen her since our separation (the particulars of which if you are not already acquainted with, your Mother will give you) I applied to Augusta for the same information respecting herself, Sir Edward and Lady Dorothea.

She told me that having a considerable taste for the Beauties of Nature, her curiosity to behold the delightful scenes it exhibited in that part of the World had been so much raised by Gilpin's Tour to the Highlands,* that she had prevailed on her Father to undertake a Tour of Scotland and had persuaded Lady Dorothea to accompany them. That they had arrived at Edinburgh a few days before and from thence had made daily Excursions into the Country around in the Stage Coach* they were then in, from one of which Excursions they were at that time returning. My next enquiries were concerning Philippa and her Husband, the latter of whom I learned having spent all her fortune, had recourse for subsistance to the talent in which, he had always most excelled, namely, Driving, and that having sold every thing which belonged to them except their Coach, had converted it into a Stage, and in order to be removed from any of his former Acquaintance, had driven it to Edinburgh from whence he went to Sterling* every other Day; That Philippa still retaining her affection for her ungratefull Husband, had followed him to Scotland and generally accompanied him in his little Excursions to Sterling. 'It has only been to throw a little money into their Pockets' (continued Augusta) 'that my Father has always travelled in their Coach to veiw the beauties of the Country since our arrival in Scotland—for it would certainly have been much more agreable to us, to visit the Highlands in a Postchaise than merely to travel from Edinburgh to Sterling and from Sterling to Edinburgh every other Day in a crouded and uncomfortable Stage.' I perfectly agreed with her in her sentiments on the Affair, and secretly blamed Sir Edward for thus sacrificing his Daughter's Pleasure for the sake of a ridiculous old Woman whose folly in marrying so young a Man ought to be punished. His Behaviour however was entirely of a peice with his general Character; for what could be expected from a Man who possessed not the smallest atom of Sensibility, who scarcely knew the meaning of Simpathy, and who actually snored—.

Adeiu
Laura.

Letter the 15th
Laura in continuation

When we arrived at the town where we were to Breakfast, I
was determined to speak with Philander and Gustavus, and
to that purpose as soon as I left the Carriage, I went to the
Basket and tenderly enquired after their Health, expressing
my fears of the uneasiness of their Situation. At first they
seemed rather confused at my Appearance, dreading no
doubt that I might call them to account for the money
which our Grandfather had left me and which they had
unjustly deprived me of, but finding that I mentioned
nothing of the Matter, they desired me to step into the
Basket as we might there converse with greater ease.
Accordingly I entered and whilst the rest of the party were
devouring Green tea* and buttered toast, we feasted
ourselves in a more refined and Sentimental* Manner by a
confidential Conversation. I informed them of every thing
which had befallen me during the course of my Life, and at
my request they related to me every incident of theirs.

'We are the sons as you already know, of the two
youngest Daughters which Lord St. Clair had by Laurina,
an Italian opera girl. Our mothers could neither of them
exactly ascertain who were our fathers; though it is
generally beleived that Philander, is the son of one Philip
Jones a Bricklayer and that my father was Gregory Staves a
Staymaker* of Edinburgh. This is however of little consequence, for as our Mothers were certainly never married
to either of them, it reflects no Dishonour on our Blood,
which is of a most ancient and unpolluted kind. Bertha (the
Mother of Philander) and Agatha (my own Mother) always
lived together. They were neither of them very rich; their
united fortunes had originally amounted to nine thousand
Pounds, but as they had always lived upon the principal of
it, when we were fifteen it was diminished to nine Hundred.
This nine Hundred, they always kept in a Drawer in one of
the Tables which stood in our common sitting Parlour, for
the Convenience of having it always at Hand. Whether it

was from this circumstance, of its being easily taken, or from a wish of being independant, or from an excess of Sensibility (for which we were always remarkable) I cannot now determine, but certain it is that when we had reached our 15th year, we took the Nine Hundred Pounds and ran away. Having obtained this prize we were determined to manage it with eoconomy and not to spend it either with folly or Extravagance. To this purpose we therefore divided it into nine parcels, one of which we devoted to Victuals, the 2d to Drink, the 3d to Housekeeping, the 4th to Carriages, the 5th to Horses, the 6th to Servants, the 7th to Amusements, the 8th to Cloathes and the 9th to Silver Buckles.* Having thus arranged our Expences for two Months (for we expected to make the nine Hundred Pounds last as long) we hastened to London and had the good luck to spend it in 7 weeks and a Day which was 6 Days sooner than we had intended. As soon as we had thus happily disencumbered ourselves from the weight of so much Money, we began to think of returning to our Mothers, but accidentally hearing that they were both starved to Death, we gave over the design and determined to engage ourselves to some strolling Company of Players,* as we had always a turn for the Stage. Accordingly we offered our services to one and were accepted; our Company was indeed rather small, as it consisted only of the Manager, his Wife and ourselves, but there were fewer to pay and the only inconvenience attending it was the Scarcity of Plays which for want of People to fill the Characters, we could perform—. We did not mind trifles however—. One of our most admired Performances was *Macbeth*, in which we were truly great. The Manager always played *Banquo* himself, his Wife my *Lady Macbeth*. I did the *Three Witches* and Philander acted *all the rest*.* To say the truth this tragedy was not only the Best, but the only Play we ever performed; and after having acted it all over England, and Wales, we came to Scotland to exhibit it over the remainder of Great Britain. We happened to be quartered in that very Town, where you came and met your Grandfather—. We were in the Inn-yard when his Carriage entered and perceiving by the Arms to whom it belonged and knowing that Lord St. Clair was our Grandfather, we agreed to endeavour to get something from him by discovering the Relationship—. You know how well it succeeded—. Having obtained the two Hundred Pounds, we instantly left the Town, leaving our Manager and his wife to act *Macbeth* by themselves, and took the road to Sterling, where we spent our little fortune with great *eclat*.* We are now returning to Edinburgh in order to get some preferment in the Acting way;* and such, my Dear Cousin, is our History.'

I thanked the amiable Youth for his entertaining Narration, and after expressing my Wishes for their Welfare and Happiness, left them in their little Habitation and returned to my other Freinds who impatiently expected me.

My Adventures are now drawing to a close my dearest Marianne; at least for the present.

When we arrived at Edinburgh Sir Edward told me that as the Widow of his Son, he desired I would accept from his Hands of four Hundred a year. I graciously promised that I would, but could not help observing that the unsimpathetic Baronet offered it more on account of my being the Widow of Edward than in being the refined and amiable Laura.

I took up my Residence in a romantic Village in the Highlands of Scotland, where I have ever since continued, and where I can uninterrupted by unmeaning Visits, indulge in a melancholy solitude, my unceasing Lamentations for the Death of my Father, my Mother, my Husband and my Freind.

Augusta has been for several Years united to Graham, the Man of all others most suited to her; she became acquainted with him during her stay in Scotland.

Sir Edward, in hopes of gaining an Heir to his Title and Estate, at the same time married Lady Dorothea—. His wishes have been answered.

Philander and Gustavus, after having raised their reputation by their Performances in the Theatrical Line at Edinburgh, removed to Covent Garden, where they still Exhibit under the assumed names of *Lewis* and *Quick*.*

Philippa has long paid the Debt of Nature,* Her

Husband however still continues to drive the Stage-Coach from Edinburgh to Sterling:—

> Adeiu my Dearest Marianne.
>
> Laura—

Finis

June 13th 1790

*To Henry Thomas Austen Esqre.**

Sir

I am now availing myself of the Liberty you have frequently honoured me with of dedicating one of my Novels to you. That it is unfinished, I greive; yet fear that from me, it will always remain so; that as far as it is carried, it Should be so trifling and so unworthy of you, is

> another concern to
> your obliged humble
>   Servant
>   The Author

Messrs Demand & Co*—pleass to pay Jane Austen Spinster* the sum of one hundred guineas on account of your Humble Servant.

                                                    H T Austen.
£105.0.0

Lesley Castle

an unfinished Novel in Letters

Letter The first is from
Miss Margaret Lesley to Miss Charlotte Lutterell.

Lesley-Castle   Janry 3d—1792.

My Brother has just left us. 'Matilda'* (said he at parting) 'you and Margaret will I am certain take all the care of my dear little one, that she might have received from an indulgent, an affectionate an amiable Mother.' Tears rolled down his cheeks as he spoke these words—the remembrance of her, who had so wantonly disgraced the Maternal character and so openly violated the conjugal Duties, prevented his adding anything farther; he embraced his sweet Child and after saluting Matilda and Me hastily broke from us—and seating himself in his Chaise, pursued the road to Aberdeen. Never was there a better young Man! Ah! how little did he deserve the misfortunes he has experienced in the Marriage State. So good a Husband to so bad a Wife! for you know my dear Charlotte that the Worthless Louisa left him, her Child and reputation a few weeks ago in company with Danvers and †dishonour. Never was there a sweeter fàce, a finer form, or a less amiable Heart than Louisa owned! Her child already possesses the personal Charms of her unhappy Mother! May she inherit from her Father all his mental ones! Lesley is at present but five and twenty, and has already given himself up to Melancholy and Despair; what a difference between him and his Father! Sir George is 57* and still remains the Beau, the flighty stripling, the gay Lad and sprightly Youngster, that his Son was really about five years back, and that *he* has affected to appear ever since my remembrance. While our father is fluttering about the streets of London, gay, dissipated, and Thoughtless at the age of 57, Matilda and I continue secluded from Mankind in our old and Mouldering Castle, which is situated two miles from Perth* on a bold projecting Rock, and commands an extensive view of the Town and its delightful Environs. But tho' retired from almost all the World, (for we visit no one but the M'Leods, The M'Kenzies, the M'Phersons, the M'Cartneys, the M'donalds, The M'Kinnons, the M'lellans, the M'Kays, the Macbeths and the Macduffs*) we are neither dull nor unhappy; on the contrary there never were two more lively, more agreable or more witty Girls, than we are; not an hour in the Day hangs heavy on our hands. We read, we work, we walk and when fatigued with these Employments releive our spirits, either by a lively song, a graceful Dance, or by some smart bon-mot, and witty repartée. We are handsome my dear Charlotte, very handsome and the greatest of our Perfections is, that we are entirely insensible of them ourselves. But why do I thus dwell on myself? Let me rather repeat the praise of our dear little Neice the innocent Louisa, who is at present sweetly smiling in a gentle Nap, as

† Rakehelly* Dishonor Esqre.

she reposes on the Sofa. The dear Creature is just turned of two years old; as handsome as tho' 2 and 20, as sensible as tho' 2 and 30, and as prudent as tho' 2 and 40. To convince you of this, I must inform you that she has a very fine complexion and very pretty features, that she already knows the two first Letters in the Alphabet, and that she never tears her frocks—. If I have not now convinced you of her Beauty, Sense and Prudence, I have nothing more to urge in support of my assertion, and you will therefore have no way of deciding the Affair but by coming to Lesley-castle, and by a personal acquaintance with Louisa, determine for yourself. Ah! my dear Freind, how happy should I be to see you within these venerable Walls! It is now four years since my removal from School has separated me from you; that two such tender Hearts, so closely linked together by the ties of simpathy and Freindship, should be so widely removed from each other, is vastly moving. I live in Perthshire, You in Sussex. We might meet in London, were my Father disposed to carry me there, and were your Mother to be there at the same time. We might meet at Bath, at Tunbridge, or anywhere else indeed, could we but be at the same place together. We have only to hope that such a period may arrive. My Father does not return to us till Autumn; my Brother will leave Scotland in a few Days; he is impatient to travel. Mistaken Youth! He vainly flatters himself that change of Air will heal the Wounds of a broken Heart! You will join with me I am certain my dear Charlotte, in prayers for the recovery of the unhappy Lesley's peace of Mind, which must ever be essential to that of your sincere freind   M. Lesley.

Letter the second
From Miss C. Lutterell to Miss M. Lesley in answer

Glenford   Feb:ry 12

I have a thousand excuses to beg for having so long delayed thanking you my dear Peggy for your agreable Letter, which beleive me I should not have deferred doing, had not every moment of my time during the last five weeks been so fully employed in the necessary arrangements for my sister's Wedding, as to allow me no time to devote either to you or myself. And now what provokes me more than anything else is that the Match is broke off, and all my Labour thrown away. Imagine how great the Dissapointment must be to me, when you consider that after having laboured both by Night and by Day, in order to get the Wedding dinner ready by the time appointed, after having roasted Beef, Broiled Mutton, and Stewed Soup* enough to last the new-married Couple through the Honey-moon, I had the mortification of finding that I had been Roasting, Broiling and Stewing both the Meat and Myself to no purpose. Indeed my dear Freind, I never remember suffering any vexation equal to what I experienced on last Monday when my Sister came running to me in the Store-room with her face as White as a Whipt syllabub,* and told me that Hervey had been thrown from his Horse, had fractured his Scull and was pronounced by his Surgeon to be in the most emminent Danger.

'Good God!' (said I) 'you don't say so? Why what in the name of Heaven will become of all the Victuals! We shall never be able to eat it while it is good. However, we'll call in the Surgeon to help us—. I shall be able to manage the Sir-loin myself; my Mother will eat the Soup, and You and the Doctor must finish the rest.' Here I was interrupted, by seeing my poor Sister fall down to appearance Lifeless upon one of the Chests, where we keep our Table linen. I immediately called my Mother and the Maids, and at last we brought her to herself again; as soon as ever she was sensible, she expressed a determination of going instantly to Henry, and was so wildly bent on this Scheme, that we had the greatest Difficulty in the World to prevent her putting it in execution; at last however more by Force than Entreaty we prevailed on her to go into her room; we laid her upon the Bed, and she continued for some Hours in the most dreadful Convulsions. My Mother and I continued in the room with her, and when any intervals of tolerable

Composure in Eloisa* would allow us, we joined in heartfelt lamentations on the dreadful Waste in our provisions which this Event must occasion, and in concerting some plan for getting rid of them. We agreed that the best thing we could do was to begin eating them immediately, and accordingly we ordered up the cold Ham and Fowls, and instantly began our Devouring Plan on them with great Alacrity. We would have persuaded Eloisa to have taken a Wing of a Chicken, but she would not be persuaded. She was however much quieter than she had been; the Convulsions she had before suffered having given way to an almost perfect Insensibility. We endeavoured to rouse her by every means in our power, but to no purpose. I talked to her of Henry.

'Dear Eloisa' (said I) 'there's no occasion for your crying so much about such a trifle' (for I was willing to make light of it in order to comfort her), 'I beg you would not mind it—. You see it does not vex me in the least; though perhaps *I* may suffer most from it after all; for I shall not only be obliged to eat up all the Victuals I have dressed already, but must if Hervey should recover (which however is not very likely) dress as much for you again; or should he die (as I suppose he will) I shall still have to prepare a Dinner for you whenever you marry any one else. So you see that tho' perhaps for the present it may afflict you to think of Henry's sufferings, Yet I dare say he'll die soon, and then his pain will be over and you will be easy, whereas my Trouble will last much longer for work as hard as I may, I am certain that the pantry cannot be cleared in less than a fortnight.' Thus I did all in my power to console her, but without any effect, and at last as I saw that she did not seem to listen to me, I said no more, but leaving her with my Mother I took down the remains of the Ham and Chicken, and sent William to ask how Hervey did. He was not expected to live many Hours; he died the same day. We took all possible Care to break the Melancholy Event to Eloisa in the tenderest manner; yet in spite of every precaution, her Sufferings on hearing it were too violent for her reason, and she continued for many hours in a high Delirium. She is still extremely ill, and her Physicians are greatly afraid of her going into a Decline.* We are therefore preparing for Bristol,* where we mean to be in the course of the next Week. And now my dear Margaret let me talk a little of your affairs; and in the first place I must inform you that it is confidently reported, your Father is going to be married; I am very unwilling to beleive so unpleasing a report, and at the same time cannot wholly discredit it. I have written to my freind Susan Fitzgerald, for information concerning it, which as she is at present in Town, she will be very able to give me. I know not who is the Lady. I think your Brother is extremely right in the resolution he has taken of travelling, as it will perhaps contribute to obliterate from his remembrance, those disagreable Events, which have lately so much afflicted him—I am happy to find that tho' secluded from all the World, neither you nor Matilda are dull or unhappy—that you may never know what it is to be either is the wish of your sincerely Affectionate   C.L.

P.S. I have this instant received an answer from my freind Susan, which I enclose to you, and on which you will make your own reflections.

The enclosed Letter

My dear Charlotte

You could not have applied for information concerning the report of Sir George Lesley's Marriage, to anyone better able to give it you than I am. Sir George is certainly married; I was myself present at the Ceremony, which you will not be surprised at when I subscribe myself your

Affectionate Susan Lesley

Letter the third
From Miss Margaret Lesley to Miss C. Lutterell

Lesley Castle   February the 16th

I *have* made my own reflections on the letter you enclosed to me, my Dear Charlotte and I will now tell you what those reflections were. I reflected that if by this second Marriage Sir George should have a second family, our fortunes must be considerably diminushed—that if his Wife should be of an extravagant turn, she would encourage him to persevere in that Gay and Dissipated way of Life to which little encouragement would be necessary, and which has I fear already proved but too detrimental to his health and fortune—that she would now become Mistress of those Jewels which once adorned our Mother, and which Sir George had always promised us*—that if they did not come into Perthshire I should not be able to gratify my curiosity of beholding my Mother-in-law, and that if they did, Matilda would no longer sit at the head of her Father's table—. These my dear Charlotte were the melancholy reflections which crouded into my imagination after perusing Susan's letter to you, and which instantly occurred to Matilda when she had perused it likewise. The same ideas, the same fears, immediately occupied her Mind, and I know not which reflection distressed her most, whether the probable Diminution of our Fortunes, or her own Consequence. We both wish very much to know whether Lady Lesley is handsome and what is your opinion of her; as you honour her with the appellation of your freind, we flatter ourselves that she must be amiable. My Brother is already in Paris. He intends to quit it in a few Days, and to begin his route to Italy. He writes in a most chearfull Manner, says that the air of France has greatly recovered both his Health and Spirits; that he has now entirely ceased to think of Louisa with any degree either of Pity or Affection, that he even feels himself obliged to her for her Elopement, as he thinks it very good fun to be single again. By this, you may perceive that he has entirely regained that chearful Gaiety, and sprightly Wit, for which he was once so remarkable. When he first became acquainted with Louisa which was little more than three Years ago, he was one of the most lively, the most agreable young Men of the age*—. I beleive you never yet heard the particulars of his first acquaintance with her. It commenced at our cousin Colonel Drummond's; at whose house in Cumberland* he spent the Christmas, in which he attained the age of two and twenty. Louisa Burton was the Daughter of a distant Relation of Mrs. Drummond, who dieing a few Months before in extreme poverty, left his only Child then about eighteen to the protection of any of his Relations who would protect her. Mrs. Drummond was the only one who found herself so disposed—Louisa was therefore removed from a miserable Cottage in Yorkshire* to an elegant Mansion in Cumberland, and from every pecuniary Distress that Poverty could inflict, to every elegant Enjoyment that Money could purchase—. Louisa was naturally ill-tempered and Cunning; but she had been taught to disguise her real Disposition, under the appearance of insinuating Sweetness by a father who but too well knew, that to be married, would be the only chance she would have of not being starved, and who flattered himself that with such an extroidinary share of personal beauty, joined to a gentleness of Manners, and an engaging address, she might stand a good chance of pleasing some young Man who might afford to marry a Girl without a Shilling. Louisa perfectly entered into her father's schemes and was determined to forward them with all her care and attention. By dint of Perseverance and Application, she had at length so thoroughly disguised her natural disposition under the mask of Innocence, and Softness, as to impose upon every one who had not by a long and constant intimacy with her discovered her real Character. Such was Louisa when the hapless Lesley first beheld her at Drummond-house. His heart which (to use your favourite comparison) was as delicate as sweet and as tender as a Whipt-syllabub, could not resist her attractions. In a very few Days, he was falling in love, shortly afterwards actually fell, and before he had known her a Month, he had married her. My Father was at first highly displeased at so hasty and imprudent a connection; but when he found that they did not mind it, he soon became perfectly reconciled to the match. The Estate near Aberdeen* which my brother possesses by the bounty of his great Uncle independant of Sir George, was entirely sufficient to support him and my Sister in Elegance and Ease. For the first twelvemonth, no one could be happier than Lesley, and no one more amiable to appearance than Louisa, and so plausibly did she act and so cautiously behave that tho' Matilda and I often spent several weeks together with them, yet we neither of us had any suspicion of her real Disposition. After the birth of Louisa however, which one would have thought would have strengthened her regard for Lesley, the mask she had so long supported was by degrees thrown aside, and as probably she then thought herself secure in the affection of her Husband (which did indeed appear if possible augmented by the birth of his Child) She seemed to take no pains to prevent that affection from ever diminishing. Our visits therefore to Dunbeath,* were now less frequent and by far less agreable than they used to be. Our absence was however never either mentioned or lamented by Louisa who in the society of young Danvers with whom she became acquainted at Aberdeen (he was at one of the Universities* there,) felt infinitely happier than in that of Matilda and your freind, tho' there certainly never were pleasanter Girls than we are. You know the sad end of all Lesley's connubial happiness; I will not repeat it—. Adeiu my dear Charlotte; although I have not yet mentioned any thing of the matter, I hope you will do me the justice to believe that I *think* and *feel*, a great deal for your Sister's affliction. I do not doubt but that the healthy air of the Bristol downs,* will intirely remove it, by erasing from her Mind the remembrance of Henry. I am my dear Charlotte yrs ever

ML—.

Letter the fourth
From Miss C. Lutterell to Miss M. Lesley

Bristol   February 27th

My dear Peggy

I have but just received your letter, which being directed to Sussex while I was at Bristol was obliged to be forwarded to me here, and from some unaccountable Delay, has but this instant reached me—. I return you many thanks for the account it contains of Lesley's acquaintance, Love and

Marriage with Louisa, which has not the less entertained me for having often been repeated to me before.

I have the satisfaction of informing you that we have every reason to imagine our pantry is by this time nearly cleared, as we left particular orders with the Servants to eat as hard as they possibly could, and to call in a couple of Chairwomen* to assist them. We brought a cold Pigeon pye, a cold turkey, a cold tongue, and half a dozen Jellies* with us, which we were lucky enough with the help of our Landlady, her husband, and their three children, to get rid of, in less than two days after our arrival. Poor Eloisa is still so very indifferent both in Health and Spirits, that I very much fear, the air of the Bristol downs, healthy as it is, has not been able to drive poor Henry from her remembrance.

You ask me whether your new Mother in law is handsome and amiable—I will now give you an exact description of her bodily and Mental charms. She is short, and extremely well-made; is naturally pale, but rouges a good deal; has fine eyes, and fine teeth, as she will take care to let you know as soon as she sees you, and is altogether very pretty. She is remarkably good-tempered when she has her own way, and very lively when she is not out of humour.* She is naturally extravagant and not very affected; she never reads anything but the letters she receives from me, and never writes anything but her answers to them. She plays, sings and Dances, but has no taste for either, and excells in none, tho' she says she is passionately fond of all. Perhaps you may flatter me so far as to be surprised that one of whom I speak with so little affection should be my particular freind; but to tell you the truth, our freindship arose rather from Caprice on her side than Esteem on mine. We spent two or three days together with a Lady in Berkshire with whom we both happened to be connected—. During our visit, the Weather being remarkably bad, and our party particularly stupid, she was so good as to conceive a violent partiality for me, which very soon settled in a downright Freindship, and ended in an established correspondence. She is probably by this time as tired of me, as I am of her; but as she is too polite and I am too civil to say so, our letters are still as frequent and affectionate as ever, and our Attachment as firm and sincere as when it first commenced.— As she had a great taste for the pleasures of London, and of Brighthelmstone,* she will I dare say find some difficulty in prevailing on herself even to satisfy the curiosity I dare say she feels of beholding you, at the expence of quitting those favourite haunts of Dissipation, for the melancholy tho' venerable gloom of the castle you inhabit. Perhaps however if she finds her health impaired by too much amusement, she may acquire fortitude sufficient to undertake a Journey to Scotland in the hope of its proving at least beneficial to her health, if not conducive to her happiness. Your fears I am sorry to say, concerning your father's extravagance, your own fortunes, your Mother's Jewels and your Sister's consequence, I should suppose are but too well founded. My freind herself has four thousand pounds,* and will probably spend nearly as much every year in Dress and Public places, if she can get it—she will certainly not endeavour to reclaim Sir George from the manner of living to which he has been so long accustomed, and there is therefore some reason to fear that you will be very well off, if you get any fortune at all. The Jewels I should imagine too will undoubtedly be hers, and there is too much reason to think that she will reside* at her Husband's table in preference to his Daughter. But as so melancholy a subject must necessarily extremely distress you, I will no longer dwell on it—.

Eloisa's indisposition has brought us to Bristol at so unfashionable a season of the year, that we have actually seen but one genteel family since we came. Mr and Mrs Marlowe are very agreable people; the ill health of their little boy occasioned their arrival here; you may imagine that being the only family with whom we can converse, we are of course on a footing of intimacy with them; we see them indeed almost every day, and dined with them yesterday. We spent a very pleasant Day, and had a very good Dinner, tho' to be sure the Veal was terribly underdone, and the Curry* had no seasoning. I could not help wishing all dinner-time that I had been at the dressing it—. A brother of Mrs Marlowe, Mr Cleveland,* is with them at present; he is a good-looking young Man, and seems to have a good deal to say for himself. I tell Eloisa that she should set her cap* at him, but she does not at all seem to relish the proposal. I should like to see the girl married and Cleveland has a very good estate. Perhaps you may wonder that I do not consider *myself* as well as my Sister in my matrimonial Projects; but to tell you the truth I never wish to act a more principal part at a Wedding than the superintending and directing the Dinner, and therefore while I can get any of my acquaintance to marry for me, I shall never think of doing it myself, as I very much suspect that I should not have so much time for dressing my own Wedding-dinner, as for dressing that of my freinds. Yrs sincerely

CL.

Letter the fifth
Miss Margaret Lesley to Miss Charlotte Lutterell

Lesley-Castle   March 18th

On the same day that I received your last kind letter, Matilda received one from Sir George which was dated from Edinburgh, and informed us that he should do himself the pleasure of introducing Lady Lesley to us on the following evening. This as you may suppose considerably surprised us, particularly as your account of her Ladyship had given us reason to imagine there was little chance of her visiting Scotland at a time that London must be so gay. As it was our business however to be delighted at such a mark of condescension as a visit from Sir George and Lady Lesley, we prepared to return them an answer expressive of the happiness we enjoyed in expectation of such a Blessing, when luckily recollecting that as they were to reach the Castle the next Evening, it would be impossible for my father to receive it before he left Edinburgh, We contented ourselves with leaving them to suppose that we were as happy as we ought to be. At nine in the Evening on the following day, they came, accompanied by one of Lady Lesley's brothers. Her Ladyship perfectly answers the description you sent me of her, except that I do not think her so pretty as you seem to consider her. She has not a bad face, but there is something so extremely unmajestic in her little diminutive figure, as to render her in comparison with the elegant height of Matilda and Myself, an insignificant Dwarf. Her curiosity to see us (which must have been great to bring her more than four hundred miles) being now perfectly gratified, she already begins to mention their return to town, and has desired us to accompany her—. We cannot refuse her request since it is seconded by the commands of our Father, and thirded by the entreaties of Mr Fitzgerald who is certainly one of the most pleasing young Men, I ever beheld, It is not yet determined when we are to go, but when ever we do we shall certainly take our little Louisa with us. Adeiu my dear Charlotte; Matilda unites in best Wishes to You and Eloisa, with your ever   M L

Letter the sixth
Lady Lesley to Miss Charlotte Lutterell

Lesley-Castle   March 20th

We arrived here my sweet Freind about a fortnight ago, and I already heartily repent that I ever left our charming House in Portman-Square* for such a dismal old Weather-beaten Castle as this. You can form no idea sufficiently hideous, of its dungeon-like form. It is actually perched upon a Rock to appearance so totally inaccessible, that I expected to have been pulled up by a rope; and sincerely repented having gratified my curiosity to behold my Daughters at the expence of being obliged to enter their prison in so dangerous and ridiculous a Manner. But as soon as I once found myself safely arrived in the inside of this tremendous building, I comforted myself with the hope of having my spirits revived, by the sight of the two beautifull Girls, such as the Miss Lesleys had been represented to me, at Edinburgh. But here again, I met with nothing but Disapointment and Surprise. Matilda and Margaret Lesley are two great, tall, out of the way, overgrown Girls, just of a proper size to inhabit a Castle almost as Large in comparison as themselves. I wish my dear Charlotte that you could but behold these Scotch Giants; I am sure they would frighten you out of your wits. They will do very well as foils to myself, so I have invited them to accompany me to London where I hope to be in the course of a fortnight. Besides these two fair Damsels, I found a little humoured Brat* here who I believe is some relation to them; they told me who she was, and gave me a long rigmerole story of her father and Miss *Somebody* which I have entirely forgot. I hate Scandal and detest Children—. I have been plagued ever since I came here with tiresome visits from a parcel of Scotch wretches, with terrible hardnames; they were so civil, gave me so many invitations, and talked of coming again so soon, that I could not help affronting them. I suppose I shall not see them any more, and yet as a family party we are so stupid, that I do not know what to do with myself. These girls have no Music, but Scotch Airs, no Drawings but Scotch Mountains, and no Books but Scotch Poems—And I hate everything Scotch.* In general I can spend half the Day at my toilett* with a great deal of pleasure, but why should I dress here, since there is not a creature in the House whom I have any wish to please—. I have just had a conversation with my Brother in which he has greatly offended me, and which as I have nothing more entertaining to send you I will give you the particulars of. You must know that I have for these 4 or 5 Days past strongly suspected William of entertaining a partiality for my eldest Daughter. I own indeed that had *I* been inclined to fall in love with any woman, I should not have made choice of Matilda Lesley for the object of my passion; for there is nothing I hate so much as a tall Woman: but however there is no accounting for some men's taste and as William is himself nearly six feet high, it is not wonderful that he should be partial to that height. Now as I have a very great Affection for my Brother and should be extremely sorry to see him unhappy, which I suppose he means to be if he cannot marry Matilda, as moreover I know that his Circumstances will not allow him to marry any one with out a fortune, and that Matilda's is entirely dependant on her Father, who will neither have his own inclination, nor my permission to give her anything at present, I thought it would be doing a good-natured action by my Brother to let him know as much, in order that he might choose for himself, whether to conquer his passion, or Love and Despair. Accordingly finding myself this Morning alone with him in one of the horrid old rooms of this Castle, I opened the Cause to him in the following Manner.

'Well my dear William what do you think of these girls? for my part, I do not find them so plain as I expected; but perhaps you may think me partial to the Daughters of my Husband and perhaps you are right—They are indeed so very like Sir George that it is natural to think. . . . .'

'My Dear Susan' (cried he in a tone of the greatest amazement), 'You do not really think they bear the least resemblance to their Father! He is so very plain!—but I beg your pardon—I had entirely forgotten to whom I was speaking—'

'Oh! pray don't mind me;' (replied I) 'every one knows Sir George is horribly ugly, and I assure you I always thought him a fright.'

'You surprise me extremely' (answered William) 'by what you say both with respect to Sir George and his daughters. You cannot think your Husband so deficient in personal Charms as you speak of, nor can you surely see any resemblance between him and the Miss Lesleys who are in my opinion perfectly unlike him and perfectly Handsome.'

'If that is your opinion with regard to the Girls it certainly is no proof of their Father's beauty, for if they are perfectly unlike him and very handsome at the same time, it is natural to suppose that he is very plain.'

'By no means,' (said he) 'for what may be pretty in a Woman, may be very unpleasing in a Man.'

'But you yourself' (replied I) 'but a few Minutes ago allowed him to be very plain.'

'Men are no Judges of Beauty in their own Sex' (said he).

'Neither Men nor Women can think Sir George tolerable.'

'Well, well', (said he) 'we will not dispute about *his* Beauty, but your opinion of his *Daughters* is surely very singular, for if I understood you right, you said you did not find them so plain as you expected to do!'

'Why, do *you* find them plainer then?' (said I).

'I can scarcely beleive you to be serious' (returned he) 'when you speak of their persons in so extroidinary a Manner. Do not you think the Miss Lesleys are two very handsome young Women?'

'Lord! No!' (cried I) 'I think them terribly plain!'

'Plain!' (replied He) 'My dear Susan, you cannot really think so! why what single Feature in the face of either of them, can you possibly find fault with?'

'Oh! trust me for that;' (replied I). 'Come, I will begin with the eldest—with Matilda. Shall I, William?' (I looked as cunning as I could when I said it, in order to shame him.)

'They are so much alike' (said he) 'that I should suppose the faults of one, would be the faults of both.'

'Well, then, in the first place, they are both so horribly tall!'

'They are *taller* than you are indeed' (said he with a saucy smile).

'Nay,' (said I); 'I know nothing of that.'

'Well, but' (he continued) 'tho' they may be above the common size, their figures are perfectly elegant; and as to their faces, their Eyes are beautifull—.'

'I never can think such tremendous, knock-me-down figures in the least degree elegant, and as for their eyes, they are so tall that I never could strain my neck enough to look at them.'

'Nay,' (replied he), 'I know not whether you may not be in the right in not attempting it, for perhaps they might dazzle you with their Lustre.'

'Oh! Certainly.' (said I, with the greatest Complacency,

for I assure you my dearest Charlotte I was not in the least offended tho' by what followed, one would suppose that William was conscious of having given me just cause to be so, for coming up to me and taking my hand, he said) 'You must not look so grave Susan; you will make me fear I have offended you!'

'Offended me! Dear Brother, how came such a thought in your head!' (returned I) 'No, really! I assure you that I am not in the least surprised at your being so warm an advocate for the Beauty of these Girls'—

'Well, but' (interrupted William) 'remember that we have not yet concluded our dispute concerning them. What fault do you find with their complexion?'

'They are so horridly pale.'

'They always have a little colour, and after any exercise it is considerably heightened.'

'Yes, but if there should ever happen to be any rain in this part of the world, they will never be able to raise more than their common stock—except indeed they amuse themselves with running up and Down these horrid old Galleries* and Antichambers—'

'Well,' (replied my Brother in a tone of vexation, and glancing an impertinent Look at me) 'if they *have* but little colour, at least, it is all their own.'

This was too much my dear Charlotte, for I am certain that he had the impudence by that look, of pretending to suspect the reality of mine. But you I am sure will vindicate my character whenever you may hear it so cruelly aspersed, for you can witness how often I have protested against wearing Rouge,* and how much I always told you I dislike it. And I assure you that my opinions are still the same—. Well, not bearing to be so suspected by my Brother, I left the room immediately, and have ever since been in my own Dressing-room writing to you. What a long Letter have I made of it! But you must not expect to receive such from me when I get to Town; for it is only at Lesley castle, that one has time to write even to a Charlotte Lutterell—. I was so much vexed by William's Glance, that I could not summon Patience enough, to stay and give him that Advice respecting his Attachment to Matilda which had first induced me from pure Love to him to begin the conversation; and I am now so thoroughly convinced by it, of his violent passion for her, that I am certain he would never hear reason on the Subject, and I shall therefore give myself no more trouble either about him or his favourite. Adeiu my dear Girl—

Yrs Affectionately Susan L.

Letter the seventh
From Miss C. Lutterell to Miss M. Lesley

Bristol the 27th of March.

I have received Letters from You and your Mother-in-Law within this week which have greatly entertained me, as I find by them that you are both downright jealous of each other's Beauty. It is very odd that two pretty Women tho' actually Mother and Daughter cannot be in the same House without falling out about their faces. Do be convinced that you are both perfectly handsome and say no more of the Matter. I suppose this Letter must be directed to Portman Square where probably (great as is your affection for Lesley Castle) you will not be sorry to find yourself. In spite of all that People may say about Green fields and the Country I was always of the opinion that London and its Amusements must be very agreable for a while, and should be very happy could my Mother's income allow her to jockey us into its Public-places,* during Winter. I always longed particularly to go to Vaux-hall,* to see whether the cold Beef there is cut so thin* as it is reported, for I have a sly suspicion that few people understand the art of cutting a slice of cold Beef so well as I do: nay it would be hard if I did not know something of the Matter, for it was a part of my Education that I took by far the most pains with. Mama always found me *her* best Scholar, tho' when Papa was alive Eloisa was *his*.* Never to be sure were there two more different Dispositions in the World. We both loved Reading. *She* preferred Histories, and *I* Receipts.* She loved drawing Pictures, and I drawing

Pullets.* No one could sing a better Song than She, and no one make a better Pye than I.—And so it has always continued since we have been no longer Children. The only difference is that all disputes on the superior excellence of our Employments *then* so frequent are now no more. We have for many years entered into an agreement always to admire each other's works; I never fail listening to *her* Music, and she is as constant in eating *my* pies. Such at least was the case till Henry Hervey made his appearance in Sussex. Before the arrival of his Aunt in our neighbourhood where she established herself you know about a twelvemonth ago, his visits to her had been at stated times, and of equal and settled Duration; but on her removal to the Hall which is within a walk from our House, they became both more frequent and longer. This as you may suppose could not be pleasing to Mrs Diana who is a professed Enemy to everything which is not directed by Decorum and Formality, or which bears the least resemblance to Ease and Good-breeding. Nay so great was her aversion to her Nephew's behaviour that I have often heard her give such hints of it before his face that had not Henry at such times been engaged in conversation with Eloisa, they must have caught his Attention and have very much distressed him. The alteration in my Sister's behaviour which I have before hinted at, now took place. The Agreement we had entered into of admiring each other's productions she no longer seemed to regard, and tho' I constantly applauded even every Country-dance,* She play'd, yet not even a pidgeon-pye* of my making could obtain from her a single word of approbation. This was certainly enough to put any one in a Passion; however, I was as cool as a Cream-cheese and having formed my plan and concerted a scheme of Revenge, I was determined to let her have her own way and not even to make her a single reproach. My Scheme was to treat her as she treated me, and tho' she might even draw my own Picture or play Malbrook* (which is the only tune I ever really liked) not to say so much as 'Thank you Eloisa;' tho' I had for many years constantly hollowed whenever she played, *Bravo, Bravissimo, Encora, Da Capo, allegretto, con*

espressione, and *Poco presto** with many other such outlandish
words, all of them as Eloisa told me expressive of my
Admiration; and so indeed I suppose they are, as I see some
of them in every Page of every Music book, being the
Sentiments I imagine of the Composer.

I executed my Plan with great Punctuality; I can not say
success, for Alas! my silence while she played seemed not in
the least to displease her; on the contrary she actually said
to me one day 'Well Charlotte, I am very glad to find that
you have at last left off that ridiculous custom of applauding
my Execution* on the Harpsichord till you made *my* head
ake, and yourself hoarse. I feel very much obliged to you for
keeping your Admiration to yourself.' I never shall forget
the very witty answer I made to this speech. 'Eloisa' (said I)
'I beg you would be quite at your Ease with respect to all
such fears in future, for be assured that I shall always keep
my Admiration to myself and my own pursuits and never
extend it to yours.' This was the only very severe thing I
ever said in my Life; not but that I have often felt myself
extremely satirical* but it was the only time I ever made my
feelings public.

I suppose there never were two young people who had a
greater affection for each other than Henry and Eloisa; no,
the Love of your Brother for Miss Burton could not be so
strong tho' it might be more violent. You may imagine
therefore how provoked my Sister must have been to have
him play her such a trick. Poor Girl! she still laments his
Death with undiminished Constancy, notwithstanding he
has been dead more than six weeks; but some people mind
such things more than others. The ill state of Health into
which his Loss has thrown her makes her so weak, and so
unable to support the least exertion, that she has been in
tears all this Morning merely from having taken Leave of
Mrs Marlowe who with Her husband, Brother and Child
are to leave Bristol this Morning. I am sorry to have them
go because they are the only family with whom we have
here any acquaintance, but I never thought of crying; to be
sure Eloisa and Mrs Marlowe have always been more
together than with me, and have therefore contracted a kind

of affection for each other, which does not make Tears so inexcusable in them as they would be in me. The Marlowes are going to Town; Cleveland accompanies them; as neither Eloisa nor I could catch him I hope you or Matilda may have better Luck. I know not when we shall leave Bristol, Eloisa's Spirits are so low that she is very averse to moving, and yet is certainly by no means mended by her residence here. A week or two will I hope determine our Measures—in the mean time believe me

&c—&c—Charlotte Lutterell

Letter the Eighth
Miss Lutterell to Mrs Marlowe

Bristol April 4th

I feel myself greatly obliged to you my dear Emma for such a mark of your affection as I flatter myself was conveyed in the proposal you made me of our Corresponding; I assure you that it will be a great releif to me to write to you and as long as my Health and Spirits will allow me, you will find me a very constant Correspondent; I will not say an entertaining one, for you know my situation sufficiently not to be ignorant that in me Mirth would be improper and I know my own Heart too well not to be sensible that it would be unnatural. You must not expect News for we see no one with whom we are in the least acquainted, or in whose proceedings we have any Interest. You must not expect Scandal for by the same rule we are equally debarred either from hearing or inventing it.—You must expect from me nothing but the melancholy effusions of a broken Heart which is ever reverting to the Happiness it once enjoyed and which ill supports its present wretchedness. The Possibility of being able to write, to speak, to you, of my lost Henry will be a Luxury to me, and your Goodness will not I know refuse to read what it will so much releive my Heart to write. I once thought that to have what is in general called a Freind (I mean one of my own Sex to whom I might speak with less reserve than to any other person) independant of my Sister would never be an object of my wishes, but how much was I mistaken! Charlotte is too much engrossed by two confidential Correspondents of that sort, to supply the place of one to me, and I hope you will not think me girlishly romantic, when I say that to have some kind and compassionate Freind who might listen to my Sorrows without endeavouring to console me was what I had for some time wished for, when our acquaintance with you, the intimacy which followed it and the particular affectionate Attention you paid me almost from the first, caused me to entertain the flattering Idea of those attentions being improved on a closer acquaintance into a Freindship which, if you were what my wishes formed you would be the greatest Happiness I could be capable of enjoying. To find that such Hopes are realised is a satisfaction indeed, a satisfaction which is now almost the only one I can ever experience.—I feel myself so languid that I am sure were you with me you would oblige me to leave off writing, and I cannot give you a greater proof of my Affection for you than by acting as I know you would wish me to do, whether Absent or Present. I am my dear Emma's sincere

freind E.L.

Letter the Ninth
Mrs Marlowe to Miss Lutterell

Grosvenor Street* April 10th*

Need I say my dear Eloisa how wellcome your Letter was to me? I cannot give a greater proof of the pleasure I received from it, or of the Desire I feel that our Correspondence may be regular and frequent than by setting you so good an example as I now do in answering it before the end of the week——. But do not imagine that I claim any merit in being so punctual; on the contrary I assure you, that it is a far greater Gratification to me to write to you, than to spend the Evening either at a Concert or a Ball. Mr Marlowe is so desirous of my appearing at some of the Public places every evening that I do not like to refuse him, but at the same time so much wish to remain at Home, that independant of the Pleasure I experience in devoting any portion of my Time to my Dear Eloisa, yet the Liberty I claim from having a Letter to write of spending an Evening at home with my little Boy, You know me well enough to be sensible, will of itself be a sufficient Inducement (if one is necessary) to my maintaining with Pleasure a Correspondence with you. As to the Subjects of your Letters to me, whether Grave or Merry, if they concern you they must be equally interesting to me; Not but that I think the Melancholy Indulgence of your own Sorrows by repeating them and dwelling on them to me, will only encourage and increase them, and that it will be more prudent in you to avoid so sad a subject; but yet knowing as I do what a soothing and Melancholy Pleasure it must afford you, I cannot prevail on myself to deny you so great an Indulgence, and will only insist on your not expecting me to encourage you in it, by my own Letters; on the contrary I intend to fill them with such lively Wit and enlivening Humour as shall even provoke a Smile in the sweet but sorrowfull Countenance of my Eloisa.

In the first place you are to learn that I have met your Sister's three freinds Lady Lesley and her Daughters, twice in Public since I have been here. I know you will be impatient to hear my opinion of the Beauty of three Ladies of whom You have heard so much. Now, as you are too ill and too unhappy to be vain, I think I may venture to inform you that I like none of their faces so well as I do your own. Yet they are all handsome—Lady Lesley indeed I have seen before; her Daughters I beleive would in general be said to have a finer face than her Ladyship, and Yet what with the charms of a Blooming Complexion, a little Affectation and a great deal of Small-talk, (in each of which She is superior to the Young Ladies) she will I dare say gain herself as many Admirers as the more regular features of Matilda, and Margaret. I am sure you will agree with me in saying that they can none of them be of a proper size for real Beauty,* when you know that two of them are taller and the other shorter than ourselves. In spite of this Defect (or rather by reason of it) there is something very noble and majestic in the figures of the Miss Lesleys, and something agreably Lively in the Appearance of their pretty little Mother-in-law. But tho' one may be majestic and the other Lively, yet the faces of neither possess that Bewitching Sweetness of my Eloisa's, which her present Languor is so far from diminushing. What would my Husband and Brother say of us, if they knew all the fine things I have been saying to you in this Letter. It is very hard that a pretty Woman is never to be told she is so by any one of her own Sex, without that person's being suspected to be either her determined Enemy, or her professed Toad-eater.* How much more amiable are women in that particular! one Man may say forty civil things to another without our supposing that he is ever paid for it, and provided he does his Duty by our Sex, we care not how Polite he is to his own.

Mrs Lutterell will be so good as to accept my Compliments, Charlotte, my Love, and Eloisa the best wishes for the recovery of her Health and Spirits that can be offered by her Affectionate Freind   E. Marlowe

I am afraid this Letter will be but a poor Specimen of my Powers in the Witty Way; and your opinion of them will not be greatly increased when I assure you that I have been as entertaining as I possibly could—.

Letter the Tenth
From Miss Margaret Lesley to Miss Charlotte Lutterell

Portman Square April 13th

My dear Charlotte

We left Lesley-Castle on the 28th of Last Month, and arrived Safely in London after a Journey of seven Days; I had the pleasure of finding your Letter here waiting my Arrival, for which you have my grateful Thanks. Ah! my dear Freind I every day more regret the serene and tranquil Pleasures of the Castle we have left, in exchange for the uncertain and unequal Amusements of this vaunted City. Not that I will pretend to assert that these uncertain and unequal Amusements are in the least Degree unpleasing to me; on the contrary I enjoy them extremely and should enjoy them even more, were I not certain that every appearance I make in Public but rivetts the Chains of those unhappy Beings whose Passion it is impossible not to pity, tho' it is out of my power to return. In short my Dear Charlotte it is my sensibility for the sufferings of so many amiable Young Men, my Dislike of the extreme Admiration I meet with, and my Aversion to being so celebrated both in Public, in Private, in Papers, and in Printshops,* that are the reasons why I cannot more fully enjoy, the Amusements so various and pleasing of London. How often have I wished that I possessed as little personal Beauty as you do; that my figure were as inelegant; my face as unlovely; and my Appearance as unpleasing as yours! But Ah! what little chance is there of so desirable an Event; I have had the Small-pox,* and must therefore submit to my unhappy fate.

I am now going to intrust you my dear Charlotte with a secret which has long disturbed the tranquility of my days, and which is of a kind to require the most inviolable Secrecy from you. Last Monday se'night Matilda and I accompanied Lady Lesley to a Rout* at the Honourable Mrs Kickabout's;* we were escorted by Mr Fitzgerald who is a very amiable Young Man in the main, tho' perhaps a little singular in his Taste—He is in love with Matilda—We had scarcely paid our Compliments to the Lady of the House and curtseyed to half a Score different people when my Attention was attracted by the appearance of a Young Man the most lovely of his Sex, who at that moment entered the Room with another Gentleman and Lady. From the first moment I beheld him, I was certain that on him depended the future Happiness of my Life. Imagine my surprise when he was introduced to me by the name of Cleveland—I instantly recognised him as the Brother of Mrs Marlowe, and the acquaintance of my Charlotte at Bristol. Mr and Mrs M. were the Gentleman and Lady who accompanied him. (You do not think Mrs Marlowe handsome?) The elegant address of Mr Cleveland, his polished Manners and Delightful Bow, at once confirmed my attachment. He did not speak; but I can imagine every thing he would have said, had he opened his Mouth. I can picture to myself the cultivated Understanding, the Noble Sentiments, and elegant Language which would have shone so conspicuous in the conversation of Mr Cleveland. The approach of Sir James Gower (one of my too numerous Admirers) prevented the Discovery of any such Powers, by putting an end to a conversation we had never commenced, and by attracting my attention to himself. But oh! how inferior are the accomplishments of Sir James to those of his so greatly envied Rival! Sir James is one of the most frequent of our Visitors, and is almost always of our Parties. We have since often met Mr and Mrs Marlowe but no Cleveland—he is always engaged some where else. Mrs Marlowe fatigues me to Death every time I see her by her tiresome conversations about You and Eloisa. She is so Stupid! I live in the hope of seeing her irrisistable Brother to night, as we are going to Lady Flambeau's,* who is I know intimate with the Marlowes. Our party will be Lady Lesley, Matilda, Fitzgerald, Sir James Gower, and myself. We see little of Sir George, who is almost always at the Gaming-table. Ah! my poor Fortune, where art thou by this time? We see more of Lady L. who always makes her appearance (highly rouged) at Dinner-time. Alas! what Delightful Jewels will she be decked in this evening at Lady Flambeau's!; Yet I wonder how she can herself delight in wearing them; surely she must be sensible of the ridiculous impropriety of loading her little diminutive figure with such superfluous ornaments; is it possible that she can not know how greatly superior an elegant simplicity is to the most studied apparel? Would she but present them to Matilda and me, how greatly should we be obliged to her. How becoming would Diamonds be on our fine majestic figures! And how surprising it is that such an Idea should never have occurred to *her*: I am sure if I have reflected in this Manner once, I have fifty times. Whenever I see Lady Lesley dressed in them such reflections immediately come across me. My own Mother's

Jewels too! But I will say no more on so melancholy a Subject—Let me entertain you with something more pleasing—Matilda had a letter this Morning from Lesley, by which we have the pleasure of finding he is at Naples, has turned Roman-catholic, obtained one of the Pope's Bulls* for annulling his 1st Marriage and had since actually married a Neapolitan Lady of great Rank and Fortune.* He tells us moreover that much the same sort of affair has befallen his first wife the worthless Louisa who is likewise at Naples has turned Roman-catholic, and is soon to be married to a Neapolitan Nobleman of great and Distinguished Merit. He says, that they are at present very good Freinds, have quite forgiven all past errors and intend in future to be very good Neighbours. He invites Matilda and me to pay him a visit in Italy and to bring him his little Louisa whom both her Mother, Step-Mother, and himself are equally desirous of beholding. As to our accepting his invitation, it is at present very uncertain; Lady Lesley advises us to go without loss of time; Fitzgerald offers to escort us there, but Matilda has some doubts of the Propriety of such a Scheme—She owns it would be very agreable. I am certain she likes the Fellow. My Father desires us not to be in a hurry, as perhaps if we wait a few months both he and Lady Lesley will do themselves the pleasure of attending us. Lady Lesley says no, that nothing will ever tempt her to forego the Amusements of Brighthelmstone for a Journey to Italy merely to see our Brother. 'No' (says the disagreable woman) 'I have once in my life been fool enough to travel I don't know how many hundred Miles to see two of the Family, and I found it did not answer, so Deuce take me, if ever I am so foolish again.' So says her Ladyship, but Sir George still perseveres in saying that perhaps in a Month or two, they may accompany us.

Adeiu my Dear Charlotte—

Yr faithful Margaret Lesley

The History of England
from the reign of Henry the 4th
to the death of
Charles the 1st*

By a partial, prejudiced, and ignorant Historian.

To Miss Austen eldest daughter of the Revd George Austen, this Work is inscribed with all due respect by

The Author

N.B. There will be very few Dates in this History.*

Henry the 4th

Henry the 4th ascended the throne of England much to his own satisfaction in the year 1399, after having prevailed on his cousin and predecessor Richard the 2d, to resign it to him, and to retire for the rest of his Life to Pomfret Castle, where he happened to be murdered. It is to be supposed that Henry was Married, since he had certainly four sons, but it is not in my power to inform the Reader who was his Wife. Be this as it may, he did not live for ever, but falling ill, his son the Prince of Wales came and took away the crown; whereupon the King made a long speech, for which I must refer the Reader to Shakespear's Plays,* and the Prince made a still longer. Things being thus settled between them the King died, and was succeeded by his son Henry who had previously beat Sir William Gascoigne.

Henry the 5th

This Prince after he succeeded to the throne grew quite reformed and Amiable, forsaking all his dissipated Companions, and never thrashing Sir William again. During his reign, Lord Cobham was burnt alive, but I forget what for. His Majesty then turned his thoughts to France, where he went and fought the famous Battle of Agincourt. He afterwards married the King's daughter Catherine, a very agreable Woman by Shakespear's account.* Inspite of all this however he died, and was succeeded by his son Henry.

Henry the 6th

I cannot say much for this Monarch's Sense—Nor would I if I could, for he was a Lancastrian. I suppose you know all about the Wars between him and The Duke of York who was of the right side; If you do not, you had better read some other History, for I shall not be very diffuse in this, meaning by it only to vent my Spleen* *against,* and shew my Hatred *to* all those people whose parties or principles do not suit with mine, and not to give information. This King married Margaret of Anjou, a Woman whose distresses and Misfortunes were so great as almost to make me who hate her, pity her. It was in this reign that Joan of Arc lived and made such a *row** among the English. They should not have burnt her—but they did. There were several Battles between the Yorkists and Lancastrians, in which the former (as they ought) usually conquered. At length they were entirely over come; The King was murdered—The Queen was sent home—and Edward the 4th Ascended the Throne.

Edward the 4th

This Monarch was famous only for his Beauty and his Courage, of which the Picture we have here given of him, and his undaunted Behaviour in marrying one Woman while he was engaged to another,* are sufficient proofs. His wife was Elizabeth Woodville, a Widow, who, poor Woman!, was afterwards confined in a Convent by that Monster of Iniquity and Avarice Henry the 7th. One of Edward's Mistresses was Jane Shore, who has had a play written about her,* but it is a tragedy and therefore not worth reading. Having performed all these noble actions, his Majesty died, and was succeeded by his Son.

Edward the 5th

This unfortunate Prince lived so little a while that no body had time to draw his picture.* He was murdered by his Uncle's Contrivance, whose name was Richard the 3d.

Richard the 3rd

The Character of this Prince has been in general very severely treated by Historians, but as he was a *York*, I am rather inclined to suppose him a very respectable Man.* It has indeed been confidently asserted that he killed his two Nephews and his Wife, but it has also been declared that he did *not* kill his two Nephews,* which I am inclined to beleive true; and if this is the case, it may also be affirmed that he did not kill his Wife, for if Perkin Warbeck* was really the Duke of York, why might not Lambert Simnel be the Widow of Richard.* Whether innocent or guilty, he did not reign long in peace, for Henry Tudor Earl of Richmond as great a Villain as ever lived, made a great fuss about getting the Crown and having killed the King at the battle of Bosworth, he suceeded to it.

Henry the 7th

This Monarch soon after his accession married the Princess Elizabeth of York, by which alliance he plainly proved that he thought his own right inferior to hers, tho' he pretended to the contrary. By this Marriage he had two sons and two daughters, the elder of which daughters was married to the King of Scotland and had the happiness of being grand-mother to one of the first Characters in the World.* But of *her,* I shall have occasion to speak more at large in future. The Youngest, Mary, married first the King of France and secondly the Duke of Suffolk, by whom she had one daughter, afterwards the Mother of Lady Jane Grey, who tho' inferior to her lovely Cousin the Queen of Scots, was yet an amiable young Woman* and famous for reading Greek while other people were hunting. It was in the reign of Henry the 7th that Perkin Warbeck and Lambert Simnel before mentioned made their appearance, the former of whom was set in the Stocks, took shelter in Beaulieu Abbey, and was beheaded with the Earl of Warwick, and the latter was taken into the King's Kitchen. His Majesty died, and was succeeded by his son Henry whose only merit was his not being *quite* so bad as his daughter Elizabeth.

Henry the 8th

It would be an affront to my Readers were I to suppose that they were not as well acquainted with the particulars of this King's reign as I am myself. It will therefore be saving *them* the task of reading again what they have read before, and *myself* the trouble of writing what I do not perfectly recollect, by giving only a slight sketch of the principal Events which marked his reign. Among these may be ranked Cardinal Wolsey's telling the father Abbott of Leicester Abbey that 'he was come to lay his bones among them', the reformation in Religion, and the King's riding through the Streets of London with Anna Bullen.* It is however but Justice, and my Duty to declare that this amiable Woman was entirely innocent of the Crimes with which she was accused, of which her Beauty, her Elegance, and her Sprightliness were sufficient proofs, not to mention her solemn protestations of Innocence, the weakness of the Charges against her, and the King's Character; all of which add some confirmation, tho' perhaps but slight ones when in comparison with those before alledged in her favour. Tho' I do not profess giving many dates, yet as I think it proper to give some and shall of course Make choice of those which it is most necessary for the Reader to know, I think it right to inform him that her letter to the King was dated on the 6th of May.* The Crimes and Cruelties of this Prince, were too numerous to be mentioned, (as this history I trust has fully shown;) and nothing can be said in his vindication, but that his abolishing Religious Houses and leaving them to the ruinous depredations of time has been of infinite use to the landscape of England in general,* which probably was a principal motive for his doing it, since otherwise why should a Man who was of no Religion himself be at so much trouble to abolish one which had for Ages been established in the Kingdom. His Majesty's 5th wife was the Duke of Norfolk's Neice who, tho' universally acquitted of the crimes for which she was beheaded, has been by many people supposed to have led an abandoned Life before her Marriage—of this however I have many doubts, since she was a relation of that noble Duke of Norfolk who was so warm in the Queen of Scotland's cause, and who at last fell a victim to it. The King's last wife contrived to survive him, but with difficulty effected it. He was succeeded by his only son Edward.

Edward the 6th

As this prince was only nine years old at the time of his Father's death, he was considered by many people as too young to govern, and the late King happening to be of the same opinion, his mother's Brother the Duke of Somerset was chosen Protector of the realm during his minority. This Man was on the whole of a very amiable Character, and is somewhat of a favourite with me, tho' I would by no means pretend to affirm that he was equal to those first of Men Robert Earl of Essex, Delamere,* or Gilpin.* He was beheaded, of which he might with reason have been proud, had he known that such was the death of Mary Queen of Scotland; but as it was impossible that He should be conscious of what had never happened, it does not appear that he felt particularly delighted with the manner of it.

After his decease the Duke of Northumberland had the care of the King and the Kingdom, and performed his trust of both so well that the King died and the Kingdom was left to his daughter in law the Lady Jane Grey, who has been already mentioned as reading Greek. Whether she really understood that language or whether such a Study proceeded only from an excess of vanity for which I beleive she was always rather remarkable, is uncertain. Whatever might be the cause, she preserved the same appearance of knowledge, and contempt of what was generally esteemed pleasure, during the whole of her Life, for she declared herself displeased with being appointed Queen, and while conducting to the Scaffold, she wrote a Sentence in Latin and another in Greek on seeing the dead Body of her Husband accidentally passing that way.

Mary

This Woman had the good luck of being advanced to the throne of England, inspite of the superior pretensions, Merit and *Beauty* of her Cousins Mary Queen of Scotland and Jane Grey. Nor can I pity the Kingdom for the misfortunes they experienced during her Reign, since they fully deserved them, for having allowed her to succeed her Brother—which was a double peice of folly, since they might have foreseen that as she died without Children, she would be succeeded by that disgrace to humanity, that pest of society, Elizabeth.* Many were the people who fell Martyrs to the protestant Religion during her reign; I suppose not fewer than a dozen. She married Philip King of Spain who in her Sister's reign was famous for building Armadas. She died without issue, and then the dreadful moment came in which the destroyer of all comfort, the deceitful Betrayer of trust reposed in her, and the Murderess of her Cousin succeeded to the Throne.

Elizabeth

It was the peculiar Misfortune of this Woman to have bad Ministers—Since wicked as she herself was, she could not have committed such extensive mischeif, had not these vile and abandoned Men connived at, and encouraged her in her Crimes. I know that it has by many people been asserted and beleived that Lord Burleigh, Sir Francis Walsingham, and the rest of those who filled the cheif offices of State were deserving, experienced, and able Ministers. But oh! how blinded such Writers and such Readers must be to true Merit, to Merit despised, neglected and defamed, if they can persist in such opinions when they reflect that these Men, these boasted Men were such Scandals to their Country and their Sex as to allow and assist their Queen in confining for the space of nineteen Years, a *Woman* who if the claims of Relationship and Merit were no avail, yet as a Queen and as one who condescended to place confidence in her, had every reason to expect Assistance and protection; and at length in allowing Elizabeth to bring this amiable Woman to an untimely, unmerited, and scandalous Death. Can any one if he reflects but for a moment on this blot, this everlasting blot upon their Understanding and their Character, allow any praise to Lord Burleigh or Sir Francis Walsingham? Oh! what must this bewitching Princess whose only freind was then the Duke of Norfolk, and whose only ones are now Mr Whitaker,* Mrs Lefroy,* Mrs Knight* and myself, who was abandoned by her son, confined by her Cousin, Abused, reproached and villified by all, what must not her most noble mind have suffered when informed that Elizabeth had given orders for her Death! Yet she bore it with a most unshaken fortitude; firm in her Mind; Constant in her Religion; and prepared herself to meet the cruel fate to which she was doomed, with a magnanimity that could alone proceed from conscious Innocence.* And yet could you Reader have beleived it possible that some hardened and zealous Protestants have even abused her for that

Steadfastness in the Catholic Religion which reflected on her so much credit? But this is a striking proof of *their* narrow Souls and prejudiced Judgements who accuse her. She was executed in the Great Hall at Fortheringay Castle (sacred Place!) on Wednesday the 8th of February—1586— to the everlasting Reproach of Elizabeth, her Ministers, and of England in general. It may not be unnecessary before I entirely conclude my account of this ill-fated Queen, to observe that she had been accused of several crimes during the time of her reigning in Scotland, of which I now most seriously do assure my Reader that she was entirely innocent; having never been guilty of anything more than Imprudencies into which she was betrayed by the openness of her Heart, her Youth, and her Education. Having I trust by this assurance entirely done away every Suspicion and every doubt which might have arisen in the Reader's mind, from what other Historians have written of her, I shall proceed to mention the remaining Events that marked Elizabeth's reign. It was about this time that Sir Francis Drake the first English Navigator who sailed round the World, lived, to be the ornament of his Country and his profession. Yet great as he was, and justly celebrated as a Sailor, I cannot help foreseeing that he will be equalled in this or the next Century by one who tho' now but young,* already promises to answer all the ardent and sanguine expectations of his Relations and Freinds, amongst whom I may class the amiable Lady to whom this work is dedicated, and my no less amiable Self.

Though of a different profession, and shining in a different Sphere of Life, yet equally conspicuous in the Character of an *Earl*, as Drake was in that of a *Sailor*, was Robert Devereux Lord Essex. This unfortunate young Man was not unlike in Character to that equally unfortunate one *Frederic Delamere*. The simile may be carried still farther, and Elizabeth the torment of Essex may be compared to the Emmeline of Delamere.* It would be endless to recount the misfortunes of this noble and gallant Earl. It is sufficient to say that he was beheaded on the 25th of February, after having been Lord Leuitenant of Ireland, after having clapped his hand on his sword, and after performing many other services to his Country. Elizabeth did not long survive his loss, and died *so* miserable that were it not an injury to the memory of Mary I should pity her.

James the 1st

Though this King had some faults, among which and as the most principal, was his allowing his Mother's death, yet considered on the whole I cannot help liking him. He married Anne of Denmark, and had several Children; fortunately for him his eldest son Prince Henry died before his father or he might have experienced the evils which befell his unfortunate Brother.

As I am myself partial to the roman catholic religion,* it is with infinite regret that I am obliged to blame the Behaviour of any Member of it; yet Truth being I think very excusable in an Historian, I am necessitated to say that in this reign the roman Catholics of England did not behave like Gentlemen to the protestants. Their Behaviour indeed to the Royal Family and both Houses of Parliament might justly be considered by them as very uncivil, and even Sir Henry Percy tho' certainly the best bred Man of the party, had none of that general politeness which is so universally pleasing, as his Attentions were entirely confined to Lord Mounteagle.

Sir Walter Raleigh flourished in this and the preceding reign, and is by many people held in great veneration and respect—But as he was an enemy of the noble Essex, I have nothing to say in praise of him, and must refer all those who may wish to be acquainted with the particulars of his Life, to Mr Sheridan's play of the Critic,* where they will find many interesting Anecdotes as well of him as of his freind Sir Christopher Hatton—. His Majesty was of that amiable disposition which inclines to Freindships, and in such points was possessed of a keener penetration in Discovering Merit than many other people. I once heard an excellent Sharade* on a Carpet, of which the subject I am now on reminds me, and as I think it may afford my Readers some Amusement to *find it out*, I shall here take the liberty of presenting it to them.

Sharade

My first is what my second was to King James the 1st, and you tread on my whole.

The principal favourites of his Majesty were Car, who was afterwards created Earl of Somerset and whose name may have some share in the above mentioned Sharade, and George Villiers afterwards Duke of Buckingham. On his Majesty's death he was succeeded by his son Charles.

Charles the 1st

This amiable Monarch seems born to have suffered Misfortunes equal to those of his lovely Grandmother; Misfortunes which he could not deserve since he was her descendant. Never certainly were there before so many detestable Characters at one time in England as in this period of its History; Never were amiable Men so scarce. The number of them throughout the whole Kingdom amounting only to *five*, besides the inhabitants of Oxford who were always loyal to their King and faithful to his interests. The names of this noble five who never forgot the duty of the Subject, or swerved from their attachment to his Majesty, were as follows,—The King himself, ever stedfast in his own support—Archbishop Laud, Earl of Strafford,* Viscount Faulkland and Duke of Ormond who were scarcely less strenuous or zealous in the cause. While the *Villains* of the time would make too long a list to be written or read; I shall therefore content myself with mentioning the leaders of the Gang. Cromwell, Fairfax, Hampden, and Pym may be considered as the original Causers of all the disturbances Distresses and Civil Wars in which England for many years was embroiled. In this reign as well as in that of Elizabeth, I am obliged in spite of my Attachment to the Scotch, to consider them as equally guilty with the generality of the English, since they dared to think differently from their Sovereign, to forget the Adoration which as *Stuarts* it was their Duty to pay them, to rebel against, dethrone and imprison the unfortunate Mary; to oppose, to deceive, and to sell the no less unfortunate Charles. The Events of this Monarch's reign are too numerous for my pen, and indeed the recital of any Events (except what I make myself) is uninteresting to me; my principal reason for undertaking the History of England being to prove the innocence of the Queen of Scotland, which I flatter myself with having effectually done, and to abuse Elizabeth, tho' I am rather fearful of having fallen short in the latter part of my Scheme—. As therefore it is not my intention to give any particular account of the distresses into which this King was involved through the misconduct and Cruelty of his Parliament, I shall satisfy myself with vindicating him from the Reproach of Arbitrary and tyrannical Government with which he has often been Charged. This, I feel, is not difficult to be done, for with one argument I am certain of satisfying every sensible and well disposed person whose opinions have been properly guided by a good Education—and this Arguement is that he was a Stuart.

Finis

Saturday Nov: 26th 1791

A Collection of Letters

To Miss Cooper*

Cousin
Conscious of the Charming Character which in every Country,
and every Clime in Christendom is Cried, Concerning you, with
Caution and Care I Commend to your Charitable Criticism this
Clever Collection of Curious Comments, which have been
Carefully Culled, Collected and Classed by your Comical Cousin
                                              The Author

A Collection of Letters

Letter the first
From a Mother to her freind*

My Children begin now to claim all my attention in a
different Manner from that in which they have been used to
receive it, as they are now arrived at that age when it is
necessary for them in some measure to become conversant
with the World. My Augusta is 17 and her Sister scarcely a
twelvemonth younger. I flatter myself that their education
has been such as will not disgrace their appearance in the
World, and that *they* will not disgrace their Education I
have every reason to beleive. Indeed they are sweet Girls—.
Sensible yet unaffected—Accomplished yet Easy—. Lively
yet Gentle—. As their progress in every thing they have
learnt has been always the same, I am willing to forget the
difference of age, and to introduce them together into
Public. This very Evening is fixed on as their first entrée
into Life, as we are to drink tea* with Mrs Cope and her
Daughter. I am glad that we are to meet no one for my Girls'
sake, as it would be awkward for them to enter too wide a

Circle on the very first day. But we shall proceed by degrees—. Tomorrow Mr Stanly's family will drink tea with us, and perhaps the Miss Phillips's will meet them. On Tuesday we shall pay Morning-Visits*—On Wednesday we are to dine at Westbrook. On Thursday we have Company at home. On Friday we are to be at a private Concert at Sir John Wynne's—and on Saturday we expect Miss Dawson to call in the Morning,—which will complete my Daughters' Introduction into Life. How they will bear so much dissipation I cannot imagine; of their Spirits I have no fear, I only dread their health.

This mighty affair is now happily over, and my Girls *are out*. As the moment approached for our departure, you can have no idea how the sweet Creatures trembled with fear and expectation. Before the Carriage drove to the door, I called them into my dressing-room, and as soon as they were seated thus addressed them. 'My dear Girls, the moment is now arrived when I am to reap the rewards of all my Anxieties and Labours towards you during your Education. You are this Evening to enter a World in which you will meet with many wonderfull Things; Yet let me warn you against suffering yourselves to be meanly swayed by the Follies and Vices of others, for beleive me, my beloved Children, that if you do—I shall be very sorry for it.' They both assured me that they would ever remember my advice with Gratitude, and follow it with Attention; That they were prepared to find a World full of things to amaze and shock them: but that they trusted their behaviour would never give me reason to repent the Watchful Care with which I had presided over their infancy and formed their Minds—.* 'With such expectations and such intentions' (cried I) 'I can have nothing to fear from you—and can chearfully conduct you to Mrs Cope's without a fear of your being seduced by her Example, or contaminated by her Follies. Come, then my Children' (added I) 'the Carriage is driving to the door, and I will not a moment delay the happiness you are so impatient to enjoy.' When we arrived at Warleigh, poor Augusta could hardly breathe, while Margaret was all Life and Rapture. 'The long-expected Moment is now arrived' (said she) 'and we shall soon be in the World.'— In a few Moments we were in Mrs Cope's parlour—, where with her daughter she sate ready to receive us. I observed with delight the impression my Children made on them—. They were indeed two sweet, elegant-looking Girls, and tho' somewhat abashed from the peculiarity of their Situation, Yet there was an ease in their Manners and Address which could not fail of pleasing—. Imagine my dear Madam how delighted I must have been in beholding as I did, how attentively they observed every object they saw, how disgusted with some Things, how enchanted with others, how astonished at all! On the whole however they returned in raptures with the World, its Inhabitants, and Manners.

Yrs Ever—A—F—.

Letter the second
From a Young lady crossed in Love to her freind*—

Why should this last disappointment hang so heavily on my Spirits? Why should I feel it more, why should it wound me deeper than those I have experienced before? Can it be that I have a greater affection for Willoughby* than I had for his amiable predecessors—? Or is it that our feelings become more acute from being often wounded? I must suppose my dear Belle that this is the Case, since I am not conscious of being more sincerely attached to Willoughby than I was to Neville, Fitzowen, or either of the Crawfords,* for all of whom I once felt the most lasting affection that ever warmed a Woman's heart. Tell me then dear Belle why I still sigh when I think of the faithless Edward, or why I weep when I behold his Bride, for too surely this is the case—. My Freinds are all alarmed for me; They fear my declining health; they lament my want of Spirits; they dread the effects of both. In hopes of releiving my Melancholy, by directing my thoughts to other objects, they have invited several of their freinds to spend the Christmas with us. Lady Bridget Dashwood* and her Sister-in-Law Miss Jane are expected on Friday; and Colonel Seaton's family will be with us next week. This is all most kindly meant by my Uncle and Cousins; but what can the presence of a dozen indifferent people do to me, but weary and distress me—. I will not finish my Letter till some of our Visitors are arrived.

———————

Friday Evening—

Lady Bridget came this Morning, and with her, her sweet Sister Miss Jane—. Although I have been acquainted with this charming Woman above fifteen years, Yet I never before observed how lovely she ɪs. She is now about 35, and in spite of sickness, Sorrow and Time is more blooming than I ever saw a Girl of 17. I was delighted with her, the moment she entered the house, and she appeared equally pleased with me, attaching herself to me during the remainder of the day. There is something so sweet, so mild in her Countenance, that she seems more than Mortal. Her Conversation is as bewitching as her appearance—; I could not help telling her how much she engaged my Admiration—. —'Oh! Miss Jane' (said I)—and stopped from an inability at the moment of expressing myself as I could wish—'Oh! Miss Jane' (I repeated)—I could not think of words to suit my feelings—She seemed waiting for my Speech—. I was confused—distressed—. My thoughts were bewildered—and I could only add 'How do you do?' She saw and felt for my Embarrassment and with admirable presence of mind releived me from it by saying—'My dear Sophia, be not uneasy at having exposed Yourself—I will turn the Conversation without appearing to notice it.' Oh! how I loved her for her kindness! 'Do you ride as much as you used to do?' said she—. 'I am advised to ride by my Physician,* We have delightful Rides round us, I have a Charming horse, am uncommonly fond of the Amusement,' replied I quite recovered from my Confusion, 'and in short I ride a great deal.' 'You are in the right my Love,' said She, Then repeating the following Line which was an extempore and equally adapted to recommend both Riding and Candour—

'Ride where you may, Be Candid where You can,'* She added, '*I* rode once, but it is many years ago'—She spoke this in so Low and tremulous a Voice, that I was silent— Struck with her Manner of Speaking I could make no reply. 'I have not ridden,' continued she fixing her Eyes on my face, 'since I was married.' I was never so surprised— 'Married, Ma'am!' I repeated. 'You may well wear that look of astonishment', said she, 'since what I have said must appear improbable to you—Yet nothing is more true than that I once was married.'

'Then why are you called Miss Jane?'

'I married, my Sophia, without the consent or knowledge of my father—the late Admiral Annesley.* It was therefore necessary to keep the secret from him and from every one, till some fortunate opportunity might offer of revealing it—. Such an opportunity alas! was but too soon given in the death of my dear Captain Dashwood—Pardon these tears,' continued Miss Jane wiping her Eyes, 'I owe them to my Husband's Memory, He fell my Sophia, while fighting for his Country in America* after a most happy Union of seven years—. My Children, two sweet Boys and a Girl, who had constantly resided with my Father and me, passing with him and with every one as the Children of a Brother (tho' I had ever been an only child) had as yet been the Comforts of my Life. But no sooner had I lossed my Henry, than these sweet Creatures fell sick and died—. Conceive, dear Sophia, what my feelings must have been when as an Aunt I attended my Children to their early Grave—. My Father did not survive them many weeks—He died, poor Good old Man, happily ignorant to his last hour of my Marriage.'*

'But did you not own it, and assume his name at your husband's death?'

'No; I could not bring myself to do it; more especially when in my Children, I lost all inducement for doing it. Lady Bridget, and Yourself are the only persons who are in the knowledge of my having ever been either Wife or Mother. As I could not prevail on myself to take the name of Dashwood (a name which after my Henry's death I could never hear without emotion) and as I was conscious of having no right to that of Annesley, I dropt all thoughts of either,* and have made it a point of bearing only my Christian one since my Father's death.' She paused—'Oh! my dear Miss Jane' (said I) 'how infinitely am I obliged to you for so entertaining a Story! You cannot think how it has diverted me! But have you quite done?'

'I have only to add, my dear Sophia, that my Henry's elder Brother dieing about the same time, Lady Bridget became a Widow like myself, and as we had always loved each other in idea from the high Character in which we had ever been spoken of, though we had never met, we determined to live together.* We wrote to one another on the same subject by the same post, so exactly did our feelings and our Actions coincide! We both eagerly embraced the proposals we gave and received of becoming one family, and have from that time lived together in the greatest affection.'

'And is this all?' said I, 'I hope you have not done.'

'Indeed I have; and did you ever hear a Story more pathetic?'

'I never did—and it is for that reason it pleases me so much, for when one is unhappy nothing is so delightful to one's sensations as to hear of equal Misery.'

'Ah! but my Sophia why *are you* unhappy?'

'Have you not heard, Madam, of Willoughby's Marriage?' 'But my Love why lament *his* perfidy, when you bore so well that of many young Men before?' 'Ah! Madam, I was used to it then, but when Willoughby broke his Engagements I had not been dissapointed for half a year.' 'Poor Girl!' said Miss Jane.

Letter the third
From A young Lady in distress'd Circumstances to her freind.

A few days ago I was at a private Ball given by Mr Ashburnham. As my Mother never goes out she entrusted me to the care of Lady Greville who did me the honour of calling for me in her way and of allowing me to sit forwards,* which is a favour about which I am very indifferent especially as I know it is considered as confering a great obligation on me. 'So Miss Maria' (said her Ladyship as she saw me advancing to the door of the Carriage) 'you seem very smart tonight—*My* poor Girls will appear quite to disadvantage by *you*.—I only hope your Mother may not have distressed herself to set *you* off. Have you got a new Gown on?'

'Yes Ma'am,' replied I with as much indifference as I could assume.

'Aye, and a fine one too I think—' (feeling it, as by her permission I seated myself by her) 'I dare say it is all very smart—But I must own, for you know I always speak my mind, that I think it was quite a needless peice of expence*—Why could not you have worn your old striped one? It is not my way to find fault with people because they are poor, for I always think that they are more to be despised and pitied than blamed for it, especially if they cannot help it, but at the same time I must say that in my opinion your old striped Gown would have been quite fine enough for its Wearer—for to tell you the truth (I always speak my mind) I am very much afraid that one half of the people in the room will not know whether you have a Gown on or not—But I suppose you intend to make your fortune tonight—: Well, the sooner the better; and I wish you success.'

'Indeed, Ma'am, I have no such intention.—'

'Who ever heard a Young Lady own that she was a

Fortune-hunter?' Miss Greville laughed, but I am sure Ellen felt for me.

'Was your Mother gone to bed before you left her?' said her Ladyship.

'Dear Ma'am' said Ellen, 'it is but nine o'clock.'

'True, Ellen, but Candles cost money, and Mrs Williams is too wise to be extravagant.'

'She was just sitting down to supper, Ma'am.'

'And what had she got for Supper?' 'I did not observe.' 'Bread and Cheese* I suppose.' 'I should never wish for a better supper,' said Ellen. 'You have never any reason' replied her Mother, 'as a better is always provided for you.' Miss Greville laughed excessively, as she constantly does at her Mother's wit.

Such is the humiliating Situation in which I am forced to appear while riding in her Ladyship's Coach—I dare not be impertinent, as my Mother is always admonishing me to be humble and patient if I wish to make my way in the world. She insists on my accepting every invitation of Lady Greville, or you may be certain that I would never enter either her House, or her Coach, with the disagreable certainty I always have of being abused for my Poverty while I am in them.— When we arrived at Ashburnham, it was nearly ten o'clock, which was an hour and a half later than we were desired to be there; but Lady Greville is too fashionable (or fancies herself to be so) to be punctual.* The Dancing however was not begun as they waited for Miss Greville. I had not been long in the room before I was engaged to dance by Mr Bernard, but just as we were going to stand up, he recollected that his Servant had got his white Gloves,* and immediately ran out to fetch them. In the mean time the Dancing began and Lady Greville in passing to another room went exactly before me.— She saw me and instantly stopping, said to me though there were several people close to us;

'Hey day, Miss Maria! What cannot you get a partner? Poor Young Lady! I am afraid your new Gown was put on for nothing. But do not despair; perhaps you may get a hop* before the Evening is over.' So saying, she passed on without hearing my repeated assurance of being engaged, and leaving me very provoked at being so exposed before every one—Mr Bernard however soon returned and by coming to me the moment he entered the room, and leading me to the Dancers, my Character I hope was cleared from the imputation Lady Greville had thrown on it, in the eyes of all the old Ladies who had heard her speech. I soon forgot all my vexations in the pleasure of dancing and of having the most agreable partner in the room. As he is moreover heir to a very large Estate I could see that Lady Greville did not look very well pleased when she found who had been his Choice.— She was determined to mortify me, and accordingly when we were sitting down between the dances, she came to me with *more* than her usual insulting importance attended by Miss Mason and said loud enough to be heard by half the people in the room, 'Pray, Miss Maria, in what way of business was your Grandfather? for Miss Mason and I cannot agree whether he was a Grocer or a Bookbinder.'* I saw that she wanted to mortify me and was resolved if I possibly could to prevent her seeing that her scheme succeeded. 'Neither Madam; he was a Wine Merchant.' 'Aye, I knew he was in some such low way—He broke,* did not he?' 'I beleive not, Ma'am.' 'Did not he abscond?' 'I never heard that he did.' 'At least he died insolvent?' 'I was never told so before.' 'Why, was not your *Father* as poor as a Rat?' 'I fancy not;' 'Was not he in the King's Bench* once?' 'I never saw him there.' *She* gave me *such* a look, and turned away in a great passion; while I was half delighted with myself for my impertinence, and half afraid of being thought too saucy. As Lady Greville was extremely angry with me, she took no further notice of me all the Evening, and indeed had I been in favour I should have been equally neglected, as she was got into a party of great folks and she never speaks to me when she can to any one else. Miss Greville was with her Mother's party at Supper,* but Ellen preferred staying with the Bernards and me. We had a very pleasant Dance and as Lady G— slept all the way home, I had a very comfortable ride.

The next day while we were at dinner* Lady Greville's

Coach stopped at the door, for that is the time of day she generally contrives it should. She sent in a message by the Servant to say that 'she should not get out but that Miss Maria must come to the Coach-door, as she wanted to speak to her, and that she must make haste and come immediately—' 'What an impertinent Message, Mama!' said I— 'Go, Maria—' replied She—Accordingly I went and was obliged to stand there at her Ladyship's pleasure though the Wind was extremely high and very cold.*

'Why I think, Miss Maria, you are not quite so smart as you were last night—But I did not come to examine your dress, but to tell you that you may dine with us the day after tomorrow—Not tomorrow, remember, do not come tomorrow, for we expect Lord and Lady Clermont and Sir Thomas Stanley's family—There will be no occasion for your being very fine for I shan't send the Carriage—If it rains you may take an umbrella—.' I could hardly help laughing at hearing her give me leave to keep myself dry— 'And pray remember to be in time, for I shan't wait—I hate my Victuals over-done—But you need not come *before* the time—How does your Mother do—? She is at dinner is not she?' 'Yes, Ma'am, we were in the middle of dinner when your Ladyship came.' 'I am afraid you find it very cold, Maria,' said Ellen. 'Yes, it is an horrible East wind'—said her Mother—'I assure you I can hardly bear the window down—But you are used to be blown about the wind, Miss Maria, and that is what has made your Complexion so ruddy and coarse. You young Ladies who cannot often ride in a Carriage never mind what weather you trudge in, or how the wind shews your legs. I would not have *my* Girls stand out of doors as you do in such a day as this. But some sort of people have no feelings either of cold or Delicacy— Well, remember that we shall expect you on Thursday at 5 o'clock—You must tell your Maid to come for you at night—There will be no Moon*—and you will have an horrid walk home—My Compliments to your Mother—I am afraid your dinner will be cold—Drive on—.' And away she went, leaving me in a great passion with her as she always does.

Maria Williams

Letter the fourth
From a young Lady rather impertinent to her freind.

We dined yesterday with Mr Evelyn where we were introduced to a very agreable looking Girl his cousin. I was extremely pleased with her appearance, for added to the charms of an engaging face, her manner and voice had something peculiarly interesting in them. So much so, that they inspired me with a great curiosity to know the history of her Life, who were her Parents, where she came from, and what had befallen her, for it was then only known that she was a relation of Mrs Evelyn, and that her name was Grenville. In the evening a favourable opportunity offered to me of attempting at least to know what I wished to know, for every one played at Cards but Mrs Evelyn, My Mother, Dr Drayton, Miss Grenville and myself, and as the two former were engaged in a whispering Conversation, and the Doctor fell asleep, we were of necessity obliged to entertain each other. This was what I wished and being determined not to remain in ignorance for want of asking, I began the Conversation in the following Manner.

'Have you been long in Essex,* Ma'am?'

'I arrived on Tuesday.'

'You came from Derbyshire?'*

'No, Ma'am!' appearing surprised at my question, 'from Suffolk.'* You will think this a good dash of mine, my dear Mary, but you will know that I am not wanting for Impudence when I have any end in veiw. 'Are you pleased with the Country, Miss Grenville? Do you find it equal to the one you have left?'

'Much superior, Ma'am, in point of Beauty.' She sighed. I longed to know for why.

'But the face of any Country however beautiful' said I, 'can be but a poor consolation for the loss of one's dearest Freinds.' She shook her head, as if she felt the truth of what I said. My Curiosity was so much raised, that I was resolved at any rate to satisfy it.

'You regret having left Suffolk then, Miss Grenville?' 'Indeed I do.' 'You were born there I suppose?' 'Yes, Ma'am, I was and passed many happy years there—.'

'That is a great comfort—'said I—'I hope Ma'am that you never spent any *un*happy one's there.'

'Perfect Felicity is not the property of Mortals, and no one has a right to expect uninterrupted Happiness*—*Some* Misfortunes I have certainly met with—.'

'*What* Misfortunes, dear Ma'am?' replied I, burning with impatience to know everything. '*None*, Ma'am, I hope that have been the effect of any wilfull fault in me.' 'I dare say not Ma'am, and have no doubt but that any sufferings you may have experienced could arise only from the cruelties of Relations or the Errors of Freinds.' She sighed—'You seem unhappy, my dear Miss Grenville—Is it in my power to soften your Misfortunes.' '*Your* power Ma'am,' replied she extremely surprised; 'it is in *no one's* power to make me happy.' She pronounced these words in so mournfull and solemn an accent, that for some time I had not courage to reply. I was actually silenced. I recovered myself however in a few moments and looking at her with all the affection I could, 'My dear Miss Grenville,' said I, 'you appear extremely young—and may probably stand in need of some one's advice whose regard for you, joined to superior Age, perhaps superior Judgement might authorise her to give it—. I am that person, and I now challenge you to accept the offer I make you of my Confidence and Freindship, in return to which I shall only ask for yours—.'

'You are extremely obliging, Ma'am'—said She—'and I am highly flattered by your attention to me—. But I am in no difficulty, no doubt, no uncertainty of situation in which any Advice can be wanted. Whenever I am, however,' continued she, brightening into a complaisant smile, 'I shall know where to apply.'

I bowed, but felt a good deal mortified by such a repulse; Still however I had not given up my point. I found that by the appearance of Sentiment and Freindship nothing was to be gained and determined therefore to renew my Attacks by Questions and Suppositions.

'Do you intend staying long in this part of England, Miss Grenville?'

'Yes, Ma'am, some time I beleive.'

'But how will Mr and Mrs Grenville bear your Absence?'

'They are neither of them alive, Ma'am.'

This was an answer I did not expect—I was quite silenced and never felt so awkward in my Life—.

Letter the fifth
From a Young Lady very much in love to her Freind.

My Uncle gets more stingy, my Aunt more particular, and I more in love every day. What shall we all be at this rate by the end of the year! I had this morning the happiness of receiving the following Letter from my dear Musgrove.*

Sackville St:* Jan:ry 7th

It is a month to day since I beheld my lovely Henrietta, and the sacred anniversary must and shall be kept in a manner becoming the day—by writing to her. Never shall I forget the moment when her Beauties first broke on my sight—No time as you well know can erase it from my Memory. It was at Lady Scudamore's.* Happy Lady Scudamore to live within a mile of the divine Henrietta! When the lovely Creature first entered the room, Oh! what were my sensations? The sight of you was like the sight of a wonderful fine Thing. I started—I gazed at her with Admiration—She appeared every moment more Charming, and the unfortunate Musgrove became a Captive to your Charms before I had time to look about me. Yes Madam, I had the happiness of adoring you, an unhappiness for which I cannot be too grateful. 'What,' said he to himself, 'is Musgrove allowed to die for Henrietta? Enviable Mortal; and may he pine for her who is the object of universal Admiration, who is adored by a Colonel, and toasted* by a Baronet!—' Adorable Henrietta how beautiful you are! I declare you are quite divine! You are more than Mortal. You are an Angel. You are Venus herself. In short, Madam, you are the prettiest Girl I ever saw in my Life—and her Beauty is encreased in her Musgrove's Eyes, by permitting him to love her and allowing me to hope. And Ah! Angelic Miss Henrietta, Heaven is my Witness how ardently I do hope for the death of your villanous Uncle and his Abandoned Wife, Since my fair one will not consent to be mine till their decease has placed her in affluence above what my fortune can procure—. Though it is an improvable Estate*—. Cruel Henrietta to persist in such a resolution! I am at present with my Sister where I mean to continue till my own house which tho' an excellent one is at present somewhat out of repair, is ready to receive me. Amiable princess of my Heart farewell—Of that Heart which trembles while it signs itself your most ardent Admirer

and devoted   humble Servt.

T. Musgrove

There is a pattern for a Love-letter, Matilda!* Did you ever read such a masterpeice of Writing? Such Sense, Such Sentiment, Such purity of Thought, Such flow of Language and such unfeigned Love in one Sheet?* No, never, I can answer for it, since a Musgrove is not to be met with by every Girl. Oh! how I long to be with him! I intend to send him the following in answer to his Letter tomorrow.

My dearest Musgrove—. Words can not express how happy your Letter made me; I thought I should have cried for Joy, for I love you better than any body in the World. I think you the most amiable, and the handsomest Man in England, and so to be sure you are. I never read so sweet a Letter in my Life. Do write me another just like it, and tell me you are in love with me in every other line. I quite die to see you. How shall we manage to see one another? for we are so much in love that we cannot live asunder. Oh! my dear Musgrove you cannot think how impatiently I wait for the death of my Uncle and Aunt—If they will not die soon, I beleive I shall run mad, for I get more in love with you every day of my Life.

How happy your Sister is to enjoy the pleasure of your Company in her house, and how happy every body in London must be because you are there. I hope you will be so kind as to write to me again soon, for I never read such sweet Letters as yours. I am, my dearest Musgrove,

most truly and faithfully Yours

for ever and ever*   Henrietta Halton

I hope he will like my answer; it is as good a one as I can write, though nothing to his; Indeed I had always heard what a dab* he was at a Love-letter. I saw him you know for the first time at Lady Scudamore's—And when I saw her Ladyship afterwards she asked me how I liked her Cousin Musgrove?

'Why upon my word' said I, 'I think he is a very handsome young Man.'

'I am glad you think so,' replied she, 'for he is distractedly in love with you.'

'Law! Lady Scudamore,' said I, 'how can you talk so ridiculously?'

'Nay, t'is very true,' answered She, 'I assure you, for he was in love with you from the first moment he beheld you.'

'I wish it may be true,' said I, 'for that is the only kind of love I would give a farthing* for—There is some Sense in being in love at first sight.'

'Well, I give you Joy of your conquest,' replied Lady Scudamore, 'and I beleive it to have been a very complete one; I am sure it is not a contemptible one, for my Cousin is a charming young fellow, has seen a great deal of the World, and writes the best Love-letters I ever read.'

This made me very happy, and I was excessively pleased with my conquest. However, I thought it proper to give myself a few Airs—So I said to her—

'This is all very pretty, Lady Scudamore, but you know that we young Ladies who are Heiresses must not throw ourselves away upon Men who have no fortune at all.'

'My dear Miss Halton,' said She, 'I am as much convinced of that as you can be, and I do assure you that I should be the last person to encourage your marrying any one who had not some pretensions to expect a fortune with you. Mr Musgrove is so far from being poor that he has an estate of Several hundreds an year* which is capable of great Improvement, and an excellent House, though at present it is not quite in repair.'

'If that is the case,' replied I, 'I have nothing more to say against him, and if as you say he is an informed young Man and can write good Love-letters, I am sure I have no reason to find fault with him for admiring me, tho' perhaps I may not marry him for all that, Lady Scudamore.'

'You are certainly under no obligation to marry him,' answered her Ladyship, 'except that which love himself will dictate to you, for if I am not greatly mistaken you are at this very moment unknown to yourself, cherishing a most tender affection for him.'

'Law, Lady Scudamore,' replied I blushing, 'how can you think of such a thing?'

'Because every look, every word betrays it,' answered She; 'Come, my dear Henrietta, consider me as a friend, and be sincere with me—Do not you prefer Mr Musgrove to any man of your acquaintance?'

'Pray do not ask me such questions, Lady Scudamore,' said I turning away my head, 'for it is not fit for me to answer them.'

'Nay my Love,' replied she, 'now you confirm my suspicions. But why, Henrietta, should you be ashamed to own a well-placed Love, or why refuse to confide in me?'

'I am not ashamed to own it;' said I taking Courage. 'I do not refuse to confide in you or blush to say that I do love your cousin Mr Musgrove, that I am sincerely attached to him, for it is no disgrace to love a handsome Man. If he were plain indeed I might have had reason to be ashamed of a passion which must have been mean since the Object would have been unworthy. But with such a figure and face, and such beautiful hair as your Cousin has, why should I blush to own that such Superior Merit has made an impression on me.'

'My sweet Girl' (said Lady Scudamore embracing me with great Affection) 'what a delicate way of thinking you have in these Matters, and what a quick discernment for one of your years! Oh! how I honour you for such Noble Sentiments!'

'Do you, Ma'am?' said I; 'You are vastly obliging. But pray, Lady Scudamore, did your Cousin himself tell you of his Affection for me? I shall like him the better if he did, for what is a Lover without a Confidante?'

'Oh! my Love' replied She, 'you were born for each other. Every word you say more deeply convinces me that your Minds are actuated by the invisible power of simpathy, for your opinions and Sentiments so exactly coincide. Nay, the colour of your Hair is not very different. Yes, my dear Girl, the poor despairing Musgrove did reveal to me the story of his Love—. Nor was I surprised at it—I know not how it was, but I had a kind of presentiment that he *would* be in love with you.'

'Well, but how did he break it to you?'

'It was not till after supper. We were sitting round the fire together talking on indifferent subjects, though to say the truth the Conversation was cheifly on my side, for he was thoughtful and silent, when on a sudden he interrupted me in the midst of something I was saying, by exclaiming in a most Theatrical tone—

"Yes I'm in love I feel it now

And Henrietta Halton has undone me*—" '

'Oh! What a sweet Way,' replied I, 'of declaring his Passion! To make such a couple of charming Lines about me! What a pity it is that they are not in rhime!'*

'I am very glad you like it,' answered She; 'To be sure there was a great deal of Taste in it. "And are you in love with her, Cousin?" said I. "I am very sorry for it, for unexceptionable as you are in every respect, with a pretty Estate capable of Great improvements, and an excellent House tho' somewhat out of repair, Yet who can hope to aspire with success to the adorable Henrietta who has had an offer from a Colonel and been toasted by a Baronet" '—
'*That* I have—' cried I. Lady Scudamore continued. ' "Ah, dear Cousin," replied he, "I am so well convinced of the little Chance I can have of winning her who is adored by thousands, that I need no assurances of yours to make me

more thoroughly so. Yet surely neither you or the fair Henrietta herself will deny me the exquisite Gratification of dieing for her, of falling a victim of her Charms. And when I am dead"—continued he—'

'Oh Lady Scudamore,' said I wiping my eyes, 'that such a sweet Creature should talk of dieing!'

'It is an affecting Circumstance indeed,' replied Lady Scudamore. ' "When I am dead," said he, "Let me be carried and lain at her feet, and perhaps she may not disdain to drop a pitying tear on my poor remains".'

'Dear Lady Scudamore' interrupted I, 'say no more on this affecting Subject. I cannot bear it.'

'Oh! how I admire the sweet sensibility of your Soul, and as I would not for Worlds wound it too deeply, I will be silent.'

'Pray go on' said I. She did so.

' "And then," added he, "Ah! Cousin, imagine what my transports will be when I feel the dear precious drops trickle on my face! Who would not die to taste such extacy! And when I am interred, may the divine Henrietta bless some happier Youth with her affection, May he be as tenderly attached to her as the hapless Musgrove and while *he* crumbles to dust, May they live an example of Felicity in the Conjugal state!" '

Did you ever hear any thing so pathetic? What a charming wish, to be lain at my feet when he was dead! Oh! what an exalted mind he must have to be capable of such a wish! Lady Scudamore went on.

' "Ah! my dear Cousin," replied I to him, "such noble behaviour as this, must melt the heart of any Woman however obdurate it may naturally be; and could the divine Henrietta but hear your generous wishes for her happiness, all gentle as is her mind, I have not a doubt but that she would pity your affection and endeavour to return it." "Oh! Cousin," answered he, "do not endeavour to raise my hopes by such flattering Assurances. No, I cannot hope to please this angel of a Woman, and the only thing which remains for me to do, is to die." "True Love is ever desponding," replied I, "but *I*, my dear Tom, will give you even greater hopes of conquering this fair one's heart, than I have yet given you, by assuring you that I watched her with the strictest attention during the whole day, and could plainly discover that she cherishes in her bosom though unknown to herself, a most tender affection for you." '

'Dear Lady Scudamore,' cried I, 'This is more than I ever knew!'

'Did I not say that it was unknown to yourself? "I did not," continued I to him, "encourage you by saying this at first, that Surprise might render the pleasure Still Greater." "No, Cousin," replied he in a languid voice, "nothing will convince me that *I* can have touched the heart of Henrietta Halton, and if you are deceived yourself, do not attempt deceiving me." In short my Love it was the work of some hours for me to persuade the poor despairing Youth that you had really a preference for him; but when at last he could no longer deny the force of my arguments, or discredit what I told him, his transports, his Raptures, his Extacies are beyond my power to describe.'

'Oh! the dear Creature,' cried I, 'how passionately he loves me! But, dear Lady Scudamore, did you tell him that I was totally dependant on my Uncle and Aunt?'

'Yes, I told him every thing.'

'And what did he say?'

'He exclaimed with virulence against Uncles and Aunts; Accused the Laws of England for allowing them to possess their Estates when wanted by their Nephews or Neices, and wished *he* were in the House of Commons, that he might reform the Legislature, and rectify all its abuses.'

'Oh! the sweet Man! What a spirit he has!' said I.

'He could not flatter himself, he added, that the adorable Henrietta would condescend for his sake to resign those Luxuries and that Splendor to which She had been used, and accept only in exchange the Comforts and Elegancies which his limitted Income could afford her, even supposing that his house were in Readiness to receive her. I told him that it could not be expected that she would; it would be doing her an injustice to suppose her capable of giving up the power she now possesses and so nobly uses of doing such extensive Good to the poorer part of her fellow Creatures,* merely for the gratification of you and herself.'

'To be sure,' said I, 'I *am* very Charitable every now and then. And what did Mr Musgrove say to this?'

'He replied that he was under a melancholy Necessity of owning the truth of what I said, and therefore if he should be the happy Creature destined to be the Husband of the Beautiful Henrietta he must bring himself to wait, however impatiently, for the fortunate day, when she might be freed from the power of worthless Relations and able to bestow herself on him.'

What a noble Creature he is! Oh! Matilda what a fortunate one *I am* who am to be his Wife! My Aunt is calling to me to come and make the pies.* So adeiu my dear freind,

and beleive me your &c.—H. Halton

Finis

[Scraps]

To Miss Fanny Catherine Austen*

My dear Neice

As I am prevented by the great distance between Rowling and Steventon* from superintending Your Education Myself, the care of which will probably on that account devolve on your Father and Mother, I think it is my particular Duty to prevent your feeling as much as possible the want of my personal instructions, by addressing to You on paper my Opinions and Admonitions on the conduct of Young Women,* which you will find expressed in the following pages.—I am my dear Neice

Your affectionate Aunt
The Author.

The female philosopher*—

a Letter

My dear Louisa

Your friend Mr Millar called upon us yesterday in his way to Bath, whither he is going for his health; two of his daughters were with him, but the oldest and the three Boys are with their Mother in Sussex. Though you have often told me that Miss Millar was remarkably handsome, you never mentioned anything of her Sisters' beauty; yet they are certainly extremely pretty. I'll give you their description.—Julia is eighteen; with a countenance in which Modesty, Sense and Dignity are happily blended, she has a form which at once presents you with Grace, Elegance and Symmetry. Charlotte who is just Sixteen is shorter than her Sister, and though her figure cannot boast the easy dignity of Julia's, yet it has a pleasing plumpness which is in a different way as estimable. She is fair and her face is expressive sometimes of softness the most bewitching, and at others of Vivacity the most striking. She appears to have infinite Wit and a good humour unalterable; her conversation during the half hour they set with us, was replete with humorous Sallies, Bonmots and repartées;* while the sensible, the amiable Julia uttered Sentiments of Morality* worthy of a heart like her own. Mr Millar appeared to answer the character I had always received of him. My Father met him with that look of Love, that social Shake, and cordial kiss* which marked his gladness at beholding an old and valued friend from whom thro' various circumstances he had been separated nearly twenty Years. Mr Millar observed (and very justly too) that many events had befallen each during that interval of time, which gave occasion to the lovely Julia for making most sensible reflections on the many changes in their situation which so long a period had occasioned, on the advantages of some, and the disadvantages of others. From this subject she made a short digression to the instability of human pleasures and the uncertainty of their duration, which led her to observe that all earthly Joys must be imperfect. She was proceeding to illustrate this doctrine by examples from the Lives of great Men when the Carriage came to the Door and the amiable Moralist* with her Father and Sister was obliged to depart; but not without a promise of spending five or six months with us on their return. We of course mentioned you, and I assure you that ample Justice was done to your Merits by all. 'Louisa Clarke' (said I) 'is in general a very pleasant Girl, yet sometimes her good humour is clouded by Peevishness, Envy and Spite. She neither wants Understanding nor is without some pretensions to Beauty, but these are so very trifling, that the value she sets on her personal charms, and the adoration she expects them to be offered are at once a striking example of her vanity, her pride, and her folly.' So said I, and to my opinion everyone added weight by the concurrence of their own.

your affe:te

Arabella Smythe

The first Act of a Comedy

Characters

Popgun	Maria
Charles	Pistoletta
Postilion*	Hostess
Chorus of Ploughboys	Cook
and	and
Strephon*	Chloe*

Scene—an Inn

Enter Hostess, Charles, Maria and Cook

Hostess to Maria. If the gentry in the Lion* should want beds, shew them number 9.—

Maria. Yes Mistress.—   exit Maria—

Hostess to Cook. If their Honours in the Moon ask for the bill of fare,* give it them.

Cook. I wull,* I wull.—   exit Cook.

Hostess to Charles. If their Ladyships in the Sun ring their Bell—answer it.

Charles. Yes, Madam.—   Exeunt Severally—.

Scene changes to the Moon, and discovers
Popgun and Pistoletta.

Pistoletta. Pray papa, how far is it to London?

Popgun. My Girl, my Darling, my favourite of all my Children, who art the picture of thy poor Mother, who died two months ago, with whom I am going to Town to marry Strephon, and to whom I mean to bequeath my whole Estate, it wants seven Miles.

Scene changes to the Sun—
Enter Chloe and a chorus of ploughboys.*

Chloe. Where am I? At Hounslow.* Where go I? To London—. What to do? To be married—. Unto whom? Unto—Strephon. Who is he? A Youth. Then I will Sing a Song.

Song

> I go to Town
> And when I come down
> I shall be married to Stree-phon*
> And that to me will be fun.

Chorus.   Be fun, be fun, be fun,
> And that to me will be fun.

Enter Cook—

Cook. Here is the bill of fare.

Chloe reads. 2 Ducks, a leg of beef, a stinking partridge,*
and a tart.— I will have the leg of beef and the
partridge.   exit Cook.

And now I will sing another song.

Song

> I am going to have my dinner,
> After which I shan't be thinner,
> I wish I had here Strephon
> For he would carve the partridge if it should
> be a tough one.

Chorus.   Tough one, tough one, tough one,
> For he would carve the partridge if it
> Should be a tough one.

Exit Chloe and Chorus—.

Scene changes to the inside of the Lion.
Enter Strephon and Postilion.

Streph. You drove me from Staines* to this place, from
whence I mean to go to Town to marry Chloe. How
much is your due?

Post. Eighteen pence.

Streph. Alas, my friend, I have but a bad guinea* with
which I mean to support myself in Town. But I will pawn
to you an undirected Letter* that I received from Chloe.

Post. Sir, I accept your offer.

End of the first Act.—

A Letter from a Young Lady, whose feelings
being too Strong for her Judgement led her into
the commission of Errors which her
Heart disapproved.*—

Many have been the cares and vicissitudes of my past life,
my beloved Ellinor, and the only consolation I feel for their
bitterness is that on a close examination of my conduct,
I am convinced that I have strictly deserved them. I
murdered my father at a very early period of my Life, I have
since murdered my Mother, and I am now going to murder
my Sister. I have changed my religion so often that at
present I have not an idea of any left. I have been a perjured
witness in every public tryal for these last twelve Years; and
I have forged my own Will.* In short there is scarcely a
crime that I have not committed—But I am now going to
reform. Colonel Martin of the Horse guards* has paid his
Addresses to me, and we are to be married in a few days. As
there is something singular in our Courtship, I will give you
an account of it. Colonel Martin is the second son of the late
Sir John Martin who died immensely rich, but bequeathing
only one hundred thousand pound a piece to his three
younger Children, left the bulk of his fortune, about eight
Million* to the present Sir Thomas. Upon his small
pittance the Colonel lived tolerably contented for nearly
four months when he took it into his head to determine on
getting the whole of his eldest Brother's Estate. A new will
was forged and the Colonel produced it in Court—but
nobody would swear to it's being the right Will except
himself, and he had sworn so much that nobody beleived
him. At that moment I happened to be passing by the door
of the Court, and was beckoned in by the Judge who told
the Colonel that I was a Lady ready to witness any thing for
the cause of Justice, and advised him to apply to me. In
short the Affair was soon adjusted. The Colonel and I swore
to its' being the right will, and Sir Thomas has been obliged
to resign all his illgotten Wealth. The Colonel in gratitude

waited on me the next day with an offer of his hand—. I am now going to murder my Sister. Yours Ever,

Anna Parker.

====

A Tour through Wales*—
in a Letter from a young Lady—

My dear Clara
I have been so long on the ramble* that I have not till now had it in my power to thank you for your Letter—. We left our dear home on last Monday Month; and proceeded on our tour through Wales, which is a principality contiguous to England and gives the title to the Prince of Wales. We travelled on horseback by preference. My Mother rode upon our little poney and Fanny and I walked by her side or rather ran, for my Mother is so fond of riding fast that She galloped all the way. You may be sure that we were in a fine perspiration* when we came to our place of resting. Fanny has taken a great many Drawings of the Country, which are very beautiful, tho' perhaps not such exact resemblances as might be wished, from their being taken as she ran along. It would astonish you to see all the Shoes we wore out in our Tour. We determined to take a good Stock with us and therefore each took a pair of our own besides those we set off in. However we were obliged to have them both capped and heelpeiced* at Carmarthen,* and at last when they were quite gone, Mama was so kind as to lend us a pair of blue Sattin Slippers,* of which we each took one and hopped home from Hereford* delightfully—

I am your ever affectionate

Elizabeth Johnson.

====

A Tale.

A Gentleman whose family name I shall conceal, bought a small Cottage in Pembrokeshire* about two Years ago. This daring Action was suggested to him by his elder Brother who promised to furnish two rooms and a Closet* for him, provided he would take a small house near the borders of an extensive Forest, and about three Miles from the Sea. Wilhelminus* gladly accepted the Offer and continued for some time searching after such a retreat when he was one morning agreably releived from his Suspence by reading this advertisement in a Newspaper.

To be Lett

A neat Cottage on the borders of an extensive forest and about three Miles from the Sea. It is ready furnished except two rooms and a Closet.

The delighted Wilhelminus posted away immediately to his brother, and shewed him the advertisement. Robertus congratulated him and sent him in his Carriage to take possession of the Cottage. After travelling for three days and six Nights without Stopping, they arrived at the Forest and following a track which led by it's side down a steep Hill over which ten Rivulets meandered, they reached the Cottage in half an hour. Wilhelminus alighted, and after knocking for some time without receiving any answer or hearing any one stir within, he opened the door which was fastened only by a wooden latch and entered a small room, which he immediately perceived to be one of the two that were unfurnished—From thence he proceeded into a Closet equally bare. A pair of Stairs* that went out of it led him into a room above, no less destitute, and these apartments he found composed the whole of the House. He was by no means displeased with this discovery, as he had the comfort of reflecting that he should not be obliged to lay out any thing on furniture himself—. He returned immediately to his Brother, who took him next day to every Shop in Town, and bought what ever was requisite to furnish the two rooms and the Closet. In a few days every thing was completed, and Wilhelminus returned to take possession of the Cottage. Robertus accompanied him, with his Lady the amiable Cecilia and her two lovely Sisters Arabella and Marina* to whom Wilhelminus was tenderly attached, and a large number of Attendants—An ordinary Genius might probably have been embarrassed in endeavouring to accomodate so large a party, but Wilhelminus with admirable presence of mind gave order for the immediate erection of two noble Tents* in an open Spot in the Forest adjoining to the house. Their Construction was both simple and elegant—A couple of old blankets, each supported by four sticks, gave a striking proof of that taste for Architecture and that happy ease in overcoming difficulties which were some of Wilhelminus's most striking Virtues.

Finis

End of the Second Volume

VOLUME THE THIRD

Jane Austen—May 6th 1792.

CONTENTS

To Miss Mary Lloyd,*
The following Novel is by permission
Dedicated,
by her Obed^t: humble Servt:
The Author

Evelyn

In a retired part of the County of Sussex there is a village (for what I know to the Contrary) called Evelyn, perhaps one of the most beautiful Spots in the south of England. A Gentleman passing through it on horseback about twenty years ago, was so entirely of my opinion in this respect, that he put up at the little Alehouse in it and enquired with great earnestness whether there were any house to be lett in the Parish.* The Landlady, who as well as every one else in Evelyn was remarkably amiable, shook her head at this question, but seemed unwilling to give him any answer. He could not bear this uncertainty—yet knew not how to obtain the information he desired. To repeat a question which had already appear'd to make the good woman uneasy was impossible—. He turned from her in visible agitation. 'What a situation am I in!' said he to himself as he walked to the window and threw up the sash. He found himself revived by the Air, which he felt to a much greater degree when he had opened the window than he had done before. Yet it was but for a moment—. The agonizing pain of Doubt and Suspence again weighed down his Spirits. The good woman who had watched in eager silence every turn of his Countenance with that benevolence which characterizes the inhabitants of Evelyn, intreated him to tell her the cause of his uneasiness. 'Is there anything, Sir, in my power to do that may releive your Greifs—Tell me in what manner I can sooth them, and beleive me that the freindly balm of Comfort and Assistance shall not be wanting; for indeed, Sir, I have a simpathetic Soul.'

'Amiable Woman' (said Mr Gower, affected almost to tears by this generous offer) 'This Greatness of mind in one to whom I am almost a Stranger, serves but to make me the more warmly wish for a house in this sweet village—. What would I not give to be your Neighbour, to be blessed with your Acquaintance, and with the farther knowledge of your virtues! Oh! with what pleasure would I form myself by such an example! Tell me then, best of Women, is there no possibility?—I cannot speak—You know my Meaning——.'

'Alas! Sir,' replied Mrs Willis, 'there is *none*. Every house in this village, from the sweetness of the Situation, and the purity of the Air, in which neither Misery, Ill health, or Vice are ever wafted, is inhabited. And yet,' (after a short pause) 'there is a Family, who tho' warmly attached to the spot, yet from a peculiar Generosity of Disposition would perhaps be willing to oblige you with their house.' He eagerly caught at this idea, and having gained a direction to the place, he set off immediately on his walk to it. As he approached the House, he was delighted with its situation. It was in the exact centre of a small circular paddock,* which was enclosed by a regular paling,* and bordered with a plantation of Lombardy poplars, and Spruce firs alternatively placed in three rows. A gravel walk ran through this beautiful Shrubbery,* and as the remainder of the paddock was unincumbered with any other Timber, the surface of it perfectly even and smooth, and grazed by four white Cows which were disposed at equal distances from each other,* the whole appearance of the place as Mr Gower entered the Paddock was uncommonly striking. A beautifully-rounded, gravel road without any turn or interruption led immediately to the house. Mr Gower rang—the Door was soon opened. 'Are Mr and Mrs Webb at home?' 'My Good Sir, they are'—replied the Servant; And leading the way, conducted Mr Gower upstairs into a very elegant Dressing room, where a Lady rising from her seat, welcomed him with all the Generosity which Mrs Willis had attributed to the Family.

'Welcome best of Men*—Welcome to this House, and to everything it contains. William, tell your Master of the happiness I enjoy—invite him to partake of it—. Bring up some Chocolate* immediately; Spread a Cloth in the dining Parlour, and carry in the venison pasty*—. In the mean time let the Gentleman have some sandwiches, and bring in a Basket of Fruit—Send up some Ices and a bason of Soup, and do not forget some Jellies and Cakes.' Then turning to Mr Gower, and taking out her purse, 'Accept this, my good Sir,—. Beleive me you are welcome to everything that is in my power to bestow.—I wish my purse were weightier, but Mr Webb must make up my deficiences—. I know he has cash in the house to the amount of an hundred pounds, which he shall bring you immediately.'* Mr Gower felt overpowered by her generosity as he put the purse in his pocket, and from the excess of his Gratitude, could scarcely express himself intelligibly when he accepted her offer of the hundred pounds. Mr Webb soon entered the room, and repeated every protestation of Freindship and Cordiality which his Lady had already made. The Chocolate, the Sandwiches, the Jellies, the Cakes, the Ice, and the Soup soon made their appearance, and Mr Gower having tasted something of all, and pocketed the rest, was conducted into the dining parlour, where he eat a most excellent Dinner and partook of the most exquisite Wines, while Mr and Mrs Webb stood by him still pressing him to eat and drink a little more. 'And now my good Sir,' said Mr Webb, when Mr Gower's repast was concluded, 'what else can we do to contribute to your happiness and express the Affection we bear you. Tell us what you wish more to receive, and depend upon our gratitude for the communication of your wishes.' 'Give me then your house and Grounds; I ask for nothing else.' 'It is yours,' exclaimed both at once; 'from this moment it is yours.' The Agreement concluded on and the present accepted by Mr Gower, Mr Webb rang to have the Carriage ordered, telling William at the same time to call the Young Ladies.

'Best of Men,' said Mrs Webb, 'we will not long intrude upon your Time.'

'Make no Apologies, dear Madam,' replied Mr Gower, 'You are welcome to stay this half hour if you like it.'

They both burst forth into raptures of Admiration at his politeness, which they agreed served only to make their Conduct appear more inexcusable in trespassing on his time.

The Young Ladies soon entered the room. The eldest of them was about seventeen, the other, several years younger. Mr Gower had no sooner fixed his Eyes on Miss Webb than he felt that something more was necessary to his happiness than the house he had just received—Mrs Webb introduced him to her daughter. 'Our dear freind Mr Gower, my Love—He has been so good as to accept of this house, small as it is, and to promise to keep it for ever.' 'Give me leave to assure you, Sir,' said Miss Webb, 'that I am highly sensible of your kindness in this respect, which from the shortness of my Father's and Mother's acquaintance with you, is more than usually flattering.'

Mr Gower bowed—'You are too obliging, Ma'am—I assure you that I like the house extremely—and if they would complete their generosity by giving me their eldest daughter in marriage with a handsome portion,* I should have nothing more to wish for.' This compliment brought a blush into the cheeks of the lovely Miss Webb, who seemed however to refer herself to her father and Mother. *They* looked delighted at each other—At length Mrs Webb breaking silence, said—'We bend under a weight of obligations to you which we can never repay. Take our girl, take our Maria, and on her must the difficult task fall, of endeavouring to make some return to so much Benefiscence.' Mr Webb added, 'Her fortune is but ten thousand pounds,* which is almost too small a sum to be offered.' This objection however being instantly removed by the generosity of Mr Gower, who declared himself satisfied with the sum mentioned, Mr and Mrs Webb, with their youngest daughter took their leave, and on the next day, the nuptials of their eldest with Mr Gower were celebrated.—This amiable Man now found himself perfectly happy; united to a very lovely and deserving young woman, with an handsome fortune, an elegant house, settled in the village of Evelyn, and by that means enabled to cultivate his acquaintance with Mrs Willis, could he have a wish ungratified?—For some months he found that he could *not*, till one day as he was walking in the Shrubbery with Maria leaning on his arm, they observed a rose full-blown lying on the gravel; it had fallen from a rose tree which with three others had been planted by Mr Webb to give a pleasing variety to the walk. These four Rose trees served also to mark the quarters of the Shrubbery, by which means the Traveller might always know how far in his progress round the Paddock he was got—. Maria stooped to pick up the beautiful flower, and with all her Family Generosity presented it to her Husband. 'My dear Frederic,' said she, 'pray take this charming rose.' 'Rose!' exclaimed Mr Gower—. 'Oh! Maria, of what does not that remind me! Alas, my poor Sister, how have I neglected you!' The truth was that Mr Gower was the only son of a very large Family, of which Miss Rose Gower was the thirteenth daughter. This Young Lady whose merits deserved a better fate than she met with, was the darling of her relations—From the clearness of her skin and the Brilliancy of her Eyes, she was fully entitled to all their partial affection. Another circumstance contributed to the general Love they bore her, and that was one of the finest heads of hair in the world. A few Months before her Brother's Marriage, her heart had been engaged by the attentions and charms of a young Man whose high rank and expectations seemed to foretell objections from his Family to a match which would be highly desirable to theirs. Proposals were made on the young Man's part, and proper objections on his Father's— He was desired to return from Carlisle* where he was with his beloved Rose, to the family seat in Sussex.* He wa. obliged to comply, and the angry father then finding from his Conversation how determined he was to marry no other woman, sent him for a fortnight to the Isle of Wight* under the care of the Family Chaplin, with the hope of overcoming his Constancy by Time and Absence in a foreign Country. They accordingly prepared to bid a long adieu to England—The young Nobleman was not allowed to see his Rosa. They set sail—A storm arose which baffled the arts of the Seamen. The Vessel was wrecked on the coast of Calshot* and every Soul on board perished. This sad Event soon reached Carlisle, and the beautiful Rose was affected by it, beyond the power of Expression. It was to soften her affliction by obtaining a picture of her unfortunate Lover that her brother undertook a Journey into Sussex, where he hoped that his petition would not be rejected, by the severe yet afflicted Father. When he reached Evelyn he was not many miles from —— Castle, but the pleasing events which befell him in that place had for a while made him totally forget the object of his Journey and his unhappy Sister. The little incident of the rose however brought everything concerning her to his recollection again, and he bitterly repented his neglect. He returned to the house immediately and agitated by Greif, Apprehension and Shame wrote the following Letter to Rosa.

July 14th——. Evelyn

My dearest Sister,

As it is now four months since I left Carlisle, during which period I have not once written to you, You will perhaps unjustly accuse me of Neglect and Forgetfulness. Alas! I blush when I own the truth of your Accusation.—— Yet if you are still alive, do not think too harshly of me, or suppose that I could for a moment forget the situation of my Rose. Beleive me I will forget you no longer, but will hasten as soon as possible to —— Castle if I find by your answer that you are still alive. Maria joins me in every dutiful and affectionate wish, and I am yours sincerely

F. Gower.

He waited in the most anxious expectation for an answer to his Letter, which arrived as soon as the great distance from Carlisle would admit of.——But alas, it came not from Rosa.

Carlisle July 17th

Dear Brother

My Mother has taken the liberty of opening your Letter to poor Rose, as she has been dead these six weeks. Your long absence and continued Silence gave us all great uneasiness and hastened her to the Grave. Your Journey to —— Castle therefore may be spared. You do not tell us

where you have been since the time of your quitting
Carlisle, nor in any way account for your tedious absence
which gives us some surprise. We all unite in Compliments
to Maria, and beg to know who she is—.

Y^r affec:^{te} Sister
M. Gower.

This Letter, by which Mr Gower was obliged to attribute
to his own conduct, his Sister's death, was so violent a shock
to his feelings, that in spite of his living at Evelyn where
Illness was scarcely ever heard of, he was attacked by a fit of
the gout,* which confining him to his own room afforded an
opportunity to Maria of shining in that favourite character
of Sir Charles Grandison's, a nurse.* No woman could ever
appear more amiable than Maria did under such circumstances, and at last by her unremitting attentions had the
pleasure of seeing him gradually recover the use of his feet.
It was a blessing by no means lost on him, for he was no
sooner in a condition to leave the house, that he mounted
his horse, and rode to —— Castle, wishing to find whether
his Lordship softened by his Son's death, might have been
brought to consent to the match, had both *he* and Rosa been
alive. His amiable Maria followed him with her Eyes till she
could see him no longer, and then sinking into her chair
overwhelmed with Greif, found that in his absence she
could enjoy no comfort.

Mr Gower arrived late in the evening at the castle, which
was situated on a woody Eminence commanding a beautiful
prospect of the Sea.* Mr Gower did not dislike the
situation, tho' it was certainly greatly inferior to that of his
own house. There was an irregularity in the fall of the
ground, and a profusion of old Timber which appeared to
him illsuited to the stile of the Castle, for it being a building
of a very ancient date, he thought it required the Paddock of
Evelyn lodge to form a Contrast,* and enliven the structure.
The gloomy appearance of the old Castle frowning on him
as he followed it's winding approach, struck him with
terror. Nor did he think himself safe, till he was introduced
into the Drawing room where the Family were assembled to

tea. Mr Gower was a perfect stranger to every one in the
Circle but tho' he was always timid in the Dark and easily
terrified when alone, he did not want that more necessary
and more noble courage which enabled him without a
Blush to enter a large party of superior Rank, whom he had
never seen before, and to take his Seat amongst them with
perfect Indifference. The name of Gower was not unknown
to Lord ——. He felt distressed and astonished; Yet rose
and received him with all the politeness of a well-bred Man.
Lady —— who felt a deeper Sorrow at the loss of her Son,
than his Lordship's harder heart was capable of, could
hardly keep her Seat when she found that he was the
Brother of her lamented Henry's Rosa. 'My Lord,' said Mr
Gower as soon as he was seated, 'You are perhaps surprised
at receiving a visit from a Man whom you could not have
the least expectation of seeing here. But my Sister, my
unfortunate Sister, is the real cause of my thus troubling
you: That luckless Girl is now no more—and tho' *she* can
receive no pleasure from the intelligence, yet for the
satisfaction of her Family I wish to know whether the Death
of this unhappy Pair has made an impression on your heart
sufficiently strong to obtain that consent to their Marriage
which in happier circumstances you would not be persuaded
to give Supposing that they now were both alive.' His
Lordship seemed lossed in astonishment. Lady —— could
not support the mention of her son, and left the room in
tears; the rest of the Family remained attentively listening,
almost persuaded that Mr Gower was distracted. 'Mr
Gower,' replied his Lordship 'This is a very odd question—
It appears to me that you are supposing an impossibility—
No one can more sincerely regret the death of my Son than I
have always done, and it gives me great concern to know
that Miss Gower's was hastened by his——. Yet to suppose
them alive is destroying at once the Motive for a change in
my sentiments concerning the affair.' 'My Lord,' replied
Mr Gower in anger, 'I see that you are a most inflexible
Man, and that not even the death of your Son can make you
wish his future Life happy. I will no longer detain your
Lordship. I see, I plainly see that you are a very vile Man—

And now I have the honour of wishing all your Lordships, and Ladyships a good Night.' He immediately left the room, forgetting in the heat of his Anger the lateness of the hour, which at any other time would have made him tremble, and leaving the whole Company unanimous in their opinion of his being Mad. When however he had mounted his horse and the great Gates of the Castle had shut him out, he felt an universal tremor through out his whole frame. If we consider his Situation indeed, alone, on horseback, as late in the year as August,* and in the day, as nine o'clock, with no light to direct him but that of the Moon almost full, and the Stars which alarmed him by their twinkling, who can refrain from pitying him?—No house within a quarter of a mile, and a Gloomy Castle blackened by the deep shade of Walnuts and Pines,* behind him.—He felt indeed almost distracted with his fears, and shutting his Eyes till he arrived at the Village to prevent his seeing either Gipsies or Ghosts, he rode on a full gallop all the way.

On his return home, he rang the housebell, but no one appeared, a second time he rang, but the door was not opened, a third and a fourth with as little success, when observing the dining parlour window open he leapt in, and persued his way through the house till he reached Maria's Dressing room, where he found all the Servants assembled at tea. Surprized at so very unusual a sight, he fainted, on his recovery he found himself on the Sofa, with his wife's maid kneeling by him, chafing his temples with Hungary water*—. From her he learned that his beloved Maria had been so much grieved at his departure that she died of a broken heart about 3 hours after his departure.

He then became sufficiently composed to give necessary orders for her funeral which took place the Monday following this being the Saturday—When Mr Gower had settled the order of the procession* he set out himself* to Carlisle, to give vent to his sorrow in the bosom of his family—He arrived there in high health and spirits, after a delightful journey of 3 days and a ½—What was his surprize on entering the Breakfast parlour to see Rosa, his beloved Rosa, seated on a Sofa; at the sight of him she fainted and would have fallen had not a Gentleman sitting with his back to the door, started up and saved her from sinking to the ground—She very soon came to herself and then introduced this gentleman to her Brother as her Husband a Mr Davenport—

'But my dearest Rosa,' said the astonished Gower, 'I thought you were dead and buried.' 'Why, my dear Frederick,' replied Rosa 'I wished you to think so, hoping that you would spread the report about the country and it would thus by some means reach —— Castle—By this I hoped some how or other to touch the hearts of its inhabitants. It was not till the day before yesterday that I heard of the death of my beloved Henry which I learned from Mr Davenport who concluded by offering me his hand. I accepted it with transport, and was married yesterday—.' Mr Gower, embraced his sister and shook hands with Mr Davenport, he then took a stroll into the town—As he passed by a public house he called for a pot of beer,* which was brought him immediately by his old friend Mrs Willis—

Great was his astonishment at seeing Mrs Willis in Carlisle. But not forgetful of the respect he owed her, he dropped on one knee, and received the frothy cup from her, more grateful to *him* than Nectar*—He instantly made her an offer of his hand and heart, which she graciously condescended to accept, telling him that she was only on a visit to her cousin, who kept the *Anchor** and should be ready to return to Evelyn, whenever he chose—The next morning they were married and immediately proceeded to Evelyn—When he reached home, he recollected that he had never written to Mr and Mrs Webb to inform them of the death of their daughter, which he rightly supposed they knew nothing of, as they never took in any newspapers—He immediately dispatched the following Letter—

Evelyn—Aug^st 19th 1809—

Dearest Madam,

How can words express the poignancy of my feelings! Our Maria, our beloved Maria is no more, she breathed her

last, on Saturday the 12th of Aug^st—I see you now in an
agony of grief lamenting not your own, but my loss—Rest
satisfied I am happy, possessed of my lovely Sarah what
more can I wish for?—

I remain

respectfully Yours

F. Gower

Westgate Buil^gs*   Aug^st 22nd

Generous, best of Men

how truly we rejoice to hear of your present welfare and
happiness! and how truly grateful are we for your unexampled
generosity in writing to condole with us on the late unlucky
accident which befel our Maria—I have enclosed a draught
on our banker for 30 pounds, which Mr Webb joins with me
in entreating you and the aimiable Sarah to accept—

Your most grateful

Anne Augusta Webb

Mr and Mrs Gower resided many years at Evelyn
enjoying perfect happiness the just reward of their virtues.
The only alteration which took place at Evelyn was that Mr
and Mrs Davenport settled there in Mrs Willis's former
abode and were for many years the proprietors of the White
Horse Inn*—

Catharine,
or the Bower

To Miss Austen*

Madam

Encouraged by your warm patronage of The beautiful Cassandra, and The History of England, which through your generous support, have obtained a place in every library in the Kingdom, and run through threescore Editions,* I take the liberty of begging the same Exertions in favour of the following Novel, which I humbly flatter myself, possesses Merit beyond any already published, or any that will ever in future appear, except such as may proceed from the pen of Your Most Grateful Humble Servt

The Author

Steventon August 1792—

Catharine had the misfortune, as many heroines have had before her,* of losing her Parents when she was very young, and of being brought up under the care of a Maiden Aunt, who while she tenderly loved her, watched over her conduct with so scrutinizing a severity, as to make it very doubtful to many people, and to Catharine amongst the rest, whether she loved her or not.* She had frequently been deprived of a real pleasure through this jealous Caution, had been sometimes obliged to relinquish a Ball because an Officer* was to be there, or to dance with a Partner of her Aunt's introduction in preference to one of her own Choice. But her Spirits were naturally good, and not easily depressed, and she possessed such a fund of vivacity and good humour as could only be damped by some very serious vexation.— Besides these antidotes against every disappointment, and consolations under them, she had another, which afforded her constant releif in all her misfortunes, and that was a fine shady Bower,* the work of her own infantine* Labours assisted by those of two young Companions who had resided in the same village—. To this Bower, which terminated a very pleasant and retired walk in her Aunt's Garden, she always wandered whenever anything disturbed her, and it possessed such a charm over her senses, as constantly to tranquillize her mind and quiet her spirits— Solitude and reflection might perhaps have had the same effect in her Bed Chamber, yet Habit had so strengthened the idea which Fancy had first suggested, that such a thought never occurred to Kitty who was firmly persuaded that her Bower alone could restore her to herself. Her imagination was warm, and in her Freindships, as well as in the whole tenure* of her Mind, she was enthousiastic.* This beloved Bower had been the united work of herself and two amiable Girls, for whom since her earliest Years, she had felt the tenderest regard. They were the daughters of the Clergyman of the Parish with whose Family, while it had continued there, her Aunt had been on the most intimate terms, and the little Girls tho' separated for the greatest part of the Year by the different Modes of their Education, were constantly together during the holidays of the Miss Wynnes. In those days of happy Childhood, now so often regretted by Kitty, this arbour had been formed, and separated perhaps for ever from these dear freinds, it encouraged more than any other place the tender and Melancholy recollections of hours rendered pleasant by *them*, at once so sorrowful, yet so soothing! It was now two years since the death of Mr Wynne, and the consequent dispersion of his Family who had been left by it in great distress. They had been reduced to a state of absolute dependance on some relations, who though very opulent and very nearly connected with them, had with difficulty been prevailed on to contribute anything towards their Support.* Mrs Wynne was fortunately spared the knowledge and participation of their distress, by her release from a painful illness a few months before the death of her husband.—The eldest daughter had been obliged to accept the offer of one of her cousins to equip her for the East Indies,* and tho' infinitely against her inclinations had been necessitated to embrace the only possibility that was offered to her, of a Maintenance;* Yet it was *one*, so opposite to all her ideas of Propriety, so contrary to her Wishes, so repugnant to her feelings, that she would almost have preferred Servitude to it, had Choice been allowed her—. Her personal Attractions had gained her a husband as soon as she had arrived at Bengal,* and she had now been married nearly a twelve month. Splendidly, yet unhappily married. United to a Man of double her own age, whose disposition was not amiable, and whose Manners were unpleasing, though his Character was respectable. Kitty had heard twice from her freind since her marriage, but her Letters were always unsatisfactory, and though she did not openly avow her feelings, yet every line proved her to be Unhappy. She spoke with pleasure of nothing, but of those Amusements which they had shared together and which could return no more, and seemed to have no happiness in veiw but that of returning to England again. Her sister had been taken by another relation the Dowager* Lady Halifax as a companion* to her Daughters, and had accompanied her family into Scotland about the same time of Cecilia's leaving England. From Mary therefore Kitty had the power of hearing more frequently, but her Letters were scarcely more comfortable—. There was not indeed that hopelessness of sorrow in her situation as in her sister's; she was not married, and could yet look forward to a change in her circumstances, but situated for the present without any immediate hope of it, in a family where, tho' all were her relations she had no freind, she wrote usually in depressed Spirits, which her separation from her Sister and her Sister's Marriage had greatly contributed to make so.— Divided thus from the two she loved best on Earth, while Cecilia and Mary were still more endeared to her by their loss, everything that brought a remembrance of them was doubly cherished, and the Shrubs they had planted, and the keepsakes they had given were rendered sacred—. The living of Chetwynde was now in the possession of a Mr

Dudley,* whose Family unlike the Wynnes were productive only of vexation and trouble to Mrs Percival and her Neice. Mr Dudley, who was the Younger Son of a very noble Family, of a Family more famed for their Pride than their opulence, tenacious of his Dignity, and jealous of his rights, was forever quarrelling, if not with Mrs Percival herself, with her Steward and Tenants concerning tythes,* and with the principal Neighbours themselves concerning the respect and parade,* he exacted. His Wife, an ill-educated, untaught Woman of ancient family, was proud of that family almost without knowing why, and like him too was haughty and quarrelsome, without considering for what. Their only daughter, who inherited the ignorance, the insolence, and pride of her parents, was from that Beauty of which she was unreasonably vain, considered by them as an irresistable Creature, and looked up to as the future restorer, by a Splendid Marriage, of the dignity which their reduced Situation and Mr Dudley's being obliged to take orders for a Country Living had so much lessened. They at once despised the Percivals as people of mean family, and envied them as people of fortune. They were jealous of their being more respected than themselves and while they affected to consider them as of no Consequence, were continually seeking to lessen them in the opinion of the Neighbourhood by Scandalous and Malicious reports. Such a family as this, was ill-calculated to console Kitty for the loss of the Wynnes, or to fill up by their Society, those occasionally irksome hours which in so retired a Situation would sometimes occur for want of a Companion. Her aunt was most excessively fond of her, and miserable if she saw her for a moment out of spirits; Yet she lived in such constant apprehension of her marrying imprudently if she were allowed the opportunity of choosing, and was so dissatisfied with her behaviour when she saw her with Young Men, for it was, from her natural disposition remarkably open and unreserved, that though she frequently wished for her Neice's sake, that the Neighbourhood were larger, and that She had used herself to mix more with it, yet the recollection of there being young Men in almost

every Family in it, always conquered the Wish. The same
fears that prevented Mrs Percival's joining much in the
Society of her Neighbours, led her equally to avoid inviting
her relations to spend any time in her House—She had
therefore constantly regretted the annual attempt of a
distant relation to visit her at Chetwynde, as there was a
young Man in the Family of whom she had heard many
traits that alarmed her. This Son was however now on his
travels, and the repeated solicitations of Kitty, joined to a
consciousness of having declined with too little Ceremony
the frequent overtures of her Freinds to be admitted, and a
real wish to see them herself, easily prevailed on her to press
with great Earnestness the pleasure of a visit from them
during the Summer. Mr and Mrs Stanley* were accordingly
to come, and Catharine, in having an object to look forward
to, a something to expect that must inevitably releive the
dullness of a constant tete a tete with her Aunt, was so
delighted, and her spirits so elevated, that for the three or
four days immediately preceding their Arrival, she could
scarcely fix herself to any employment. In this point Mrs
Percival always thought her defective, and frequently
complained of a want of Steadiness and perseverance in her
occupations, which were by no means congenial to the
eagerness of Kitty's Disposition, and perhaps not often met
with in any young person. The tediousness too of her Aunt's
conversation and the want of agreable Companions greatly
increased this desire of Change in her Employments, for
Kitty found herself much sooner tired of Reading, Working,
or Drawing, in Mrs Percival's parlour than in her own
Arbour, where Mrs Percival for fear of its being damp never
accompanied her.

As her Aunt prided herself on the exact propriety and
Neatness with which everything in her Family was conducted,
and had no higher Satisfaction than that of knowing her
house to be always in complete Order, as her fortune was
good, and her Establishment* Ample, few were the
preparations necessary for the reception of her Visitors. The
day of their arrival so long expected, at length came, and
the Noise of the Coach and 4 as it drove round the sweep,*

was to Catharine a more interesting sound, than the Music of an Italian Opera, which to most Heroines is the hight of Enjoyment.* Mr and Mrs Stanley were people of Large Fortune and high Fashion. He was a Member of the house of Commons, and they were therefore most agreably necessitated to reside half the Year in Town;* where Miss Stanley had been attended by the most capital Masters from the time of her being six years old to the last Spring, which comprehending a period of twelve Years had been dedicated to the acquirement of Accomplishments which were now to be displayed and in a few Years entirely neglected. She was elegant in her appearance, rather handsome, and naturally not deficient in Abilities; but those Years which ought to have been spent in the attainment of useful knowledge and Mental Improvement, had been all bestowed in learning Drawing, Italian and Music, more especially the latter, and she now united to these Accomplishments, an Understanding unimproved by reading and a Mind totally devoid either of Taste or Judgement.* Her temper was by Nature good, but unassisted by reflection, she had neither patience under Disappointment, nor could sacrifice her own inclinations to promote the happiness of others. All her Ideas were towards the Elegance of her appearance, the fashion of her dress, and the Admiration she wished them to excite. She professed a love of Books without Reading, was Lively without Wit, and generally Good humoured without Merit. Such was Camilla Stanley; and Catharine, who was prejudiced by her appearance, and who from her solitary Situation was ready to like anyone, tho' her Understanding and Judgement would not otherwise have been easily satisfied, felt almost convinced when she saw her, that Miss Stanley would be the very companion She wanted, and in some degree make amends for the loss of Cecilia and Mary Wynne. She therefore attached herself to Camilla from the first day of her arrival, and from being the only young People in the house, they were by inclination constant Companions. Kitty was herself a great reader, tho' perhaps not a very deep one,* and felt therefore highly delighted to find that

Miss Stanley was equally fond of it. Eager to know that their sentiments as to Books were similar, she very soon began questioning her new Acquaintance on the subject; but though She was well read in Modern history* herself, she chose rather to speak first of Books of a lighter kind, of Books universally read and Admired.

'You have read Mrs Smith's Novels,* I suppose?' said she to her Companion—. 'Oh! Yes,' replied the other, 'and I am quite delighted with them—They are the sweetest things in the world—' 'And which do you prefer of them?' 'Oh! dear, I think there is no comparison between them— Emmeline* is *so much* better than any of the others—' 'Many people think so, I know; but there does not appear so great a disproportion in their Merits to *me*; do you think it is better written?' 'Oh! I do not know anything about *that*— but it is better in *every thing*—Besides, Ethelinde* is so long—' 'That is a very common Objection I believe,' said Kitty, 'but for my own part, if a book is well written, I always find it too short.' 'So do I, only I get tired of it before it is finished.' 'But did not you find the story of Ethelinde very interesting? And the Descriptions of Grasmere,* are not they Beautiful?' 'Oh! I missed them all, because I was in such a hurry to know the end of it'—. Then from an easy transition she added, 'We are going to the Lakes* this Autumn, and I am quite Mad with Joy; Sir Henry Devereux has promised to go with us, and that will make it so pleasant, you know—'

'I dare say it will; but I think it is a pity that Sir Henry's powers of pleasing were not reserved for an occasion where they might be more wanted.—However I quite envy you the pleasure of such a Scheme.'

'Oh! I am quite delighted with the thoughts of it; I can think of nothing else. I assure you I have done nothing for this last Month but plan what Cloathes I should take with me, and I have at last determined to take very few indeed besides my travelling Dress,* and so I advise you to do, when ever you go; for I intend in case we should fall in with any races, or stop at Matlock* or Scarborough,* to have some Things made for the occasion.'

'You intend then to go into Yorkshire?'

'I beleive not—indeed I know nothing of the Route, for I never trouble myself about such things. I only know that we are to go from Derbyshire to Matlock and Scarborough, but to which of them first, I neither know nor care—I am in hopes of meeting some particular freinds of mine at Scarborough—Augusta told me in her last Letter that Sir Peter talked of going; but then you know that is so uncertain. I cannot bear Sir Peter, he is such a horrid Creature—'

'He *is*, is he?' said Kitty, not knowing what else to say.

'Oh! he is quite Shocking.' Here the Conversation was interrupted, and Kitty was left in a painful Uncertainty, as to the particulars of Sir Peter's Character; She knew only that he was Horrid and Shocking, but why, and in what, yet remained to be discovered. She could scarcely resolve what to think of her new Acquaintance; She appeared to be shamefully ignorant as to the Geography of England, if she had understood her right, and equally devoid of Taste and Information. Kitty was however unwilling to decide hastily; she was at once desirous of doing Miss Stanley justice, and of having her own Wishes in her answered; she determined therefore to suspend all Judgement for some time. After Supper, the Conversation turning on the state of Affairs in the political World, Mrs Percival, who was firmly of opinion that the whole race of Mankind were degenerating, said that for her part, Everything she beleived was going to rack and ruin, all order was destroyed over the face of the World,* The house of Commons she heard did not break up sometimes till five in the Morning, and Depravity never was so general before; concluding with a wish that she might live to see the Manners of the People in Queen Elizabeth's reign, restored again. 'Well, Ma'am,' said her Neice, 'but I hope you do not mean with the times to restore Queen Elizabeth herself.'

'Queen Elizabeth,' said Mrs Stanley, who never hazarded a remark on History that was not well founded, 'lived to a good old age, and was a very Clever Woman.' 'True, Ma'am,' said Kitty; 'but I do not consider either of those

Circumstances as meritorious in herself, and they are very far from making me wish her return, for if she were to come again with the same Abilities and the same good Constitution She might do as much Mischeif and last as long as she did before—.'* Then turning to Camilla who had been sitting very silent for some time, she added, 'What do *you* think of Elizabeth, Miss Stanley? I hope you will not defend her.'

'Oh! dear,' said Miss Stanley, 'I know nothing of Politics,* and cannot bear to hear them mentioned.' Kitty started at this repulse, but made no answer; that Miss Stanley must be ignorant of what she could not distinguish from Politics she felt perfectly convinced.—She retired to her own room, perplexed in her opinion about her new Acquaintance, and fearful of her being very unlike Cecilia and Mary. She arose the next morning to experience a fuller conviction of this, and every future day encreased it—. She found no variety in her conversation; She received no information from her but in fashions, and no Amusement but in her performance on the Harpsichord;* and after repeated endeavours to find her what she wished, she was obliged to give up the attempt and to consider it as fruitless. There had occasionally appeared a something like humour in Camilla which had inspired her with hopes, that she might at least have a natural genius, tho' not an improved one, but these Sparklings of Wit happened so seldom, and were so ill-supported that she was at last convinced of their being merely accidental. All her stock of knowledge was exhausted in a very few Days, and when Kitty had learnt from her, how large their house in Town was, when the fashionable Amusements began, who were the celebrated Beauties and who the best Millener, Camilla had nothing further to teach, except the Characters of any of her Acquaintance as they occurred in Conversation, which was done with equal Ease and Brevity, by saying that the person was either the sweetest Creature in the world, and one of whom she was doatingly fond, or horrid, shocking and not fit to be seen.*

As Catharine was very desirous of gaining every possible information as to the Characters of the Halifax Family,*

and concluded that Miss Stanley must be acquainted with
them, as she seemed to be so with every one of any
Consequence, she took an opportunity as Camilla was one
day enumerating all the people of rank that her Mother
visited, of asking her whether Lady Halifax were among the
number.

'Oh! Thank you for reminding me of her; She is the
sweetest Woman in the world, and one of our most intimate
Acquaintance, I do not suppose there is a day passes during
the six Months that we are in Town, but what we see each
other in the course of it—. And I correspond with all the
Girls.'

'They *are* then a very pleasant Family?' said Kitty. 'They
ought to be so indeed, to allow of such frequent Meetings,
or all Conversation must be at end.'

'Oh! dear, not at all,' said Miss Stanley, 'for sometimes
we do not speak to each other for a Month together. We
meet perhaps only in Public,* and then you know we are
often not able to get near enough; but in that case we always
nod and smile.'

'Which does just as well—. But I was going to ask you
whether you have ever seen a Miss Wynne with them?'

'I know who you mean perfectly—she wears a blue
hat*—. I have frequently seen her in Brook Street,* when I
have been at Lady Halifax's Balls—She gives one every
Month during the Winter*—. But only think how good it is
in her to take care of Miss Wynne, for she is a very distant
relation, and so poor that, as Miss Halifax told me, her
Mother was obliged to find her in Cloathes.* Is not it
shameful?'

'That she should be so poor? it is indeed, with such
wealthy connexions as the Family have.'

'Oh! no; I mean, was not it shameful in Mr Wynne to
leave his Children so distressed, when he had actually the
Living of Chetwynde and two or three Curacies,* and only
four Children to provide for—. What would he have done if
he had had ten, as many people have?'

'He would have given them all a good Education and
have left them all equally poor.'

'Well I do think there never was so lucky a Family. Sir George Fitzgibbon you know sent the eldest girl to India entirely at his own Expence, where they say she is most nobly married and the happiest Creature in the World— Lady Halifax you see has taken care of the youngest and treats her as if she were her Daughter; She does not go out into Public with her to be sure; but then she is always present when her Ladyship gives her Balls, and nothing can be kinder to her than Lady Halifax is; she would have taken her to Cheltenham* last year, if there had been room enough at the Lodgings, and therefore I do not think that *she* can have anything to complain of. Then there are the two Sons; one of them the Bishop of M—— has got into the Army as a Leiutenant I suppose; and the other is extremely well off I know, for I have a Notion that somebody puts him to School somewhere in Wales.* Perhaps you knew them when they lived here?'

'Very well, We met as often as your Family and the Halifaxes do in Town, but as we seldom had any difficulty in getting near enough to speak, we seldom parted with merely a Nod and a Smile. They were indeed a most charming Family, and I beleive have scarcely their Equals in the World; The Neighbours we now have at the Parsonage, appear to more disadvantage in coming after them.'

'Oh! horrid Wretches! I wonder you can endure them.'

'Why, what would you have one do?'

'Oh! Lord, If I were in your place, I should abuse them all day long.'

'So I do, but it does no good.'

'Well, I declare it is quite a pity that they should be suffered to live. I wish my Father would propose knocking all their Brains out, some day or other when he is in the House. So abominably proud of their Family! And I dare say after all, that there is nothing particular in it.'

'Why Yes, I beleive thay *have* reason to value themselves on it, if any body has; for you know he is Lord Amyatt's Brother.'

'Oh! I know all that very well, but it is no reason for their being so horrid. I remember I met Miss Dudley last Spring with Lady Amyatt at Ranelagh,* and she had such a frightful Cap* on, that I have never been able to bear any of them since.—And so you used to think the Wynnes very pleasant?'

'You speak as if their being so were doubtful! Pleasant! Oh! they were every thing that could interest and attach. It is not in my power to do Justice to their Merits, tho' not to feel them, I think must be impossible. They have unfitted me for any Society but their own!'

'Well, That is just what I think of the Miss Halifaxes; by the bye, I must write to Caroline tomorrow, and I do not know what to say to her. The Barlows too are just such other sweet Girls; but I wish Augusta's hair was not so dark. I cannot bear Sir Peter—Horrid Wretch! He is *always* laid up with the Gout, which is exceedingly disagreable to the Family.'

'And perhaps not very pleasant to *himself*—. But as to the Wynnes; do you really think them very fortunate?'

'Do I? Why, does not every body? Miss Halifax and Caroline and Maria all say that they are the luckiest Creatures in the World. So does Sir George Fitzgibbon and so do Every body.'

'That is, Every body who have themselves conferred an obligation on them. But do you call it lucky, for a Girl of Genius and Feeling to be sent in quest of a Husband to Bengal, to be married there to a Man of whose Disposition she has no opportunity of judging till her Judgement is of no use to her, who may be a Tyrant, or a Fool or both for what she knows to the Contrary.* Do you call *that* fortunate?'

'I know nothing of all that; I only know that it was extremely good in Sir George to fit her out and pay her Passage, and that she would not have found Many who would have done the same.'

'I wish she had not found *one*,' said Kitty with great Eagerness, 'she might then have remained in England and been happy.'

'Well, I cannot conceive the hardship of going out in a very agreable Manner with two or three sweet Girls for

Companions, having a delightful voyage to Bengal or Barbadoes* or wherever it is, and being married soon after one's arrival to a very charming Man immensely rich—. I see No hardship in all that.'

'Your representation of the Affair,' said Kitty laughing, 'certainly gives a very different idea of it from Mine. But supposing all this to be true, still, as it was by no means certain that she would be so fortunate either in her voyage, her Companions, or her husband; in being obliged to run the risk of their proving very different, she undoubtedly experienced a great hardship—. Besides, to a Girl of any Delicacy, the voyage in itself, since the object of it is so universally known, is a punishment that needs no other to make it very severe.'

'I do not see that at all. She is not the first Girl who has gone to the East Indies for a Husband, and I declare I should think it very good fun if I were as poor.'

'I beleive you would think very differently *then*. But at least you will not defend her Sister's situation? Dependant even for her Cloathes on the bounty of others, who of course do not pity her, as by your own account, they consider her as very fortunate.'

'You are extremely nice* upon my word; Lady Halifax is a delightful Woman, and one of the sweetest tempered Creatures in the World; I am sure I have every reason to speak well of her, for we are under most amazing Obligations to her. She has frequently chaproned me when my Mother has been indisposed, and last Spring she lent me her own horse three times, which was a prodigious favour, for it is the most beautiful Creature that ever was seen, and I am the only person she ever lent it to.'

'And then,' continued she, 'the Miss Halifaxes are quite delightful. Maria is one of the cleverest Girls that ever were known—Draws in Oils,* and plays anything by sight. She promised me one of her Drawings before I left Town, but I entirely forgot to ask her for it. I would give anything to have one.'

'But was not it very odd,' said Kitty, 'that the Bishop should send Charles Wynne to sea, when he must have had a much better chance of providing for him in the Church, which was the profession that Charles liked best, and the one for which his Father had intended him? The Bishop I know had often promised Mr Wynne a living, and as he never gave him one, I think it was incumbant on him to transfer the promise to his Son.'

'I beleive you think he ought to have resigned his Bishopric to him; you seem determined to be dissatisfied with every thing that has been done for them.'

'Well,' said Kitty, 'this is a subject on which we shall never agree, and therefore it will be useless to continue it farther, or to mention it again—' She then left the room, and running out of the House was soon in her dear Bower where she could indulge in peace all her affectionate Anger against the relations of the Wynnes, which was greatly heightened by finding from Camilla that they were in general considered as having acted particularly well by them—. She amused herself for some time in Abusing, and Hating them all, with great spirit, and when this tribute to her regard for the Wynnes, was paid, and the Bower began to have its usual influence over her Spirits, she contributed towards settling them, by taking out a book, for she had always one about her, and reading—. She had been so employed for nearly an hour, when Camilla came running towards her with great Eagerness, and apparently great Pleasure—. 'Oh! my Dear Catharine,' said she, half out of Breath—'I have such delightful News for You—But you shall guess what it is—We are all the happiest Creatures in the World; would you beleive it, the Dudleys have sent us an invitation to a Ball at their own House—. What Charming People they are! I had no idea of there being so much sense in the whole Family—I declare I quite doat upon them—. And it happens so fortunately too, for I expect a new Cap from Town tomorrow which will just do for a Ball—Gold Net*—It will be a most angelic thing— Every Body will be longing for the pattern—'. The expectation of a Ball was indeed very agreable intelligence to Kitty, who fond of Dancing and seldom able to enjoy it, had reason to feel even greater pleasure in it than her

Freind; for to *her*, it was now no novelty—. Camilla's delight however was by no means inferior to Kitty's, and she rather expressed the most of the two. The Cap came and every other preparation was soon completed; while these were in agitation the Days passed gaily away, but when Directions were no longer necessary, Taste could no longer be displayed, and Difficulties no longer overcome, the short period that intervened before the day of the Ball hung heavily on their hands, and every hour was too long. The very few Times that Kitty had ever enjoyed the Amusement of Dancing was an excuse for *her* impatience, and an apology for the Idleness it occasioned to a Mind naturally very Active; but her Freind without such a plea was infinitely worse than herself. She could do nothing but wander from the house to the Garden, and from the garden to the avenue, wondering when Thursday would come, which she might easily have ascertained, and counting the hours as they passed which served only to lengthen them—. They retired to their rooms in high Spirits on Wednesday night, but Kitty awoke the next Morning with a violent Toothake. It was in vain that she endeavoured at first to deceive herself; her feelings were witnesses too acute of it's reality; with as little success did she try to sleep it off, for the pain she suffered prevented her closing her Eyes—. She then summoned her Maid and with the Assistance of the Housekeeper, every remedy that the receipt book* or the head of the latter contained, was tried, but ineffectually; for though for a short time releived by them, the pain still returned. She was now obliged to give up the endeavour, and to reconcile herself not only to the pain of a Toothake, but to the loss of a Ball; and though she had with so much eagerness looked forward to the day of its arrival, had received such pleasure in the necessary preparations, and promised herself so much delight in it, Yet she was not so totally void of philosophy as many Girls of her age, might have been in her situation. She considered that there were Misfortunes of a much greater magnitude than the loss of a Ball, experienced every day by some part of Mortality,* and that the time might come when She would herself look back with Wonder and perhaps with Envy on her having known no greater vexation.* By such reflections as these, she soon reasoned herself into as much Resignation and Patience as the pain she suffered, would allow of, which after all was the greatest Misfortune of the two, and told the sad Story when she entered the Breakfast room, with tolerable Composure. Mrs Percival more greived for her toothake than her Disappointment, as she feared that it would not be possible to prevent her Dancing with a *Man* if she went, was eager to try everything that had already been applied to alleviate the pain, while at the same time She declared it was impossible for her to leave the House. Miss Stanley who joined to her concern for her Freind, felt a mixture of Dread lest her Mother's proposal that they should all remain at home, might be accepted, was very violent in her sorrow on the occasion, and though her apprehensions on the subject were soon quieted by Kitty's protesting that sooner than allow any one to stay with her, she would herself go, she continued to lament it with such unceasing vehemence as at last drove Kitty to her own room. Her Fears for herself being now entirely dissipated left her more than ever at leisure to pity and persecute her Freind who tho' safe when in her own room, was frequently removing from it to some other in hopes of being more free from pain, and then had no opportunity of escaping her—.

'To be sure, there never was anything so shocking,' said Camilla; 'To come on such a day too! For one would not have minded it you know had it been at *any other* time. But it always is so. I never was at a Ball in my Life, but what something happened to prevent somebody from going! I wish there were no such things as Teeth in the World; they are nothing but plagues to one, and I dare say that People might easily invent something to eat with instead of them; Poor Thing! what pain you are in! I declare it is quite Shocking to look at you. But you won't have it out, will you? For Heaven's sake don't; for there is nothing I dread so much. I declare I had rather undergo the greatest Tortures in the World than have a tooth drawn.* Well! how patiently you do bear it! how can you be so quiet? Lord, if I were in your place I should make such a fuss, there would be no bearing me. I should torment you to Death.'

'So you do, as it is,' thought Kitty.

'For my own part, Catharine' said Mrs Percival 'I have not a doubt but that you caught this toothake by sitting so much in that Arbour, for it is always damp. I know it has ruined your Constitution entirely; and indeed I do not beleive it has been of much service to mine; I sate down in it last May to rest myself, and I have never been quite well since—. I shall order John* to pull it all down I assure you.'

'I know you will not do that, Ma'am,' said Kitty, 'as you must be convinced how unhappy it would make me.'

'You talk very ridiculously, Child; it is all whim and Nonsense. Why cannot you fancy this room an Arbour?'

'Had this room been built by Cecilia and Mary, I should have valued it equally, Ma'am, for it is not merely the name of an Arbour, which charms me.'

'Why indeed, Mrs Percival,' said Mrs Stanley, 'I must think that Catharine's affection for her Bower is the effect of a Sensibility that does her Credit. I love to see a Freindship between Young Persons and always consider it as a sure mark of an aimiable affectionate disposition. I have from Camilla's infancy taught her to think the same, and have taken great pains to introduce her to young people of her own age who were likely to be worthy of her regard. Nothing forms the taste more than sensible and Elegant Letters—. Lady Halifax thinks just like me—. Camilla corresponds with her Daughters, and I beleive I may venture to say that they are none of them *the worse* for it.'

These ideas were too modern to suit Mrs Percival who considered a correspondence between Girls as productive of no good, and as the frequent origin of imprudence and Error by the effect of pernicious advice and bad Example.* She could not therefore refrain from saying that for her part, she had lived fifty Years in the world without having ever had a correspondent, and did not find herself at all the less respectable for it—. Mrs Stanley could say nothing in answer to this, but her Daughter who was less governed by

Propriety, said in her thoughtless way, 'But who knows what you might have been, Ma'am, if you *had* had a Correspondent; perhaps it would have made you quite a different Creature. I declare I would not be without those I have for all the World. It is the greatest delight of my Life, and you cannot think how much their Letters have formed my taste as Mama says, for I hear from them generally every week.'

'You received a Letter from Augusta Barlow to day, did not you, my Love?' said her Mother—. 'She writes remarkably well I know.'

'Oh! Yes Ma'am, the most delightful Letter you ever heard of. She sends me a long account of the new Regency* walking dress* Lady Susan has given her, and it is so beautiful that I am quite dieing with envy for it.'

'Well, I am prodigiously happy to hear such pleasing news of my young freind; I have a high regard for Augusta, and most sincerely partake in the general Joy on the occasion. But does she say nothing else? it seemed to be a long Letter—Are they to be at Scarborough?'

'Oh! Lord, she never once mentions it, now I recollect it; and I entirely forgot to ask her when I wrote last. She says nothing indeed except about the Regency.' 'She *must* write well' thought Kitty, 'to make a long Letter upon a Bonnet and Pelisse.'* She then left the room tired of listening to a conversation which tho' it might have diverted her had she been well, served only to fatigue and depress her, while in pain. Happy was it for *her*, when the hour of dressing* came, for Camilla satisfied with being surrounded by her Mother and half the Maids in the House did not want her assistance, and was too agreably employed to want her Society. She remained therefore alone in the parlour, till joined by Mr Stanley and her Aunt, who however after a few enquiries, allowed her to continue undisturbed and began their usual conversation on Politics. This was a subject on which they could never agree, for Mr Stanley who considered himself as perfectly qualified by his Seat in the House, to decide on it without hesitation, resolutely maintained that the Kingdom had not for ages been in so flourishing and prosperous a state,* and Mrs Percival with equal warmth, tho' perhaps less argument, as vehemently asserted that the whole Nation would speedily be ruined, and everything as she expressed herself be at sixes and sevens. It was not however unamusing to Kitty to listen to the Dispute, especially as she began then to be more free from pain, and without taking any share in it herself, she found it very entertaining to observe the eagerness with which they both defended their opinions, and could not help thinking that Mr Stanley would not feel more disappointed if her Aunt's expectations were fulfilled, than her Aunt would be mortified by their failure. After waiting a considerable time Mrs Stanley and her daughter appeared, and Camilla in high Spirits, and perfect good humour with her own looks, was more violent than ever in her lamentations over her Freind as she practised her Scotch Steps* about the room—. At length they departed, and Kitty better able to amuse herself than she had been the whole Day before, wrote a long account of her Misfortunes to Mary Wynne. When her Letter was concluded she had an opportunity of witnessing the truth of that assertion which says that Sorrows are lightened by Communication, for her toothake was then so much releived that she began to entertain an idea of following her Freinds to Mr Dudley's. They had been gone an hour, and as every thing relative to her Dress was in complete readiness, She considered that in another hour since there was so little a way to go, She might be there—. They were gone in Mr Stanley's Carriage and therefore She might follow in her Aunt's. As the plan seemed so very easy to be executed, and promising so much pleasure, it was after a few Minutes deliberation finally adopted, and running up stairs, She rang in great haste for her Maid. The Bustle and Hurry which then ensued for nearly an hour was at last happily concluded by her finding herself very well-dressed and in high Beauty. Anne was then dispatched in the same haste to order the Carriage, while her Mistress was putting on her gloves, and arranging the folds of her dress. In a few Minutes she heard the Carriage drive up to the Door, and tho' at first surprised at the expedition with which it had been got ready, she concluded after a little reflection that the Men had received some hint of her intentions beforehand, and was hastening out of the room, when Anne came running into it in the greatest hurry and agitation, exclaiming 'Lord, Ma'am! Here's a Gentleman in a Chaise and four* come, and I cannot for my Life conceive who it is! I happened to be crossing the hall when the Carriage drove up, and I knew nobody would be in the way to let him in but Tom, and he looks so awkward you know, Ma'am, now his hair is just done up,* that I was not willing the gentleman should see him, and so I went to the door myself. And he is one of the handsomest young Men you would wish to see; I was almost ashamed of being seen in my Apron,* Ma'am, but however he is vastly handsome and did not seem to mind it at all.——And he asked me whether the Family were at home; and so I said everybody was gone out but you, Ma'am, for I would not deny you because I was sure you would like to see him. And then he asked me whether Mr and Mrs Stanley were not here, and so I said Yes, and then——'

'Good Heavens!' said Kitty, 'what can all this mean! And who can it possibly be! Did you never see him before? And Did not he tell you his Name?'

'No, Ma'am, he never said anything about it——So then I asked him to walk into the parlour, and he was prodigious agreable, and——'

'Whoever he is,' said her Mistress, 'he has made a great impression upon you, Nanny——But where did he come from? and what does he want here?'

'Oh! Ma'am, I was going to tell you, that I fancy his business is with you; for he asked me whether you were at leisure to see anybody, and desired I would give his Compliments to you, and say he should be very happy to wait on you——However I thought he had better not come up into your Dressing room, especially as everything is in such a litter, so I told him if he would be so obliging as to stay in the parlour, I would run up stairs and tell you he was come, and I dared to say that you would wait upon *him*. Lord, Ma'am, I'd lay anything that he is come to ask you to dance with him tonight, and has got his Chaise ready to take you to Mr Dudley's.'

Kitty could not help laughing at this idea, and only wished it might be true, as it was very likely that she would be too late for any other partner—'But what, in the name of wonder, can he have to say to me? Perhaps he is come to rob the house—he comes in stile at least; and it will be some consolation for our losses to be robbed by a Gentleman in a Chaise and 4—. What Livery* has his Servants?'

'Why that is the most wonderful thing about him, Ma'am, for he has not a single servant with him, and came with hack horses;* But he is as handsome as a Prince for all that, and has quite the look of one.* Do, dear Ma'am, go down, for I am sure you will be delighted with him—'

'Well, I beleive I must go; but it is very odd! What can he have to say to me.' Then giving one look at herself in the Glass, she walked with great impatience, tho' trembling all the while from not knowing what to expect, down Stairs, and after pausing a moment at the door to gather Courage for opening it, she resolutely entered the room. The Stranger, whose appearance did not disgrace the account she had received of it from her Maid, rose up on her entrance, and laying aside the Newspaper he had been reading, advanced towards her with an air of the most perfect Ease and Vivacity,* and said to her, 'It is certainly a very awkward circumstance to be thus obliged to introduce myself, but I trust that the necessity of the case will plead my Excuse, and prevent your being prejudiced by it against me—. *Your* name, I need not ask, Ma'am—. Miss Percival is too well known to me by description to need any information of that.' Kitty, who had been expecting him to tell his own name, instead of hers, and who from having been little in company, and never before in such a situation, felt herself unable to ask it, tho' she had been planning her speech all the way down stairs, was so confused and distressed by this unexpected address that she could only return a slight curtesy to it, and accepted the chair he reached her, without knowing what she did. The gentleman then continued. 'You are, I dare say, surprised to see me returned from France so soon, and nothing indeed but business could have brought me to England; a very Melancholy affair has now occasioned it, and I was unwilling to leave it without paying my respects to the Family in Devonshire* whom I have so long wished to be acquainted with—.' Kitty, who felt much more surprised at his supposing her *to be so*,* than at seeing a person in England, whose having ever left it was perfectly unknown to her, still continued silent from Wonder and Perplexity, and her visitor still continued to talk. 'You will suppose, Madam, that I was not the *less* desirous of waiting on you, from your having Mr and Mrs Stanley with you—. I hope they are well? And Mrs Percival, how does *she* do?' Then without waiting for an answer he gaily added, 'But my dear Miss Percival, you are going out I am sure; and I am detaining you from your appointment. How can I ever expect to be forgiven for such injustice! Yet how can I, so circumstanced, forbear to offend! You seem dressed for a Ball? But this is the Land of gaiety I know; I have for many years been desirous of visiting it. You have Dances I suppose at least every week—But where are the rest of your party gone, and what kind Angel in compassion to me, has excluded *you* from it?'

'Perhaps Sir,' said Kitty extremely confused by his manner of speaking to her, and highly displeased with the freedom of his Conversation towards one who had never seen him before and did not *now* know his name, 'perhaps Sir, you are acquainted with Mr and Mrs Stanley; and your business may be with *them*?'

'You do me too much honour, Ma'am,' replied he laughing, 'in supposing me to be acquainted with Mr and Mrs Stanley; I merely know them by sight; very distant relations; only my Father and Mother. Nothing more I assure you.'

'Gracious Heaven!' said Kitty, 'are *you* Mr Stanley then?—I beg a thousand pardons—Though really upon recollection I do not know for what—for you never told me your name——'

'I beg your pardon—I made a very fine speech when you

entered the room, all about introducing myself; I assure you it was very great for *me*.'

'The speech had certainly great Merit,' said Kitty smiling; 'I thought so at the time; but since you never mentioned your name in it, as an *introductory one* it might have been better.'

There was such an air of good humour and Gaiety in Stanley, that Kitty, tho' perhaps not authorized to address him with so much familiarity on so short an acquaintance, could not forbear indulging the natural Unreserve* and Vivacity of her own Disposition, in speaking to him, as he spoke to her. She was intimately acquainted too with his Family who were her relations, and she chose to consider herself entitled by the connexion to forget how little a while they had known each other. 'Mr and Mrs Stanley and your Sister are extremely well,' said she, 'and will I dare say be very much surprised to see you—But I am sorry to hear that your return to England has been occasioned by an unpleasant circumstance.'

'Oh, Don't talk of it,' said he, 'it is a most confounded shocking affair, and makes me miserable to think of it; But where are my Father and Mother, and your Aunt gone? Oh! Do you know that I met the prettiest little waiting maid in the World, when I came here; she let me into the house; I took her for you at first.'

'You did me a great deal of honour, and give me more credit for good nature than I deserve, for I *never* go to the door when any one comes.'*

'Nay do not be angry; I mean no offence. But tell me, where are you going to so smart?* Your carriage is just coming round.'

'I am going to a Dance at a Neighbour's, where your Family and my Aunt are already gone.'

'Gone, without you! what's the meaning of *that*? But I suppose you are like myself, rather long in dressing.'

'I must have been so indeed, if that were the case for they have been gone nearly these two hours; The reason however was not what you suppose—I was prevented going by a pain——'

'By a pain!' interrupted Stanley, 'Oh! heavens, that is dreadful indeed! No Matter where the pain was. But my dear Miss Percival, what do you say to my accompanying you? And suppose you were to dance with me too? *I* think it would be very pleasant.'

'I can have no objection to either I am sure,' said Kitty laughing to find how near the truth her Maid's conjecture had been; 'on the contrary I shall be highly honoured by both, and I can answer for Your being extremely welcome to the Family who give the Ball.'*

'Oh! hang them; who cares for that; they cannot turn me out of the house. But I am afraid I shall cut a sad figure among all your Devonshire Beaux in this dusty, travelling apparel,* and I have not wherewithal to change it. You can procure me some powder* perhaps, and I must get a pair of Shoes from one of the Men, for I was in such a devil of a hurry to leave Lyons* that I had not time to have anything pack'd up but some linen.'* Kitty very readily undertook to procure for him everything he wanted, and telling the footman to shew him into Mr Stanley's dressing room, gave Nanny orders to send in some powder and pomatum,* which orders Nanny chose to execute in person. As Stanley's preparations in dressing were confined to such very trifling articles, Kitty of course expected him in about ten minutes; but she found that it had not been merely a boast of vanity in saying that he was dilatory in that respect, as he kept her waiting for him above half an hour, so that the Clock had struck ten before he entered the room and the rest of the party had gone by eight.*

'Well,' said he as he came in, 'have not I been very quick? I never hurried so much in my Life before.'

'In that case you certainly have,' replied Kitty, 'for all Merit you know is comparative.'

'Oh! I knew you would be delighted with me for making so much haste—. But come, the Carriage is ready; so, do not keep me waiting.' And so saying he took her by the hand, and led her out of the room.

'Why, my dear Cousin,' said he when they were seated, 'this will be a most agreable surprize to everybody to see you enter the room with such a smart Young Fellow as I am—I hope your Aunt won't be alarmed.'

'To tell you the truth,' replied Kitty, 'I think the best way to prevent it, will be to send for her, or your Mother before we go into the room, especially as you are a perfect stranger, and must of course be introduced to Mr and Mrs Dudley—'

'Oh! Nonsense,' said he; 'I did not expect *you* to stand upon such Ceremony; Our acquaintance with each other renders all such Prudery,* ridiculous; Besides, if we go in together, we shall be the whole talk of the Country—'

'To *me*' replied Kitty, 'that would certainly be a most powerful inducement; but I scarcely know whether my Aunt would consider it as such—. Women at her time of life, have odd ideas of propriety you know.'

'Which is the very thing that you ought to break them of; and why should you object to entering a room with me where all our relations are, when you have done me the honour to admit me without any chaprone into your Carriage? Do not you think your Aunt will be as much offended with you for one, as for the other of these mighty crimes?'

'Why really' said Catharine, 'I do not know but that she may; however, it is no reason that I should offend against Decorum a second time, because I have already done it once.'

'On the contrary, that is the very reason which makes it impossible for you to prevent it, since you cannot offend for the *first time* again.'

'You are very ridiculous,' said she laughing, 'but I am afraid your arguments divert me too much to convince me.'

'At least they will convince you that I am very agreable, which after all, is the happiest conviction for me, and as to the affair of Propriety we will let that rest till we arrive at our Journey's end—. This is a monthly Ball* I suppose. Nothing but Dancing here—.'

'I thought I had told you that it was given by a Mr Dudley—'

'Oh! aye so you did; but why should not Mr Dudley give one every month? By the bye who *is that* Man? Everybody gives Balls now I think; I beleive I must give one myself soon—. Well, but how do you like my Father and Mother? And poor little Camilla too, has not she plagued you to death with the Halifaxes?' Here the Carriage fortunately stopped at Mr Dudley's, and Stanley was too much engaged in handing her out of it, to wait for an answer, or to remember that what he had said required one. They entered the small vestibule which Mr Dudley had raised to the Dignity of a Hall,* and Kitty immediately desired the footman who was leading the way upstairs, to inform either Mrs Percival, or Mrs Stanley of her arrival, and beg them to come to her, but Stanley unused to any contradiction and impatient to be amongst them, would neither allow her to wait, or listen to what she said, and forcibly seizing her arm within his, overpowered her voice with the rapidity of his own, and Kitty half angry, and half laughing was obliged to go with him up stairs, and could even with difficulty prevail on him to relinquish her hand before they entered the room. Mrs Percival was at that very moment engaged in conversation with a Lady at the upper end of the room, to whom she had been giving a long account of her Neice's unlucky disappointment, and the dreadful pain that she had with so much fortitude, endured the whole Day—'I left her however,' said She, 'thank heaven!, a little better, and I hope she has been able to amuse herself with a book, poor thing! for she must otherwise be very dull. She is probably in bed by this time, which while she is so poorly, is the best place for her you know, Ma'am.' The Lady was going to give her assent to this opinion, when the Noise of voices on the stairs, and the footman's opening the door as if for the entrance of Company, attracted the attention of every body in the room; and as it was in one of those Intervals between the Dances when every one seemed glad to sit down, Mrs Percival had a most unfortunate opportunity of seeing her Neice whom she had supposed in bed, or amusing herself as the height of gaity with a book, enter the room most elegantly dressed, with a smile on her Countenance, and a glow of mingled Chearfulness and Confusion on her Cheeks, attended by a young Man uncommonly handsome, and who without any of her Confusion, appeared to have all her vivacity. Mrs Percival, colouring with anger and astonishment, rose from her Seat, and Kitty walked eagerly towards her, impatient to account for what she saw appeared wonderful to every body, and extremely offensive to *her*, while Camilla on seeing her Brother ran instantly towards him, and very soon explained who he was by her words and her actions. Mr Stanley, who so fondly doated on his Son, that the pleasure of seeing him again after an absence of three Months prevented his feeling for the time any anger against him for returning to England without his knowledge, received him with equal surprise and delight; and soon comprehending the cause of his Journey, forbore any further conversation with him, as he was eager to see his Mother, and it was necessary that he should be introduced to Mr Dudley's family. This introduction to any one but Stanley would have been highly unpleasant, for they considered their dignity injured by his coming uninvited to their house, and received him with more than their usual haughtiness: But Stanley who with a vivacity of temper seldom subdued, and a contempt of censure not to be overcome, possessed an opinion of his own Consequence,* and a perseverance in his own schemes which were not to be damped by the conduct of others, appeared not to perceive it. The Civilities therefore which they coldly offered, he received with a gaiety and ease peculiar to himself, and then attended by his Father and Sister walked into another room where his Mother was playing at Cards,* to experience another Meeting, and undergo a repetition of pleasure, surprise and Explanations. While these were passing, Camilla eager to communicate all she felt to some one who would attend to her, returned to Catharine, and seating herself by her, immediately began—'Well, did you ever know anything so delightful as this? But it always is so; I never go to a Ball in my Life but what something or other happens unexpectedly that is quite charming!'

'A Ball' replied Kitty, 'seems to be a most eventful thing to you—'

'Oh! Lord, it is indeed—But only think of my brother's

returning so suddenly—And how shocking a thing it is that has brought him over! I never heard anything so dreadful—!'

'What is it pray that has occasioned his leaving France? I am sorry to find that it is a melancholy event.'

'Oh! it is beyond anything you can conceive! His favourite Hunter* who was turned out in the park on his going abroad, somehow or other fell ill—No, I beleive it was an accident, but however it was something or other, or else it was something else, and so they sent an Express immediately to Lyons where my Brother was, for they knew that he valued this Mare more than anything else in the World besides; and so my Brother set off directly for England, and without packing up another Coat; I am quite angry with him about it; it was so shocking you know to come away without a change of Cloathes—'

'Why indeed,' said Kitty, 'it seems to have been a very shocking affair from beginning to end.'

'Oh! it is beyond anything You can conceive! I would rather have had *anything* happen than that he should have lossed that mare.'

'Except his coming away without another coat.'

'Oh! yes, that has vexed me more than you can imagine.— Well, and so Edward got to Brampton* just as the poor Thing was dead; but as he could not bear to remain there *then*, he came off directly to Chetwynde on purpose to see us—. I hope he may not go abroad again.'

'Do you think he will not?'

'Oh! dear, to be sure he must, but I wish he may not with all my heart—. You cannot think how fond I am of him! By the bye are not you in love with him yourself?'

'To be sure I am,' replied Kitty laughing, 'I am in love with every handsome Man I see.'

'That is just like me—*I* am always in love with every handsome Man in the World.'

'There you outdo me,' replied Catharine 'for I am only in love with those I *do* see.' Mrs Percival who was sitting on the other side of her, and who began now to distinguish the words, *Love* and *handsome Man*, turned hastily towards them, and said 'What are you talking of, Catharine?' To which Catharine immediately answered with the simple artifice of a Child, 'Nothing, Ma'am.' She had already received a very severe lecture from her Aunt on the imprudence of her behaviour during the whole evening; She blamed her for coming to the Ball, for coming in the same Carriage with Edward Stanley, and still more for entering the room with him.* For the last-mentioned offence Catharine knew not what apology to give, and tho' she longed in answer to the second to say that she had not thought it would be civil to make Mr Stanley *walk*, she dared not so to trifle with her aunt, who would have been but the more offended by it. The first accusation however she considered as very unreasonable, as she thought herself perfectly justified in coming. This conversation continued till Edward Stanley entering the room came instantly towards her, and telling her that every one waited for *her* to begin the next Dance led her to the top of the room,* for Kitty, impatient to escape from so unpleasant a Companion, without the least hesitation, or one civil scruple at being so distinguished, immediately gave him her hand, and joyfully left her Seat. This Conduct however was highly resented by several young Ladies present, and among the rest by Miss Stanley whose regard for her brother tho' *excessive*, and whose affection for Kitty tho' *prodigious*, were not proof against such an injury to her importance and her peace. Edward had however only consulted his own inclinations in desiring Miss Percival to begin the Dance, nor had he any reason to know that it was either wished or expected by anyone else in the Party. As an heiress she was certainly of consequence, but her Birth gave her no other claim to it, for her Father had been a Merchant. It was this very circumstance which rendered this unfortunate affair so offensive to Camilla, for tho' she would sometimes boast in the pride of her heart, and her eagerness to be admired that she did not know who her grandfather had been, and was as ignorant of everything relative to Genealogy as to Astronomy, (and she might have added, Geography) yet she was really proud of her family and Connexions, and easily offended if they were treated with Neglect. 'I should not have minded it,' said she to her Mother, 'if she had been *anybody* else's daughter; but to see her pretend to be above *me*, when her Father was only a tradesman,* is too bad! It is such an affront to our whole Family! I declare I think Papa ought to interfere in it, but he never cares about anything but Politics. If I were Mr Pitt* or the Lord Chancellor,* he would take care I should not be insulted, but he never thinks about *me*; And it is so provoking that *Edward* should let her stand there. I wish with all my heart that he had never come to England! I hope she may fall down and break her neck, or sprain her Ancle.' Mrs Stanley perfectly agreed with her daughter concerning the affair, and tho' with less violence, expressed almost equal resentment at the indignity. Kitty in the meantime remained insensible of having given any one Offence, and therefore unable either to offer an apology, or make a reparation; her whole attention was occupied by the happiness she enjoyed in dancing with the most elegant young Man in the room, and every one else was equally unregarded. The Evening indeed to *her*, passed off delightfully; he was her partner during the greatest part of it, and the united attractions that he possessed of Person, Address and vivacity, had easily gained that preference from Kitty which they seldom fail of obtaining from every one. She was too happy to care either for her Aunt's illhumour which she could not help remarking, or for the Alteration in Camilla's behaviour which forced itself at last on her observation. Her Spirits were elevated above the influence of Displeasure in any one, and she was equally indifferent as to the cause of Camilla's, or the continuance of her Aunt's. Though Mr Stanley could never be really offended by any imprudence or folly in his Son that had given him the pleasure of seeing him, he was yet perfectly convinced that Edward ought not to remain in England, and was resolved to hasten his leaving it as soon as possible; but when he talked to Edward about it, he found him much less disposed towards returning to France, than to accompany them in their projected tour, which he assured his Father would be infinitely more pleasant to him, and that as to the affair of travelling he considered it of no importance, and what might be pursued at any little odd time, when he had nothing better to do. He advanced these objections in a manner which plainly shewed that he had scarcely a doubt of their being complied with, and appeared to consider his father's arguments in opposition to them, as merely given with a veiw to keep up his authority, and such as he should find little difficulty in combating. He concluded at last by saying, as the chaise in which they returned together from Mr Dudley's reached Mrs Percival's, 'Well Sir, we will settle this point some other time, and fortunately it is of so little consequence, that an immediate discussion of it is unnecessary.' He then got out of the chaise and entered the house without waiting for his Father's reply. It was not till their return that Kitty could account for that coldness in Camilla's behaviour to her, which had been so pointed as to render it impossible to be entirely unnoticed. When however they were seated in the Coach with the two other Ladies, Miss Stanley's indignation was no longer to be suppressed from breaking out into words, and found the following vent.

'Well, I must say *this*, that I never was at a stupider Ball in my Life! But it always is so; I am always disappointed in them for some reason or other. I wish there were no such things.'

'I am sorry, Miss Stanley,' said Mrs Percival drawing herself up, 'that you have not been amused; every thing was meant for the best I am sure, and it is a poor encouragement for your Mama to take you to another if you are so hard to be satisfied.'

'I do not know what you mean, Ma'am, about Mama's *taking* me to another. You know I am come out.'*

'Oh! dear Mrs Percival,' said Mrs Stanley, 'you must not beleive everything that my lively Camilla says, for her spirits are prodigiously high sometimes, and she frequently speaks without thinking. I am sure it is impossible for *any one* to have been at a more elegant or agreable dance, and so she wishes to express herself I am certain.'

'To be sure I do,' said Camilla very sulkily, 'only I must

say that it is not very pleasant to have any body behave so
rude to one as to be quite shocking! I am sure I am not at all
offended, and should not care if all the World were to stand
above me, but still it is extremely abominable, and what I
cannot put up with. It is not that I mind it in the least, for I
had just as soon stand at the bottom as at the top all Night
long, if it was not so very disagreable—. But to have a
person come in the middle of the Evening and take
everybody's place is what I am not used to, and tho' I do
not care a pin about it myself, I assure you I shall not easily
forgive or forget it.'

This speech which perfectly explained the whole affair to
Kitty, was shortly followed on her side by a very submissive
apology, for she had too much good Sense to be proud of her
family, and too much good Nature to live at variance with
any one. The Excuses she made, were delivered with so
much real concern for the Offence, and such unaffected
Sweetness, that it was almost impossible for Camilla to
retain that anger which had occasioned them; She felt
indeed most highly gratified to find that no insult had been
intended and that Catharine was very far from forgetting
the difference in their birth for which she could *now* only
pity her, and her good humour being restored with the same
Ease in which it had been affected, she spoke with the
highest delight of the Evening, and declared that she had
never before been at so pleasant a Ball. The same
endeavours that had procured the forgiveness of Miss
Stanley ensured to her the cordiality of her Mother, and
nothing was wanting but Mrs Percival's good humour to
render the happiness of the others complete; but She,
offended with Camilla for her affected Superiority, Still
more so with her brother for coming to Chetwynde, and
dissatisfied with the whole Evening, continued silent and
Gloomy and was a restraint on the vivacity of her
Companions. She eagerly seized the very first opportunity
which the next Morning offered to her of speaking to Mr
Stanley on the subject of his son's return, and after having
expressed her opinion of its being a very silly affair that he
came at all, concluded with desiring him to inform Mr

Edward Stanley that it was a rule with her never to admit a young Man into her house as a visitor for any length of time.

'I do not speak, Sir,' she continued, 'out of any disrespect to You, but I could not answer it to myself to allow of his stay; there is no knowing what might be the consequence of it, if he were to continue here, for girls nowadays will always give a handsome young Man the preference before any other, tho' for why, I never could discover, for what after all is Youth and Beauty? It is but a poor substitute for real worth and Merit; Beleive me Cousin that, what ever people may say to the contrary, there is certainly nothing like Virtue for making us what we ought to be, and as to a young Man's, being young and handsome and having an agreable person, it is nothing at all to the purpose for he had much better be respectable. I always *did* think so, and I always *shall*, and therefore you will oblige me very much by desiring your son to leave Chetwynde, or I cannot be answerable for what may happen between him and my Neice. You will be surprised to hear *me* say it,' she continued, lowering her voice, 'but truth will out, and I must own that Kitty is one of the most impudent Girls that ever existed. I assure you Sir, that I have seen her sit and laugh and whisper with a young Man whom she has not seen above half a dozen times. Her behaviour indeed is scandalous, and therefore I beg you will send your Son away immediately, or everything will be at sixes and sevens.' Mr Stanley, who from one part of her Speech had scarcely known to what length her insinuations of Kitty's impudence* were meant to extend, now endeavoured to quiet her fears on the occasion, by assuring her, that on every account he meant to allow only of his son's continuing that day with them, and that she might depend on his being more earnest in the affair from a wish of obliging her. He added also that he knew Edward to be very desirous himself of returning to France, as he wisely considered all time lost that did not forward the plans in which he was at present engaged, tho' he was but too well convinced of the contrary himself. His assurance in some degree quieted Mrs Percival, and left her tolerably releived of her Cares and Alarms, and better disposed to behave with civility towards his Son during the short remainder of his stay at Chetwynde. Mr Stanley went immediately to Edward, to whom he repeated the Conversation that had passed between Mrs Percival and himself, and strongly pointed out the necessity of his leaving Chetwynde the next day, since his word was already engaged for it. His son however appeared struck only by the ridiculous apprehensions of Mrs Percival; and highly delighted at having occasioned them himself, seemed engrossed alone in thinking how he might encrease them, without attending to any other part of his Father's Conversation. Mr Stanley could get no determinate Answer from him, and tho' he still hoped for the best, they parted almost in anger on his side. His Son though by no means disposed to marry, or any otherwise attached to Miss Percival than as a good natured lively Girl who seemed pleased with him, took infinite pleasure in alarming the jealous fears of her Aunt by his attentions to her, without considering what effect they might have on the Lady herself. He would always sit by her when she was in the room, appear dissatisfied if she left it, and was the first to enquire whether she meant soon to return. He was delighted with her Drawings, and enchanted with her performance on the Harpsichord; Everything that she said, appeared to interest him; his Conversation was addressed to her alone, and she seemed to be the sole object of his attention. That such efforts should succeed with one so tremblingly alive to every alarm of the kind as Mrs Percival, is by no means unnatural, and that they should have equal influence with her Neice whose imagination was lively, and whose Disposition romantic,* who was already extremely pleased with him, and of course desirous that he might be so with her, is as little to be wondered at. Every moment as it added to the conviction of his liking her, made him still more pleasing, and strengthened in her Mind a wish of knowing him better. As for Mrs Percival, she was in tortures the whole Day; Nothing that she had ever felt before on a similar occasion was to be compared to the sensations which then distracted her; her fears had never been so strongly, or indeed so reasonably excited.—Her dislike of Stanley, her anger at her Neice, her impatience to have them separated conquered every idea of propriety and Good breeding, and though he had never mentioned any intention of leaving them the next day, she could not help asking him after Dinner, in her eagerness to have him gone, at what time he meant to set out.

'Oh! Ma'am,' replied he, 'if I am off by twelve at night, you may think yourself lucky; and if I am not, you can only blame yourself for having left so much as the *hour* of my departure to my own disposal.' Mrs Percival coloured very highly at this speech, and without addressing herself to any one in particular, immediately began a long harangue on the shocking behaviour of modern young Men, and the wonderful Alteration that had taken place in them, since her time, which she illustrated with many instructive anecdotes of the Decorum and Modesty which had marked the Characters of those whom she had known, when she had been young. This however did not prevent his walking in the Garden with her Neice, without any other companion for nearly an hour in the course of the Evening. They had left the room for that purpose with Camilla at a time when Mrs Percival had been out of it, nor was it for some time after her return to it, that she could discover where they were. Camilla had taken two or three turns with them in the walk which led to the Arbour, but soon growing tired of listening to a Conversation in which she was seldom invited to join, and from its turning occasionally on Books, very little able to do it, she left them together in the arbour, to wander alone to some other part of the Garden, to eat the fruit, and examine Mrs Percival's Greenhouse. Her absence was so far from being regretted, that it was scarcely noticed by them, and they continued conversing together on almost every subject, for Stanley seldom dwellt long on any, and had something to say on all, till they were interrupted by her Aunt.

Kitty was by this time perfectly convinced that both in Natural Abilities, and acquired information, Edward Stanley was infinitely superior to his Sister. Her desire of knowing that he was so, had induced her to take every opportunity of turning the Conversation on History and they were very soon engaged in an historical dispute, for which no one was more calculated than Stanley who was so far from being really of any party, that he had scarcely a fixed opinion on the Subject. He could therefore always take either side, and always argue with temper. In his indifference on all such topics he was very unlike his Companion, whose judgement being guided by her feelings which were eager and warm, was easily decided, and though it was not always infallible, she defended it with a Spirit and Enthouisasm which marked her own reliance on it. They had continued therefore for sometime conversing in this manner on the character of Richard the 3rd*, which he was warmly defending when he suddenly seized hold of her hand, and exclaiming with great emotion, 'Upon my honour you are entirely mistaken,' pressed it passionately to his lips, and ran out of the arbour. Astonished at this behaviour, for which she was wholly unable to account, she continued for a few Moments motionless on the seat where he had left her, and was then on the point of following him up the narrow walk through which he had passed, when on looking up the one that lay immediately before the arbour, she saw her Aunt walking towards her with more than her usual quickness. This explained at once the reason of his leaving her, but his leaving her in such Manner was rendered still more inexplicable by it. She felt a considerable degree of confusion at having been seen by her in such a place with Edward, and at having that part of his conduct, for which she could not herself account, witnessed by one to whom all gallantry was odious. She remained therefore confused, distressed and irresolute, and suffered her Aunt to approach her, without leaving the Arbour. Mrs Percival's looks were by no means calculated to animate the spirits of her Neice, who in silence awaited her accusation, and in silence meditated her Defence. After a few Moments suspence, for Mrs Percival was too much fatigued to speak immediately, she began with great Anger and Asperity, the following harangue. 'Well; *this* is beyond anything I could have supposed. *Profligate** as I *knew* you to be, I was not prepared for such a sight. This is beyond any thing you ever did *before*; beyond any thing I ever heard of in my Life! Such Impudence, I never witnessed before in such a Girl! And this is the reward for all the cares I have taken in your Education; for all my troubles and Anxieties; and Heaven knows how many they have been! All I wished for, was to breed you up virtuously; I never wanted you to play upon the Harpsichord, or draw better than any one else; but I had hoped to see you respectable and good; to see you able and willing to give an example of Modesty and Virtue to the Young people here abouts. I bought you Blair's Sermons,* and Cœlebs in Search of a Wife,* I gave you the key to my own Library,* and borrowed a great many good books of my Neighbours for you, all to this purpose. But I might have spared myself the trouble—Oh! Catharine, you are an abandoned Creature, and I do not know what will become of you. I am glad however,' she continued softening into some degree of Mildness, 'to see that you have some shame for what you have done, and if you are really sorry for it, and your future life is a life of penitence and reformation perhaps you may be forgiven. But I plainly see that every thing is going to sixes and sevens and all order will soon be at an end throughout the Kingdom.'

'Not however, Ma'am, the sooner, I hope, from any conduct of mine,' said Catharine in a tone of great humility, 'for upon my honour I have done nothing this evening that can contribute to overthrow the establishment of the kingdom.'

'You are Mistaken, Child,' replied she; 'the welfare of every Nation depends upon the virtue of it's individuals, and any one who offends in so gross a manner against decorum and propriety is certainly hastening it's ruin.* You have been giving a bad example to the World, and the World is but too well disposed to receive such.'

'Pardon me, Madam,' said her Neice; 'but I *can* have given an Example only to *You*, for *You* alone have seen the offence. Upon my word however there is no danger to fear from what I have done; Mr Stanley's behaviour has given me as much surprise, as it has done to You, and I can only suppose that it was the effect of his high spirits, authorized in his opinion by our relationship. But do you consider, Madam, that it is growing very late? Indeed You had better return to the house.' This speech as she well knew, would be unanswerable with her Aunt, who instantly rose, and hurried away under so many apprehensions for her own health, as banished for the time all anxiety about her Neice, who walked quietly by her side, revolving within her own Mind the occurrence that had given her Aunt so much alarm. 'I am astonished at my own imprudence,' said Mrs Percival; 'How could I be so forgetful as to sit down out of doors at such a time of night? I shall certainly have a return of my rheumatism after it—I begin to feel very chill already. I must have caught a dreadful Cold by this time—I am sure of being lain-up all the winter after it—' Then reckoning with her fingers, 'Let me see; This is July; the cold weather will soon be coming in—August—September—October—November—December — January— February — March—April—Very likely I may not be tolerable again before May. I must and will have that arbour pulled down—it will be the death of me; who knows *now*, but what I may never recover—Such things *have* happened—My particular freind Miss Sarah Hutchinson's death was occasioned by nothing more—She staid out late one Evening in April, and got wet through for it rained very hard, and never changed her Cloathes when she came home—It is unknown how many people have died in consequence of catching Cold!* I do not beleive there is a disorder in the World except the Smallpox which does not spring from it.' It was in vain that Kitty endeavoured to convince her that her fears on the occasion were groundless; that it was not yet late enough to catch cold, and that even if it were, she might hope to escape any other complaint, and to recover in less than ten Months. Mrs Percival only replied that she hoped she knew more of Ill health than to be convinced in such a point by a Girl who had always been perfectly well, and hurried up stairs leaving Kitty to make her apologies to Mr and Mrs Stanley

for going to bed——. Tho' Mrs Percival seemed perfectly
satisfied with the goodness of the Apology herself, yet Kitty
felt somewhat embarrassed to find that the only one she
could offer to their Visitors was that her Aunt had *perhaps*
caught cold, for Mrs Percival charged her to make light of
it, for fear of alarming them. Mr and Mrs Stanley however
who well knew that their Cousin was easily terrified on that
Score, received the account of it with very little surprise,
and all proper concern. Edward and his Sister soon came
in, and Kitty had no difficulty in gaining an explanation of
his Conduct from him, for he was too warm on the subject
himself, and too eager to learn its success, to refrain from
making immediate Enquiries about it; and She could not
help feeling both surprised and offended at the ease and
Indifference with which he owned that all his intentions had
been to frighten her Aunt by pretending an affection for *her*,
a design so very incompatible with that partiality which she
had at one time been almost convinced of his feeling for her.
It is true that she had not yet seen enough of him to be
actually in love with him, yet she felt greatly disappointed
that so handsome, so elegant, so lively a young Man should
be so perfectly free from any such Sentiment as to make it
his principal Sport.* There was a Novelty in his character
which to *her* was extremely pleasing; his person was
uncommonly fine, his Spirits and Vivacity suited to her
own, and his Manners at once so animated and insinuating,
that she thought it must be impossible for him to be
otherwise than amiable, and was ready to give him Credit
for being perfectly so. He knew the powers of them himself;
to them he had often been endebted for his father's
forgiveness of faults which had he been awkward and
inelegant would have appeared very serious; to them, even
more than to his person or his fortune, he owed the regard
which almost every one was disposed to feel for him, and
which Young Women in particular were inclined to
entertain. Their influence was acknowledged on the present
occasion by Kitty, whose Anger they entirely dispelled, and
whose Chearfulness they had power not only to restore, but
to raise——. The Evening passed off as agreably as the one

that had preceded it; they continued talking to each other, during the cheif part of it, and such was the power of his Address, and the Brilliancy of his Eyes, that when they parted for the Night, tho' Catharine had but a few hours before totally given up the idea, yet she felt almost convinced again that he was really in love with her. She reflected on their past Conversation, and tho' it had been on various and indifferent subjects, and she could not exactly recollect any speech on his side expressive of such a partiality, she was still however nearly certain of it's being so; But fearful of being vain enough to suppose such a thing without sufficient reason, she resolved to suspend her final determination on it, till the next day, and more especially till their parting which she thought would infallibly explain his regard if any he had—. The more she had seen of him, the more inclined was she to like him, and the more desirous that he should like *her*. She was convinced of his being naturally very clever and very well disposed, and that his thoughtlessness and Negligence, which tho' they appeared to *her* as very becoming in *him*, she was aware would by many people be considered as defects in his Character, merely proceeded from a vivacity always pleasing in Young Men, and were far from testifying a weak or vacant Understanding. Having settled this point within herself, and being perfectly convinced by her own arguments of it's truth, she went to bed in high Spirits, determined to study his Character, and watch his Behaviour still more the next day. She got up with the same good resolutions and would probably have put them in execution, had not Anne informed her as soon as she entered the room that Mr Edward Stanley was already gone. At first she refused to credit the information, but when her Maid assured her that he had ordered a Carriage the evening before to be there at seven o'clock in the Morning and that she herself had actually seen him depart in it a little after eight, she could no longer deny her beleif to it. 'And this,' thought she to herself blushing with anger at her own folly, 'this is the affection for me of which I was so certain. Oh! what a silly Thing is Woman! How vain, how unreasonable!* To suppose that a young Man would be seriously attached in the course of four and twenty hours, to a Girl who has nothing to recommend her but a good pair of eyes! And he is really gone! Gone perhaps without bestowing a thought on me! Oh! why was not I up by eight o'clock? But it is a proper punishment for my Lazyness and Folly, and I am heartily glad of it. I deserve it all, and ten times more for such insufferable vanity. It will at least be of service to me in that respect; it will teach me in future *not* to think Every Body is in love with me. Yet I *should* like to have seen him before he went, for perhaps it may be many Years before we meet again. By his Manner of leaving us however, he seems to have been perfectly indifferent about it. How very odd, that he should go without giving us Notice of it, or taking leave of any one! But it is just like a Young Man, governed by the whim of the moment, or actuated merely by the love of doing anything oddly!* Unaccountable Beings indeed! And Young Women are equally ridiculous! I shall soon begin to think like my Aunt that everything is going to sixes and sevens, and that the whole race of Mankind are degenerating.' She was just dressed, and on the point of leaving her room to make her personal enquiries after Mrs Percival, when Miss Stanley knocked at her door, and on her being admitted began in her Usual Strain a long harangue upon her Father's being so shocking as to make Edward go at all, and upon Edward's being so horrid as to leave them at such an hour in the Morning. 'You have no idea,' said she, 'how surprised I was, when he came into my Room to bid me good bye—'

'Have you seen him then, this Morning?' said Kitty.

'Oh Yes! And I was so sleepy that I could not open my eyes. And so he said, "Camilla, goodbye to you for I am going away—. I have not time to take leave of any body else, and I dare not trust myself to see Kitty, for then you know I should never get away—" '

'Nonsense,' said Kitty; 'he did not say that, or he was in joke if he did.'

'Oh! no I assure you he was as much in earnest as he ever was in his life; he was too much out of spirits to joke *then.*

And he desired me when we all met at Breakfast to give his Compliments to your Aunt, and his Love to you, for you was a nice* Girl he said, and he only wished it were in his power to be more with You. You were just the Girl to suit him, because you were so lively and good-natured, and he wished with all his heart that you might not be married before he came back, for there was nothing he liked better than being here. Oh! You have no idea what fine things he said about you, till at last I fell asleep and he went away. But he certainly is in love with you—I am sure he is—I have thought so a great while I assure You.'

'How can you be so ridiculous?' said Kitty smiling with pleasure; 'I do not beleive him to be so easily affected. But he *did* desire his Love to me then? And wished I might not be married before his return? And said I was a Nice Girl, did he?'

'Oh! dear, Yes, and I assure You it is the greatest praise in his opinion, that he can bestow on any body; I can hardly ever persuade him to call *me* one, tho' I beg him sometimes for an hour together.'

'And do You really think that he was sorry to go?'

'Oh! you can have no idea how wretched it made him. He would not have gone this Month, if my Father had not insisted on it; Edward told me so himself yesterday. He said that he wished with all his heart he had never promised to go abroad, for that he repented it more and more every day; that it interfered with all his other schemes, and that since Papa had spoke to him about it, he was more unwilling to leave Chetwynde than ever.'

'Did he really say all this? And why would your father insist upon his going?' 'His leaving England interfered with all his other plans, and his Conversation with Mr Stanley had made him still more averse to it.' 'What can this Mean?' 'Why that he is excessively in love with you to be sure; what other plans can he have? And I suppose my father said that if he had not been going abroad, he should have wished him to marry you immediately.—But I must go and see your Aunt's plants—There is one of them that I quite doat on—and two or three more besides—'.

'Can Camilla's explanation be true?' said Catharine to herself, when her freind had left the room. 'And after all my doubts and Uncertainties, can Stanley really be averse to leaving England for *my sake* only? "His plans interrupted." And what indeed can his plans be, but towards Marriage? Yet *so soon* to be in love with me!—But it is the effect perhaps only of a warmth of heart which to *me* is the highest recommendation in any one. A Heart disposed to love— And such under the appearance of so much Gaity and Inattention, is Stanley's! Oh! how much does it endear him to me! But he is gone—Gone perhaps for Years—Obliged to tear himself from what he most loves, his happiness is sacrificed to the vanity of his Father! In what anguish he must have left the house! Unable to see me, or to bid me adieu, while I, senseless wretch, was daring to sleep. This, then explained his leaving us at such a time of day—. He could not trust himself to see me—. Charming Young Man! How much must you have suffered! I *knew* that it was impossible for one so elegant, and so well bred, to leave any Family in such a Manner, but for a Motive like this unanswerable.' Satisfied, beyond the power of Change, of this, She went in high spirits to her Aunt's apartment, without giving a Moment's recollection on the vanity of Young Women, or the unaccountable conduct of Young Men.

Kitty continued in this state of satisfaction during the remainder of the Stanley's visit—Who took their leave with many pressing invitations to visit them in London, when as Camilla said, she might have an opportunity of becoming acquainted with that sweet girl Augusta Halifax—Or Rather (thought Kitty,) of seeing my dear Mary Wynne again—. Mrs Percival in answer to Mrs Stanley's invitation replied—That she looked upon London as the hot house of Vice where virtue had long been banished from Society and Wickedness of every description was daily gaining ground*— that Kitty was of herself sufficiently inclined to give way to, and indulge in vicious inclinations*—and therefore was the last girl in the world to be trusted in London, as she would be totally unable to withstand temptation——.

After the departure of the Stanleys Kitty returned to her usual occupations, but Alas! they had lost their power of pleasing. Her bower alone retained its interest in her feelings, and perhaps that was oweing to the particular remembrance it brought to her mind of Edward Stanley.

The Summer passed away unmarked by any incident worth narrating, or any pleasure to Catharine save one, which arose from the reciept of a letter from her friend Cecilia now Mrs Lascelles,* announcing the speedy return of herself and Husband to England.

A correspondance productive indeed of little pleasure to either party had been established between Camilla and Catharine. The latter had now lost the only satisfaction she had ever received from the letters of Miss Stanley, as that young Lady having informed her Friend of the departure of her Brother to Lyons now never mentioned his name—Her letters seldom contained any Intelligence except a description of some new Article of Dress, an enumeration of various engagements, a panegyric on Augusta Halifax and perhaps a little abuse of the unfortunate Sir Peter—.

The Grove, for so was the Mansion of Mrs Percival at Chetwynde denominated, was situated within five miles from Exeter,* but though that Lady possessed a carriage and horses of her own, it was seldom that Catharine could prevail on her to visit that town for the purpose of shopping, on account of the many Officers perpetually Quartered* there and who infested the principal Streets—. A company of strolling players in their way from some Neighbouring Races* having opened a temporary Theatre there, Mrs Percival was prevailed on by her Niece to indulge her by attending the performance once during their stay—Mrs Percival insisted on paying Miss Dudley the compliment of inviting her to join the party, when a new difficulty arose, from the necessity of having some Gentleman to attend them——.

Scene to be in the Country, Heroine the Daughter of a
[1]Clergyman, one who after having lived much in the World
had retired from it, and settled on a Curacy, with a very
small fortune of his own.—He, the most excellent Man that
can be imagined, perfect in Character, Temper and
Manners—without the smallest drawback or peculiarity to
prevent his being the most delightful companion to his
Daughter from one year's end to the other.—Heroine a
[2]faultless Character herself—, perfectly good, with much
tenderness and sentiment, and not the least [3]Wit—very
highly [4]accomplished, understanding modern Languages
and (generally speaking) everything that the most accomplished young Women learn, but particularly excelling in
Music—her favourite pursuit—and playing equally well on
the Piano Forte and Harp—and singing in the first stile.
Her Person, quite beautiful—[5]dark eyes and plump
cheeks.*—Book to open with the description of Father and
Daughter—who are to converse in long speeches, elegant
Language—and a tone of high, serious sentiment.—The
Father to be induced, at his Daughter's earnest request, to
relate to her the past events of his Life.* This Narrative will
reach through the greatest part of the 1st vol.—as besides all
the circumstances of his attachment to her Mother and
their Marriage, it will comprehend his going to Sea as
[6]Chaplain to a distinguished Naval Character about the
Court, his going afterwards to Court himself, which
introduced him to a great variety of Characters and
involved him in many interesting situations, concluding
with his opinion of the Benefits to result from Tythes* being

[1] Mr. Gifford.* [2] Fanny Knight.* [3] Mary Cooke.*
[5] Mary Cooke. [4] Fanny K. [6] Mr. Clarke.*

done away, and his having buried his own Mother
(Heroine's lamented Grandmother) in consequence of the
High Priest of the Parish in which she died, refusing to pay
her Remains the respect due to them. The Father to be of a
very literary turn, an Enthusiast in Literature, nobody's
Enemy but his own*—at the same time most zealous in the
discharge of his Pastoral Duties, the model of an [7]exemplary
Parish Priest.—The heroine's friendship to be sought after
by a young Woman in the same Neighbourhood, of
[8]Talents and Shrewdness, with light eyes and a fair skin,
but having a considerable degree of Wit, Heroine shall
shrink from the acquaintance.—From this outset, the Story
will proceed, and contain a striking variety of adventures.*
Heroine and her Father never above a [9]fortnight together in
one place, *he* being driven from his Curacy by the vile arts of
some totally unprincipled and heart-less young Man,
desperately in love with the Heroine, and pursuing her with
unrelenting passion—no sooner settled in one Country of
Europe than they are necessitated to quit it and retire to
another—always making new acquaintance, and always
obliged to leave them.—This will of course exhibit a wide
variety of Characters—But there will be no mixture; the
scene will be for ever shifting from one Set of People to
another—but All the [10]Good will be unexceptionable in
every respect—and there will be no foibles or weaknesses
but with the Wicked, who will be completely depraved and
infamous, hardly a resemblance of Humanity left in
them.—Early in her career, in the progress of her first
removals, Heroine must meet with the Hero—all [11]perfection
of course—and only prevented from paying his addresses to
her, by some excess of refinement.—Wherever she goes,
somebody falls in love with her, and she receives repeated
offers of Marriage—which she always refers wholly to her
Father, exceedingly angry that [12]*he* should not be first
applied to.—Often carried away by the anti-hero, but

[7] Mr. Sherer.*   [8] Mary Cooke.
[9] Many Critics.   [10] Mary Cooke.
[11] Fanny Knight.   [12] Mrs. Pearse of Chilton-Lodge.*

rescued either by her Father or the Hero—often reduced to support herself and her Father by her Talents, and work for her Bread;*—continually cheated and defrauded of her hire, worn down to a Skeleton, and now and then starved to death—. At last, hunted out of civilized Society, denied the poor Shelter of the humblest Cottage, they are compelled to retreat into Kamschatka* where the poor Father, quite worn down, finding his end approaching, throws himself on the Ground, and after 4 or 5 hours of tender advice and parental Admonition to his miserable Child, expires in a fine burst of Literary Enthusiasm,* intermingled with Invectives against Holder's of Tythes.—Heroine inconsolable for some time—but afterwards crawls back towards her former Country—having at least 20 narrow escapes of falling into the hands of Anti-hero—and at last in the very nick of time, turning a corner to avoid him, runs into the arms of the Hero himself, who having just shaken off the scruples which fetter'd him before, was at the very moment setting off in pursuit of her.—The Tenderest and completest Eclaircissement takes place, and they are happily united.— Throughout the whole work, Heroine to be in the most [13]elegant Society and living in high style. The name of the work *not* to be [14]*Emma* but of the same sort as [15]S & S. and P & P.

[13] Fanny Knight.   [14] Mrs. Craven.*
[15] Mr H. Sanford.*

The Verses of Jane Austen

This little bag

This little bag* I hope will prove
    To be not vainly made—
For, if you should a needle want
    It will afford you aid.

And as we are about to part
    T'will serve another end,
For when you look upon the Bag
    You'll recollect your friend.*

                    Jan:ʳʸ 1792

[Thro' the rough ways of Life

Thro' the rough ways of Life,* with a patten* your Guard,
    May you safely and pleasantly jog;
May the ring never break, nor the Knot press too hard,
    Nor the Foot find the Patten a Clog.*]

Miss Lloyd has now sent to Miss Green

Miss Lloyd* has now sent to Miss Green,
As, on opening the box, may be seen,
Some yards of a Black Ploughman's Gauze,*
To be made up directly,* because
Miss Lloyd must in mourning appear
For the death of a Relative dear—
Miss Lloyd must expect to receive
This license to mourn and to grieve,
Complete, ere the end of the week—
It is better to write than to speak.

Oh! M^r. Best, you're very bad

Oh! M^r. Best,* you're very bad
    And all the world shall know it;
Your base behaviour shall be sung
    By me, a tunefull Poet.—

You used to go to Harrowgate*
    Each summer as it came,
And why I pray should you refuse
    To go this year the same?—

The way's as plain, the road's as smooth,
    The Posting* not increased;
You're scarcely stouter* than you were,
    Not younger Sir at least.—

If e'er the waters were of use
    Why now their use forego?
You may not live another year,
    All's mortal here below.—

It is your duty M^r. Best
    To give your health repair.
Vain else your Richard's pills* will be,
    And vain your Consort's care.*

But yet a nobler Duty calls
    You now towards the North.
Arise ennobled—as Escort
    Of Martha Lloyd stand forth.

She wants your aid—she honours you
    With a distinguished call.
Stand forth to be the friend of her
    Who is the friend of all.—

Take her, and wonder at your luck,
    In having such a Trust.
Her converse sensible and sweet
    Will banish heat and dust.—

So short she'll make the journey seem
    You'll bid the Chaise stand still.
T'will be like driving at full speed
    From Newb'ry to Speen Hill.*—

Convey her safe to Morton's wife*
    And I'll forget the past,
And write some verses in your praise
    As finely and as fast.

But if you still refuse to go
    I'll never let you rest,
But haunt you with reproachful song
    Oh! wicked M^r. Best!—

                                    J. A.
                            Clifton* 1806

See they come, post haste from Thanet

See they come, post haste from Thanet,*
    Lovely couple, side by side;
They've left behind them Richard Kennet*
    With the Parents of the Bride!

Canterbury they have passed through;
    Next succeeded Stamford-bridge;*
Chilham village* they came fast through;
    Now they've mounted yonder ridge.

Down the hill they're swift proceeding,
    Now they skirt the Park around;
Lo! The Cattle sweetly feeding
    Scamper, startled at the sound!

Run, my Brothers, to the Pier gate!*
   Throw it open, very wide!
Let it not be said that we're late
   In welcoming my Uncle's Bride!*

To the house the chaise advances;
   Now it stops—They're here, they're here!
How d'ye do, my Uncle Francis?
   How does do your Lady dear?

Happy the lab'rer*

Happy the lab'rer in his Sunday clothes!
In light-drab* coat, smart waistcoat, well-darn'd hose,
And hat upon his head, to church he goes;
As oft, with conscious pride, he downward throws
A glance upon the ample cabbage rose*
That, stuck in button-hole, regales his nose,
He envies not the gayest London beaux.
In church he takes his seat among the rows,*
Pays to the place the reverence he owes,
Likes best the prayers whose meaning least he knows,
Lists to the sermon in a softening doze,
And rouses joyous at the welcome close.

Of a Ministry pitiful, angry, mean

Of a Ministry* pitiful, angry, mean,
A gallant commander* the victim is seen.
For promptitude, vigour, success, does he stand
Condemn'd to receive a severe reprimand!
To his foes I could wish a resemblance in fate:
That they, too, may suffer themselves, soon or late,
The injustice they warrant. But vain is my spite,
They cannot *so* suffer who never do right.

Cambrick! with grateful blessings*

Cambrick!* with grateful blessings would I pay
    The pleasure given me in sweet employ:—
Long may'st thou serve my Friend without decay,
    And have no tears to wipe, but tears of joy!—

J. A.—Aug:ˢᵗ 26.—1808—

Cambrick! thou'st been to me a good*

Cambrick! thou'st been to me a good,
And I would bless thee if I could.
Go, serve thy mistress with delight,
Be small in compass, soft and white;
Enjoy thy fortune, honour'd much
To bear her name and feel her touch;
And that thy worth may last for years.
Slight be her colds, and few her tears.

To the Memory of Mʳˢ. Lefroy,
who died Dec:ʳ 16—my Birthday.—written 1808

The day returns again, my natal day;*
What mix'd emotions with the Thought arise!
Beloved friend, four years have pass'd away
Since thou wert snatch'd forever from our eyes.—

The day, commemorative of my birth
Bestowing Life and Light and Hope on me,
Brings back the hour which was thy last on Earth.
Oh! bitter pang of torturing Memory!—

Angelic Woman! past my power to praise
In Language meet, thy Talents, Temper, mind.
Thy solid Worth, thy captivating Grace!—
Thou friend and ornament of Humankind!—

At Johnson's death* by Hamilton* t'was said,
'Seek we a substitute—Ah! vain the plan,
No second best remains to Johnson dead—
None can remind us even of the Man.'*

So we of thee—unequall'd in thy race
Unequall'd thou, as he the first of Men.
Vainly we search around the vacant place,
We ne'er may look upon thy like again.

Come then fond Fancy, thou indulgent Power,—
—Hope is desponding, chill, severe to thee!—
Bless thou, this little portion of an hour,
Let me behold her as she used to be.

I see her here, with all her smiles benign,
Her looks of eager Love, her accents sweet.
That voice and Countenance almost divine!—
Expression, Harmony, alike complete.—

I listen—'tis not sound alone—'tis sense,
'Tis Genius, Taste and Tenderness of Soul.
'Tis genuine warmth of heart without pretence
And purity of Mind that crowns the whole.

She speaks; 'tis Eloquence—that grace of Tongue
So rare, so lovely!—Never misapplied
By *her* to palliate Vice, or deck a Wrong,
She speaks and reasons but on Virtue's side.

Her's is the Energy of Soul sincere.
Her Christian Spirit ignorant to feign,
Seeks but to comfort, heal, enlighten, chear,
Confer a pleasure, or prevent a pain.—

Can ought enhance such Goodness?—Yes, to me,
Her partial favour from my earliest years
Consummates all.—Ah! Give me yet to see
Her smile of Love.—the Vision disappears.

'Tis past and gone—We meet no more below.
Short is the Cheat of Fancy o'er the Tomb.
Oh! might I hope to equal Bliss to go!
To meet thee Angel! in thy future home!—

Fain would I feel an union in thy fate,
Fain would I seek to draw an Omen fair
From this connection in our Earthly date.
Indulge the harmless weakness—Reason, spare.—

J. A.

'Alas! poor Brag'*

'Alas! poor Brag,* thou boastful Game!—What now avails
    thine empty name?
Where now thy more distinguish'd fame?—My day is o'er,
    and Thine the same.—
For thou like me art thrown aside, At Godmersham, this
    Christmas Tide;
And now across the Table wide, Each Game, save Brag or
    Spec:* is tried.'—
Such is the mild Ejaculation, Of tender hearted
    Speculation.—

My dearest Frank, I wish you joy

Chawton, July 26—1809

My dearest Frank,* I wish you joy
Of Mary's safety with a Boy,*
Whose birth has given little pain
Compared with that of Mary Jane.*—
May he a growing Blessing prove,
And well deserve his Parents' Love!—
Endow'd with Art's and Nature's Good,
Thy Name possessing with thy Blood,
In him, in all his ways, may we
Another Francis William see!—

Thy infant days may he inherit,
Thy warmth, nay insolence of spirit;—
We would not with one fault dispense
To weaken the resemblance.
May he revive thy Nursery sin,
Peeping as daringly within,
His curley Locks but just descried,
With 'Bet, my be not come to bide.'*—
  Fearless of danger, braving pain,*
And threaten'd very oft in vain,
Still may one Terror daunt his Soul,
One needful engine of Controul
Be found in this sublime array,
A neighbouring Donkey's aweful Bray.*
So may his equal faults as Child,
Produce Maturity as mild!
His saucy words and fiery ways
In early Childhood's pettish days,
In Manhood, shew his Father's mind
Like him, considerate and Kind;
All Gentleness to those around,
And eager only not to wound.
  Then like his Father too, he must,
To his own former struggles just,
Feel his Deserts with honest Glow,
And all his self-improvement know.
A native fault may thus give birth
To the best blessing, conscious Worth.

  As for ourselves we're very well;
As unaffected prose will tell.—
Cassandra's pen will paint our state,
The many comforts that await
Our Chawton home,* how much we find
Already in it, to our mind;
And how convinced, that when complete
It will all other Houses beat
That ever have been made or mended,
With rooms concise, or rooms distended.

You'll find us very snug next year,
Perhaps with Charles and Fanny* near,
For now it often does delight us
To fancy them just over-right us.*—

J. A.—

'I've a pain in my head'

'I've a pain in my head'
  Said the suffering Beckford;*
To her Doctor so dread.
  'Oh! what shall I take for't?'

Said this Doctor so dread
  Whose name it was Newnham.*
'For this pain in your head
  Ah! What can you do Ma'am?'

Said Miss Beckford, 'Suppose
  If you think there's no risk,
I take a good Dose
  Of calomel* brisk.'—

'What a praise worthy Notion.'
  Replied Mr. Newnham.
'You shall have such a potion
  And so will I too Ma'am.'

Feb 7. 1811.

'I am in a Dilemma'

'I am in a Dilemma, for want of an Emma,'*
Escaped from the Lips, of Henry Gipps*—

Between Session* and Session

Between Session and Session	And the villainous Bill*
The first Prepossession	May be forced to lie still
May rouse up the Nation,	Against Wicked Men's will.*

At Eastbourne Mr. Gell

At Eastbourne* Mr. Gell, From being perfectly well,
Became dreadfully ill, For love of Miss Gill.*
So he said, with some sighs, I'm the slave of your *iis*;
Oh, restore, if you please, By accepting my *ees*.

When stretch'd on one's bed

When stretch'd on one's bed
With a fierce-throbbing head,
Which precludes alike thought or repose,
How little one cares
For the grandest affairs
That may busy the world as it goes!

How little one feels
For the waltzes and reels
Of our Dance-loving friends at a Ball!
How slight one's concern
To conjecture or learn
What their flounces or hearts* may befall.

How little one minds
If a company dines
On the best that the Season affords!
How short is one's muse
O'er the Sauces and Stews,
Or the Guests, be they Beggars or Lords.

How little the Bells,
Ring they Peels,* toll they Knells,*
Can attract our attention or Ears!
The Bride may be married,
The Corse* may be carried
And touch nor our hopes nor our fears.

Our own bodily pains
Ev'ry faculty chains;
We can feel on no subject beside.
Tis in health and in ease
We the power must seize
For our friends and our souls to provide.

Maria, good-humoured, and handsome, and tall

Maria,* good-humoured, and handsome, and tall,
　　For a husband was at her last stake;
And having in vain danced at many a ball,
　　Is now happy to *jump at a Wake*.

In measured verse I'll now rehearse

In measured verse I'll now rehearse
　　The charms of lovely Anna:*
And, first, her mind is unconfined
　　Like any vast savannah.

Ontario's lake* may fitly speak
　　Her fancy's ample bound:
Its circuit may, on strict survey
　　Five hundred miles be found.

Her wit descends on foes and friends
　　Like famed Niagara's Fall,*
And travellers gaze in wild amaze,
　　And listen, one and all.

Her judgment sound, thick, black, profound,
  Like transatlantic* groves,
Dispenses aid, and friendly shade
  To all that in it roves.

If thus her mind to be defined
  America exhausts,
And all that's grand in that great land
  In similes it costs—

Oh how can I her person try
  To image and portray?
How paint the face, the form how trace
  In which those virtues lay?

Another world must be unfurled,
  Another language known,
Ere tongue or sound can publish round
  Her charms of flesh and bone.

Charades*

1

When my first is a task to a young girl of spirit,
And my second confines her to finish the piece,
How hard is her fate! but how great is her merit,
If by taking my whole she effects her release!

2

Divided, I'm a gentleman
  In public deeds and powers;
United, I'm a monster, who
  That gentleman devours.

3

You may lie on my first by the side of a stream,
  And my second compose to the nymph you adore,
But if, when you've none of my whole, her esteem
  And affection diminish—think of her no more!

When Winchester races*

When Winchester races* first took their beginning
It is said the good people forgot their old Saint
Not applying at all for the leave of Saint Swithin*
And that William of Wykeham's* approval was faint.

The races however were fixed and determined
The company came and the Weather was charming
The Lords and the Ladies were satine'd and ermined
And nobody saw any future alarming.—

But when the old Saint was informed of these doings
He made but one Spring from his Shrine to the Roof
Of the Palace* which now lies so sadly in ruins*
And then he addressed them all standing aloof.

'Oh! subjects rebellious! Oh Venta* depraved
When once we are buried you think we are gone
But behold me immortal! By vice you're enslaved
You have sinned and must suffer, then farther he said

These races and revels and dissolute measures
With which you're debasing a neighboring Plain
Let them stand—You shall meet with your curse in your
      pleasures
Set off for your course, I'll pursue with *my* rain.

Ye cannot but know my command o'er July*
Henceforward I'll triumph in shewing my powers
Shift your race as you will it shall never be dry
The curse upon Venta is July in showers—'.

Prayers*

1

Give us Grace Almighty Father, so to pray, as to deserve to be heard, to address thee with our hearts, as with our lips.* Thou art every where present, from thee no secret can be hid.* May the knowledge of this, teach us to fix our thoughts on thee, with reverence and devotion that we pray not in vain.

Look with mercy on the sins we have this day committed and in mercy make us feel them deeply, that our repentance may be sincere, and our resolutions steadfast of endeavouring against the commission of such in future. Teach us to understand the sinfulness of our own hearts, and bring to our knowledge every fault of temper and every evil habit in which we have indulged to the discomfort of our fellow-creatures, and the danger of our own souls. May we now, and on each return of night, consider how the past day has been spent by us, what have been our prevailing thoughts, words and actions during it, and how far we can acquit ourselves of evil. Have we thought irreverently of thee, have we disobeyed thy commandments, have we neglected any known duty, or willingly given pain to any human being? Incline us to ask our hearts these questions oh! God, and save us from deceiving ourselves by pride or vanity.

Give us a thankful sense of the blessings* in which we live, of the many comforts of our lot; that we may not deserve to lose them by discontent or indifference.

Be gracious to our necessities, and guard us, and all we love, from evil this night.* May the sick and afflicted, be now, and ever thy care; and heartily do we pray for the safety of all that travel by land or by sea, for the comfort and protection of the orphan and widow and that thy pity may be shewn upon all captives and prisoners.*

Above all other blessings oh! God, for ourselves, and our fellow-creatures, we implore thee to quicken our sense of thy mercy in the redemption of the world, of the value of that Holy Religion in which we have been brought up, that we may not, by our own neglect, throw away the salvation thou hast given us, nor be Christians only in name. Hear us Almighty God, for His sake who has redeemed us, and taught us thus to pray. Our Father Which Art in heaven &c.

2

Almighty God! Look down with mercy on thy servants here assembled and accept the petitions now offered up unto thee. Pardon oh God! The offences of the past day. We are conscious of many frailties; we remember with shame and contrition, many evil thoughts and neglected duties; and we have perhaps sinned against thee and against our fellow-creatures in many instances of which we have no remembrance. Pardon Oh God! Whatever thou hast seen amiss in us, and give us a stronger desire of resisting every evil inclination and weakening every habit of sin. Thou knowest the infirmity of our nature, and the temptations which surround us. Be thou merciful, Oh Heavenly Father! To creatures so formed and situated. We bless thee for every comfort of our past and present existence, for our health of body and of mind and for every other source of happiness which thou hast bountifully bestowed on us and with which we close this day, imploring their continuance from thy Fatherly goodness,* with a more grateful sense of them, than they have hitherto excited. May the comforts of every day, be thankfully felt by us, may they prompt a willing obedience of thy commandments and a benevolent spirit toward every fellow-creature.

Have Mercy Oh Gracious Father! Upon all that are now suffering from whatsoever cause, that are in any circumstance of danger or distress. Give them patience under every affliction,* strengthen, comfort and relieve them.

To thy goodness we commend ourselves this night

beseeching thy protection of us through its darkness and dangers. We are helpless and dependent; graciously preserve us. For all whom we love and value, for every friend and connection, we equally pray; However divided and far asunder, we know that we are alike before thee, and under thine eye, may we be equally united in thy faith and fear,* in fervent devotion towards thee, and in thy merciful protection this night. Pardon Oh Lord! The imperfections of these our prayers, and accept them through the mediation of our blessed saviour, in whose holy words, we further address thee; our Father &c.

3

Father of Heaven! Whose goodness has brought us in safety to the close of this day,* dispose our hearts in fervent prayer, another day is now gone, and added to those, for which we were before accountable. Teach us Almighty Father, to consider this solemn truth, as we should do, that we may feel the importance of every day, and every hour as it passes, and earnestly strive to make a better use of what thy goodness may yet bestow on us, than we have done of the time past.

Give us grace to endeavour after a truly christian spirit to seek to attain that temper of forbearance and patience of which our blessed saviour has set us the highest example; and which, while it prepares us for the spiritual happiness of the life to come, will secure to us the best enjoyment of what this world can give. Incline us Oh God! To think humbly of ourselves, to be severe only in the examination of our own conduct, to consider our fellow-creatures with kindness, and to judge of all they say and do with that charity which we would desire from them ourselves.

We thank thee with all our hearts for every gracious dispensation, for all the blessings that have attended our lives, for every hour of safety, health and peace, of domestic comfort and innocent enjoyment. We feel that we have been blessed far beyond any thing that we have deserved; and though we cannot but pray for a continuance of all these mercies, we acknowledge our unworthiness of them and implore thee to pardon the presumption of our desires.

Keep us Oh! Heavenly Father from evil this night.* Bring us in safety to the beginning of another day* and grant that we may rise again with every serious and religious feeling which now directs us.

May thy mercy be extended over all mankind, bringing the ignorant to the knowledge of thy truth,* awakening the impenitent, touching the hardened. Look with compassion upon the afflicted of every condition, assuage the pangs of disease, comfort the broken in spirit.

More particularly do we pray for the safety and welfare of our own family and friends wheresoever dispersed, beseeching thee to avert from them all material and lasting evil of body or mind; and may we by the assistance of thy holy spirit so conduct ourselves on earth as to secure an eternity of happiness with each other in thy heavenly kingdom. Grant this most merciful Father, for the sake of our blessed saviour in whose holy name and words we further address thee. Our Father Which Art in Heaven &c.

TEXTUAL NOTES

VOLUME THE FIRST

1. l. 20	*muslin Cloak*:	'muslin' added above line.
3. l. 4	*Father*:	orig. 'Mother', crossed out.
3. l. 11	*either . . . beloved, or*:	added above line.
4. l. 29	*rightly imagined them*:	'them' added above line.
6. l. 10	*Patches*:	orig. 'Rouge'.
6. l. 30	*she should return*:	'should' orig. 'would'.
7. l. 6	*he accordingly did*:	'did' added above line.
8. l. 22	*Roger first*:	'first' substituted for word crossed out (? 'must').
11. l. 7	*once upon*:	'up' in 'upon' added above line.
11. l. 20	*of the party*:	added above line.
12. l. 2	*to be pleasing*:	'pleasing' orig. 'agreable', crossed out.
12. l. 22	*feirceness*:	orig. 'inconvenience'.
12. l. 23	*concourse*:	orig. 'concourse of masks'.
13. l. 4	*in their hand*:	orig. 'by his side'.
14. l. 5	*so much her Junior*:	'Junior' orig. 'inferior'.
14. l. 28	*unreturned affection*:	'unreturned' added above line.
15. l. 23	*and might perhaps*:	'might' orig. 'had not'.
15. l. 30	*following year*:	'year' orig. 'Xmas'.
16. l. 8	*too red a look*:	orig. 'much colour'.
16. l. 10	*I'll tell you why*:	'tell' added by Chapman and present editors.
16. ll. 23–4	*my idea of the case is*:	orig. 'my ideas of the case are'.
16. l. 36	*so hot*:	orig. 'so hot that'.
16. l. 37	*she almost*:	'she' orig. 'they'.
16. l. 38	*forced her away*:	orig. 'forced away his Daughter'.
17. l. 10	*Lady Williams called*:	'Lady Williams' orig. 'her ladyship'.
17. l. 17	*roused from the reflection*:	'the' orig. 'a'.
17. l. 32	*what they may do*:	in MS the following words have been crossed out: 'a woman (?) in *such* a situation is particularly off her guard because

her head is not strong enough to support intoxication'.

18. l. 1   *angry at the time, because*: 'because' added above line.

18. l. 29   *a sister . . . who is*: 'is' orig. 'was'.

18. l. 32   *I have lived*: 'have' added above line.

18. l. 33   *during which time*: orig. 'during which time some'.

20. l. 4   *any thing else*: 'thing else' substituted for 'other reason'.

20. l. 8   *I should shortly*: 'shortly' orig. 'soon'.

20. l. 21   *since we might otherwise*: 'since' orig. 'or'; 'otherwise' added above line.

20. l. 24   *screamed as you may*: 'may' added above line.

21. l. 21   *of Lucy her*: 'her' orig. 'on'.

21. l. 22   *as soon as*: orig. 'when'.

21. l. 31   *I fancy*: orig. 'I fancy that'.

21. l. 35   *the other Evening*: 'the other' orig. 'yesterday'.

22. l. 1   *tho' I am very partial to her*: orig. 'tho' I may be partial; indeed I believe I am; yes I am *very* partial to her'.

22. l. 19   *tour to you—I hope*: 'I' orig. 'I'll'.

23. l. 19   *expected to appear*: 'appear' amended from 'appeared' in MS.

23. l. 19   *pleased at*: 'at' added above line.

23. l. 20   *you have made me*: 'me' added above line.

23. l. 32   *sketch . . . of her*: 'of' added above line.

24. l. 5   *obliged to Mr Adams*: 'Mr Adams' orig. 'him'.

24. l. 14   *conquering every*: 'every' amended from 'ever' in MS.

24. l. 19   *she determined to do*: 'to do' added above line.

24. l. 23   *having accomplished*: 'having' added above line.

24. l. 35   *That one should receive*: 'That' added above line.

25. l. 2   *instilled into my mind*: 'mind' added above line.

25. l. 24   *be united*: phrase repeated, the second crossed out.

25. ll. 29–32   *Altho' . . . happy*: all substituted for phrase crossed out (partly illegible). Austen substituted the phrase 'yet, let me beg . . . happy' for 'less deeply felt for want of sufficient [illegible]'.

25. l. 30   *I admire your*: 'your' added above line

25. l. 36	*or refuse*: orig. '& refuse'.
26. l. 9	*blemish*: orig. 'plot'.
26. l. 13	*2 first of whom had*: 'had' orig. 'having'.
26. l. 34	*at present the favourite Sultana*: 'at present' added above line.
27. ll. 20–1	*'indeed, has been'*: added above line.
28. l. 29	*Mr Willmot was*: orig. 'Mr. Willmot was a younger'.
29. l. 12	*tremble*: orig. 'fear'.
29. l. 26	*much against*: orig. 'much' crossed out; 'most' inserted and crossed out; 'much' restored.
30. l. 2	*so faltering a voice*: orig. 'so faultering a manner'.
32. l. 6	*Having amused herself*: orig. followed by 'with', crossed out.
32. l. 14	*Mrs Wilson*: here 'Willson', elsewhere 'Wilson'; in every case, 'Wilson' was orig. 'Jones'.
32. l. 15	*was no sooner*: 'was' orig. 'had'.
32. l. 27	*obliging her and*: orig. followed by 'of expressing the Love she bore her'.
33. l. 11	*introduce her to Lady Harriet*: 'Harriet' here orig. 'Hariet'.
33. l. 18	*effected, as*: 'as' added above line.
33. l. 19	*Dutchess's chaplain being*: orig. followed by 'likewise'.
33. l. 29	*as soon as she had read*: orig. 'after having read it'.
33. l. 33	*sent out after them 300*: 'after' written twice, the first crossed out.
33. l. 34	*not to return without*: 'out' in 'without' written above line.
34. ll. 10–11	*able to save*: 'save' substituted for another word (? 'render').
34. l. 34	*nor would it be possible*: 'be' added above line.
35. l. 1	*her little boys*: 'little' added above line.
35. ll. 26–7	*steps at the door*: 'at' orig. 'of'.
36. l. 24	*than you had*: 'had' orig. 'do'.
36. ll. 26–7	*now strikes me as*: orig. 'never before struck me with'.
36. l. 37	*with which she*: 'she' added above line.
38. l. 26	*enamoured of*: 'of' orig. 'with'.
38. l. 28	*Husband, whom*: 'whom' added above line.

39. ll. 5–6	*as he knew that he should*: this phrase was orig. 'should'.
39. l. 6	*greived by*: 'by' orig. 'at'.
39. l. 10	*the Village*: 'the' added above line.
39. l. 28	*Lady Percival, at*: 'at' orig. 'with'.
41. l. 2	*a dangerous fever*: 'dangerous' orig. 'violent'.
41. l. 23	*Manners are*: 'are' added above line.
42. l. 12	*Mother's shop*: 'shop' added above line.
43. l. 12	*peremptory*: orig. 'arrogant'.
46. l. 19	*inform you of besides*: 'besides' added above line.
47. l. 16	*veiw when it*: 'it' orig. 'they'.
47. l. 18	*Dramatis Personae*: in the MS, characters' names are given in one long column.
49. l. 4	*never went any farther*: 'any' added above line.
49. l. 7	*he has always*: 'always' orig. 'ever'.
49. l. 8	*adherent to Truth*: after this in MS, the following has been crossed out: 'He never told a Lie but once, & that was merely to oblige me. Indeed I may truly say there never was such a Brother!'
49. l. 28	*and Sophy my Brother*: orig. 'and Sophy take my Brother'.
50. l. 25	*but Sophy*: orig. 'but however Sophy', 'however' crossed out.
50. l. 29	*toast and*: added above line.
51. l. 3	*too savoury for him*: 'him' substituted for word or words crossed out, probably 'Sir Arthur'.
51. l. 9	*never eats suet pudding*: 'suet' added above line.
51. l. 12	*take away the Pudding*: 'suet' crossed out before 'Pudding'.
52. l. 15	*Patronage to*: 'to' orig. 'of'.
53. l. 3	*Dramatis Personae*: list of characters orig. in one column.
54. l. 20	*I'll go*: followed by 'and dress' crossed out.
55. l. 5	*His obedient*: orig. 'obediant', 'ant' crossed out.
56. l. 19	*hates dancing and*: orig. followed by 'has a great idea of Womens never going from home' ('never' added above line).
56. l. 20	*talks a great deal*: orig. 'has a great idea'.
56. l. 38	*I don't like it*: 'it' orig. 'him'.
57. l. 1	*I am not going*: 'not' added above line.

58. l. 19   *from herself, he told her he should do*: 'he should do' substituted for 'that he should' or perhaps 'that he would'.

58. ll. 28–9   *If Mary won't have him*: 'him' added above line.

58. l. 32   *more strictly*: 'more' orig. 'most'.

60. l. 11   *three thousand a year.*: there follows in the MS, crossed out: 'who keeps a postchaise & pair, with silver Harness, a boot before before and a window to look out at behind?'

60. l. 25   *ensure it in reality*: substituted for 'have made it really so'.

61. ll. 22–3   *if he will be so cross*: illegible word or words crossed out before 'so cross'.

62. l. 11   *never were seen!*: there follows in MS the following passage, crossed out: 'Pearls as large as those of the Princess Badroulbadour, as in the 4th Volume of the Arabian Nights and Rubies, Emeralds, Toppazes, Sapphires, Amythists, Turkey stones, Agate, Beads, Bugles & Garnets'. In 'The Story of Aladdin, or the Wonderful Lamp' in the *Arabian Nights*, Aladdin's mother offers the princess he attempts to woo the jewels he carried from the cave, where he had found them growing like fruit on a tree: these include pearls, diamonds, rubies, emeralds, sapphires, amethysts. Later the genie of the lamp offers Aladdin yet more jewels with which to win the princess, sending 'forty black slaves, each with a bason on his head full of pearls, diamonds, rubies, and emeralds, all larger than those presented to the sultan before'. 'Turkey stones' are turquoises, and a 'bugle' is a 'tube-shaped glass bead, usually black' (*OED*).

64. l. 20   *have with Mary*: 'with' added above line.

64. l. 23   *Leicestershire.*: The following sentence is crossed out: 'Not related to the Family & even but distantly connected with it. His Sister is married to John Dutton's Wife's Brother. When you have puzzled over this account a little you will understand it.'

65. l. 13   *object of every one's*: 'every one's' orig. 'general'.
66. l. 19   *encouraged her*: orig. followed by 'in doing so'.
67. l. 23   *[Detached pieces]*: title not in MS added to agree with JA's title-page.
68. l. 6   *The Author*: after this introduction follows a fragment entirely crossed out:

A Fragment

written to inculcate the practise of Virtue

We all know that many are unfortunate in their progress through the world, but we do not know all that are so. To seek them out to study their wants, & to leave them unsupplied is the duty, and ought to be the Business of Man. But few have time, fewer still have inclination, and no one has either the one or the other for such employments. Who amidst those that perspire away their Evenings in crouded assemblies can have leisure to bestow a thought on such as sweat under the fatigue of their daily Labour.

69. l. 9   *she cannot think to*: 'to' orig. 'of'.
69. l. 14   *Warwick*: orig. 'Warwickshire'.

VOLUME THE SECOND

75. l. 11   *dreadful ones*: 'dreadful' orig. 'cruel'.
75. ll. 14–15 *cruel Persecutions*: 'cruel' substituted for another word, illegible, crossed out.
75. l. 25   *Afflictions of my past Life*: orig. 'many Afflictions of that', 'that' crossed out.
76. l. 19   *Acquirements had been*: 'had been' orig. 'were'.
76. l. 20   *I had shortly surpassed*: 'had' added above line.
76. l. 21   *that could adorn it*: 'adorn' added above line.
76. l. 22   *Rendezvous of every good Quality*: orig. 'Quality & the place of appointment', 'place of appointment' crossed out.
77. ll. 12–13 *and had supped one night in Southampton*: 'had supped' orig. 'had slept'.
78. l. 1   *greatly astonished*: orig. 'greatly astonished, considerably amazed and somewhat sur-

prized', 'considerably . . . surprized' crossed out.

78. ll. 11–12   *We must not . . . partly convinced*: orig. 'I cannot pretend to assert that any one knocks, tho' for my own part I own I rather imagine it is a Knock at the Door that somebody does. Yet as we have no ocular Demonstration . . . .' all crossed out. The four dots are JA's.

78. ll. 20–1   *Oh! let no time be lost.*: orig. 'Oh! let us go immediately.', crossed out.

79. ll. 2–3   *that on him the happiness . . . depend*: substituted for partially illegible original, possibly 'I felt myself [instantaneously] in Love with him' ('in Love with him' is clearly the end of the old sentence).

79. l. 23   *in compliance with your Wishes*: orig. 'if you wish I should'.

79. l. 27   *he had perhaps*: 'perhaps' added above line.

79. l. 28   *to meet with*: orig. 'to have met with'.

80. ll. 8–9   *what might have befallen me*: 'me' added above line.

80. l. 34   *never even had the*: orig. 'not even the'.

81. l. 1   *I found her*: orig. 'Her I found'.

81. ll. 29–30   *acquit you of ever having*: 'ever' added above line.

81. ll. 35–6   *(said Edward)*: added above line.

82. l. 6   *returned Augusta*: 'returned' orig. 'replied'.

82. l. 8   *Does it appear*: 'Does' orig. 'Did'.

82. l. 9   *vile and corrupted*: 'corrupted' orig. 'Vulgar'.

82. l. 15   *Here I was prevented*: 'prevented' orig. 'interrupted'.

83. ll. 6–7   *dared to unite*: 'to' added above line.

83. l. 18   *doubtless reflecting*: squeezed in below line.

83. l. 26   *most particular freind*: 'freind' added above line.

83. l. 28   *in a few hours*: orig. 'in less than an hour'.

84. l. 17   *Towards the close of the Day*: Letter the 9th originally began 'When we were somewhat recovered from the overpowering effusions of our': 'overpowering' substituted for illegible word, crossed out. NB: this clause now begins Letter the 10th.

84. l. 21   *charming Society, I*: orig. 'charming Society, yet I', 'yet' crossed out.

85. l. 2	*that fortune which*: 'which' added above line.
85. l. 20	*as I then enjoyed*: 'then' added above line.
85. l. 25	*there never were a happier Couple*: 'were' orig., changed to 'was', then back to 'were'.
85. l. 29	*with those whom they*: 'whom' added above line.
85. ll. 31–2	*to such despotic Power*: 'such' substituted above line for illegible word crossed out, possibly 'their'; another illegible word, possibly 'rule', crossed out before 'Power'.
85. l. 35	*the good opinion*: 'good' added above line.
85. l. 36	*in so doing*: 'in' orig. 'by'.
86. l. 16	*Sensibility of Edward*: 'Edward' orig. 'Augus'; JA originally starts to write 'Augustus'.
86. l. 30	*We promised that we*: orig. 'we promised that he'.
87. l. 11	*within twelve miles*: 'twelve' orig. 'six'.
87. l. 13	*Holbourn*: orig. 'Piccadilly'.
87. l. 29	*unprovided*: : 'un' added above line.
88. l. 29	*to follow it*: 'it' orig. 'him'.
88. l. 36	*he was my Grandfather*: 'Grandfather' squeezed in below line.
91. l. 5	*the natural noble*: 'noble' added above line.
91. ll. 33–4	*no other young Man*: 'young Man' orig. 'Person'.
91. l. 39	*and assured her that*: 'that' added above line.
92. ll. 3–4	*to imagine that*: 'that' added above line.
92. l. 15	*with Confusion*: orig. 'with with', second 'with' crossed out.
92. l. 18	*any other Person*: orig. 'other People'.
93. ll. 5–6	*although it was at a considerable distance from Macdonald-Hall*: orig. 'as it was a most agreable Drive', crossed out; JA probably then substituted 'from its wonderful Celebrity', also crossed out.
93. l. 13	*suspected it*: orig. 'suspected it, had it not', 'had it not' crossed out.
93. l. 17	*amongst*: orig. 'with'.
93. l. 26	*majestically*: orig. 'magestically'.
94. l. 21	*must desire that*: 'that' added above line.
96. ll. 7–8	*to be silent would be cruel*: 'cruel' crossed out, then restored.
96. l. 13	*melancholy reflections*: orig. 'melancholy reflections of Augustus', 'of Augustus' crossed out.

97. l. 24   *on my Edward's Death*: 'Edward's' added above line.

98. l. 23   *proceeding to relate*: 'to relate' squeezed in at the end of the page.

99. l. 6   *allotted us*: 'us' orig. 'her'.

99. l. 12   *her sweet face:*: 'sweet' orig. 'fair'.

99. l. 28   *the last words*: 'words' added above line.

99. l. 33   *Village in which*: 'in which' orig. 'where'.

100. l. 4   *A general Silence prevailed—*: orig. 'A mutual Silence prevailed amongst us all—'.

100. l. 23   *when on looking behind*: 'on' added above line.

101. ll. 5–6   *of Sir Edward and*: 'and' (in JA's MS '&') added above line.

101. l. 13   *singular Service*: 'Service' added above line.

101. l. 27   *reflected Honour*: 'Honour' added above line.

101. l. 31   *unjustifiable Reproaches*: 'unjustifiable' probably orig. 'unmanly'.

102. l. 2   *delightful scenes*: 'delightful' orig. 'Beautifull'.

102. l. 6   *from thence had made daily Excursions*: 'made' orig. 'many'.

102. l. 11   *subsistance*: orig. 'subsistence', 'ence' crossed out, 'ance' substituted.

102. l. 19   *generally accompanied*: 'generally' orig. 'always'.

103. ll. 6–7   *expressing my fears of*: 'of' orig. 'for'.

103. l. 18   *befallen me*: 'me' orig. 'them'.

103. l. 30   *Agatha (my own Mother)*: 'Mother' added above line.

104. l. 14   *we expected*: orig. 'we were determined'.

104. l. 20   *starved to Death*: orig. 'dead'.

104. l. 35   *England, and Wales*: orig. 'England, Ireland, and Wales'.

104. l. 37   *We happened to be quartered*: orig. 'We happened to quit'.

105. l. 5   *left the Town*: 'Town' orig. 'room'.

105. l. 15   *drawing to a close*: 'drawing' struck out and re-inserted.

105. l. 23   *I took up my Residence*: 'Residence' orig. 'Lodging'.

105. ll. 29–30   *united to . . . suited to her*: orig. 'united to the Man of all others most suited to her, Graham'; JA changed the position of the word 'Graham'.

105. ll. 37–8	*still Exhibit*: orig. 'still continue to Exhibit'.
107. ll. 5–6	*it will always remain so*: 'always' added above line.
107. l. 6	*it is carried*: 'is' added above line.
107. ll. 11–14	*Messrs . . . £105. 0. 0*: written in a different hand, apparently by Henry Austen.
107. ll. 18–19	*to Miss Charlotte Lutterell*: in 'Letter the fifth' in MS, JA alters the spelling of 'Lutterell' to 'Luttrell'; we are sustaining the first form throughout for consistency.
109. l. 15	*two such tender*: 'two' orig. 'too'.
109. l. 21	*or anywhere else*: 'else' added above line.
109. l. 22	*We have only to hope*: 'We' orig. 'I'; 'to' added above line.
110. ll. 12–13	*Honeymoon, I had the*: 'I had the' substituted for orig. 'to find that'.
110. ll. 32–3	*going instantly to Henry*: 'instantly' added above line.
110. l. 36	*room; we laid*: orig. 'room; where we laid', 'where' crossed out.
110. ll. 37–8	*in the most dreadful*: 'the' added above line.
111. l. 2	*dreadful Waste in our provisions*: 'in our provisions' added above line.
111. l. 13	*but to no purpose*: 'to' added above line.
111. ll. 17–18	*I may suffer most from it*: 'from' substituted for the original 'for'.
111. ll. 31–2	*but leaving her . . . I took down*: orig. 'I left her with my Mother and taking down'.
111. l. 35	*Melancholy Event*: 'Event' substituted for 'Account', heavily crossed out.
113. l. 17	*reflection distressed her most*: 'her' substituted for orig. 'us'.
113. l. 24	*a most chearfull Manner*: 'chearfull' orig. 'lively'.
113. l. 30	*cheerful Gaiety*: the 'e' in this latter word is added above line.
114. l. 29	*afterwards actually fell*: 'fell' orig. 'fallen'.
115. l. 17	*there certainly never were*: 'never' added above line.
116. l. 31	*Caprice on her side*: 'on her side' orig. 'in herself'.
116. l. 36	*a violent partiality*: 'partiality' orig. 'freindship'.

117. l. 3	*as when it first commenced*: orig. 'as when it was first commenced'.
117. l. 4	*the pleasures of London, and of Brightelmstone*: orig. 'the pleasures of London and the amusements of Brighthelmstone'.
117. ll. 5–6	*even to satisfy the curiosity*: 'curiosity' substituted for 'certainly' heavily crossed out.
118. l. 11	*my acquaintance to marry*: 'acquaintance' orig. 'freinds'.
118. l. 18	*Miss Margaret Lesley to*: 'to' orig. 'and'.
118. l. 27	*to imagine there was*: orig. 'to imagine that there was'.
118. l. 35	*We contented*: orig. 'We therefore contented'.
119. l. 6	*unmajestic*: orig. 'unmagestic'.
119. l. 7	*in comparison with*: 'with' orig. 'to'.
119. l. 10	*to bring her*: orig. 'to have brought *us*'.
119. l. 28	*dungeon-like form*: 'form' orig. 'appearance'.
119. l. 29	*a Rock to appearance so*: 'to appearance' added above line.
120. l. 1	*Girls, such as*: 'such' added above line.
121. l. 10	*conquer his passion*: 'his' added above line.
121. l. 31	*resemblance between*: 'between' orig. 'with'.
122. l. 7	*you said you did not*: orig. 'you said that you did not'.
122. l. 12	*Do not you think the Miss Lesleys*: 'think the' orig. 'think that the'.
123. l. 1	*Charlotte I was not*: orig. 'Charlotte that I was not'.
123. l. 32	*to be so suspected*: 'so' added above line.
124. l. 18	*I suppose this Letter*: orig. 'I suppose that this Letter'.
124. l. 25	*its Public-places*: 'its' orig. 'her'.
124. l. 31	*my Education that I took by far the*: orig. 'my Education I always took'.
125. l. 2	*so it has always*: 'has' added above line.
125. ll. 12–13	*equal and*: orig. 'equal of'.
125. l. 25	*Agreement*: JA scratched out second 'e', then reinserted it above line.
125. l. 30	*approbation*: orig. 'Praise'.
125. l. 36	*which is the only tune*: 'is' orig. 'was'.
126. l. 18	*the only very severe thing*: 'thing' orig. 'speech'.
126. l. 39–127. l. 1	*a kind of affection*: orig. 'an affection'.

127. l. 4	*I hope you or Matilda*: orig. 'I hope that you or Matilda'.
127. ll. 21–2	*I know my own Heart too well*: 'too well' orig. 'well enough'.
127. l. 31	*to write, to speak*: 'to speak' added above line.
128. l. 33	*write to you*: 'to' added above line.
129. l. 36	*sure you will agree*: orig. 'I am sure that you will'.
130. l. 10	*by any one of her own Sex*: 'one' added above line.
130. l. 13	*one Man*: 'one' added above line.
130. l. 17	*my Compliments*: orig. 'my best Compliments'.
130. l. 21	*I am afraid*: orig. 'I am afraid that'.
131. l. 13	*the reasons why I cannot*: 'why' added above line.
131. l. 23	*Last Monday se'night*: 'se'night' orig. 'sennet'.
132. ll. 9–10	*a conversation we had never*: 'never' added above line.
132. l. 13	*one of the most frequent*: 'frequent' added above line.
133. l. 6	*his 1st Marriage*: '1st' added above line.
133. ll. 10–11	*turned Roman-catholic . . . married*: orig. 'obtained another of the Pope's Bulls for annulling'.
133. l. 21	*She owns*: orig. 'She owns me to'.
135. ll. 20–1	*should not have burnt her*: 'have' added above line.
135. l. 28	*we have here given*: 'here' added above line.
136. ll. 12–13	*his two Nephews*: 'two' added above line.
137. ll. 9–10	*the former of whom*: 'whom' orig. 'which'.
137. l. 14	*daughter Elizabeth*: 'daughter' orig. 'Granddaughter'.
137. l. 21	*giving only a slight sketch*: 'only' added above line.
137. ll. 28–9	*Crimes with which she was accused*: orig. 'Crimes she was accused with'.
137. l. 34	*those before alledged*: 'before' added above line.
138. l. 36	*the manner of it*: 'it' substituted for 'his own (?) death'.
139. l. 7	*excess of vanity*: 'vanity' substituted for '*Cockylorum*' crossed out.
139. l. 29	*reign was famous for*: 'was' is Chapman's emendation, substituted for original MS 'for'; MS phrase is 'for famous for'.

141. l. 24	*in this or the next Century*: 'the' added above line.
141. l. 24	*tho' now but young*: 'now' added above line.
143. l. 31	*may be considered*: orig. 'may be all considered'.
144. l. 8	*uninteresting*: orig. 'tedious'.
144. ll. 22–3	*he was a Stuart*: in the MS, the letters composing the word 'Stuart' are written emphatically, in large size (not caps.) with spaces between them.
145. l. 3	*Cousin*: orig. 'Madam', erased.
145. ll. 13–14	*a different Manner from*: 'from' orig. 'to'.
146. ll. 2–3	*drink tea with us*: 'tea' added above line.
146. ll. 34–5	*seduced by her Example, or contaminated by her Follies*: this construction is the third stage, which in its very first version was 'contaminated by her Example, or her Follies'; JA changed 'contaminated' to 'seduced' and then altered the whole to obtain the two balanced phrases in the text.
149. l. 22	*wiping her Eyes*: orig. 'my Eyes'.
150. l. 6	*have made it a point*: 'have' added above line.
151. l. 8	*a favour about which*: 'about' orig. 'for'.
151. l. 22	*Why could not you have worn*: 'you' added above line.
151. l. 24	*poor, for*: 'for' orig. 'because'.
152. ll. 1–2	*I am sure Ellen felt for me*: throughout, 'Ellen' is written over another name crossed out, apparently 'Fanny'.
153. l. 9	*of having the most*: 'having' added above line.
153. ll. 25–6	*Why, was not your Father*: what follows is different in the orig. MS: 'I fancy not; but your Ladyship knows best.' 'Was not he in the Kings Bench once?' [the reply crossed out is difficult to read but appears to be 'Just as your Ladyship pleases—it is the same to me.']
153. ll. 29–30	*half afraid of being*: orig. 'half afraid of having'.
154. l. 30	*shews your legs*: 'legs' written over 'ancles'.
154. ll. 31–2	*some sort of people*: 'some sort' orig. 'your sort' crossed out, the word 'low' substituted and crossed out, 'some sort' inserted above line.
156. l. 7	*Happiness*: orig. 'Felicity'.
156. l. 20	*I was actually silenced*: orig. followed by 'Could you have beleived it Mary'

157. l. 4   *your Absence*: orig. 'your Absence during a long stay in Essex?'

157. ll. 23–4   *what were my sensations*: 'were' added above line.

158. l. 8   *my fair one*: 'one' added above line.

158. l. 13   *my own house which tho' an excellent one*: 'one' orig. 'House'.

158. l. 18   *T. Musgrove*: after the signature the following postscript, crossed out: 'May I hope to receive an answer to this e'er many days have tortured me with Suspence! Any Letter (post paid) will be most welcome.'

158. l. 38   *every day of my life*: after this sentence two-and-a-half lines have been heavily and repeatedly crossed out. We offer this partial and highly conjectural reading: 'T[ire]d [tho'] we shall be of one another when we are [marrie]d [illegible] do not you long for the spring?'

161. l. 28   *To be sure*: substituted for 'Indeed'.

161. l. 31   *as you are in every*: 'in' added above line.

162. l. 23   *example of Felicity*: 'Felicity' substituted for orig. 'conjugal'.

162. l. 39   *my dear Tom*: 'Tom' orig. 'Cousin'.

163. ll. 6–7   *I ever knew*: 'ever' orig. 'never'.

164. ll. 3–4   *Charitable every now and then*: originally followed by this sentence: 'I gave away two pence this Morning.'

166. l. 5   *He replied*: 'replied' orig. 'said'.

164. l. 7   *destined to be the Husband*: 'to be' orig. 'as'.

165. l. 1   *[Scraps]*: title not in MS, added to agree with JA's title-page.

165. l. 30   *estimable*: orig. 'pleasing'.

166. l. 29   *Understanding nor is without*: 'is' added above line.

167. l. 2   *Characters*: in the MS, characters' names are given in one long column.

169. l. 3   *Errors*: replaces a word crossed out, possibly 'several'.

169. ll. 15–16   *I am now going to reform*: 'now' added above line.

170. l. 10   *through Wales, which is*: Austen writes 'with is'; we have printed Chapman's emendation 'which is'.

171. l. 26	*only by a wooden latch*: 'by' added above line.
171. ll. 33–4	*to lay out any thing on furniture himself*: 'himself' orig. 'herself', corrected (in a different ink).

VOLUME THE THIRD

173. l. 1	*Volume the Third*: There is a pencilled note on the inside cover of the vellum notebook containing 'Volume the Third':

> Effusions of Fancy
> by a very Young Lady
> Consisting of Tales
> in a Style entirely new

Deirdre Le Faye believes this to be in the hand of the Revd George Austen; see *Jane Austen: A Family Record* (London, 1989), 73.

173. l. 2	*Jane Austen—May 6th 1792.*: on the index page above this phrase is written in pencil 'for James Edward Austen', presumably in Cassandra Austen's hand; see Le Faye, *A Family Record*, 244.
173. l. 10	*The Author*: this dedication is on the verso of JA title-page.
175. l. 20	*pain*: orig. 'idea'.
175. ll. 27–8	*that the freindly balm*: 'the' added above line.
176. l. 12	*oblige you with their house* : orig. 'oblige you with the remainder of their house'.
176. l. 13	*a direction to the place*: 'place' orig. 'House'.
177. l. 10	*excess*: orig. 'effusions'.
177. l. 14	*already made*: substituted for 'before expressed'.
177. ll. 23–4	*we bear you*: orig. 'we bear for you'.
178. l. 8	*to promise to keep it*: 'promise to' added above line.
180. l. 11	*agitated by*: 'by' orig. 'with'.
180. l. 21	*I will forget you no longer*: 'will' added above line.
180. l. 28	*not from Rosa*: 'from' orig. 'for' crossed out, 'from' written in pencil below line, probably not by JA.
181. l. 29	*certainly greatly inferior*: 'inferior' orig. 'superior'.

181. l. 33   *very ancient date*: 'ancient' orig. 'old'.
182. l. 13   *lamented Henry's Rosa*: word crossed out before 'Rosa', probably 'Brother'.
183. l. 19   *On his return home*: from here on, 'Evelyn' is written with a different pen and ink, and in a different hand. It is most probable that the continuation was written in 1809, taking the clue from the date given to Mr Gower's letter in this continuation. But as to the authorship of this continuation, we can offer only informed conjecture. Deirdre Le Faye, a biographer of JA well acquainted with the Austens' handwritings, suggests that the continuation from this point is in the hand of James Edward Austen, JA's nephew. In 1809 James Edward would have been 11 years old. On the other hand, it has been suggested that the handwriting might be another form of the same hand which produced the other continuation of 'Evelyn', printed in Chapman, *Minor Works*, 240–2; that continuation is signed with the initials of Anna Lefroy, née Austen, James Edward's older half-sister. Anna Austen was 16 in 1809; she could have attempted a continuation at that early date, and then tried to refine upon it years later, after her marriage in 1814.

The nephew or niece who composed these final pages of 'Evelyn' might have undertaken the task alone, or in consultation with JA. See 'Introduction', pp. xix–xx.

183. l. 22   *window open*: 'open' orig. 'opened'.
183. l. 39   *seated on a Sofa*: an illegible word crossed out before 'Sofa', probably 'chaiselong'.
184. l. 12   *inhabitants*: 'itants' written above line.
184. l. 22   *respect*: orig. 'respectful', 'ful' crossed out.
186. ll. 1–2   *Catharine, or the Bower*: the title was originally 'Kitty, or the Bower'. JA changed 'Kitty' to 'Catharine' here and elsewhere in the text, but 'Kitty' was not replaced on all occasions. In this case, we have differed from our usual policy of keeping names uniform: where JA has changed the name to 'Catharine', we

sustain 'Catharine' but where JA has not changed 'Kitty' we retain 'Kitty'. (Another problem is offered by JA's inconsistency in spelling the name both 'Catharine' and 'Catherine': we have maintained the spelling 'Catharine' throughout.)

187. l. 4   *To this Bower*: 'Bower' orig. 'Garden'.

187. ll. 23–4   *the Miss Wynnes*: there originally followed a passage crossed out: 'they were companions in their walks, their Schemes & Amusements, and while the sweetness of their dispositions had prevented any serious Quarrels, the trifling disputes which it was impossible wholly to avoid, had been far from lessening their affection.' *had prevented*: 'had' inserted above line.

187. l. 29   *at once so*: 'once' actually 'one' in MS.

188. l. 8   *gained her a husband*: 'a' added above line.

189. l. 2   *to Mrs. Percival*: JA seems originally to have given the surname 'Peterson' to the niece and aunt and then to have substituted the more interesting and aristocratic 'Percival'. JA herself did not correct all the appearances of the old name, as in this instance, but we have written 'Percival' throughout; JA sometimes crosses out the 'eterson', letting 'P' stand alone, e.g. 'Mrs. P'.

189. l. 14   *pride of her parents*: 'her' inserted above line.

189. l. 20   *people of mean family*: 'mean' substituted for orig. 'no'.

189. l. 29   *sometimes occur*: an addition above the line has been scratched out, 'to Kitty' (?).

189. ll. 33–4   *and was so dissatisfied*: 'was' inserted above line.

190. l. 11   *overtures*: substituted for 'endeavours'.

190. l. 38   *at length came*: 'came' substituted for orig. 'arrived'.

191. l. 2   *is the hight*: 'is' added above the line.

191. l. 4   *Member of the house*: orig. 'and' followed 'house'.

191. l. 12   *She was elegant*: orig. 'She was about Kitty's age, elegant', 'about Kitty's age' crossed out. (Chapman has the final version as 'She was

not inelegant'; 'not in' appears to be crossed out, and we believe we have the correct reading.)

191. ll. 31–2   *almost convinced when she saw her*: 'when she saw her' added above line.

192. l. 2   *as to Books*: 'to' inserted in pencil above line, possibly not by JA.

192. l. 6   *universally read and Admired*: followed by 'and that have given rise perhaps to more frequent Arguments than any other of the same sort', crossed out.

192. ll. 21–2   *are not they*: 'they' written as 'the' in MS.

192. l. 30   *However I quite envy*: 'However' added above line.

192. l. 33   *I have done nothing*: 'done' added above line.

192. ll. 33–4   *said her Neice*: orig. followed by 'I beleive you have as good a chance of it as any one else', crossed out.

192. l. 35   *Queen Elizabeth*: 'Elizabeth' written as 'Eliz:^{th}' here and in next instance.

194. ll. 11–12   *distinguish from Politics*: 'Politics' orig. 'History'.

194. l. 30   *Amusements began*: 'began' orig. 'again', altered in pencil.

195. ll. 18–19   *we are often not able*: 'often not' substituted for orig. 'not always'.

195. l. 22   *ever seen*: 'ever' inserted above line.

196. ll. 13–14   *got into the Army*: substituted for orig. 'sent to Sea'.

196. l. 15   *I have a Notion*: 'a' added above line.

196. l. 18   *Very well*: substituted for orig. 'Slightly'.

197. l. 13   *Barlows*: orig. 'Barkers'.

197. l. 36   *she might then have remained*: 'then' inserted above line.

198. l. 31   *she ever lent it to'*: after this there follows this retort: 'If so, *Mary Wynne* can receive very little adventage from *her* having it.'

198. l. 32   *and then, continued she*: 'continued she' added above line.

198. ll. 36–7   *to have one.'*: there follows the original retort, crossed out, 'Why indeed, if Maria will give my Freind a drawing, she can have nothing to complain of, but as she does not write in

	Spirits, I suppose she has not yet been fortunate enough to be so distinguished'.
198. l. 38	*odd,' said Kitty*: 'said Kitty' inserted above line.
199. l. 20	*her regard*: 'her' orig. 'the'; 'her' added above line.
199. l. 25	*towards her with great*: 'her' added above line.
199. l. 35	*Gold Net*: inserted above line.
200. l. 39	*that the time*: 'that' inserted above line.
201. l. 32	*I dare say that People*: 'that' inserted above line.
202. l. 22	*Young Persons*: 'Persons' orig. 'Ladies'.
202. l. 23	*of an aimiable affectionate disposition*: substituted for orig. 'of their being disposed to like one another'.
202. l. 26	*worthy of her regard.*: there follows in the MS, crossed out: 'There is something mighty pretty I think in young Ladies corresponding with each other, and'.
203. l. 9	*Augusta Barlow*: 'Barlow' added above line.
203. ll. 13–14	*Regency walking dress*: added above line, substituted for an indecipherable word or words, possibly 'Parasol' mis-spelled as 'Parisol'.
202. l. 23	*about the Regency*: 'Regency' substituted for the same indecipherable word.
203. ll. 24–5	*Bonnet and Pelisse*: orig. 'Jacket & petticoat'.
203. l. 25	*left the room*: 'the' added above line.
203. l. 27	*depress her*: 'her' added above line.
203. l. 34	*to continue undisturbed*: 'continue' orig. 'remain'.
204. l. 25	*gone an hour*: orig. 'gone but half an hour', 'but half' crossed out.
204. l. 25	*as every thing*: 'thing' written above line.
204. ll. 26–7	*in another hour*: orig. 'in an hour and a half'.
204. ll. 30–1	*so much pleasure, it*: after 'pleasure' and before 'it', an expression crossed out (? 'even delight,').
204. ll. 33–4	*ensued for nearly*: 'nearly' orig. 'about'.
204. l. 35	*Anne*: here and in several places elsewhere, orig. 'Nanny', altered by JA.
204. l. 37	*gloves, and arranging*: 'and' (actually '&') inserted above line.
204. l. 38	*folds of her dress,.*: orig. followed by 'and providing herself with Lavender water'

crossed out. (Water and crushed lavender leaves heated and distilled was used as a perfume and mild stimulant, applied both internally and externally [*Plocacosmos*, 339–43]. As Henry Tilney tells Catherine Morland in *Northanger Abbey*, in dances the woman 'furnishes the fan and the lavender water' [p. 57].)

205. ll. 8–9   *and I knew nobody*: orig. 'and as I knew nobody', 'as' crossed out.

205. l. 14   *in my Apron, Ma'am*: substituted for 'because you know Ma'am I am all over powder'.

206. l. 20   *entered the room*: squeezed in below line.

208. l. 4   *but since you*: 'since' orig. 'as'.

208. l. 7   *Gaiety*: 'e' added to this word above line.

208. l. 32   *at a Neighbour's*: orig. 'at a Neighbour's of ours'.

209. l. 15   *procure*: orig. 'lend'.

209. ll. 17–18   *have anything pack'd up*: substituted above line for 'pack up anything'.

209. l. 35   *so much haste*: JA writes 'must' in MS; we have emended to 'much'.

209. l. 37   *led her out*: 'her' added above line.

212. l. 20   *Stanley who with a vivacity*: orig. 'Stanley who joined to a vivacity', 'with' substituted above line for 'joined to'.

212. l. 26   *gaiety*: orig. 'gaity', 'e' added above line.

213. l. 22   *his coming away*: 'his' orig. 'your Brother's'.

215. l. 26   *could not help remarking*: 'remarking' orig. 'observing'.

215. l. 32   *in his Son*: phrase added above line.

219. ll. 32–3   *seeing him*: 'him' orig. 'his Son'; 'Son' crossed out, 'his' made into 'him'.

215. l. 33   *he was yet*: orig. 'but he was yet'.

215. l. 36   *he found him*: inserted above line.

217. l. 2   *rude to one*: Chapman has 'rude to me'; the words 'one' and 'me' are practically indistinguishable in JA's hand, but we believe 'one' is the correct reading.

217. ll. 35–6   *opportunity which the next Morning offered to her*: orig. 'opportunity which offered the next Morning'; 'offered to her' added above line.

218. l. 10   *Youth and Beauty?*: after this follows in the MS,

	crossed out, 'Why in fact, it is nothing more than being Young and Handsome—and that'.
218. l. 10	*It*: added above line to make a full sentence after the first part was deleted.
218. ll. 13–14	*a young Man's*: orig. 'a handsome young Man's'.
218. l. 23	*ever existed.*: here follows in the MS crossed out, 'Her intimacies with Young Men are abominable; and it is all the same to her, who it is, no one comes amiss to her—'.
219. ll. 13–14	*Answer from him*: 'from him' added above the line.
220. l. 2	*reasonably excited*: phrase originally followed by word 'before', crossed out.
220 l. 30	*together in the arbour*: inserted above the line.
221. l. 5	*Stanley who was so far*: 'was' inserted above line.
222. l. 14	*Coelebs in Search of a Wife*: substituted for 'Seccar's explanation of the Catechism'.
223. l. 36	*only replied*: 'only' inserted above line.
224. l. 10	*in gaining an explanation*: 'in' orig. 'of'; 'an explanation' added above line.
224. l. 28	*otherwise than amiable*: 'than' inserted above line.
224. l. 29	*perfectly*: orig. 'completely'.
224. ll. 35–6	*inclined to entertain*: orig. 'disposed to feel'.
227. l. 6	*might not be married*: 'be' added above line.
228. l. 26	*Kitty continued in this state of satisfaction*: from this point to the end, the handwriting differs from that found earlier in the MS of 'Catharine'. Two hands appear to be involved; the first new hand writes the two paragraphs down to 'to her mind of E^wd Stanley'. According to Deirdre Le Faye and Sally Brown, the hand is that of JA's nephew, James Edward, and these two paragraphs were probably written between 1809 and JA's death. The authorship of the ending is a vexed question—see note to 'the Summer passed away', below.
228. l. 30	*Augusta Halifax*: Halifax in MS as 'Hallifax'.
228. l. 31	*Mary Wynne*: 'Wynne' in MS as 'Wynn'.
229. l. 5	*it brought to her mind*: inserted above line.

229. l. 6   *the Summer passed away*: here the handwriting changes once again. Again, Deirdre Le Faye and Sally Brown believe the hand is that of James Edward, but, according to Deirdre Le Faye, these last paragraphs are now in his 'mature hand', and these paragraphs were probably written after JA's death. Le Faye's knowledge of the Austens' handwriting makes her a good judge, and it is easy to believe that these last sentences of 'Catharine' were written without JA's participation. We wish, however, to record our own sense that the language of the first two paragraphs of this continuation (see note above) is livelier than that in the passage offered in the 'mature hand'. The first section of the continuation also contains the kind of literary allusion likely to be found in Austen's work. The first two paragraphs of added material might have been partly dictated by JA, or composed in committee with her. See 'Introduction', pp. xix–xx. The identification of James Edward as author of the first two paragraphs of this puzzling 'ending' or as author of the ending of 'Evelyn' is not altogether without doubt. Anna Austen has also been suggested as a possible author (or scribe) of the first two paragraphs of the added conclusion to 'Catharine'—as of the material at the end of 'Evelyn'. (See note to p. 183.)

229. l. 17   *except a description*: 'a description' orig. 'the account'.

229. l. 19   *a panegyric on Augusta Halifax*: we here follow Chapman's reading of 'panegyric' for an indecipherable expression.

229. ll. 22–3   *five miles from Exeter*: orig. 'from the town Exeter'.

229. l. 24   *of her own*: orig. 'of her her own'.

229. l. 27   *there and who infested*: 'who' not in MS, added for grammatical clarity.

229. l. 31   *attending the performance*: after this phrase, the expression '& un' is crossed out.

229. ll. 34–5   *to attend them*: orig. 'of their party'.

Plan of a Novel

The manuscript of 'Plan of Novel' probably dates from 1816, when JA was in correspondence with the Revd James Stanier Clarke, the librarian to the Prince Regent. The MS, in JA's hand, is now in the Pierpont Morgan Library, New York, MS No. MA 1034. The footnotes, originally sidenotes, are JA's own, indicating the source of each suggestion.

230. l. 3	*Daughter*: orig. 'only Child'.
230. l. 8	*Manners*—: originally followed by 'doing infinite good in his Parish, a Blessing to every body connected with him, &'.
230. l. 17	*Piano Forte and Harp*: '& Harp' added above line.
230. ll. 19–20	*Father and Daughter—who are*: 'who are' added above line.
231. l. 1	*his own Mother*: 'own' added above line.
231. l. 15	*driven*: added above line.
231. l. 22	*Characters—But there will be no mixture*: 'But there will be no mixture' added above line.
231. l. 24	*another—but All*: 'but' added above line.
231. l. 25	*respect—and there*: 'and' added above line.
231. l. 27	*Humanity*: orig. 'Mortal'.
231. l. 30	*of course—and only*: 'and only' added above line.
232. l. 8	*finding his end*: the beginning of 'finding' is written over the word 'after'.
232. l. 12	*Invectives against*: we have supplied the 'st'.

Verses

234. l. 1	*This little bag*: entitled in Chapman, *Minor Works*, 'Verses given with a Needlework Bag to Mrs. James Austen'. The text was first published in ch. 5 of the *Memoir* (1870) by J. E. Austen-Leigh (see *Memoir* [1926], 93). The surviving MS is described and reproduced in a photograph in Joan Austen-Leigh, 'Jane Austen's Housewife', *Country Life*, 28 Oct. 1982, p. 1323. Our text is taken from a reading of this photograph.
234. l. 11	*Thro' the rough ways of Life*: the text given here is taken from the MS of this verse in the Pierpont Morgan Library, New York (MA

1034, V9B). It bears the title 'On Capt. Foote's Marriage with Miss Patton'. The handwriting is probably not JA's, and the MS exhibits the formal penmanship used in copying for circulation. The authorship of this piece has been doubtful. In the *Memoir*, J. E. Austen-Leigh cites it as an 'epigram, written by Jane Austen's uncle, Mr. Leigh-Parrot, on reading in a newspaper the marriage of Captain Foote to Miss Patton' (pp. 40–1). Family tradition is not, however, universally accurate, and the piece did survive among papers attributed to JA. B. C. Southam includes this verse among JA's works in the 1969 edition of *Minor Works*, but offers no explanation of his decision. As the verse has so often been considered among JA's works, we reproduce it here, but bracketed to indicate uncertainty.

The marriage between Captain Foote and Miss Patton took place in 1803, which supplies a probable date.

234. l. 16   *Miss Lloyd has now sent to Miss Green*: this verse is printed by Deirdre Le Faye in the *TLS*, 20 Feb. 1987, p. 185. Le Faye informs us by letter that this and 'See they come' 'were copied by Anna Lefroy into her commonplace book . . . at some time between 1854 (watermarks) and her death in 1872'. This commonplace book, largely a collection of notes on family history, is now known as the Lefroy MS. Anna Lefroy provided titles for both this text and 'See they come', Lefroy's title for this poem being 'Lines *supposed* to have been sent to an uncivil Dressmaker'. JA's mother wrote a reply in the imagined voice of the dressmaker: 'Miss Green's reply—by Mrs. Austen':

> I've often made clothes
> For those who write prose,
> But 'tis the first time
> I've had orders in rhyme.—

Depend on't, fair Maid,
You shall be obeyed;
Your garment of black
Shall sit close to your back,
And in every part
I'll exert all my art;
It shall be the neatest,
And eke the completest
That ever was seen—
Or my name is not Green!

(*TLS*, p. 185)

We base the dating of these poems on Le Faye's contention that the bereavement alluded to is the loss of Martha Lloyd's mother, who died 16 Apr. 1805.

235. l. 1   *Oh M^r. Best*: entitled in Chapman, *Minor Works*, 'Lines to Martha Lloyd' and there printed only as the short version found in W. and R. A. Austen-Leigh, *Jane Austen, her Life and Letters: A family record* (1913), 70. Our text is that which appears in Donald Greene, 'New Verses by Jane Austen', *Nineteenth-Century Fiction*, 30 (1975), 257–60. Greene saw the original MS, in the possession of Joan Austen-Leigh, which he describes as 'written on a single sheet of paper approximately 9 inches in width and 7½ inches in height. . . . On the reverse is written "To Martha" ' (p. 258). Greene argues that the paper indicates that this verse was composed close to the time in which *The Watsons* was written.

236. l. 15   *See they come*: as printed by Deirdre Le Faye in *TLS*, 20 Feb. 1987, p. 185. Le Faye's text is from the Lefroy MS, a compilation of information on family history collected by Anna Lefroy. The title supplied by Anna Lefroy is 'Lines written by Jane Austen for the amusement of a Niece (afterwards Lady Knatchbull) on the arrival of Captn. & Mrs. Austen at Godmersham Park soon after their marriage July 1806'. Le Faye says that young Fanny Knight 'recorded in her diary on July

29 "I had a bit of a letter from Aunt Jane with some verses of hers" '.

237. l. 5   *Happy the lab'rer*: entitled 'Verses to Rhyme with Rose' in Chapman, *Minor Works*. The original surviving MS, sold at Sotheby's in Oct. 1962 and now the property of the Fondation Martin Bodmer, Cologny-Genève (now called the Bodmer MS), has not been seen by the present editors, but this verse has been checked against a Xerox of that MS in the British Museum. The Bodmer MS contains (*inter alia*) four sets of verses rhyming with 'rose'. The handwriting is JA's throughout, but the verses are by JA, Cassandra Austen, JA's mother, and JA's sister-in-law Elizabeth. The verses rhyming with 'rose' were first published by Lord Brabourne (in *Letters of Jane Austen* [1884], 341); Brabourne refers to them as 'enclosed in one of the letters of 1807'. Brabourne's texts of various verses differ from those in the Bodmer MS in spelling, punctuation, and capitals—all important indicators that he was probably looking at a different MS. (See Gilson, 'Jane Austen's Verses', 31.) The Bodmer MS is a compilation, containing material definitely written in 1808 (see verses on 'Cambrick' below), but there is no reason to believe that some of the material could not have been first composed in 1807, as Brabourne suggests.

237. l. 18   *Of a Ministry*: entitled 'On Sir Home Popham's Sentence, April 1807' in Chapman, *Minor Works*; the date of Popham's sentence dates the poem. The text was first published in Brabourne, *Letters of Jane Austen*, 344. According to Brabourne, this verse was enclosed in the same 1807 letter as 'Happy the lab'rer'. Our text is based on a Xerox of the Bodmer MS. Chapman added an 'and' as the penultimate word in the first line, but we have deleted this. See Gilson, 'Jane Austen's Verses', 31.

237. l. 27   *Cambrick! with grateful blessings*: entitled 'To

Miss Bigg with some Pockethandkerchiefs' in *Minor Works*. The text is taken from a Xerox of the MS supplied by the Jane Austen Memorial Trust at Chawton. This MS is addressed on the other side to 'Miss Bigg'; the MS was found by Ernest de Selincourt in an album belonging to Bertha Hill, a descendant of Catherine Bigg (fifth daughter of Lovelace Bigg-Wither of Marydown) who married the Revd Herbert Hill in 1808. This MS bears a date supplied by JA.

238. l. 1   *Cambrick! thou'st been to me a good*: this second poem survives in the Bodmer MS, along with 'Happy the lab'rer' and 'Of a Ministry'. As Gilson says, 'The Bodmer manuscript is presumably a fair copy done for retention by the writer' ('Jane Austen's Verses', 32). Brabourne printed both 'Cambrick! with grateful blessings' and 'Cambrick! thou'st been to me a good' from that MS, including the title by JA, 'To Miss Bigg, previous to her Marriage, with some Pocket handkerchieves I had hemmed for her', and the comment-title before the second of the two verses, 'On the same occasion, but not sent'. The source for Chapman is Brabourne's *Letters*. We have had to rely on the Brabourne version of the second verse on 'Cambrick' as we have not seen the MS. The date is pretty certainly 1808, though the composition may be later than that of the preceding verse.

238. l. 10   *To the Memory of M^rs. Lefroy*: the present text is transcribed from the MS now in the possession of the Dean and Chapter of Winchester Cathedral, and reproduced by them in photographic facsimile in *Jane Austen in Winchester*, 5th edn. (Winchester: The Friends of Winchester Cathedral, 1991), pp. 12–13. The MS, given to the Cathedral in 1956 by Jessie Lefroy, great-grand-daughter of Mrs Lefroy, was accompanied by a letter from James Edward Austen Leigh's son William, testifying that this copy 'is certainly Jane Austen's

handwriting' (p. 11). The MS appears to be written out in JA's fairest hand, as a present to a friend, probably a member of Anne Lefroy's family.

Gilson lists four MSS, two apparently autograph, one a transcript in an unknown hand included in a collection compiled by Anne Lefroy's son, C. E. Lefroy, and another in an album signed by Mrs Rice, i.e. Lucy Jemima Lefroy, daughter of Anne Lefroy.

Eleven quatrains of this poem were printed in J. E. Austen-Leigh's *Memoir*, the author's nephew offering the verses 'not for their merits of poetry, but to show how deep and lasting was the impression made by the older friend on the mind of the younger' (p. 57).

240. l. 1   *'Alas! poor Brag'*: the original MS of the letter in which this verse occurs is now in the Pierpont Morgan Library, and has been seen by the present editors; the MS is also reproduced in *Jane Austen's Manuscript Letters in Facsimile*, ed. Jo Modert, F—187. (Compare Chapman, *Letters*, No. 64, pp. 252–3.) The letter, of 17 Jan. 1809, is addressed to Cassandra Austen. JA introduces these lines as follows: 'I have just received some verses in an unknown hand, & am desired to forward them to my nephew Edwd at Godmersham . . .' (the three dots are JA's). The 'unknown hand' seems a joke, and there is no reason to think the lines were not composed by JA, who in the winter of 1808–9 was lamenting the decline of Speculation's popularity: 'The preference of Brag over Speculation does not greatly surprise me, I believe, because I feel the same myself; but it mortifies me deeply, because Speculation was under my patronage; and, after all, what is there so delightful in a pair royal of Braggers? . . . When one comes to reason upon it, it cannot stand its ground against Speculation—of which I hope Edward is now convinced' (Letter to Cassandra, 10 Jan. 1809, *Letters*, 247).

When including a verse on the page of a
letter, JA usually sets it off by surrounding
each line with quotation marks. We have
deleted these marks and regularized punctuation by including quotation marks only when
there is a speaker (as here Speculation is a
speaker).

240. l. 11   *My dearest Frank*: this text is derived from the
verse letter of 26 July 1809, now in the British
Museum. This MS is reproduced in *Jane
Austen's Manuscript Letters in Facsimile* (F—199–
201). Another version is owned by the Jane
Austen Memorial Trust and is to be found at
Chawton; Jean K. Bowden, the curator of the
house, believes this version is also in JA's
hand. The only substantial difference is in
line 41: the Chawton version reads
'Cassandra's pen will give our state'.

241. l. 32   *I've a pain in my head*: entitled 'Lines on Maria
Beckford' in *Minor Works*; the present text is
from a MS in the Winchester City Museum.

242. l. 14   *'I . . . Dilemma'*: the original MS of the letter
of 30 Apr. 1811 in which this and the
following verse occur is now in the Pierpont
Morgan Library, and has been seen by the
present editors; the MS is also reproduced in
Letters in Facsimile, F—214. (Cf. Chapman,
Letters, 278.) The MS places quotation marks
around both lines; we have left quotation
marks only for Mr. Gipps.

242. l. 17   *Between Session and Session*: in the same MS
letter of 30 Apr. as above. We are following
the original layout of the verses; Chapman
prints one set of lines (on the right) below the
others instead of in parallel (p. 279). We have
removed JA's quotation marks around the
lines.

242. l. 21   *At Eastbourne Mr. Gell*: this text is derived
from Austen-Leigh, *Memoir*, p. 93. We have
not seen either of the surviving MSS. The
verse was first published in the *Memoir* in
1870, with the title 'On reading in the
Newspapers the Marriage of Mr. Gell to Miss

Gill, of Eastbourne': Chapman in *Minor Works* uses this title and bases his text presumably on the MS now in the possesion of the Bath City Council, in which 'eyes' and 'ease' are written out at the end of the 3rd and 4th lines respectively. The second surviving MS (now the property of Park Honan) was written on the verso of a print illustrating a novel of 1810; it bears the title 'On the Marriage of Mr Gell of East Bourn to Miss Gill' and ends the punning lines in question with 'i.s' and 'e.s'. As Gilson admits, a third MS may have existed as a source for Austen-Leigh (Gilson, 'Jane Austen's Verses', pp. 28–9). We prefer the form in the *Memoir* to that in the *Minor Works*, as it restores pun and playfulness.

243. l. 1   *When stretch'd on one's bed*: entitled 'On a Headache' in *Minor Works*. This piece, like 'Of Eastbourne Mr. Gell', is found in a MS belonging to the Bath City Council; the lines are dated 'Octr 27. 1811' (Gilson, 'Jane Austen's Verses', 32). We have not seen the MS. Gilson informs us that 'the last three lines of the second stanza are written above an earlier deleted text ... there is also an earlier text of the last stanza' (p. 32). At present, we are using the text offered by Chapman.

244. l. 1   *Maria, good-humoured, and handsome*: our text comes from the *Memoir* (p. 93). No surviving MS is presently known. JA refers to this verse in a letter of 29 Nov. 1812, now in the Henry W. and Albert A. Berg Collection in the New York Public Library (Astor, Lenox and Tilden Foundations). See *Letters in Facsimile*, F—230: 'The 4 lines on Miss W. which I sent you were all my own, but James afterwards suggested what I thought a great improvement & as it stands in the Steventon Edition.' Chapman's note to this letter (*Letters*, 500–1) supplies an alternative version of this verse, which, as Gilson more fully explains, Chapman found in *The Diaries of Dummer*:

Reminiscences of an Old Sportsman, Stephen Terry of Dummer, ed. A. M. Sterling (London: Unicorn Press, 1934). Gilson tells us that this verse is reproduced from Stephen Terry's diary for 11 Apr. 1866. Terry explained his entry: 'These lines were given me this day by Mrs. Ben Lefroy'. That is, JA's niece Anna had kept the earlier version. We may readily surmise that it is earlier because the name is not 'Maria' but 'Camilla', a reference to the real Camilla Wallop who married the Revd Henry Wake on 26 Mar. 1813, after being engaged to him in Nov. 1812. See Gilson, 'Jane Austen's Verses', 29–30. This is the alternative version as Chapman prints it, derived from Terry:

Camilla, good humoured and merry and small,
For a husband, it happened, was at her last stake,
And having in vain danced at many a ball
Is now very happy to jump at a Wake.

(Note to Letter 74)

The changes to conceal identity, including the alteration of the name to 'Maria' and the change in her stature from 'small' to 'tall', were probably among the alterations contributed by James in his 'improvement' of the verse so that it could be allowed to circulate: the 'Steventon Edition' to which JA jokingly refers could allude to suitability for public consumption.

The *Memoir* supplies a title (all in capital letters): 'On the Marriage of a Middle-Aged Flirt with a Mr. Wake, whom, it was supposed, she would scarcely have accepted in her Youth', a title repeated by Chapman.

244. l. 6 *In measured verse I'll now rehearse*: no MS for this piece is known. Chapman reproduces the version given in the *Memoir* (pp. 94–5), and so do we. Chapman supplies the title 'Mock Panegyric on a Young Friend', taken from

J. E. Austen-Leigh's introduction to the piece: 'Once, too, she took it into her head to write the following mock panegyric on a young friend, who really was clever and handsome' (*Memoir*, p. 94). After quoting the verses, J. E. Austen-Leigh adds, 'I believe that all this nonsense was nearly extempore' (p. 95).

245. l. 5   *Charades*: we follow Chapman in reproducing three verses attributed to JA in *Charades Written a Hundred years ago by Jane Austen and Her Family* (1895). No MS containing any of these particular pieces is known, and the attribution must be entertained with some caution. All of the Austen family were fond of written charades. On 29 Jan. 1813 JA writes of having received a set of charades from Cassandra, probably by a number of members of the Godmersham group: 'We admire your Charades excessively—but as yet have guessed only the 1ˢᵗ' (*Letters*, 298). Two Austen family MSS of charades, not containing work by JA, are still extant; see Chapman, *Minor Works*, 450, and Gilson, 'Jane Austen's Verses', 34–5.

245. l. 21   *When Winchester races*: 'When Winchester races' is taken from MS 209715B (No. 410–412) in the Henry W. and Albert Berg Collection in the New York Public Library. On the front of the folder, after the librarian's description, is a note in an unidentified hand: 'This was apparently dictated by her, probably to her sister, Cassandra, who wrote it down'. We entirely concur in this judgement and have chosen this version of the poem because we believe it is closest to JA's own composition. Problems with the text discussed below are all entirely consonant with the conditions of dictation. The version presented by R. W. Chapman in *Minor Works* is based on a MS probably by James Austen and now at Chawton. The Chawton version, neater and more 'correct' than the earlier, demonstrates James's tendency to edit his

sister's work, to offer 'improvement' (see note to 'Maria, good-humoured, and handsome' pp. 275–6). Neither of these two MSS bears the title 'Venta' offered by Chapman.

246. l. 5   *Oh Venta depraved*: 'Venta' in this MS is actually written 'Ventar'; the person taking the dictation was evidently not familiar with the word, and in spoken English of the Austens' region and class the 'ar' and 'a' sounds on the ends of words are nearly identical. This is one of several indications that the MS was taken from dictation.

246. l. 7   *you're enslaved*: 'you're' orig. 'you'r'.

246. l. 8   *You have sinned*: in the MS, written with several false starts: 'Yove [crossed out] You've have'.

246. l. 8   *farther he said*: 'he said' added above line.

246. l. 11   *You shall*: 'h' in 'shall' added above line.

246. l. 11   *curse in your pleasures*: 'pleasures' added above line.

246. l. 12   *Set off for your course*: instead of 'course', the scribe writes 'curse', then crosses it out and continues with 'course'.

246. l. 12   *I'll pursue*: 'I'll' orig. 'Ill'.

246. l. 16   *the curse upon Venta*: 'Venta' orig. 'Ventar'.

246. l. 16   *July in showers—.*: after the verses, a pencilled line is drawn, beneath which is a note in another hand: 'written July 15:th 1817: by Jane Austen who died early in the morning (½ past 4) of July 18.th 1817 aged 41 y:rs'.

Prayers

We have not seen the MSS of these prayers, which are now in the possession of Mills College, Oakland, California. Our text is based on a transcription sent to us by the Special Collections Librarian; this appears to be the typed transcription made by William Matson Roth when he was preparing the version printed in 1940 by The Colt Press. Examination of a photograph of part of the third prayer, published in the Colt Press volume, shows, however, that Roth eliminated almost all capitals from the pieces transcribed; it was doubtless Roth's version that formed the basis of Chapman's printing (*Minor Works*, 453–7).

The prayers are found in two MSS, first described by Chapman

(*TLS*, 14 Jan. 1926, p. 27). Across the back of the folded sheet on which the first prayer is written are the words 'Prayers composed by my ever dear sister Jane'. There seems no doubt that this prayer was transcribed by Cassandra from some earlier MSS some while after JA's death; the watermark of the paper is dated 1818. The second MS, containing prayers 2 and 3, is in two hands. The first of the prayers is in a hand which both Chapman and William Matson Roth presume to be that of the Revd Henry Austen; the third prayer begins in that hand but then continues in another hand which is perhaps that of JA. R. A. Austen-Leigh was quite sure that the latter part of the third prayer is in JA's hand in this MS. See William Matson Roth, 'Introduction' to *Three Evening Prayers by Jane Austen* (San Francisco, 1940), [pp. 2–3, unnumbered].

249 l. 30   *of all they say and do*: after the word 'do' the handwriting changes from what is presumably Henry's handwriting to that attributed to JA.

EXPLANATORY NOTES

We have attempted to supply information about places, customs, activities, and language not necessarily familiar to today's world-wide audience of English readers, as well as to give complete references for literary quotations. Citations from Jane Austen's novels are all taken from the latest World's Classics Editions. The following works are cited in the Notes by short titles:

The Accomplish'd Housewife	*The Accomplish'd Housewife or, the Gentle-woman's Companion* (London, 1745).
Berkebile, *Carriage Terminology*	Don H. Berkebile, *Carriage Terminology: An Historical Dictionary* (Washington, DC, 1978).
Cecilia	Frances Burney, *Cecilia, or Memoirs of an Heiress*, ed. Peter Sabor and Margaret Anne Doody (Oxford, 1988).
Clarissa	Samuel Richardson, *Clarissa, or the History of a Young Lady* [reproduction of the 3rd edn., 1751], ed. Florian Stuber, vols 1–8 of *The Clarissa Project*, (New York, 1990).
Cunnington, *Handbook*	C. Willet Cunnington and Phillis Cunnington, *Handbook of English Costume*, rev. edn. (London, 1972).
An Elegant Art	*An Elegant Art: Fashion and Fantasy in the Eighteenth Century* (Los Angeles, 1983).
Evelina	Frances Burney, *Evelina*, ed. Edward A. Bloom (Oxford, 1982).
Felton, *Treatise*	William Felton, *A Treatise on Carriages; comprehending coaches, chariots, phaetons, curricles, gigs, whiskies, &c.*, 2 vols. (London, 1796).
Glasse, *The Art of Cookery*	Hannah Glasse, *The Art of Cookery, Made Plain and Easy* (London, 1747).
Hibbert and Weinreb, *London Encyclopedia*	Christopher Hibbert and Ben Weinreb, *The London Encyclopedia* (London, 1983).

Honan, *Life*	Park Honan, *Jane Austen: Her Life* (London, 1987).
Jane Austen's Beginnings	*Jane Austen's Beginnings*, ed. J. David Grey (Ann Arbor, Mich., 1989).
Johnson	Samuel Johnson, *The Works of Samuel Johnson*, ed. Arthur Murphy, 12 vols. (London, 1824).
Johnson, *Dictionary*	Samuel Johnson, *A Dictionary of the English Language*, 2 vols. (London, 1755).
Joseph Andrews	Henry Fielding, *Joseph Andrews and Shamela*, ed. Douglas Brooks-Davies (Oxford, 1980).
Lennox, *Female Quixote*	Charlotte Lennox, *The Female Quixote*, ed. Margaret Dalziel, rev. edn. (Oxford, 1989).
Letters	Jane Austen, *Jane Austen's Letters to her Sister Cassandra and Others*, ed. R. W. Chapman (2nd edn., London, 1952; repr. 1979).
Lewis, *Topographical Dictionary*	Samuel Lewis, *Topographical Dictionary of England*, 5th edn. 4 vols. (London, 1839).
Memoir	James Edward Austen-Leigh, *Memoir of Jane Austen*, ed. R. W. Chapman (Oxford, 1926).
Minor Works	Jane Austen, *Minor Works*, ed. R. W. Chapman, with revisions by B. C. Southam (Oxford, 1969).
OED	*The Compact Edition of the Oxford English Dictionary* (Oxford, 1987).
Plocacosmos	James Stewart, *Plocacosmos, or the Whole Art of Hairdressing* (London, 1782).
Pope	Alexander Pope, *The Poems of Alexander Pope*, ed. John Butt (London, 1963).
Porter, *English Society*	Roy Porter, *English Society in the Eighteenth Century*, rev. edn. (Harmondsworth, 1990).
Shakespeare	William Shakespeare, *The Complete Works: Compact Edition*, ed. Stanley Wells and Gary Taylor (Oxford, 1988).

Sheridan	Richard Brinsley Sheridan, *The Dramatic Works*, ed. Cecil Price, 2 vols. (Oxford, 1973).
Sir Charles Grandison	Samuel Richardson, *The History of Sir Charles Grandison*, ed. Jocelyn Harris, 3 vols. (Oxford, 1972).
Southam, *Literary MSS*	B. C. Southam, *Jane Austen's Literary Manuscripts: A Study of the Novelist's Development through the Surviving Papers* (Oxford, 1964).
Tom Jones	Henry Fielding, *Tom Jones*, ed. Sheridan Baker (New York, 1973).
Tristram Shandy	Laurence Sterne, *The Life and Opinions of Tristram Shandy, Gentleman*, ed. Ian Watt (Boston, 1955).
Tucker, *Goodly Heritage*	George Holbert Tucker, *A Goodly Heritage: A History of Jane Austen's Family* (Manchester, 1983).
Woodforde, *Diary*	James Woodforde, *The Diary of a Country Parson*, ed. John Beresford, 5 vols. (Oxford, 1968).

Frederic and Elfrida

3   *rules of Propriety*: see Samuel Richardson, *Rambler*, 97 (19 Feb. 1751): 'That a young lady should be in love, and the love of the young gentleman undeclared, is an heterodoxy which prudence, and even policy, must not allow' (Johnson, *Works*, v. 168).

  so much alike: near-identical siblings are a romance convention, as with Viola and Sebastian in *Twelfth Night*.

  fashionable Bonnet: 'This term [bonnet] was applied to a hat with a small brim often tied under the chin with ribbon strings' (Cunnington, *Handbook*, 352). Full-dress bonnets could be very elaborate, adorned with beads and flowers.

4   *Crankhumdunberry . . . sweet village*: a little echo of Oliver Goldsmith's 'Sweet Auburn, loveliest village of the plain' in 'The Deserted Village' (1770), l. 1 (*Goldsmith: Selected Works*, ed. Richard Garnett (London, 1967), 607). The farcical name makes fun of Irish place-names.

  verdant Lawn . . . purling Stream: artificial language in high pastoral mode derived from late Renaissance poetry.

  Valley of Tempé: a vale celebrated for its beauty, running between the mountains of Olympus and Ossa in Greece; in classical times the site of the worship of Apollo. This famous site is used as a setting in Madeleine de Scudéry's *Clélie* (1654–60). Scudéry's scenes are referred to by Charlotte Lennox's Arabella, who compares the site of Bath to the 'Valley of Tempé' (*The Female Quixote* [1752], 259).

  Damon: long a name for a swain in pastoral poetry.

5   *artificial flowers*: artificial flowers were fashionable adornments for hats etc.; Cunnington quotes the *Ipswich Journal* of 1787, which refers to a 'Nosegay, very large, of artificial flowers' (Cunnington, *Handbook*, 402). Jezalinda and Rebecca show a garish taste, but perhaps they have heard that fine ladies have real flowers in their rooms.

  Indian and English Muslins: although JA here does not seem to place much value on knowing muslins, she gives such expertise to Henry Tilney in *Northanger Abbey*; Henry, who is 'allowed to be an excellent judge', had recently bought a

gown for his sister and 'gave but five shillings for it, and a
true Indian Muslin' (p. 14).

6 *parents of Frederic proposed*: here parents, usually in fiction
impediments of children's happiness, neatly cut the Gordian
knot wrought by the young people's unusual delicacy.

Powder: powder for the hair; based on starch or orris root, it
could be scented with various spices; James Stewart suggests
clove, cinnamon, and ginger; hair powder could be made in
many colours, including black, blue, or purple, 'the fair, the
rose, and the red' (*Plocacosmos*, 321).

Pomatum: an oil-based dressing for the hair. James Stewart's
favourite pomatum contains 'veal fat, lamb's ditto, eels ditto
. . . linseed oil, an infusion of onions, an infusion of Bayonne
honey, Castile soap, etc.' (*Plocacosmos*, 170).

Patches, Powder, Pomatum and Paint: an echo of 'Puffs, Powder,
Patches, Bibles, Billet-doux' in Pope's *Rape of the Lock* (i.
139).

post-chaise: (JA's note); a four-wheeled carriage, using from
one to six horses, which could be changed at posting
stations. A hired post-chaise was the fastest and most
expensive mode of eighteenth-century transport.

postilion: 'one who rides the near horse of the leaders when
four or more are used in a carriage or post-chaise'
(*OED*).

7 *Portland Place*: the grandest street in the London of JA's day,
laid out by the Adam brothers in 1778, running north from
Langham Place and Oxford Street to the present-day
Regent's Park.

old pink Coat: presumably 'hunting pink', i.e. red.

new blue coat: blue was a fashionable colour; Charles Bingley
wears a blue coat at his first appearance in *Pride and Prejudice*
(p. 7) and Lydia Bennet wonders if Wickham will wear a
blue coat at their wedding (p. 282).

Leveret: 'a young hare, strictly one in its first year' (*OED*).

leash: 'a set of three' (*OED*).

8 *stream . . . pleasure Grounds in Portland Place*: there is no stream
in Portland Place; houses in the new squares and streets had
very small areas in front and to the rear—certaintly not
pleasure grounds.

8 *smelling Bottle*: a small ornamental phial containing aromatic vinegar, or smelling salts (carbonate of ammonia), or hartshorn (an aqueous solution of ammonia) to revive one suffering from faintness.

   dagger: parody of the alternatives offered by Eleanor, wife of Henry II, to her husband's mistress, the Fair Rosamund— either the bowl of poison or the dagger.

9 *Corydon*: traditional Greek name for a swain in pastoral poetry, in contrast to 'Bess', which is English and rustic.

   fess: a dialectal word from southern and south-western England, 'Lively, active, strong; gay, "smart", clever' (*English Dialect Dictionary*, ed. Joseph Wright (London, 1898– 1905), ii. 338).

   Stage Waggon: the poor man's stage-coach. 'A primitive type of public traveling carriage . . . The earliest forms were nothing more than ordinary covered wagons, with several transverse benches inside' (Berkebile, *Carriage Terminology*, 258).

   seat: a family estate, used only of a considerable holding.

   Buckinghamshire: a pastoral and agricultural county in the southern middle region of England, containing many famous estates.

10 *spluttered*: imitative of 'sputter'; noted by Samuel Johnson (*Dictionary*) as a 'low word'.

Jack and Alice

11 *Francis William Austen Esq'*: JA's brother, Frank (1774– 1865), who had left the Royal Naval Academy in Portsmouth in 1788 and had volunteered as a midshipman on the *Perseverance*, bound for the East Indies.

   Johnson: Brigid Brophy thinks the name was derived from the Revd Augustus Johnson, who in 1791 became rector of a living in the gift of the Leigh family; Brophy suggests the Austens may have been 'speculating how old Mr. Johnson might be, with a view to calculating how long a relation of their own might have to wait before stepping into his pulpit' ('Jane Austen and the Stuarts', *Critical Essays*, 23). However, B. C. Southam dates 'Jack and Alice' somewhat earlier (*Literary MSS*, 15–16).

Masquerade: a masked ball; a favourite eighteenth-century entertainment for all classes. Characters in eighteenth-century novels often attend masquerades with bad effect. Cf. Richardson's *Sir Charles Grandison* (1753–4), i. 115–16 and 150–3; Fielding's *Tom Jones* (1749), XIII. vii; pp. 545–9; *Amelia* (1751), x. ii–iv; pp. 410–29); and Frances Burney's *Cecilia* (1782), 106–28. See also Terry Castle, *Masquerade and Civilization* (Stanford, Calif., 1986).

55th year: JA's father, the Revd George Austen, became 55 on 1 May 1787; 'Jack and Alice' possibly began as part of the birthday celebrations.

tickets: calling cards with invitations written on them, or actual printed 'tickets' such as were put out for subscription balls or assemblies, and public masquerades; see *Evelina* (1778), 179 and 315.

Pammydiddle: nonsense word, probably based on 'Pam' as the name for the knave of clubs and for the card game in which that card is the highest trump; to 'diddle' a person is to cheat him, so the whole word indicates cheating at cards.

none but Eagles . . . Face: traditionally, eagles are able to look into the sun; note that later Charles appears to wear a 'Mask representing the Sun' (p. 12).

Sukey: familiar form of 'Susan'.

12 *Cecilia*: perhaps in reminiscence of Frances Burney's *Cecilia, or Memoirs of an Heiress*.

Lady Williams: Park Honan interprets JA's presentation of Lady Williams as a complimentary portrait of Mrs Anne Brydges Lefroy (1749–1804), JA's neighbour, friend, and older confidante (*Life*, 71).

Jointure: property settled on a wife at marrige, to be used by her at the death of her husband.

Tho' Benevolent . . . Entertaining: a parody of Johnsonian symmetry and antithesis.

family of Love: a phrase used in Richardson's *Sir Charles Grandison* to describe the Grandisons, perhaps derived from 'the Family of Love', the name of a sixteenth-century pietistical sect. For a complete discussion of JA's relation to Richardson, see Jocelyn Harris, *Jane Austen's Art of Memory* (Cambridge, 1989); in '*Sir Charles Grandison* in the juvenilia'

Harris illustrates the many references to that novel, especially in 'Jack and Alice' (pp. 228–38).

12 *Sultana*: wife, concubine, or favourite mistress of a sultan. Oriental costumes were especially popular at masquerades; see Terry Castle, *Masquerade and Civilization*, 60–1.

female Masks: an unusual use of 'mask' to represent the person wearing a costume; also found in *Tom Jones*, xiii, vii; pp. 546–8.

Mask representing the Sun: the resplendent Charles Adams here is a parodic version of Richardson's Sir Charles Grandison; Harriet Byron writes that the hero's 'face is overspread with a manly sunniness' (*Sir Charles Grandison*, i. 181). Sir Charles Grandison is incessantly referred to in terms of the sun, e.g. 'here comes the sun darting into all the crooked and obscure corners of my heart; and I shrink from his dazling eye; and, compared to Him . . . appear to myself such a Nothing—' (ibid., iii. 132).

2 Dominos: a domino, worn by either men or women, was a 'Loose cloak, of Venetian origin, chiefly worn at masquerades by people not impersonating a character' (*An Elegant Art*, 226). See Frances Burney's *Cecilia*, 'Dominos of no character, and fancy-dresses of no meaning, made, as is usual at such meetings, the general herd of the company' (p. 106).

Flora: goddess of flowers and plants, associated with springtime.

13 *tout ensemble*: total effect.

14 *like the great Sir Charles Grandison . . . Home*: Richardson's hero 'never perverts the meaning of words. He never, for instance, suffers his servants to deny him, when he is at home' (*Sir Charles Grandison*, ii. 388).

Bigamy: the solution which the reader is tempted to offer to Sir Charles Grandison, torn between the English Harriet Byron and the Italian Clementina della Porretta.

out of spirits: a pun, 'spirits' being the common English word for strong drink (American 'hard liquor').

15 *second attachment*: Marianne Dashwood 'does not approve of second attachments', but she lives 'to counteract, by her conduct, her most favourite maxims' and to marry a second love (*Sense and Sensibility*, 47; 333).

Life and Adventures: a phrase often used in the titles of novels. Fictional characters encountered in states of distress often recount their lives and adventures.

Berkshire: county slightly west of London, in JA's time bounded on the north by the Thames; the county containing Windsor Castle and the Berkshire Downs.

Winter . . . town: after the New Year, the fashionable world returned from country estates to the 'Town': the West End, or Westminster, not the vulgar 'City'. The fashionable 'Winter' then comprised the 'Season', which lasted until 4 June, the King's official birthday.

16 *too much colour*: JA's natural complexion, when in health, seems to have inclined to the rosy; comic self-description may also be present in the 'dark eyes and plump cheeks' awarded the heroine of 'Plan of a Novel' (p. 230).

'From Words she almost came to Blows': adaptation of 'From words they almost came to blows' in James Merrick's 'The Camelion: A Fable, after Monsieur De La Motte', in which two men dispute the colour of a chameleon. Merrick's poem received wide circulation in Robert Dodsley's *Collection of Poems* (1748; frequently reissued thereafter). We cite *A Collection of Poems in six volumes by several hands* (London, 1782), v. 242.

17 *Claret*: red wine imported from Bordeaux; a gentleman's drink.

Citron Grove: literally a grove of trees of the genus *Citrus Medica*, or a grove of any other citrus trees—such as lemon, orange, or lime. Such groves are not to be met with in England, though they form popular settings for scenes in novels set abroad, like 'the Orange-grove' which appears in the Italian section of *Sir Charles Grandison* (ii. 150).

Horsepond: a pond for horses to drink from; an unromantic feature of a farm.

18 *favour us . . . Life and adventures?*: as the Countess reminds the heroine of *The Female Quixote*, who entreats the Countess 'to favour her with the Recital of her Adventures', the word is suspect: 'the Word Adventures carries in it so free and licentious a Sound . . . that it can hardly with Propriety be apply'd to those few and natural Incidents which compose the History of a Woman of Honour' (p. 327). Yet often in

fiction a secondary female character will relate a harrowing tale containing some element of sexual 'Adventure'. Charlotte Smith's *Emmeline* (1788) seems to be one of JA's fictional sources here: Emmeline and her friend Mrs Stafford, taking a walk 'among these natural shrubberies and solitary shades', see a young lady at a cottage window, 'half obscured by the pendant trees' (p. 202). Consumed with curiosity, they search out the mysterious young lady, who is beautiful, ill and in distress, and Mrs Stafford, who believes the sick (or rather pregnant) woman must be her husband's mistress, urges her to give an account of herself; the unhappy Adelina does so at some length. See *Emmeline, or The Orphan of the Castle*, ed. Anne Henry Ehrenpreis (Oxford, 1971), 206–17.

18 *North Wales*: location of the picturesque and the sublime, not usually associated with tailors' daughters.

19 *accomplishments requisite . . . rank*: the daughter of a tailor would not be expected to possess any genteel accomplishments.

rents . . . Estate: the source of a gentleman's income was rent from tenants who farmed his estates. The steward was generally in charge of collecting rents; Charles Adams does not act like a gentleman in collecting the money himself.

Place: position in domestic service, here as cook.

Youth, Beauty, Birth, Wit, Merit, and Money: JA often satirizes unrealistic attributes which qualify a woman as accomplished. See Caroline Bingley's and Darcy's lengthy list of essential female accomplishments in *Pride and Prejudice*, p. 34.

20 *offering him . . . hand and heart*: Lucy's bold offer to Charles Adams looks back to the bold offer of Olivia to Sir Charles Grandison: 'She owned, that her chief motive for coming to England [from Italy] was, to cast her fortune at [Sir Charles's] feet' (*Sir Charles Grandison*, ii. 365). Lucy's proposal also comically assumes woman's right to equality in proposing, anticipating an issue much debated in novels of the 1790s.

steel traps: to catch poachers, deer-stealers, and wood-gatherers. Throughout the eighteenth century, increasingly harsh game laws were enacted. According to Sir William Blackstone, these laws, 'founded upon the . . . unreasonable notions of permanent property in wild creatures . . . have raised a little Nimrod in every manor' (*Commentaries on the Laws of England* [Oxford, 1765–9], iv. 409).

21 *her having never performed such a one before*: here the resourceful Lady Williams recalls Lady Bountiful in Sir George Farquhar's *The Beaux' Stratagem* (1707).

22 *Bath*: the major English spa and fashionable resort of JA's time. See *Northanger Abbey* and *Persuasion*.

Jaunt: pleasure trip.

23 *a peculiar sweetness . . . cannot describe*: Charles Adams's self-praise here paraphrases and mocks the hyperbolical praise lavished upon Sir Charles Grandison by other observers: e.g. Harriet Byron's first description of him: 'Were kings to be chosen for beauty and majesty of person, Sir Charles Grandison would have few competitors. . . . What is beauty in a man to me? . . . And yet, this grandeur in his person and air is accompanied with so much ease and freedom of manners, as engages one's love with one's reverence' (*Sir Charles Grandison*, i. 181)

24 *She flew to her Bottle . . . forgot*: see Mrs Slipslop in *Joseph Andrews* (1742), who, after the hero rejects her advances, 'with great Tranquility paid a visit to a Stone-Bottle, which is of sovereign use to a Philosophical Temper' (p. 39).

25 *How nobly . . . account!*: cf. Mrs Bennet's excited response to the news of Elizabeth's engagement to Darcy: 'I can think of nothing else! Ten thousand a year, and very likely more! 'Tis as good as a Lord!' (p. 337).

26 *interceding freind*: in eighteenth-century usage, a 'friend' is primarily a person with some unavoidable connection to the person befriended (as a member of the family, the lord of the manor, etc.) and in a position to do good to that person; in such a sense a 'friend' need feel no equality or personal warmth of amity.

Gallows: hanging from a gallows was in JA's time the punishment for women and men convicted of major felonies, including murder.

cheifly engaged: the amatory adventures of Prince George (later George IV) were well known, including his affairs with 'Perdita' Robinson and his marriage with Maria Fitzherbert in 1785, a marriage denied by the Prince to conciliate Parliament, although its validity was an open secret. Frederick, the Duke of York, married the daughter of the King of Prussia in 1791, but he was better known for his relation with Mary Anne Clarke.

26 *Mogul*: 'the emperor of Delhi, whose empire at one time included most of Hindustan' (*OED*).

Edgar and Emma

27 *said Sir Godfrey to his Lady*: a narrative expression later to be used in the first chapter of *Pride and Prejudice*: ' "My dear Mr. Bennet," said his lady to him one day . . .' (p. 1).

Market-town: the centre of a country area, holding regular markets.

28 *three pair of Stairs high*: Sir Godfrey and his Lady live on the third floor by British standards, the fourth by American, up three pairs, i.e. flights, of stairs. The fashionable floor was the first above ground level. The upper storeys of a town building were usually the habitation of servants or poor lodgers.

Sussex: pastoral county south of London.

Marlhurst: the fictional name of the Marlows' country seat, concocted from the first syllable of their name (with a Whiggish accent derived from sharing a first syllable with 'Marlborough') added to 'hurst', from the 'OE *hyrst* "hill, wood, wooded hill" ' (*The Concise Oxford Dictionary of English Place-Names*, ed. Eilert Ekwall, 4th edn. (Oxford, 1960), 259).

ninepence among the Ringers: the ringing of a peal of church bells marked events of importance in the eighteenth-century village. But by late-century standards, ninepence was a low payment indeed, merely a penny or so per ringer. On 15 Jan. 1764, the Revd James Woodforde paid ringers 2*s*. 6*d*. and 'a pail of Cyder' to celebrate his entry into his curacy at Babcary in Somerset (Woodforde, *Diary*, i. 24).

Villa: a country mansion, inspired by the Northern Italian country houses of Andrea Palladio. Usually, villas were built by persons of taste and were smaller than the great country houses of the eighteenth century. Sometimes, however, the term was used ironically of pretentious structures, as in 'Timon's villa' in Pope's *Epistle to Burlington: Of the Use of Riches* (1731).

Willmot: the name derives aristocratic associations from the poet John Wilmot, the Earl of Rochester (1647–80).

Lead mine: this share might indeed have been valuable, as the eighteenth century saw the expansion of lead mining in England, 'from Allendale south to the Peak' (Porter, *English Society*, 176). JA also brings to lead its traditional association with heaviness, as in Pope's *Dunciad*, where Dulness's 'mighty wings out-spread/To hatch a new Saturnian age of Lead' (i. 27–8).

ticket in the Lottery: 'The state ran a lottery from 1709 to 1824, national institutions from the British Museum to Westminster Bridge being partly funded from the proceeds' (Porter, *English Society*, 238).

29 *Sopha*: a sofa, a form of furniture in use since the early eighteenth century. In *Mansfield Park*, Aunt Norris scolds Fanny Price for 'idling away all the evening upon a sofa' (p. 64).

confidante: a male confidante violates linguistic, fictional, and social rules; an example of JA's interest in crossing genders. Compare 'The History of England', p. 136.

30 *Eton*: Eton College, a 'public' (private in American usage) school for boys situated on the Thames near Windsor, founded by Henry VI in 1440.

Winchester: Winchester College, in Winchester, another 'public' school, founded by William of Wykeham in 1382.

Queen's Square: presumably Queen Square, a square in Bloomsbury, fashionable in the eighteenth century, open to the north and thus offering an unobstructed view of Highgate and Hampstead. A girl's school (the 'ladies' Eton') stood on the east side from the mid-eighteenth until the mid-nineteenth century (Hibbert and Weinreb, *London Encyclopedia*, 629–30).

Convent at Brussells: English and Irish Roman Catholic families sent daughters to foreign convent schools.

college: one of the colleges at Oxford or Cambridge.

at Nurse: infants of upper classes, including the Austen children, were sent out to a wet nurse. Often, children did not return to their parents' home until the age of 2.

Henry and Eliza

31 *Eliza*: the character of Eliza probably derives much of its vivacity and unpredictability from JA's cousin Eliza, the Comtesse de Feuillide, née Hancock (1761–1813), who at the age of 19 married a French Comte, Jean Gabriel Capotte. Eliza visited the Austens at Steventon in 1787 and in subsequent years. She was a clever conversationalist, writer, and comic actress. In 'Henry and Eliza', JA provides an uncannily accurate anticipation of Eliza de Feuillide's biography. In the story, Eliza becomes a widow (p. 34); Eliza de Feuillide's husband was guillotined in Paris in 1794. The fictional Eliza flirts with the fictional Henry; the widow Eliza de Feuillide married JA's brother Henry in 1797.

Miss Cooper: JA's cousin Jane Cooper (d. 1798), who often participated in the family theatricals (Honan, *Life*, 72). See 'Introduction', xiii.

rewarding the industry ... approbation: the common and expected reward for haymaking in the eighteenth century was food and drink: in Shropshire in 1794, for example, harvesters were daily given 'from 5 to 8 quarts of strong and small beer' (J. Bishton, *General View of the Agriculture of the County of Salop* [Brentford, 1794], 36).

cudgel: 'short thick stick, used as a weapon; a club' (*OED*).

Haycock: 'A conical heap of hay in the field' (*OED*).

stealing ... 50£: since stealing even small sums was a capital offence, being 'turned out of doors' was hardly an 'inhuman' punishment. Had her benefactors brought her to court, Eliza could have been hanged.

32 *red Lion*: an inn or alehouse; commonly, its emblem would appear on its sign.

Humble Companion: a highly specific phrase, describing the job of a poor gentlewoman, hired for room, board, clothes, and a small annual salary to perform tasks such as reading aloud, attending to pets, and fetching objects for a richer gentlewoman who often felt entitled to humiliate her 'companion'.

33 *private union*: this marriage is not legal. Lord Hardwicke's Marriage Act (1753) required either the publication of banns or a special licence from the Archbishop of Canterbury. Here the duchess's chaplain is guilty of a felony; he is

liable to fourteen years' transportation (see William Allen Jowitt, first Earl, and Clifford Walsh, *Jowitt's Dictionary of English Law*, ed. John Burke, 2nd edn. [London, 1977], ii. 1151).

34 *the Continent*: continental Europe.

18,000£ a year: for JA's time, an unbelievably vast amount. Mr Darcy's income in *Pride and Prejudice* is only £10,000 a year (p. 337).

man of War of 55 Guns: Gino Galuppini's *Warships of the World: An Illustrated Encyclopedia* (Milan, 1986) makes no mention of vessels with an odd number of guns: balance would be difficult. It is probable that JA intends this description to be a joke.

Newgate: the most famous London prison of the eighteenth century gave its name to any prison; a private keep such as this one 'for the reception of . . . private prisoners' is mock-medieval, deriving from fairy tales and Gothic fiction.

private Prisoners: it would, of course, be illegal to distrain prisoners without due process of law.

35 *gold Watch for herself*: gold watches could be extremely expensive: Horace Walpole in 1759 lists the price of a gold watch as 134 guineas (Letter to Sir Horace Mann, 8 June 1759, Horace Walpole, *Correspondence*, ed. W. S. Lewis *et al.*, 42 vols. (1937–83), 21: 295).

biting off two of her fingers: references to mothers eating their children are common enough (see the Lamentations of Jeremiah 2: 20, and Daniel Defoe's *Roxana* [Oxford, 1981], 18), but not children eating their mothers.

cold collation: a collection of cold meats and salads.

Junketings: slang expression for 'feasting, banqueting, merry-making' (*OED*).

36 *our real Child*: the revelation of true parentage figures large at the conclusion of many eighteenth-century novels, for example *Joseph Andrews*, *Tom Jones*, and *Evelina*.

37 *Applause of her own Heart*: a sentiment suited to the philosophy of benevolence, similar to that in Pope's *Essay on Man*:

> One self-approving hour whole years out-weighs
> Of stupid starers, and of loud huzzas. (iv. 255–6).

The adventures of Mr Harley

37 *Harley*: the name perhaps derives from that of the hero of Henry Mackenzie's *The Man of Feeling* (1771).

Francis William Austen: see note to p. 11.

Midshipman: 'In the navy, the designation of a rank intermediate in the line of promotion between that of naval cadet and that of the lowest commissioned officer' (*OED*).

Hogsworth Green: supposedly 'the seat of Emma', though no woman could really own a 'seat', the centre of a family; a woman might act as trustee for the real heir, the closest male relative.

Sir William Mountague

38 *Mountague*: a family name as 'Montague' associated with Romeo, and with Lovelace's family in Samuel Richardson's *Clarissa* (1747–8).

Charles John Austen Esqre: JA's youngest brother (1779–1852), still at home in Steventon when 'Sir William Mountague' was written between 1787 and 1790.

Park well stocked with Deer: deer were originally kept to be hunted, later as a necessary component of picturesque landscape; only gentlemen of wealth and property could keep deer. The grounds of Grandison Hall, among their other perfections, are supplied with deer: 'Clementina . . . diverts herself often with feeding the deer, which gather about her, as soon as she enters the park' (*Sir Charles Grandison*, iii. 433).

Kilhoobery Park: an absurd mock-Irish name.

Sir William was equally in Love with them all: a recollection of the dilemma faced by Sir Charles Grandison; see note to p. 14.

first of September: the traditional beginning of the partridge season. See *Pride and Prejudice*, where the recently married Lydia is confident that her new husband Wickham 'would kill more birds on the first of September, than any body else in the country' (p. 281).

39 *Surry*: Surrey; one of the 'home counties', south of London. *Emma* is set in Surrey, and JA there describes the landscape's 'English verdure, English culture [i.e. agriculture], English

comfort, seen under a sun bright, without being oppressive'
(p. 325).

Stanhope: family name of Philip Dormer Stanhope, Lord
Chesterfield.

Sir William shot Mr Stanhope: one would expect this action to
take place in a duel. But Sir William may have assassinated
Mr Stanhope. In either case, he is subject to a charge of
murder.

privately married: since Sir William is only 17, the marriage is
invalid. See note to p. 33.

Chariot: in the eighteenth century, 'a light four-wheeled
carriage with only back seats, and differing from the post-
chaise in having a coach-box' (*OED*).

Brook Street: fashionable street, extending from Hanover
Square to Grosvenor Square, taking its name from Tyburn
Brook which flows beneath it.

Memoirs of Mr Clifford

40 *Coach and Four*: a coach was a large, closed carriage, offering
seating for many; often, as here, powered by four horses.
Coaches 'for families, are the most convenient of any in use,
as they can accommodate twice the number of passengers at
one time' (Felton, *Treatise*, ii. 32). The heavy coach was an
expensive vehicle, ranging in price from £105 (plain) to
£188. 19s. (ornamented) (*ibid.*, ii. 37).

Chaise: a light, fast vehicle for one to three passengers,
powered by one to six horses, the driver sitting on one of the
horses.

Landeau: 'A Landau is a carriage in the form of a Coach, the
upper part of which may be opened at pleasure, for the
advantage of air and prospect in the summer time, principally
intended for country use . . .' (Felton, *Treatise*, ii. 38).
Landaus were among the most expensive vehicles of the day,
an ornamented landau costing £185. 16s. 6d. (ii. 40).

Landeaulet: or landaulet, a demi- or half landau, for two
rather than four passengers, so light that sometimes one
horse sufficed (Berkebile, *Carriage Terminology*, 188). 'The
difference of this body from that of the landau is very simple:
it has no division on the roof, but opens all from the fore
part, and throws down behind; whereas the other has two,

and opens nearly in the middle of the roof' (Felton, *Treatise*, i. 25).

40 *Phaeton*: a four-wheeled chaise holding two passengers, lighter than a coach, safer and more comfortable than two-wheelers, driven by its owner. 'Phaetons, for some years, have deservedly been regarded as the most pleasant sort of carriage in use, as they contribute, more than any other, to health, amusement, and fashion, with the superior advantage of lightness, over every other sort of four-wheeled carriages, and are much safer, and more easy to ride in than those of two wheels' (Felton, *Treatise*, ii. 68). Phaetons cost from £37. 8s. (unadorned) to £61. 9s. 6d. (ornamented) (*ibid.*, ii. 5).

Gig: 'all one-horse chaises, that are neat and fancifully constructed, are named Gigs' (Felton, *Treatise*, ii. 107). Gigs, fashionable in the 1790s, cost from £31. 14s. 6d. to £54. 1s. 6d. (ibid., ii. 7 and 112).

Whisky: 'Whiskies are one-horse chaises of the lightest construction, with which the horses may travel with ease and expedition, and quickly pass other carriages on the road, for which reason they are called whiskies' (Felton, *Treatise*, ii. 113). Whiskies were comparatively inexpensive, with costs reported from £22. 12s. 6d. to £48. 19s. (*ibid.*, ii. 117).

Italian Chair: a chair is 'A light, one-horse, two wheel vehicle used extensively in England and America in the eighteenth and early nineteenth centuries', lacking a top (Berkebile, *Carriage Terminology*, 80). 'For lawns or parks these sort of chaises have been mostly used, and for that reason, do not require to have springs, or to be lined, as they are frequently left out, exposed to the weather' (Felton, *Treatise*, ii. 122).

Buggy: 'A Buggy is a cant name given to phaetons or chaises which can only contain one person on the seat; they are particularly intended for lightness in draught, for the rider to sit snug in' (Felton, *Treatise*, ii. 121).

Curricle: 'A two-wheel carriage, drawn by two horses abreast' (Felton, *Treatise*, ii, Glossary, p. 5); 'from their novelty, and being generally used by persons of eminence, [curricles] are, on that account, preferred as a more genteel kind of carriage than the phaeton' (*ibid.*, ii. 95).

wheelbarrow: though wheelbarrows in the twentieth-century

sense did exist in the eighteenth century, in the seventeenth century the term could refer to a light and inexpensive horse-drawn carriage (Berkebile, *Carriage Terminology*, 298), which may be the meaning here.

six Greys, 4 Bays, eight Blacks and a poney: bays and black horses were generally more expensive than greys; ponies were the least expensive.

Devizes: a small market town in Wiltshire, east of Bath, a frequent stop for travellers between Bath and London. See Christopher Anstey's *New Bath Guide* (1766):

> What tho' at *Devizes* I fed pretty hearty
> And made a good meal, like the rest of the party.
> (10th edn. [London, 1776], p. 13.)

41   *Overton*: town in Hampshire, 3 miles from Steventon, where JA's eldest brother James became a curate early in 1790 (Tucker, *Goodly Heritage*, 105). Overton, approximately 50 miles east of Devizes, is not three days' hard journey away.

Dean Gate: probably modern Deane, 3 miles east of Overton, 5½ miles west of Basingstoke.

Basingstoke: the largest town close to Steventon (with a population of 4,066 early in the nineteenth century), 'a municipal borough, market-town, and parish' (Lewis, *Topographical Dictionary*, i. 162).

Clarkengreen: Clarken Green, 5 miles west of Basingstoke.

Worting: a parish half-way between Deane and the centre of Basingstoke.

Mr. Robins's: Mr Robins kept the Crown Inn at Basingstoke; see Deirdre Le Faye, *Jane Austen: A Family Record* (London, 1989), 63.

The Beautifull Cassandra

Miss Austen: JA's sister, Cassandra Elizabeth (1773–1845), called here simply 'Miss Austen', without first name, since she is the eldest Austen daughter (as Jane Bennet is called 'Miss Bennet').

42   *Bond Street*: street running north from Piccadilly to Oxford Street, a fashionable shopping venue then as now. Many shopkeepers let their upper storeys as lodgings. In *Sense and*

Sensibility John Willoughby apparently lives there; it is from Bond Street that he dates his cruel letter to Marianne (p. 158).

42 *fall in love with . . . Bonnet*: cf. Leonora, the Unfortunate Jilt, in *Joseph Andrews*, who, on seeing 'a Coach and Six' pass by, exclaims '*O I am in love with that Equipage!*' (p. 95).

six ices: pastry-cooks sold ice-cream and water ices. In *Northanger Abbey*, James Morland, Isabella, Maria, and John Thorpe adjourned from the Pump-room in Clifton 'to eat ice at a pastry-cook's' (p. 91).

43 *Hackney Coach*: the word 'hackney' indicates that the coach is for hire.

Hampstead: a distance of some 4 miles from Bond Street; site of a famous prospect of London. Instead of walking on Hampstead Heath and admiring the view, as did Lovelace and Clarissa in Samuel Richardson's novel (*Clarissa*, iv. 269), Cassandra is merely indolently driven.

Bloomsbury Square: one of the earliest squares in London, a fashionable address in the eighteenth century.

Amelia Webster

45 *Mrs Austen*: JA's mother, Cassandra Leigh Austen (1739–1827).

Beverley: a name with romantic association: Captain Absolute assumes it in Sheridan's *The Rivals* (1775) and it is the surname of the heroine of Frances Burney's *Cecilia*.

two thousand Pounds: c.£120, in current value. Note that this sum represents Maud's total dowry; it is not an annual income.

46 *private Correspondence*: eighteenth-century novels frequently include hidden repositories for letters: see 'the side of the wood-house [where] the boards are rotted away down to the floor' which allows Clarissa to correspond with Anna Howe (*Clarissa*, i. 52).

my Paper reminds me of concluding: hackneyed and vulgar way of concluding a letter, later used by Lucy Steele in *Sense and Sensibility* (p. 242). Amelia's brief note can hardly have covered a whole sheet of paper.

The Visit

47 *the Revd James Austen*: JA's oldest brother (1765–1819), who had been ordained on 7 June 1789. James ('Jemmy' to the family) often provided prologues and epilogues for the amateur theatricals presented in the Austen household at Steventon (Tucker, *Goodly Heritage*, 100–5).

'The School for Jealousy' and 'The travelled Man': these titles recall many eighteenth-century plays: see Arthur Murphy's *The School for Guardians* (1767), Sheridan's *The School for Scandal* (1777), Hannah Cowley's *School for Eloquence* (1780), Goldsmith's *The Good-Natur'd Man* (1768), and Richard Cumberland's *The Choleric Man* (1774). These titles in JA's dedication may be burlesques, or may be titles of James Austen's plays, now lost.

Curate: originally, a priest entrusted with the cure (care) of souls; in the eighteenth century, the assistant to the rector of a parish. At the time *The Visit* was written, James Austen was or was about to become curate at Stoke Charity, near Steventon (Tucker, *Goodly Heritage*, 103–4).

48 *'The more free, the more Wellcome'*: probably a proverb.

discovered: a term commonly used in stage directions, indicating that the characters are already on the scene when the curtain opens.

49 *Chairs . . . row*: in old-fashioned houses, chairs were ranged along the wall, ready to be moved as required; setting chairs round in conversational groups was the new and fashionable way of arranging furnishings.

50 *Stanly hands*: to hand is to lead or conduct by the hand, to escort.

Miss Fitzgerald at top. Lord Fitzgerald at bottom: i.e. at the dinner table. Precise location at the dining table indicated rank. See *Pride and Prejudice*, where the recently married Lydia Wickham takes precedence over the still-unmarried Jane (p. 280). Here Lord Fitzgerald and Miss Fitzgerald act as hosts—at the head and foot of the table—although they are not married.

fried Cowheel and Onion: startlingly vulgar food; cowheel (often marketed as 'trotters') was generally stewed to make a broth or jelly.

50 *bumper*: 'A cup or glass of wine, etc., filled to the brim, *esp.* when drunk as a toast' (*OED*).

Elder wine: 'Put a Gallon of Water, and two Pounds of Sugar, to a Quart of Syrup of Elder-Berries; take a Crust of Bread, and spread a little Ale-Yeast upon it to work it' (*The Accomplish'd Housewife*, 269); a drink with rural, not fashionable, associations.

Mead: 'Take eight Gallons of Water, and as much Honey as will make it bear an Egg; add to this the Rind of six Lemons, and boil it well, and scum it carefully as it rises. When 'tis off the Fire, put to it the Juice of six Lemons, and pour it into a clean Tub or open Earthen Vessel . . . in three Months time it will be fine, and fit for bottling' (*The Accomplish'd Housewife*, 275–6).

warm ale . . . nutmeg: a comforting drink for invalids, not usual at dinner parties.

51 *Tripe*: 'The first or second stomach of a ruminant, especially of the ox, prepared as food; formerly including also the entrails of swine and fish' (*OED*); coarse food of the very poor.

Crow: giblets, as in modern Dutch 'kroos', modern English 'craw'. Crow, the carrion bird, was not eaten in England. The following recipe is offered in *The Accomplish'd Housewife*: 'Hogs-Liver, Crow *and* Sweet-Bread *fry'd*. Pepper and salt it and cut red Sage small; serve it with Butter and Mustard' (p. 191).

suet pudding: Hannah Glasse's recipe in *The Art of Cookery Made Plain and Easy* (London, 1747), pp. 189–90, calls for a quart of milk, four spoonfuls of flour, one pound of shredded suet, four eggs, a spoon of 'beaten ginger', and a teaspoon of salt. These ingredients are to be boiled two hours, probably tied in a cloth. Again, not the food of the genteel.

Wine: claret, for serious drinking, after the meal and after the ladies have gone.

Desert: i.e. dessert, fruit and nuts, not a sweet course.

Hothouse: where grapes, oranges, and even pineapples (the makings of 'Desert') could be grown. See *Northanger Abbey*, where General Tilney possesses 'a village of hot-houses' (p. 142).

Closet: probably a cupboard.

Gooseberry Wine: 'To every Pound of *Gooseberries*, pick'd and bruis'd, put a Quart of Water, and let it stand two or three Days, stirring it up every Day. To every Gallon of Wine, when clean'd, put in three Pounds of Sugar, and put it into a sweet Barrel; let it stand six Months, then bottle it; put a Pound of *Malaga* Raisins into every Gallon, when it is put into the Barrel' (*The Accomplish'd Housewife*, 271–2). Gooseberry wine was rustic and antiquated; it was never substituted for fine French wine at dinner parties.

The Mystery

52   *the Revd George Austen*: JA's father (1731–1805), rector of Steventon.

53   *Spangle*: a small round piece of glittering metal, sewn on fabric for a sparkle; name indicates clown or showman.

Humbug: eighteenth-century slang for a hoax or imposition, or for someone who practises deception or is simply a fraud.

Corydon ... Daphne: male and female names from the pastoral tradition.

54   *reclined ... asleep*: earlier in the eighteenth century, proper carriage was an essential quality of the gentleman; stances derived from dance positions. *The Polite Academy* advises gentlemen: 'Sit in a genteel and easy posture, do not stretch out your Legs, nor loll: Put one Hand in the Bosom of your Waistcoat, and let the other fall easily upon your Knee' (London, 1762, p. 22). But by the later part of the century an elegant indolence had become fashionable. See the portrait of Sir Brooke Boothby by Joseph Wright of Derby (1781) and Burney's description of Mr Meadows, who 'flung himself all along upon the form in such a lounging posture, while he rested one arm upon the table, that ... he filled up a space meant for three' (*Cecilia*, 287).

So I'll e'en venture: 'The Mystery' recalls two famous Restoration and eighteenth-century burlesque plays, George Villiers, Duke of Buckingham's *The Rehearsal* (1672) and Sheridan's *The Critic* (1779).

The Three Sisters

55   *Edward Austen Esqre*: the third Austen son (1767–1852), already by the time of 'The Three Sisters' under the

protection of the wealthy Knight family; Edward was later to be legally adopted by them. In 1791—the year before the composition of 'The Three Sisters'— Edward had married the wealthy Elizabeth Bridges and had come into possession of Rowling, a small estate in Kent.

55 *Settlements*: property legally settled by pre-nuptial contract on the wife and her children (if any) for her use in the event of the husband's death. As Mary realizes, this wealth will be no good to her while her husband lives.

56 *blue spotted with silver . . . plain Chocolate*: it is difficult to determine whether JA refers to the interior or exterior of the coach. A carriage could be painted and varnished a plain brown or elaborately ornamented, often with silver-plate (see note to p. 63). Interior upholstery could likewise be fancy or plain.

low as his old one: Mary Stanhope wants a tall carriage, which will provide a grand view.

to chaprone: a chaperone was a married woman who could properly accompany single women to parties. See *Pride and Prejudice*, where the hastily married Lydia expects to chaperone her sisters—even the older ones—to balls in Newcastle (p. 280).

Winter Balls: winter was the height of 'the season' in towns and a favourite time for large private parties and public assemblies, such as masquerades.

57 *Law*: a linguistic vulgarism used by Anne Steele in *Sense and Sensibility*: 'Oh, la' (pp. 239–40).

Tea: not generally a meal but rather the drinking of tea after dinner, which during the eighteenth century was gradually moved from 12 o'clock until the end of the afternoon. Teatime seems to have been established long before the Victorian period to which some social historians would allocate it. Sometimes guests came for the tea after a meal, as today guests might come for coffee. In *Evelina*, the heroine writes of Madame Duval coming to tea 'near five o'clock, for we never dine till the day is almost over' (p. 56).

58 *Miss XXX*: JA creates the impression of elaborate secrecy found in eighteenth-century novels, in which fictional characters' names are withheld, as if they were real people.

Proposals . . . receive: here the superficial Mary should be contrasted with Richardson's Clarissa Harlowe. In her rejection of the wealthy Mr Solmes, Richardson's heroine knows her own mind, and does know how to receive proposals from a suitor who offers wealth but not affection.

59 *genteel figure*: an elegant shape of the body.

Three thousand a year: a considerable income, now approximately £180,000 per year. Note that Mrs Stanhope's income, a sixth of this figure, is only £500, approximately that of Mrs Dashwood in *Sense and Sensibility* (p. 25).

Phaeton: see note to p. 40.

61 *Chaise*: see note to p. 40.

62 *Jointure*: see note to p. 12.

pinmoney: 'an annual sum allotted to a woman for personal expenses in dress, etc.' (*OED*).

two hundred a year: c.£12,000 in today's value.

a wreath of silver flowers round it: perhaps silver-plated ornaments on carriages. See p. 63 and note.

Winter in Bath: to spend the winter in Bath, like Lady Russell in *Persuasion* (p. 19).

Spring in Town: see note to p. 15.

Tour: a prolonged excursion for pleasure, generally in search of picturesque scenery; favourite late-century destinations included the Lake District, the Peak District in Derbyshire, or the Continent. The volumes of William Gilpin, whose titles all include the word 'tour', describe journeys to Wye and South Wales (1782), the Lakes (1789), and the Highlands of Scotland (1789).

Watering Place: spa or seaside resort.

a Theatre to act Plays in: the heroine of Frances Brooke's *The Excursion* (1777) gets her husband-to-be to promise her a private theatre. Putting on plays had become a fashionable amusement, as JA later depicts in *Mansfield Park*.

Which is the Man: play by Hannah Cowley, published in 1783, acted at Steventon at Christmas 1787 (Southam, *Literary MSS*, 7).

Lady Bell Bloomer: in *Which is the Man?*, a vivacious widow wooed by the rake Sparkish; she is as demanding as JA's

Mary Stanhope: in the play we hear that 'the hair-dresser has been with her these three hours, and her maid is running here and there, and Mr. *John* flying about to milliners and perfumers, and the new *vis-a-vis* at the door to carry her Ladyship to court' (*Which is the Man? A Comedy* [London, 1783], 10).

63 *silver Border*: probably silver-plating; according to William Felton, 'Nothing has ever been introduced with a better effect than . . . silver plating, which is now become so general, that almost every hackney carriage exhibits some portion of it' (*Treatise*, i. 164).

Special Licence: permission, available only from the Archbishop of Canterbury, which dispenses with the reading of banns before a wedding. Cf. Mrs Bennet's excited comment in *Pride and Prejudice*: 'Ten thousand a year, and very likely more! 'Tis as good as a Lord! And a special licence. You must and shall be married by a special licence' (p. 337).

Banns: proclamation or public notice given in church of an intended marriage; the Book of Common Prayer requires the banns to be read on three Sundays before the marriage. The rich and powerful could avoid the public and hence, in their minds, slightly vulgar reading of the banns by means of the special or common licence.

common Licence: an ordinary licence, granted by an archbishop or bishop, for marriage in any church or chapel within his diocese, permitting marriage without banns.

Saddle horse: a horse broken for riding.

in return . . . three Years: recalls the marriage agreements of Walter and Mrs Shandy (*The Life and Opinions of Tristram Shandy* [1759–67], i. xv; pp. 29–31). Mrs Shandy was allowed to visit London only to give birth.

64 *Stoneham*: South and North Stonham are parishes 3 and 4 miles north-north-east of Southampton (Lewis, *Topographical Dictionary*, iv, 226–7).

Leicestershire: a county in the Midlands of England; one of the 'shires' famous for fox-hunters; thus, JA quickly characterizes Sir Henry as another fox-hunting squire, such as Fielding's Squire Western in *Tom Jones*.

my appearance: the bride's first public appearance after her wedding, usually at church.

67   *Vixen*: literally, a bitch fox.

   Blackguard: originally, a vagabond, a criminal, or a low-life
   character.

   dressed: i.e. dressed for the evening.

To Miss Jane Anna Elizabeth Austen

   Miss Jane Anna Elizabeth Austen: JA's niece Anna (1793–
   1872), the daughter of James Austen, later Mrs Benjamin
   Lefroy.

   Infancy: Anna was indeed an infant, having been born on 15
   Apr. 1793.

68   *Treatises for your Benefit*: works for the advice of young ladies
   by writers such as Hannah More (1745–1833) and Hester
   Chapone (1721–1801) poured off late eighteenth-century
   presses. Mrs Percival, the aunt of the heroine of Austen's
   'Catharine', recommends several such texts (p. 222).

A beautiful description of the different effects of Sensibility on different Minds

   Sensibility: a major word in the philosophy and aesthetics of
   the eighteenth century, referring to sensitivity of body and
   mind, and capacity to respond emotionally to beauty and
   pathos.

   object: eighteenth-century art as well as literature generates
   many affecting objects, particularly persons in a state of
   distress calculated to affect, to move the emotions of the
   sensitive—who should be moved to generosity also.

   book muslin: 'a fine kind of muslin owing its name to the
   book-like manner in which it is folded when sold in the piece'
   (*OED*).

   chambray gauze: a semi-transparent cloth made of cambric, a
   fine white linen (*An Elegant Art*, 239 and 242).

   shift: a plain undergarment of linen or cotton.

   French net nightcap: the 'dormeuse' or 'French Nightcap' was
   in style 1750–90; it was a day cap, not a dress cap. A crown,
   trimmed with ribbon, fitted over the head, with flaps (called
   'wings') at each side (Cunnington, *Handbook*, 347). The
   headgear referred to is a 'dormeuse' made of net, an open-
   work fabric.

68   *hashing up*: cutting up, heating, and serving with sauce.

      Curry: this dish had been brought to England from India.
      Hannah Glasse provides two recipes for chicken curry, one
      seasoned with curry powder, the other with 'an ounce of
      turmeric, a large spoonful of ginger and beaten pepper
      together, and a little salt to your palate' (*The Art of Cookery*,
      129). This is hardly a dish for an invalid.

69   *Warwick*: 'Woody' or 'Leafy Warwickshire', a county in
      central England known for its forests.

      living: a clergyman's income from farm lands owned by the
      parish and rented out. The livings of parishes varied a great
      deal in the eighteenth century, and £200 per annum was not
      a large sum. At the time JA wrote 'The Generous Curate',
      her brother, the Revd James Austen (and the father of Anna
      Austen: see p. 67), was experiencing financial difficulties.
      He and his wife Anne had a combined yearly income of £300
      (Honan, *Life*, 90–1).

      The portrait of the generous Curate derives from Henry
      Fielding's Parson Abraham Adams in *Joseph Andrews*, who
      has a yearly income of £23. Like the Revd Mr Williams,
      Adams is 'a little incumbered with a Wife and six Children'
      (p. 19) but does not complain.

      Royal Academy for Seamen at Portsmouth: The Royal Naval
      Academy (later the Royal Naval College) accepted boys of
      11 to 17 (Lewis Michael, *A Social History of the Navy, 1793–
      1815* [London, 1960], 145).

      Newfoundland Dog: a breed of dog apparently approved by
      JA since she gives a large Newfoundland puppy to Henry
      Tilney in *Northanger Abbey* (p. 171).

70   *Dame's School*: an elementary private school kept by an old
      woman or widow, attended by the poor who wanted to learn
      the elements of reading, arithmetic, and perhaps writing.
      Here the fee is two pence per week.

      brickbats: 'A piece or fragment of a brick. . . . It is the typical
      ready missile, where stones are scarce' (*OED*). Young
      Williams's youthful tricks recall those of the young Tom
      Jones (III. ii; p. 89).

Ode to Pity

      Miss Austen: Cassandra Austen. See note to p. 41.

Ode to Pity: JA echoes the titles of William Collins's well-known *Ode to Pity* (1747).

Myrtle: associated with love, its leaves having been pierced in desperation by Phaedra, in love with Hippolytus, her stepson.

Philomel: the nightingale.

71 *brawling down the turnpike road*: an aspect of England's progress in the later eighteenth century was a proliferation of new turnpike roads paid for by tolls on vehicles. JA later makes a similar joke in 'Love and Freindship', pp. 95–6.

Cot . . . Chapel queer: images made fashionable and hackneyed by the mid-century Graveyard Poets and later by Gothic novelists.

Cot: cottage.

Grot: grotto.

Abbey: another favourite image of the Graveyard Poets and Gothic novelists. In *Northanger Abbey*, Catherine Morland finds it 'delightful to be really in an abbey', where 'her imagination . . . hoped for . . . the heaviest stone-work, for painted glass, dirt and cobwebs' (p. 128).

VOLUME THE SECOND

73 *Ex dono mei Patris*: 'A gift from my father'; the notebook containing the manuscript of 'Volume the Second' was a gift from the Revd George Austen.

74 *Madame La Comtesse De Feuillide*: see note to p. 31.

Love and Freindship

75 *'Deceived in Freindship and Betrayed in Love'*: unidentified quotation.

Laura: since the time of Petrarch, the name Laura has been common among literary heroines.

76 *natural*: illegitimate.

Opera-girl: 'a girl or woman who dances in the ballet of an opera' (*OED*).

romantic: here, wild and picturesque, as in William Gilpin's *Observations on the River Wye and Several Parts of South Wales*

(London, 1782): '*Brecknoc* is a very romantic place, abounding with broken grounds, torrents, dismantled towers, and ruins of every kind' (p. 51).

76 *Vale of Uske*: generally 'Usk'; river valley north of Newport in the present Welsh counties of Gwent and Powys. JA's notion of the Vale perhaps derives from William Gilpin: 'The vale of Usk, is a delightful place. The river, from whence it borrows its name, winds through the middle of it; and the hills, on both sides, were diversified with woods, and lawns. In many places, they were partially cultivated. We could distinguish little cottages, and farms, faintly traced along their shadowy side; which, at such a distance, rather varied, and inriched the scene; than impressed it with any regular, and unpleasing shapes' (*Observations on the River Wye*, 50).

accustomary: usual (an archaic usage in JA's time).

Rendez-vous: an appointed meeting or meeting-place, primarily referring to the assembly of troops.

Minuet Dela Cour: literally, the minuet of the court; the fashionable, stately, formal dance of the age, to be distinguished from country dances.

77 *Boarding schools*: increasingly common for girls with any pretence to gentility. See 'Introduction', pp. xiii–xiv. Perhaps Isabel—and Charlotte Palmer in *Sense and Sensibility*—attended the famous 'ladies' Eton' in Queen Square in London. See note to p. 30.

Stinking . . . Southampton: Southampton is a port city in the south of England in Hampshire. See 'Introduction', p. xiii

78 *rustic Cot*: country cottage; poetical language of the pastoral and picturesque.

79 *Lindsay*: a noble Scottish name, family name of the Earls of Balcarres; the first Earl of Balcarres, Alexander Lindsay, declared for the King in the Civil War and died in exile at Breda.

Talbot: an eminently English and heroic name; the most famous Talbot was John, first Earl of Shrewsbury, who fought the French under Henry V (see Shakespeare's *Henry V*) and Henry VI (see 1 *Henry VI*, IV. vii).

Baronet: a holder of the lowest hereditary rank.

middle size: JA in her later fiction always concerns herself with height; Fitzwilliam Darcy, for example, is tall (*Pride and Prejudice*, 7). See also note to p. 129.

Polydore: name of the youngest son of King Priam, often used for characters in romance. In Shakespeare's *Cymbeline* (printed 1623), it is the name taken by the disguised Guiderius in the Welsh forest. One of the rival brothers in Otway's *The Orphan* (1680) is also a Polydore.

Claudia: Roman name, female equivalent of 'Claudius' (crippled), associated with Quinta Claudia, a Roman matron suspected of lack of chastity, who vindicated herself by drawing a vessel containing the image of Cybele out of the shallows.

obliged my Father: such a difference of opinion between fathers (or sometimes guardians) and offspring is traditional in comedies; for example, in Sheridan's *The Rivals* (1771), a play in which JA acted, Sir Anthony Absolute demands obedience in matters matrimonial from his son, Captain Absolute.

studying Novels I suspect: Sir Edward accuses his son of being quixotic, of deriving strange and 'romantic' ideas from his reading of novels. Novels were often blamed for youthful misbehaviour: as JA writes in *Northanger Abbey*, 'no species of composition has been so much decried' (p. 21).

Bedfordshire . . . Middlesex: Bedfordshire is one of the eastern Midland counties; Middlesex lies just north and west of London. South Wales lies in the extreme west of the island. Clearly Edward is not proficient in geography.

80 *distant Light*: a light often announces the nocturnal hospitality scenes in eighteenth-century novels; for example, in *Joseph Andrews*, a large 'number of Lights' lead Parson Adams, Fanny Goodwill, and Joseph to the home of the generous Mr Wilson (p. 173).

never taken orders: as Laura's father is not an ordained clergyman, Laura and Edward are not legally married; for other examples of invalid marriage ceremonies, see pp. 33, 39, 133, 149–50.

84 *inward Secrets of our Hearts*: JA regards with suspicion the sudden flaming of friendship, as between Catherine Morland and Isabella Thorpe in *Northanger Abbey*: 'they passed so

rapidly through every gradation of increasing tenderness, that there was shortly no fresh proof of it to be given to their friends or themselves. They called each other by their Christian name, were always arm in arm when they walked, pinned up each other's train for the dance, and were not to be divided in the set' (p. 21).

84 *We fainted alternately on a Sofa*: See *The Critic*, III, i.

'MOTHER

'O ecstasy of bliss!

'SON

'O most unlook'd for happiness!

'JUSTICE

'O wonderful event!

[*They faint alternately in each other's arms.*
(*The Dramatic Works of Richard Brinsley Sheridan*, ed. Cecil Price [Oxford, 1973], ii, 540–1.)

85 *Clandestine Marriage*: the phrase derives from the play *The Clandestine Marriage* (1766), by George Colman the elder and David Garrick. Hardwicke's Marriage Act of 1753 prohibited the secret marriage of minors (see note to p. 33). Thus, parents and guardians were generally apprised of the forthcoming marriages of their children and wards; they had the power to stop such marriages as they disapproved. The clandestine marriages of the sort JA here describes were of dubious legality.

86 *purloined*: stolen; to purloin is 'to steal, especially under circumstances which involve a breach of trust' (*OED*).

Escritoire: writing-desk.

would have blushed . . . paying their Debts: perhaps this 'gentle-manly' attribute derives from Charles Surface in Sheridan's *School for Scandal* (1777), a play in which JA had acted the part of Mrs Candour. When Careless, one of Charles's spendthrift friends, mentions 'tradesmen', Charles replies, 'Very true, and paying them is only Encouraging them' (IV. i; Sheridan, *Dramatic Works*, i. 408).

arrested: since Augustus is sent to Newgate and may be sentenced to hang, he is probably arrested for theft, not for debt.

Execution in the House: the seizure of a debtor's goods by a sheriff's officer in execution of writ.

Officers of Justice: sheriff's officers.

87 *Holbourn*: Holborn; district in London, between the City and the West End.

Postilion: see note to p. 6.

Newgate: see note to p. 34.

Annuity: an annual return of a set sum, the payment ceasing upon the death of the recipient. Annuities did not generally provide large amounts; during periods of inflation—such as the 1790s—the set sum's buying power was considerably reduced.

88 *travel Post*: the quickest and most expensive mode of transportation.

coroneted Coach: coach ornamented with the family crest of a peer.

instinctive Sympathy: the 'natural' instinct which impels the finding of lost relatives was a prominent narrative element in ancient fiction. The Romantic era also saw a new interest in emotional affinities and sympathies, while the idealization of the family so often supported by conservative theorists of the 1790s led to an emphasis on the supposedly innate and 'instinctive' affections that draw family members together.

89 *Matilda*: Matilda is one of the heroines of Horace Walpole's *Castle of Otranto* (1764). JA associated the name with romantic fiction: in *Northanger Abbey*, when Henry Tilney improvises on Gothic themes, he imagines that Catherine Morland will find in manuscript the 'memoirs of the wretched Matilda' (p. 126).

St. Clair: name reminiscent of Sinclair, the assumed name of the bawd in Richardson's *Clarissa*.

Philander: play on the noun 'philanderer'.

Gustavus: the name had heroic associations. See Henry Brooke's *Gustavus Vasa* (1739).

89–90 *'But tell . . . other Grand-Children in the House'*: cf., in Burney's *Evelina*, the scene where Sir John Belmont resists Mrs Selwyn's efforts to persuade him to acknowledge Evelina as his daughter: 'I have already a daughter . . . and it is not three days since, that I had the pleasure of discovering a son; how many more sons and daughters may be brought to me, I am yet to learn, but I am, already, perfectly satisfied with the size of my family' (p. 371).

90 *Janetta*: here JA plays with her own name. 'Janetta' is a manufactured, romanticized version of Janet, a Scottish form of Jane.

91 *Graham*: Graham, like many of the names that appealed to JA, has Royalist associations, as the name of the celebrated and unfortunate first Marquis of Montrose. It is also further evidence of the eighteenth-century vogue for things Scottish, a fashion particularly evident in the last half of 'Love and Freindship'. See notes to 'Lesley Castle', pp. 108 and 120.

Sorrows of Werter: Wolfang von Goethe's *Sorrows of Young Werther* (1774) recounted in epistolary form the title character's hopeless love for Lotte. The novel ends with Werther's suicide. *Werther* exemplifies the sensibility and love of wild, romantic Nature which JA satirizes in 'Love and Freindship'.

93 *Gretna-Green*: town in Dumfries in southern Scotland, north of Carlisle, where marriages of parties under 21 could be quickly performed; the destination of many English elopers: 'the great resort of such unfortunate nymphs, as differ with their parents and guardians on the subject of marriage' (Gilpin, *Observations, Relative Chiefly to Picturesque Beauty . . . On Several Parts of Great Britain; Particularly the High-Lands of Scotland* [London, 1789], 107). Hardwicke's Marriage Act, 1753 (see note to p. 33) did not apply to Scotland. Thus, Scottish marriage laws did not require the public reading of banns and therefore the permission of parents or guardians of minors.

Wherefore . . . broken in on?: a parodic version of a conflict often found in eighteenth-century novels, where women often try to create private spaces. For example, Richardson's Clarissa enjoys solitude in her room at Harlowe Place and in her room at Mrs Sinclair's. Clarissa, of course, has the right to ask such a haughty question when she is disturbed; Sophia the thief does not.

94 *sate down . . . stream*: this description involves a recollection of a passage in Samuel Johnson's *Journey to the Western Isles of Scotland* (1775): 'I sat down on a bank, such as a writer of romance might have delighted to feign. I had indeed no trees to whisper over my head, but a clear rivulet streamed at my feet. The day was calm, the air was soft, and all was

rudeness, silence, and solitude. Before me, and on either side, were high hills, which, by hindering the eye from ranging, forced the mind to find entertainment for itself. Whether I spent the hour well I know not; for here I first conceived the thought of this narration' (Johnson, *Works*, viii. 255). R. W. Chapman notes this parallel (*Minor Works*, 459).

95 *murmuring brook . . . turn-pike road*: see 'Ode to Pity', p. 71.

Eastern Zephyr: since 'Zephyr' is a poetical name for the west wind, this phrase is nonsensical.

blue sattin Waistcoat striped with white!: according to the Cunningtons, 'stripes were very prevalent' on waistcoats of the 1780s. They quote the *Ipswich Journal* for June 1788, referring to the fashion of 'white striped Manchester dimity waistcoats trimmed with a small white fringe' (Cunnington, *Handbook*, 208). JA is particularly likely to refer to blue: see the 'blue hat' on p. 195, Bingley's blue coat (see note to p. 7), and the blue shoes in the shop window of *Sanditon*.

96 *apropos*: from French *à propos*, to the point, opportune.

Life of Cardinal Wolsey . . . Mind!: suggested by *The Vanity of Human Wishes*, in which Samuel Johnson meditates on Wolsey's fall from power:

> In full-blown dignity, see Wolsey stand,
> Law in his voice, and fortune in his hand . . .
> At length his sov'reign frowns—the train of state
> Mark the keen glance, and watch the sign to hate.
> Where'er he turns he meets a stranger's eye,
> His suppliants scorn him and his followers fly.
>
> (ll. 99–100, 109–12)

(*The Poems of Samuel Johnson*, ed. David Nichol Smith and Edward McAdam [Oxford, 1941], 34–5.) Perhaps also suggested by Wolsey's soliloquy in Shakespeare's *Henry VIII* (III. ii, 351–73):

> Farewell, a long farewell to all my greatness!
> This is the state of man. Today he puts forth
> The tender leaves of hopes; tomorrow blossoms,
> And bears his blushing honours thick upon him;
> The third day comes a frost, a killing frost. (ll.352–6)

97 *sensible*: in possession of his senses; conscious.

97 *Talk not . . . Cucumber*: the scene here repeats effects found in Ophelia's mad scene in *Hamlet* (IV. v) and especially in Tilburina's final speech in Sheridan's *The Critic*:

> The wind whistles—the moon rises—see,
> They have kill'd my squirrel in his cage!
> Is this a grasshopper!—Ha! no, it is my
> Whiskerandos—you shall not keep him—
> I know you have him in your pocket—
> An oyster may be crossed in love!—Who says
> A whale's a bird? (III, i)

(Sheridan, *Dramatic Works*, 548.)

98 *Seventeen*: B. C. Southam suggests that this passage compliments JA's sister Cassandra, who was to turn 17 at her next birthday, in Jan. 1791 (*Minor Works*, 459).

Bridget: cf. the quixotic heroine in Richard Steele's play *The Tender Husband* (1705), who objects to her own name:

AUNT. Alack a day, Cousin *Biddy*, these Idle Romances have quite turn'd your Head.

NIECE. How often must I desire you, Madam, to lay aside that familiar Name, Cousin *Biddy*? I never hear it without Blushing—Did you ever meet with an Heroine in those Idle romances as you call 'em, that was term'd *Biddy*?

. . . .

AUNT. Looky', *Biddy* . . . your Mother was a *Bridget* afore you, and an excellent House-Wife.

NIECE. Good Madam, don't upbraid me with my Mother *Bridget*, and an Excellent House-Wife. (II, ii)

(*The Plays of Richard Steele*, ed. Shirley Strum Kenny [Oxford, 1971], 233–4.

99 *galloping Consumption*: rapidly developing tuberculosis or any wasting disease.

100 *Coach-box*: on a coach, 'The fixture on which the driver sits' (Felton, *Treatise*, ii, Glossary, p. 4).

Basket: the overhanging back compartment on the outside of a stage-coach; the most uncomfortable seat(s), primarily intended for luggage or for passengers paying the cheapest fare.

Relations and Connections: Juliet McMaster offers a genealogical chart of the families in 'Love and Freindship' and finds that the chart 'demonstrates a balanced familial symmetry among the figures of Sensibility and Sense' ('Teaching "Love and Freindship" ', *Jane Austen's Beginnings*, 145–6).

102 *Gilpin's . . . Highlands*: *Observations, Relative Chiefly to Picturesque Beauty . . . On Several Parts of Great Britain; Particularly the High-Lands of Scotland* (London, 1789).

Stage Coach: a coach that runs according to scheduled stages, offering transportation to paying passengers; not the way genteel families did their touring.

Edinburgh . . . Sterling: Sterling (generally Stirling) is an ancient Scottish city in central Scotland, north-east of Edinburgh, an early capital of the country; the distance between Edinburgh and Sterling is some 40 miles.

103 *Green tea*: tea treated by heat as soon as it is picked from the plant, thus not allowed to wither and ferment. Cf. *Sanditon*, 370–1.

Sentimental: pertaining to the feelings, or to feeling and thought mixed; an important eighteenth-century term with varying significance. In 1749 Lady Dorothy Bradshaigh wrote to Samuel Richardson: 'Pray, Sir . . . what . . . is the meaning of the word *sentimental* so much in vogue amongst the polite, both in town and country? . . . I have . . . generally received for answer, it is—it is—*sentimental*. Every thing clever and agreeable is comprehended in that word. . . . I am frequently astonished to hear such a one is a *sentimental* man; we were a *sentimental* party; I have been taking a *sentimental* walk'. (*The Correspondence of Samuel Richardson*, ed. Anna Laetitia Barbauld [London, 1804], iv. 282–3).

Staymaker: a maker of women's corsets.

104 *the 9th to Silver Buckles*: thus, Laurina, Philander, and Gustavus have £100 to spend on silver buckles. Since a typical 1788 price of a pair was £3. 8s. (Cunnington, *Handbook*, 424), they could have purchased about 30 pairs.

Company of Players: a travelling troupe of actors, usually ill-paid and (in fiction, at least) dramatically inept. Characters in eighteenth-century novels who become strolling players include Lydia Bramble's lover Wilson in Tobias Smollett's *Humphry Clinker* (1771) and George Primrose in Goldsmith's *The Vicar of Wakefield* (1766).

104 *all the rest*: Philander thus plays many significant characters who appear together on stage, including Macbeth and his first victim, King Duncan.

105 *eclat*: from French *éclat*, burst or flash, a dazzling effect; the term is associated with theatrical effects, as in *Mansfield Park* (p. 164).

preferment in the Acting way: an unusual usage of the word 'preferment', which usually refers to advancement in the Church.

Lewis and Quick: two of the best-known and most versatile actors and theatre managers of the late eighteenth century were William Thomas Lewis (*c.*1746–1811) and John Quick (1748–1831). Both were often seen on stage at Covent Garden; Quick was the first Tony Lumpkin in *She Stoops to Conquer*. See Philip H. Highfill, Jr., Kalman A. Burnim, and Edward A. Langhans, *A Bibliographical Dictionary of Actors, Actresses, Musicians, Dancers, Managers and Other Stage Personnel in London, 1660–1800* (Carbondale, Ill., 1973), ix. 281–92 and xii. 217–25.

paid . . . Nature: a euphemism for 'died'.

Lesley Castle

107 *Henry Thomas Austen Esqre*: JA's fourth brother (1771–1850), awarded his BA at Oxford in 1792, the possible occasion of JA's dedicating 'Lesley Castle' to him. Henry seems to have written the note which follows the dedication, pretending to be a patron who could order a payment to his sister.

Demand & Co: a parodic name for a bank.

Spinster: the general and legal term for an unmarried woman.

Matilda: see note to p. 89.

108 *Rakehelly*: cf. 'rakehell': 'a thorough scoundrel or rascal; an utterly immoral or dissolute person; a vile debauchee or rake' (*OED*). The short form is 'rake'.

Sir George is 57: cf. the character Sir Thomas Grandison in Richardson's *Sir Charles Grandison*, who remains a rake and a beau and who leaves his daughters in the country while he enjoys himself in London (i. 320).

Perth: the county town of Perthshire in Scotland, known in JA's time for picturesque beauty.

M'Leods . . . Macduffs: a salmagundi of Scottish names from diverse sources such as Shakespeare and Frances Burney's *Evelina*, from which 'M'Cartney' derives.

110 *Stewed Soup*: i.e. made stock, by simmering meat and bones in water.

Whipt syllabub: a frothy sweet; 'Take a quart of thick cream, and half a pint of sack [sherry], the juice of two Seville oranges or lemons, grate in the peel of two lemons, half a pound of double-refined sugar, pour it into a broad earthen pan, and whisk it well' (Glasse, *The Art of Cookery*, 327).

111 *Eloisa*: literary name reminiscent of characters in Pope's poem *Eloisa and Abelard* (1717) and in Rousseau's novel *La Nouvelle Héloïse* (1761) and thus suited for a lachrymose female in love and in distress.

112 *Decline*: any wasting disease, often tuberculosis or anaemia.

Bristol: Bristol Hotwells, 1½ miles west of the port city of Bristol; an eighteenth-century spa, less fashionable and cheaper than the nearby Bath; scene of the final volume of Burney's *Evelina*.

113 *Mistress . . . promised us*: a mother's jewels usually went to her daughter(s), but here the jewels are in Sir George's disposal; they can go to his second wife.

most agreable . . . age: like Sir Charles Grandison in the novel by Richardson.

Cumberland: a county in north-west England, now part of Cumbria.

114 *Yorkshire*: a large county in north-east England.

Aberdeen: the principal city on the north-east coast of Scotland, in the Grampian region, noted for its old university, not for 'Elegance and Ease'.

115 *Dunbeath*: a fishing village in Caithness.

Universities: Aberdeen is a centre for education in Scotland, King's College having been founded in 1495.

the healthy air of the Bristol downs: the hills or 'downs' in and around Bristol had various names such as 'Leigh-down', 'Clifton-down', 'Kingsdown', 'Durdham-down', etc. Bristol Hotwell boasted of the restorative powers of its air: 'the valetudinarian seems to breathe new life, and to enjoy again the blessings that await returning health and cheerfulness'

(E. Shercliff, *The Bristol and Hotwell Guide* [Bristol, 1793], 66).

116 *Chairwomen*: or 'charwoman'; a charwoman is 'a woman hired by the day to do odd jobs of household work' (*OED*).

Jellies: aspic; not sweet jellies.

out of humour: out of temper, out of patience, deriving from the old but still accredited 'humours' theory, according to which good temper and a sense of well-being were supposed to result from a proper balance of the four 'humours' (black bile, yellow bile [choler], phlegm, and blood).

117 *Brighthelmstone*: the modern Brighton, in Sussex, south of London; a seaside resort since the mid-eighteenth century, when Dr Richard Russell's recommendation of its healthy air and sea-bathing drew visitors such as Samuel Johnson, Frances Burney, and Hester Thrale; in 1784, the Prince of Wales (later Regent and George IV) moved there and two years later began constructing the first of several Royal Pavilions.

four thousand pounds: a capital sum, no doubt put out at 5 per cent interest, drawing £200 per annum.

reside: presumably 'preside', but ironically appropriate for Charlotte, who does reside at table.

Curry: see note to p. 68.

118 *Cleveland*: JA later uses this name for the Palmers' Somerset estate in *Sense and Sensibility* (p. 264).

set her cap: a phrase rejected by Marianne Dashwood: 'That is an expression . . . which I particularly dislike. I abhor every common-place phrase by which wit is intended; and "setting one's cap at a man," or "making a conquest," are the most odious of all' (*Sense and Sensibility*, 38).

119 *Portman-Square*: fashionable London square, north of Oxford Street; developed 1764–84 with houses by Robert Adam, James Wyatt, and others; its most illustrious resident in the eighteenth century was the 'bluestocking' writer Elizabeth Montagu.

120 *Brat*: insignificant or small child; also, a spoiled child.

Scotch Airs . . . everything Scotch: the interest in Scotland and things Scottish preceded the novels of Sir Walter Scott. James Macpherson's *Fingal* (1762), supposedly the work of the ancient Gaelic bard Ossian, brought Scotland to an international audience: Macpherson's works were praised by readers as diverse as Schiller, Goethe, and Napoleon. Other popular works with a Scottish setting include Johnson's *Journey to the Western Islands of Scotland* (1775); Sophia Lee's novel about Mary, Queen of Scots, *The Recess* (1783–5); James Boswell's *Journal of a Tour to the Hebrides* (1785); and Ann Radcliffe's first novel, *The Castles of Athlin and Dunbayne* (1789). The interest in 'Scotch Airs' perhaps dates to Allan Ramsay's inclusion of them in his *Tea-table Miscellany* (Edinburgh, 1724; 18 edns.) and in his comedy *The Gentle Shepherd* (1725). Later, publishers commissioned settings of Scottish folk-songs by well-known foreign composers: W. Napier's *Selection of Original Scots Songs* (London, 1792–5) included arrangements by Franz Joseph Haydn. Collections of Scots traditional music figure prominently among JA's own music books, now at Chawton (see Mollie Sands, 'Jane Austen and her Music Books', *Jane Austen Society Report* [1956], 92–3).

toilett: commonly 'toilette'; literally, the dressing table (as in *The Rape of the Lock*, i. 121–48); by extension the act of dressing and putting on make-up.

123 *Galleries*: long passages, a common feature of medieval and Elizabethan domestic architecture, prized by lovers of the picturesque and the Gothic. Charlotte Smith's *The Old Manor House* (1793) sets episodes in 'a long gallery which reached the whole length of the South wing, and which was hung with a great number of family pictures' (ed. Anne Henry Ehrenpreis [Oxford, 1969], 15).

Rouge: a fine red powder, derived from safflower, used on the cheeks and lips. Also cf. the 'highly rouged' Lady L. (p. 132). Wearing rouge is generally frowned upon in novels. See Orville's comment in *Evelina*: 'the difference of natural and of artificial colour, seems to me very easily discerned' (pp. 79–80).

124 *Public-places*: places of public assembly where women are allowed, such as pleasure gardens, theatres, concert halls, and churches.

Vaux-hall: more usually 'Vauxhall'; a London pleasure garden, in Lambeth, south of the Thames; the prototype of today's amusement or theme parks.

cold Beef . . . thin: the paper-thin slices of beef and ham at

Vauxhall were notorious; cf. the fifth act of Frances Burney's *The Witlings* (written 1779):

MRS. VOLUBLE. . . . I think this is the nicest cold Beef I ever Tasted,—You *must* eat a bit, or I shall take it quite ill.
MRS. WHEEDLE. Well it must be [a] *leetle* tiny Morsel, then.
MRS. VOLUBLE. I shall cut you quite a *fox-hall* Slice.

(Margaret Anne Doody, *Frances Burney: The Life in the Works* [New Brunswick, NJ, 1988], 87.)

124 *Mama . . . Eloisa was his*: in such cases of parental favouritism in the eighteenth-century novel, the advantage generally goes to the father's favourite: see the heroine in Sarah Scott's *Agreeable Ugliness* (1754) and Elizabeth in *Pride and Prejudice*.

Receipts: recipes.

124–5 *drawing Pullets*: eviscerating young hens in preparation for cooking them.

125 *Country-dance*: a square or round dance, of country origin, popular in seventeenth- and eighteenth-century England, to be contrasted with the more formal minuet. See 'Minuet Dela Cour', p. 76.

pidgeon-pye: pigeon-pie: 'Make a puff-paste crust, cover your dish, let your pigeons be very nicely picked and cleaned, season them with pepper and salt, and put a good piece of fine fresh butter, with pepper and salt in their bellies; lay them in your pans, the necks, gizzards, livers, pinions, and hearts, lay between, with the yolk of a hard egg and beef-steak in the middle; put as much water as will almost fill the dish, lay on the top-crust and bake it well; this is the best way to make a pigeon-pie' (Glasse, *The Art of Cookery*, 194).

Malbrook: the song 'Malbrouck s'en va-t-en guerre' (Marlborough is going to battle), a French folk-song, sung to the same tune as 'The bear went over the mountain' and 'For he's a jolly good fellow'. This tune, very popular in JA's period, is used by Chérubin for his own romantic text in Act II of Beaumarchais' *Le Mariage de Figaro* (1784).

125–6 *Bravo, Bravissimo, Encora, Da Capo, allegretto, con espressione, and Poco presto*: a pot-pourri of musical terms, some legitimate and typically used to mark instrumental music, especially for the pianoforte: *Da Capo*, *allegretto*, and *con espressione*.

The pertinent volumes of *The London Pianoforte School, 1766–1860*, ed. Nicholas Temperley, 20 vols. (New York, 1984–7), containing reproductions of music of the period, offer many examples of such markings, especially the latter. *Bravo*, *Bravissimo*, and *Encora* are the traditional Italian calls to hail an excellent performance. *Poco presto* is not to be found in *The London Pianoforte School* and is probably one of JA's jokes: *presto* is the fastest possible tempo marking; *poco* means 'a little'; how can anything be played a little as fast as possible?

Such 'outlandish words' are also found in the margins of Parson Yorick's sermon in *Tristram Shandy*, as indications of tempi and expressions to be adopted in its reading (pp. 325–6).

126   *Execution*: performance, as on the harpsichord. In her family, only JA played.

      satirical: cf. *Sense and Sensibility*: 'because they were fond of reading, she fancied them satirical: perhaps without exactly knowing what it was to be satirical; but *that* did not signify. It was censure in common use, and easily given' (p. 215).

128   *Grosvenor Street*: fashionable London street, developed 1720s–1750s, running from Hyde Park in the west to New Bond Street; in 1735 it was described as 'a spacious well built street, inhabited chiefly by People of Distinction' (Hibbert and Weinreb, *London Encyclopedia*, 342).

      April 10th: a date familiar to novel readers of JA's time, the date on which Clarissa runs away with Lovelace in Richardson's novel, and the date which she has engraved on her coffinplate.

129   *proper size for real Beauty*: a running joke in JA's fiction: cf. 'Love and Freindship', p. 79, and *Pride and Prejudice*, 33, 43–4; see also *Emma*, where the proper Jane Fairfax is of a 'pretty' height, 'just such as almost everybody would think tall, and nobody could think very tall' (p. 149). Harriet Smith is apparently short, though Emma's drawing gives her the ideal stature (p. 42).

130   *Toad-eater*: a sycophant, from the act put on by a mountebank's assistant who would pretend to swallow a toad; cf. the word 'toady'.

131   *celebrated . . . in Printshops*: printshops offered for sale engravings of portraits of actresses, noble beauties, and beautiful and notorious female criminals.

131 *Small-pox*: a disease which often disfigured the face; one who had survived the disease possessed immunity.

Rout: 'a fashionable gathering or assembly, a large evening party or reception, much in vogue in the eighteenth and early nineteenth centuries' (*OED*); not a dinner party.

Mrs Kickabout's: Kickabout is a descriptive name for a high-stepping fashionable woman. Cf. Moll Hackabout, the subject of Hogarth's *Harlot's Progress* (1732).

132 *Lady Flambeau's*: a 'flambeau' is a lighted wax torch which illuminated guests when they alighted from carriages at parties.

133 *Pope's Bulls*: a bull in this sense is any document with the papal seal affixed. Lesley could argue that his marriage to a Protestant heretic is invalid, providing another variety of the invalid marriage, a theme which runs through these early works (see pp. 33, 39, 80, 149–50, and notes).

Neapolitan . . . Fortune: cf. Sir Charles Grandison, who has the chance to marry the Florentine Olivia, 'nobly born . . . mistress of a great fortune' (ii. 117).

The History of England

134 *Charles the 1st*: instead of arranging a conventional Whig narrative, which interpreted English history as a gradual march towards increased liberty and as a progressive defeat of absolutism, JA sets up history as pro-Stuart tragedy by placing the execution of Charles I as its climax and conclusion. As Christopher Kent writes, JA 'brashly inverts the Whig view of history' ('Learning History with, and from, Jane Austen', in *Jane Austen's Beginnings*, 64).

One source of JA's suspicion of culturally approved accounts of the past is Horace Walpole's *Historic Doubts on the Life and Reign of King Richard the Third*. There Walpole writes, 'If we take a survey of our own history, and examine it with any attention, what an unsatisfactory picture does it present to us! How dry, how superficial, how void of information! How little is recorded besides battles, plagues, and religious foundations!' (p. ix). In *Northanger Abbey* Catherine Morland voices Austen's scepticism when she tells Eleanor and Henry Tilney that she reads 'real solemn history' 'as a duty, but it tells me nothing that does not either vex or weary me. The quarrels of popes and kings, with wars or pestilences, in every page; the men all so good for nothing, and hardly any women at all—it is very tiresome: and yet I often think it odd that it should be so dull, for a great deal of it must be invention' (p. 84).

few Dates . . . History: cf. Oliver Goldsmith's popular schoolroom *History of England* (1764), which contained only two dates.

Shakespear's Plays: See *2 Henry IV*, iv iii. 221–66 for the King's speech; see ll. 267–305 for Prince Hal's speech.

135 *Shakespear's account*: see the conversation between the Princess Katherine and an old gentlewoman in *Henry V*, iii. iv and the bilingual wooing scene between Katherine and Henry in v. ii.

Spleen: the bodily organ once regarded as the seat of melancholy, ill-humour, ill-nature, ill-temper, and peevishness. See Pope's 'Cave of Spleen' in *The Rape of the Lock*, iv. 11–88.

row: rhymes with 'how', not 'hoe'; a very new slang word (*OED* gives 1787 as the date of first use) meaning fight or disturbance. For the disturbance among the English brought about by Joan of Arc, see Shakespeare *1 King Henry VI*, iv. vii.

marrying . . . engaged to another: Edward IV's council wished him to marry Bona of Savoy, but he secretly wed Elizabeth Woodville, widow of Sir John Grey. JA makes Edward a male Lucy Steele.

135–6 *Jane Shore . . . her*: see the tragedy by Nicholas Rowe, 1714, 'Written in Imitation of Shakespear's Style'. Note that JA sustains the use of dramas as sources for history.

136 *draw his picture*: Cassandra Austen illustrated the 'History' with 13 water-colour portraits of the monarchs of England but did not provide a picture of Edward V.

respectable Man: there seems to have been an Austen family joke about the name Richard. See *Letters* (15 Sept. 1796): 'Mr. Richard Harvey's match is put off till he has got a Better Christian name, of which he has great Hopes' (p. 15). Also see the beginning of *Northanger Abbey*, where Catherine Morland's father is 'a very respectable man, though his name was Richard' (p. 1).

declared . . . two Nephews: Whig history found it necessary to depict Richard III as a villain, since he was replaced by the Tudors, the family which brought about English Protestantism and expansion into the New World. Horace Walpole, in *Historic Doubts* (see above, note to p. 134), was the most vocal eighteenth-century opponent of the Tudors and defender of Richard III. He writes: 'It occurred to me some years ago, that the picture of Richard the third, as drawn by historians, was a character formed by prejudice and invention. I did not take Shakespeare's tragedy for a genuine representation. . . . Many of the crimes imputed to Richard seemed improbable; and what was stronger, contrary to his interest. . . . [A]s it was easy to perceive, under all the glare of encomiums which historians have heaped on the wisdom of Henry the Seventh, that he was a mean and unfeeling tyrant, I suspected that they had blackened his rival, till Henry, by the contrast, should appear in a kind of amiable light' (pp. xiii–xiv).

136 *Perkin Warbeck*: pretended to be Richard, Duke of York, son of Edward IV; was recognized as monarch by some foreign powers; confessed his imposture in 1497.

Widow of Richard: another gender-crossing joke in the manner of those on pp. 3 and 29 (see textual note to p. 3).

grandmother . . in the World: Margaret, daughter of Henry VII, married James IV of Scotland in 1503 and became the grandmother of Mary, Queen of Scots, the heroine of JA's 'History'. Here JA parodies the Whig historian's interest in tracing patterns of growth and development, for example in viewing tribal councils as anticipations of modern parliaments. As Christopher Kent notes, the Whig historian's 'preoccupation with anticipations and forerunners can easily stray into absurdity' ('Learning History with, and from, Jane Austen', 65).

137 *amiable young Woman*: as Kent notes (p. 67), David Hume in his *History of Great Britain* (1754) had described Lady Jane Grey as 'amiable'.

Bullen: Shakespeare uses the spelling 'Bullen' in *King Henry VIII*.

138 *6th of May*: one of the two dates found in Goldsmith's *History*. Note that the year is not given.

infinite use to the landscape of England in general: reference to the eighteenth-century fondness for ruins and for country houses which had once been religious establishments. Later, in

Northanger Abbey, Catherine Morland admires abbeys for providing the scenery and atmosphere of Gothic fiction (pp. 127–8); in *Emma* JA praises Mr Knightley's Donwell Abbey, which must derive from a medieval monastic building, as 'rambling and irregular, with many comfortable and one or two handsome rooms' (p. 323).

Delamere: the anti-hero of Charlotte Smith's *Emmeline*. The heroine is first engaged to her ardent suitor, Frederic Delamere; she later breaks the engagement and marries the hero because of his rash and impetuous temper. The hero has the very Whig name of Godolphin.

Gilpin: William Gilpin. See notes to pp. 62, 76, 102.

139 *pest . . . Elizabeth*: cf. the argument between Mrs Percival and her niece in 'Catharine', pp. 193–4.

140 *Mr Whitaker*: 'Probably John Whitaker, 1735–1806, author of *Mary Queen of Scots Vindicated*, 1787. Jane Austen may have been led to his work by a reference in Gilpin's Highland *Observations* [see above, p. 102], where he writes sympathetically of "that unfortunate princess, Mary, Queen of Scots" and refers the reader to "A late historian, Mr. Whitacre" who has "thrown the guilt on Elizabeth" (i. 92, and note)' (B. C. Southam in *Minor Works*, 461).

Mrs Lefroy: Anne, née Brydges (1749–1804), wife of Isaac Peter George Lefroy, rector of Ashe, near Steventon. See 'To the Memory of M^{rs}. Lefroy', pp. 238–9 and note.

Mrs Knight: Catherine Knatchbull Knight (born *c*.1753), wife of Thomas Knight the younger, who adopted JA's brother Edward.

magnanimity . . . conscious Innocence: this presentation of Mary, Queen of Scots (and of Elizabeth I) resembles that in Sophia Lee's *The Recess, or a Tale of other Times* (1783–5). Elizabeth, 'she who oppressed her equal, and a Queen' (i. 81) is presented as unattractive: 'a severe, satirical smile marked her countenance, and an absurd gaiety her dress' (i. 205). Beautiful, hapless Mary inspires the admiration of all: 'I saw friends and enemies united in the eulogium of the royal Martyr.—What magnanimity, what sweetness, what sanctitude did they assign to her—she became a bright example in the most awful of trials' (4th edn. [London, 1792], ii. 56).

141 *one . . . but young*: complimentary reference to JA's brother Francis, then serving on the *Perseverance*.

141   *Emmeline of Delamere*: see notes to pp. 18 and 138.

142   *partial to the roman catholic religion*: an audaciously unusual
      partiality, as the English were customarily fond of emphasiz-
      ing their Protestantism, and schoolroom history was supposed
      to stress Protestant values. Here again JA rejects Whig
      progressivist ideas; see notes to pp. 134 and 136.

      Mr Sheridan's play of the Critic: once again, JA cites drama
      rather than history. Sheridan's *The Critic; Or, A Tragedy
      Rehearsed* (1779) contains within it Mr Puff's tragedy entitled
      The Spanish Armada. Sir Walter Raleigh and Sir Christopher
      Hatton open the play-within-a-play (II, ii) and appear
      frequently thereafter.

      Sharade: charade (from Provençal or Spanish *charrada*, or
      chatter); a riddle in which individual syllables of a word are
      described or acted out. For charades written by JA herself,
      see p. 245 and *Emma* (pp. 64–5).

143   *Strafford*: Sir Thomas Wentworth, first Earl of Strafford,
      impeached by the House of Commons and executed in 1641,
      was of particular interest to the Austen family, because the
      Leighs, the family of JA's mother, were connected to the
      Wentworths. JA was to combine the names of the hero of
      Emmeline and the ancestral martyr to Charles I's cause in the
      name of the hero of *Persuasion*, Frederick Wentworth.

A Collection of Letters

145   *Miss Cooper*: see 'Introduction', pp. xii–xiii.

      From a Mother to her freind: this letter seems a parody of all the
      novels treating the entrance of young girls into the world,
      most particularly Frances Burney's *Evelina*, which begins
      with the anxious letters between Lady Howard and Mr
      Villars about the latter's ward, whom Villars reluctantly
      allows to go on a visit, writing, 'the time draws on for
      experience and observation to take place of instruction'
      (p. 18).

      drink tea: see note to p. 57.

146   *Morning-Visits*: or afternoon calls; the period between break-
      fast and dinner was called 'morning'; breakfast was late, and
      dinner was served at 4 or 5, so calls were paid between 12
      and 3 p.m.

      Watchful Care . . . Minds——.: the eighteenth century became almost obsessed with the power of education, and there were many books, including Rousseau's *Émile* (1762), on the delightful and important task of forming the mind and character of young persons of both sexes, or as Thomson phrases it, 'Delightful task! to rear the tender Thought,/To teach the young Idea how to shoot' (*The Seasons*, ed. James Sambrook [Oxford, 1981], 'Spring', ll. 1152–3; p. 55).

147 *Young lady . . . freind*: cf. Mr Bennet's comments on Jane's disappointments in *Pride and Prejudice* (p. 123).

Willoughby: possibly suggested by the name of the rakish Sir Clement Willoughby in *Evelina*; it was to be the name of the anti-hero of *Sense and Sensibility*.

Crawfords: a name recurring in *Mansfield Park*.

Lady Bridget Dashwood: for 'Bridget', see note to p. 98; 'Dashwood' is the surname of the heroines of *Sense and Sensibility*.

148 *advised . . . Physician*: riding was considered a beneficial open-air exercise; Fanny Price in *Mansfield Park* suffers a deterioration in health when her pony is gone, and her cousin Edmund, determined that she must be able to ride for the sake of her health, purchases a mare for her use (pp. 31–3).

149 *Ride where you may . . . can*: parodic variation of Pope's well-known line in *Essay on Man*: 'Laugh where we must, be candid where we can' (i. 15).

Annesley: suggested by the Annesley claimant, James Annesley, who claimed to be the legitimate son and thus heir of Lord Altham; Altham's brother and successor had the claimant sent to America as a slave. He escaped, joined the navy, and prosecuted his claim in the courts, but died in 1743 without recovering property, though he had been declared legitimate. The case attracted much attention and continued to be well known.

149 *fighting . . . America*: Captain Dashwood was in the British Army fighting against the 'rebels' in the North American colonies; this war, the American War for Independence, lasted from 1776 to 1783, so if Miss Jane has been weeping for 10 years, the date of the action can be no later than 1793.

ignorant . . . Marriage: like so many unions in JA's early works, the status of this marriage is questionable, and Miss

Jane, who attended the funerals of her own children in the guise of their aunt, seems to have a very uncertain idea of the marital or maternal tie. Cf. pp. 33, 39, 80, 133.

150   *dropt . . . either*: whether the Annesley claimant had any right to his name was an essential point of legal contention; like Burney's heroine Evelina, who complains of her namelessness in her very first letter, as the world considers her illegitimate, 'Miss Jane' has no patronym. Her aversion to her husband's surname is a fine instance of sentimental delicacy, but it suggests that on a more practical level she had no legal right to his surname.

we . . . live together: in women's novels of the eighteenth century, female characters who have suffered the vicissitudes of love and fate often decide to live together, like the characters in Eliza Heywood's *The British Recluse* (1722); Anna Howe and Clarissa Harlowe think of doing so. The most striking celebration of such an arrangement is Sarah Scott's *Millenium Hall* (1762), written by an author who left her husband and lived with her friend Lady Barbara Montagu. Real-life women who followed this paradigm were 'The Ladies of Llangollen', Lady Eleanor Butler and Miss Sarah Ponsonby, who in 1779 defied their families by taking up residence together in Plas Newydd in Llangollen Vale; their story was frequently cited in periodicals of the late 1780s and early 1790s and celebrated in Anna Seward's 'Llangollen Vale' (1795).

151   *sit forwards*: to sit facing the horses, and not facing backwards; the latter position, which often caused mild sickness or discomfort, was given to the less-favoured members of a carriage party.

needless . . . expence: cf. Mr Collins's exposition of Lady Catherine de Bourgh's preferences: 'Lady Catherine will not think the worse of you for being simply dressed. She likes to have the distinction of rank preserved' (*Pride and Prejudice*, 143).

152   *Bread and Cheese*: the simplest and cheapest sort of food, the typical food of the poor; not only cheap in itself, it also requires no cookery.

too fashionable . . . punctual: fashionable and wealthy folk who had acquired town manners were in the habit of keeping late hours. Cf. *The Watsons* for the behaviour of the fashionable

Osbornes. Mr Edwardes tells his wife and the heroine about to go to a ball, 'We are always at home before Midnight. They would laugh at Osborne Castle to hear you call that late; they are but just rising from dinner at midnight' (p. 284). The ball is well under way when the Osbornes make their expected and affected entrance: 'the returning sound of Carriages after a long interruption, called general notice, and "the Osbornes are coming, the Osbornes are coming"—was repeated round the room' (p. 288).

white Gloves: gentlemen were supposed to wear white gloves at any formal dance; in Frances Burney's *Camilla* (1796) the vulgar Mr Dubster is prevented from dancing with Camilla (to her relief) because he has lost one of his gloves (p. 71).

get a hop: have a dance; in this situation she cannot participate in terpsichorean pleasures without a partner, so her getting 'a hop' depends on her acquiring one. For the use of 'hop' for 'dance', compare *Camilla*'s Mr Dubster: 'I thought I might as well come and see the hop' (p. 77). Burney's use reflects the use of 'hop' for a dancing party, as given in the *OED*, but JA's use of the word for a single dance seems unusual.

153   *Grocer or a Bookbinder*: low occupations, involving manual labour and handling raw materials in retail; the occupation of 'Wine Merchant' is socially much superior, as a 'Merchant' deals wholesale, not retail.

broke: went bankrupt.

King's Bench: King's Bench Prison, where an insolvent debtor could be imprisoned at the suit of creditors.

Supper: here, a very late evening meal, constituted by the refreshment offered at an entertainment at a late hour, around midnight, sometimes as late as 2 a.m. Ordinary 'supper' was served as Frances Burney had it in Norfolk in the 1760s: 'we Breakfast always at 10, & rise as much before as we please—we Dine precisely at 2 Drink Tea about 6—& sup exactly at 9' (*Early Journals and Letters*, ed. Lars E. Troide [Oxford, 1988], i. 14). Some people boasted that they never ate supper at all.

next day . . . dinner: Lady Greville may have chosen to call at this awkward time to show that she herself does not dine at such an unfashionably early hour as Maria and her mother. Lady Greville regards the time of day as still morning, the time for 'Morning Visits' (see note to p. 146). In *The Watsons*, Tom Musgrave with similar rudeness brings Lord Osborne to call upon the Watson girls just as they are about to have their early dinner. Unpretentious Elizabeth Watson simply says, 'you know what early hours we keep' and Tom Musgrave is almost abashed: 'he knew it very well, and such honest simplicity, such shameless Truth rather bewildered him' (*The Watsons*, 304).

154 *Wind . . . very cold*: Lady Greville conducts herself with the discourtesy shown by Miss de Bourgh who, with her companion Mrs Jenkinson, makes Charlotte Collins stand outside and talk to her while she remains in her phaeton. Elizabeth Bennet comments bluntly, 'She is abominably rude to keep Charlotte out of doors in all this wind' (*Pride and Prejudice*, 142).

no Moon: coachmen did not care for driving carriages on dark nights, and the phases of the moon were consulted when journeys were planned. See the planning of the journey to Sotherton in *Mansfield Park*, and Aunt Norris's eager emphasis on the ease of the journey, with 'a pleasant drive home by moonlight' (p. 56).

155 *Essex*: the low-lying, fertile county east of London, between the Thames and the sea.

Derbyshire: a county in the North Midlands, between Staffordshire and Nottinghamshire; noted for picturesque rock formations and rocky heights, it is the site of Mr Darcy's estate, Pemberley, in *Pride and Prejudice*. When Elizabeth and her aunt and uncle, the Gardiners, go on a tour to the picturesque county, she thinks 'of Pemberley and its owner'. ' "But surely," said she, "I may enter his country with impunity, and rob it of a few petrified spars without his perceiving me" ' (p. 212).

Suffolk: a county on the east coast of England, south of Norfolk, known for picturesque medieval villages, gentle countryside, and seascape—a great contrast to Derbyshire and the much nearer Essex.

156 *Perfect Felicity . . . uninterrupted Happiness*: a Johnsonian sentiment, reflecting views found everywhere in his writing; e.g. *Rambler*, No. 32 (1750): 'The cure for the greatest part of human miseries is not radical, but palliative. Infelicity is involved in corporeal nature, and interwoven with our

being; all attempts therefore to decline it wholly are useless and vain' (Johnson, *Works*, iv. 209). See also the 'History of Seged', *Rambler*, Nos. 204–5 (1752).

157 *Musgrove*: a name later used in *Persuasion*, in which the heroine's sister Mary has married into the Musgrove family.

Sackville St: a street extending from Piccadilly to Vigo Street. Sackville Street, dating from the 1670s and rebuilt in the 1730s, was both residential and commerical: Marianne and Elinor Dashwood visit a jeweller's in Sackville Street (*Sense and Sensibility*, 192).

Lady Scudamore's: John Scudamore and his wife (née Westcomb) were friends and correspondents of Samuel Richardson, as JA may have known; in Spenser's *Faerie Queene*, Sir Scudamour is the lover of Amoret.

toasted: had her health drunk and beauty celebrated by a baronet (at an all-male party); being a 'toast' was thought a mixed blessing at best, and girls were urged to shun by their own modesty any such loud demonstrations of their charms.

158 *improvable Estate*: an estate capable of giving increased yield by better management either of its farming methods or of its rentals and accounting. JA usually refers to improvement of the estate in terms of rendering it more beautiful in modern ways, particularly in accord with the picturesque landscaping practised and made fashionable by Humphrey Repton, as in *Mansfield Park*, where Mr Rushworth complains of his estate, Sotherton: 'It wants improvement, ma'am, beyond any thing' (p. 47). The rectory at Steventon later underwent 'improvement' in 1800 (*Letters*, 76–77).

Matilda: see note to pp. 89 and 107.

one Sheet: one sheet of paper; paper was expensive, and young Musgrove shows his discretion in economizing in paper, if in nothing else.

159 *faithfully Yours for ever and ever*: Henrietta is sinning against all discretion in responding to Musgrove's letter at all, let alone in writing back so warmly; a young lady was not supposed to correspond with a young gentleman until the two were engaged. Henrietta's closing sentiments seem reminiscent of those of the naïve Margery in William Wycherley's *The Country Wife* (first acted 1675); discussing with her husband the severe response she is to write back to her admirer, Mr Horner, Margery asks, concerning the

conclusion of her letter, 'What, shan't I say your most faithful humble Servant till death?' (*Complete Plays of William Wycherley*, ed. Gerald Weales [New York, 1967], Act IV; p. 321).

dab: an expert, an adept.

farthing: a quarter of a penny.

160 *Several hundreds an year*: not much, according to JA's standards; the Dashwood women have £500 a year to live on, and JA considers them to be living in reduced circumstances (*Sense and Sensibility*, 25).

161 *Yes I'm in love . . . undone me—*: from 'The je ne scai quoi' by William Whitehead (1715–85):

> Yes, I'm in love, I feel it now,
> And CAELIA has undone me;
> And yet I'll swear I can't tell how
> The pleasing plague stole on me.

(*Eighteenth-Century English Literature*, ed. Geoffrey Tillotson *et al.* [New York, 1969], 1521.) JA later alludes to the fourth line of this stanza in *Mansfield Park* (p. 264).

not in rhime: had Henrietta known the entire stanza, her objection would have been met.

164 *extensive Good . . . fellow Creatures*: the language of benevolence here derives generally from the expectation that genteel women will be charitable to the poor. See Emma Woodhouse's 'charitable visit to a poor sick family, who lived a little way out of Highbury' (*Emma*, 75); see also the satire of Lady Bountiful (see note to p. 21). Here particular reference may be made to Frances Burney's *Cecilia*, in which the heroine, an heiress, does plan on doing good to her fellow creatures, a power that will be severely curtailed if she marries.

make the pies: by now an unladylike occupation, although an ability to make puddings and pies was a hackneyed subject in praises of the old-fashioned female virtue. Mrs Bennet boasts that 'her daughters had nothing to do in the kitchen' (*Pride and Prejudice*, 58).

To Miss Fanny Catherine Austen

165 *Miss Fanny Catherine Austen*: Frances (Fanny) Knight (1793–1882), eldest daughter of Jane Austen's brother Edward.

Fanny, when married, was to become Lady Knatchbull-Hugesson and was to write rather condescendingly of her aunts' vulgarity and provinciality. Born 23 Jan. 1793, Fanny is in her infancy when JA jokes about superintending her education.

Rowling and Steventon: Rowling was the estate in east Kent which the Knights had given Edward and his bride, who lived there until 1798, at some distance from Steventon in Hampshire.

Admonitions . . . Young Women: works of solemn advice to young women on their conduct abounded in the eighteenth century, and the matter of female conduct was stressed with increasing urgency after the French Revolution (see note to p. 222).

The female philosopher

female philosopher: a phrase reminiscent of both Jacobin and anti-Jacobin sentiment. Those against advanced liberal opinions made fun of female philosophers, whereas writers who advocated a better position for women often urged women to learn philosophy, both moral and scientific.

166 *Bonmots and repartées*: 'bonmots' (from French *bons mots* or good words) had become naturalized into English, meaning clever or witty sayings; 'repartée' (from French *repartir*, to set out again) means 'a ready, witty, or smart reply; a quick and clever retort' (*OED*).

Sentiments of Morality: moral reflections, generally derived from reading. Characters in late eighteenth-century literature who utter 'sensible reflections' are either hypocritical (like Joseph Surface in Sheridan's *The School for Scandal*) or superficial (like Mary Bennet in *Pride and Prejudice*).

166 *cordial kiss*: highly improbable; English gentlemen did not kiss or engage in demonstrations of emotion with each other; cf. the meeting of the Knightley brothers 'burying under a calmness that seemed all but indifference, the real attachment which would have led either of them . . . to do every thing for the good of the other' (*Emma*, 90).

amiable Moralist: Julia goes on in a stream of commonplaces that make her a rival to Mary Bennet (see *Pride and Prejudice*, 53, 255).

The first Act of a Comedy

167 *Postilion*: see note to p. 6.

Strephon: name of a pastoral hero (later used by W. S. Gilbert in *Iolanthe*).

Chloe: typical pastoral heroine, as in the antique pastoral novel *Daphnis and Chloe*; the name actually means 'green shoot'.

the Lion: inn chambers were given names, not numbers, a source of comedy in Shakespeare and elsewhere. 'Moon' and 'Sun' below also refer to rooms.

bill of fare: menu.

I wull: 'I will'; spelling indicates dialect pronunciation.

chorus of ploughboys: like the chorus of rustic harvesters who sing the harvest-home song in Dryden and Purcell's *King Arthur* (1691), but more likely suggested by choruses in Frances Brooke's successful ballad-opera *Rosina*, first produced in Dec. 1782, and published in 1783.

Hounslow: village west of London on the road to Bath; travellers over Hounslow Heath were frequently preyed upon by highwaymen. It was a rural area; Pope speaks of mutton coming from Hounslow (*Imitations of Horace*, II. ii. 143–4).

168 *Stree-phon*: the spelling here indicates the rhyme sound.

stinking partridge: some gourmands believed that game should be hung for a long time. See Pope's line: 'Our Fathers prais'd rank Ven'son' (*Imitations of Horace*, II. ii 91). Game birds well hung could be considered a delicacy or a failure in cleanliness, depending on taste.

Staines: a village 17 miles west-south-west of London, where JA's carriage often stopped for the night during trips to London (*Letters*, 7, 22).

bad guinea: a counterfeit of the valuable gold coin, worth 21 shillings. Uttering false currency was a capital offence: in 1789 a woman was burned at Tyburn for coining (Porter, *English Society*, 152).

undirected Letter: a letter without an address, presumably hand-delivered.

A Letter from a Young Lady

169 *feelings being too Strong ... Heart disapproved*: the fault of
excessive capacity for feeling is a fashionable one among
heroines of novels; cf., for example, Ann Radcliffe's *The
Mysteries of Udolpho* (1794), in which the dying St Aubert
warns his daughter Emily not to give way to feeling: 'do not
indulge in the pride of fine feeling, the romantic error of
amiable minds. Those, who really possess sensibility, ought
early to be taught, that it is a dangerous quality' (*The
Mysteries of Udolpho*, ed. Bonamy Dobrée [Oxford, 1980],
79). Marianne Dashwood in *Sense and Sensibility* shares this
elegant defect. No other heroines of feeling fall into the sort
of 'Errors' that Anna Parker commits.

forged my own Will: an impossible 'crime' (cf. W. S. Gilbert's
Ruddigore [1887]).

Horse guards: the cavalry brigade of the English Household
troops: especially the third regiment of this body, the Royal
Horse Guards (*OED*); horse guards protected royal palaces,
and membership has traditionally been upper-class.

eight Million: a sum considerably beyond any private fortune
at the time.

A Tour through Wales

170 *A Tour through Wales*: Wales was already a popular and
romantic region for tourists in search of the picturesque. The
Thrales and Samuel Johnson had toured Wales in 1774; cf.
the references to the Vale of Usk in 'Love and Freindship',
p. 76.

on the ramble: an unusual locution for 'rambling', i.e. taking
an excursion without any planned route or objective, purely
for pleasure.

fine perspiration: an indelicate matter for a lady to mention,
but the Johnson women are indelicate altogether, in their
riding alone and in walking and running.

capped and heelpeiced: repaired by covering the toe with
leather and furnishing with a new heel.

Carmarthen: county town of the old county of Carmarthen-
shire, in south-west Wales.

blue Sattin Slippers: slippers of blue satin would be elegant
evening wear entirely unsuited to walking on the road.

170 *Hereford*: county town of Herefordshire, famous for its
     cathedral and other medieval remains; the distance from
     Carmarthen to Hereford is some 70 miles, and the distance
     from the Johnsons' home, presumably in the south of
     England, would be much greater.

A Tale

171 *Pembrokeshire*: a western Welsh county (now Dyfed) border-
     ing the sea, noted for medieval remains and beautiful
     scenery and seascapes.

     Closet: either a small, private chamber or a closet in the
     modern sense of a place for storage; a closet would not really
     require furnishing.

     Wilhelminus: not the English name William or the German
     name Wilhelm but an extraordinary Latinized version;
     'Robertus' below is a Latin form of 'Robert'.

     pair of Stairs: common locution for a flight of stairs, from the
     original meaning of 'pair' as a set, not limited to two.

172 *Marina*: an unusual name, probably taken from Shakespeare's
     Pericles, Prince of Tyre (composed between 1606 and 1608).

     two noble Tents: tents or marquees were used for shelter
     during elaborate entertainments, but this instance alludes
     rather to the ingenious contrivances of heroes of adventure
     stories; see, for example, the hero of Robert Paltock's *Peter
     Wilkins* (1750), when he is visited by a multitude of in-laws,
     and their retinue, and has to think how to quarter them: 'I
     told him [his father-in-law], I had purposely erected a Tent,
     which would, with great ease, accomodate a greater number'
     (*Peter Wilkins*, ed. Christopher Bentley [Oxford, 1990], 208).

VOLUME THE THIRD

Evelyn

174 *Miss Mary Lloyd*: along with her elder sister Martha, Mary
     Lloyd (1771–1843) was a close friend of the Austen family.
     See verse 'This little bag' and note to p. 234. Despite the
     dedication of 'Volume the Third' to Mary, she 'distrusted
     books and read very few of them' (Honan, *Life*, 77).

175 *Parish*: a subdivision of an English county, with its own
     church and clergyman.

176 *paddock*: a small enclosed pasture, especially for horses.

paling: a fence made of vertical rails or stakes.

beautiful Shrubbery: the introduction of evergreens in shrubbery was popular in the new landscape gardening. Fanny Price in *Mansfield Park* praises the Grants' shrubbery and walk (p. 187). Lines of shrubbery with a gravel walk running straight through them would be more convenient than ornamental, defying the rules of picturesque taste, which valued the curved and wayward.

four white Cows . . . equal distances from each other: William Gilpin, in his *Observations on the Mountains and Lakes of Cumberland and Westmoreland* (1786), describes his 'doctrine of grouping larger cattle' in asserting, 'with three, you are almost sure of a good group . . . *Four* introduces a new difficulty in grouping . . . The only way in which they will group well, is to *unite three* . . . and to *remove the fourth* (*Observations*, ii. 259). John McAleer refers to this passage in Gilpin in commenting upon this description in 'Evelyn' and suggests that the completely symmetrical circle recalls the name of the owners, the Webbs: 'the analogy to a spider's web is inescapable' ('What a Biographer can Learn about Jane Austen', *Jane Austen's Beginnings*, 9). Elizabeth Bennet alludes to Gilpin's desire to escape the tyrannical symmetry of four when she refuses to join Miss Bingley, Mr Darcy, and Mrs Hurst in a walk, declaring, 'The picturesque would be spoilt by admitting a fourth' (*Pride and Prejudice*, 46 and note).

best of Men: Sir Charles Grandison is frequently thus described or addressed; see, e.g., ii. 142; 164; 176. Mr Gower is addressed throughout 'Evelyn' as if he were the generous and noble Sir Charles, while all his actions exhibit him as a sponging, indolent (and cowardly) egotist.

Chocolate: a drink of hot chocolate, popular since the late seventeenth century.

venison pasty: 'make a good rich puff-paste crust, and rim your dish, then lay in your venison, put in a half a pound of butter, about a quarter of a pint of water, then put a very thick paste over, and ornament it in any form you please with leaves, & cut in paste, and let it be baked three hours in a very quick oven; put a sheet of buttered paper over it to keep it from scorching' (Glasse, *The Art of Cookery*, 197).

177   *an hundred pounds ... immediately*: a parody of novelistic displays of generosity.

178   *a handsome portion*: a good dowry.

ten thousand pounds: not a small fortune: Mrs Elton brings to her marriage 'so many thousands as would always be called ten' (*Emma*, 162).

179   *Carlisle*: a county town in north-west England, very near the Scottish border.

Sussex: a county on the south coast of England, south of Surrey and Kent, at an extreme distance from Carlisle.

Isle of Wight: an island just south of Southampton, a popular resort during the eighteenth century; Anna Howe and her mother go for a tour to the Isle of Wight (*Clarissa*, vii. 102). Lovers inconveniently attached were sometimes sent to take a tour on the Continent; the Isle of Wight, however, is not a foreign country and not very far from Sussex.

Calshot: site of Calshot Castle, one of Henry VIII's coast defences, at the mouth of Southampton Water, opposite the Isle of Wight.

181   *fit of the gout*: not the typical disease of a young man, or of the emotionally distressed, but most unromantically associated in eighteenth-century medical doctrine with over-eating and over-drinking, and usually (in fiction at least) the malady of middle-aged portly gentlemen.

that favourite character of Sir Charles Grandison's, a nurse: Sir Charles advises his elderly uncle, Lord W., to marry: 'You are often indisposed with the gout: Servants will not always *be* servants when they find themselves of use. ... There is such a tenderness, such an helpfulness, such a sympathy in suffering, in a good woman, that I am always for excusing men in years, who marry prudently; while I censure, for the same reason, women in years. Male nurses are unnatural creatures! ... Womens sphere is the house, and their shining-place the sick chamber, in which they can exert all their amiable, and, shall I say, lenient qualities? Marry, my Lord, by all means' (*Sir Charles Grandison*, ii. 58).

castle ... beautiful prospect of the Sea: this castle has all the elements of the most highly considered views and picturesque location to recommend it, as well as being an utterly romantic building. Mr Gower, however, stubbornly and unfashionably prefers the fearful symmetry of Evelyn Lodge.

Evelyn lodge . . . Contrast: Ellen E. Martin points out that the image of symmetrical Evelyn Lodge and its grounds is Mr Gower's 'touchstone for his tastes and identity' and that 'the perfect symbol of Mr. Gower's cozy mental cosmos consoles him' when he is terrified by the too-sublime castle. ('The Madness of Jane Austen: Metonymic Style', in *Jane Austen's Beginnings*, 92.)

183 *as late . . . August*: not really late or cold: there is nothing remarkable in being out at nine o'clock, and journeys were constantly taken by the light of a full moon. See note to p. 154.

Walnuts and Pines: not trees which provide deep leafy shade.

Hungary water: a restorative distilled from wine and rosemary. It 'had its name from wonderful effects it is said to have had on a Queen of Hungary, at the age of 72 years: it is good aginst faintings, palsies, lethargies, apoplexies, and hysterical disorders' (Steward, *Plocacosmos*, 339).

order of the procession: the Revd James Woodforde describes a funeral procession: 'The Corpse first in an Hearse and Pair of Horses, then followed six Chaises. . . . The Underbearers and Servants all in Hatbands black closed the Procession and an handsome appearance the whole Procession made' (Woodforde, *Diary* [12 Feb. 1782], ii. 7–8).

set out himself: Mr Gower is the chief mourner, and his absence from the funeral of his wife is highly irregular.

184 *pot of beer*: it is not genteel for a man of Mr Gower's station to drink beer in public houses.

Nectar: the fabled drink of the gods on Olympus.

Anchor: name of an inn.

185 *Westgate Buil^{gs}*: Westgate Buildings, a fairly new and jerry-built block in Bath, in which the Austens had considered taking lodgings. In a letter of 3 Jan. 1801, JA writes to Cassandra: 'Westgate Buildings, tho' quite in the lower part of the Town are not badly situated . . .' (*Letters*, 100). But in *Persuasion* the impoverished Mrs Smith lives in Westgate Buildings, and Sir Walter Elliot is annoyed to hear that his daughter Anne visits her former school-friend there (p. 149). The Webbs are somewhat down on their luck since giving up

their fortune and estate to Mr Gower, though they still retain their insanely determined cheerful benevolence.

185 *White Horse Inn*: a common name for a public house.

Catharine, or the Bower

186 Miss Austen: Cassandra Austen; see note to p. 41.

threescore Editions: sixty editions; only devotional works like *The Whole Duty of Man* went into so many editions in the eighteenth century: see J. Paul Hunter, *Before Novels: The Cultural Contexts of Eighteenth-Century English Fiction* [London, 1990], 235. No work of fiction could hope for such success.

heroines . . . before her: a few years later, JA recalls the expectation that heroines will be orphans when she writes at the beginning of *Northanger Abbey* that Catherine Morland's mother, 'instead of dying in bringing the latter into the world, as any body might expect . . . still lived on' (p. 1).

watched over her . . . whether she loved her or not: the severe Mrs Percival ignores John Locke's advice in *Some Thoughts Concerning Education* (1693): 'Children (earlier perhaps than we think) are very sensible of *Praise* and Commendation. They find a Pleasure in being esteemed and valued, especially by their Parents, and those whom they depend on. If therefore the Father *caress and commend them, when they do well* . . . And this accompanied by a like Carriage of the Mother, and all others that are about them, it will in a little Time make them sensible of the Difference [between good and ill]' (*Some Thoughts Concerning Education*, ed. James L. Axtell [Cambridge, 1968], 153).

Officer: in eighteenth-century fiction, officers are not always good matches. Captain Anderson, who courts Charlotte Grandison in Richardson's *Sir Charles Grandison*, is prepossessing but illiterate (i. 407, 415). JA herself presents the predatory Wickham in *Pride and Prejudice*. She later contradicts these views with Captain Frederick Wentworth in *Persuasion* but he is a *naval* officer.

187 *Bower*: heroines often have special places of retreat. Clarissa resorts to the summer house at Harlowe Place, especially in winter, when the family will avoid her there. JA recalls the heroine's desire for a place of her own when Charlotte Collins (née Lucas), to avoid her husband, spends time in a

small, backwards-facing room, without a pleasant aspect (*Pride and Prejudice*, 150).

infantine: jocular use of a word strictly applying to the period of infancy, below 7 years, but also to the age of minority, below 21 (which Kitty still is).

tenure: tenor.

enthousiastic: enthusiastic, responding with enthusiasm, in the contemporary sense. In the late seventeenth and early eighteenth centuries, 'enthusiasm' primarily referred to 'religious enthusiasm', and thus the word is defined by Samuel Johnson as 'a vain confidence of divine favour or communication' (*Dictionary*); in the latter part of the eighteenth century, however, 'enthusiasm' took on a more positive aspect, and referred to the capacity to respond to the sublime in nature and to the pathetic quality of other human beings. Marianne Dashwood in *Sense and Sensibility* is 'enthusiastic' in that sense.

had with difficulty . . . Support: in *Sense and Sensibility*, the heroines' relatives are likewise grudging about financial support.

188 *The eldest daughter . . . equip her for the East Indies*: JA may have in mind here the fate of her cousin, Philadelphia Hancock, who was orphaned in early childhood and who, in 1752 at the age of 21, was sent to India (the East Indies) by relations. Tucker suggests that she was 'shipped out' as a prospective bride for her uncle's bachelor client. She was married to a much older man within a few days of her arrival (Tucker, *Goodly Heritage*, 36–8).

Maintenance: provision with the necessities of life. JA here demystifies the marriage arrangement by showing it as a search for the minimum food, clothing, and shelter.

Bengal: the British name for a province in north-east India, now partly in Pakistan and partly in Bangladesh.

Dowager: a widow in enjoyment of a title or property which came from her deceased husband.

companion: see note to p. 32.

Dudley: as a younger son of a noble family, probably related to Robert Dudley, the Earl of Leicester, Queen Elizabeth's favourite. Note that JA does not like characters associated with Elizabeth I: see pp. 139–42. A further reason for JA's dislike derives from her family history: a member of her mother's family, the Leighs, married Robert Dudley, son of Elizabeth I's Earl of Leicester, and was deserted by him (Tucker, *Goodly Heritage*, 56).

189 *tythes*: or tithes, literally 'tenths', the tithe being supposed to be one-tenth of the produce of the land, to be paid to the rector of a parish for the support of the church and community; in practice, certain specific assessments which landholders were supposed to pay to the rector, constituting his income. This practice led to severe inequalities between rich and poor parishes. Under the system, curates, who did most of the work, could be paid next to nothing, while the rector or vicar had a very genteel income.

parade: show, display.

190 *Stanley*: another surname with Elizabethan connections. Henry Stanley, fourth Earl of Derby, was commissioner at the trial of Mary, Queen of Scots, an event deplored by JA on p. 139.

Establishment: 'an organized staff of employees or servants including, or occasionally limited to, the building in which they are located' (*OED*).

sweep: a curved carriage drive. This passage pre-dates the first usage noted in the *OED*, which is in *Sense and Sensibility*: after their marriage, Edward and Elinor, in preparing their parsonage, 'could chuse papers, project shrubberies, and invent a sweep' (p. 329).

191 *Italian Opera . . . the hight of Enjoyment*: at the opera, Evelina, in Frances Burney's novel, 'could have thought [herself] in paradise' (p. 38); in Burney's *Cecilia*, her heroine 'gave to the whole Opera an avidity of attention almost painful from its own eagerness' (p. 64).

half the Year in Town: in London during the 'Winter' season, from New Year until 4 June, the King's official birthday, which marked the end of the London season; cf. p. 15.

the acquirement of Accomplishments . . . Judgement: a number of women writers in the latter part of the century criticized the empty 'accomplishments' which genteel women of the era were encouraged to cultivate. Catherine Macaulay had advised parents, 'Confine not the education of your daughters to what is regarded as the ornamental parts of it' (*Letters on Education* [London, 1790], 49: Letter IV, 'Amusement and

Instruction of Boys and Girls to Be the Same'). Mary Wollstonecraft wrote that men 'have been more anxious to make [women] alluring mistresses than affectionate wives and rational mothers' (*A Vindication of the Rights of Women*, 1792 [New York, 1988], 7). JA continues this theme in *Emma*, in which Augusta Elton, now that she is suitably married, seems determined to give up playing her piano (p. 249).

a great reader, tho' perhaps not a very deep one: this could have been JA's deprecating description of herself. She mocks the pretensions of ladies who read 'those enormous great stupid thick quarto volumes' in which comprehensive and significant scholarly works were printed (*Letters*, 304).

192 *well read in Modern history*: 'Modern history' can mean all history that is not of antiquity, or at least all that deals with European events after the Middle Ages. In being fond of history, Kitty is unlike that other Catherine, the heroine of *Northanger Abbey*, who complains of history: 'I read it a little as a duty, but it tells me nothing that does not either vex or weary me' (p. 84).

Mrs Smith's Novels: Charlotte Smith (1749–1806), poet and novelist, produced her first novel, *Emmeline*, in 1788, followed by *Ethelinde* in 1789 and *Celestina* in 1791. These JA could have read by 1792, the date of the beginning of 'Catharine', but she would also have continued reading Smith's later works, such as *The Old Manor House* (1793), *The Banished Man* (1794), *Montalbert* (1795), and *Marchmont* (1796). Charlotte Smith's style was much admired, and her poetry is thought to have influenced Wordsworth.

Emmeline: a favourite novel of JA; see 'The History of England', p. 141 and note.

Ethelinde: slightly longer (five volumes) than the four-volume *Emmeline*, *Ethelinde* exhibits more of Smith's interest in natural description; the description of stars reflected in the lake was a notable beauty.

Grasmere: a small circular lake in the Lake District in Lancashire, an area now in Cumbria. Wordsworth lived in Dove Cottage near Grasmere.

Lakes: the Lake District, in north-west England, much in vogue in the middle- and late-eighteenth century as a destination for those who loved sublime and picturesque scenery (see Ian Ousby, *The Englishman's England: Taste, Travel and the Rise of Tourism* [Cambridge, 1990], 143–94). In *Pride and Prejudice*, Elizabeth anticipates her visit to the Lakes: 'What are men to rocks and mountains? Oh! what hours of transport we shall spend!' (p. 138).

192 *travelling Dress*: probably a Spencer, a 'coat without tails, being a short-waisted jacket with a stand-fall collar and cuffed sleeves; buttoned by a few buttons down the front. It was worn out of doors over the coat or frock.' Spencers were popular from 1790 on into the nineteenth century (Cunnington, *Handbook*, 225).

Matlock: a picturesque town in the Peak District of Derbyshire; one of the popular tourist destinations during the development of tourism in the later eighteenth century (Ousby, *Englishman's England*, 131–43). In *Pride and Prejudice*, Elizabeth and the Gardiners plan to visit Matlock on the way to the Lakes.

Scarborough: a seaside village in eastern Yorkshire, on the opposite side of England from the Lakes, Scarborough was Britain's first seaside resort. Camilla Stanley apparently thinks Scarborough to be on the west coast.

193 *all order was destroyed over the face of the World*: Mrs Percival gives a hyperbolic and parodic version of the conservative perspective on the French Revolution and the Jacobin threat in the 1790s.

194 *if she were to come again . . . as much Mischeif and last as long as she did before—*: for JA on Queen Elizabeth, see 'The History of England', pp. 139–42.

Politics: ladies might discuss history but were not supposed to speak about politics, an entirely male subject; cf. Henry Tilney talking to his sister and to Catherine Morland: 'he shortly found himself arrived at politics; and from politics, it was an easy step to silence' (*Northanger Abbey*, 87).

no variety . . . fashions . . . Harpsichord: compare the even more trifling Isabella Thorpe in *Northanger Abbey*: 'Miss Thorpe, however, being four years older than Miss Morland, and at least four years better informed . . . could compare the balls of Bath with those of Tunbridge; its fashions with the fashions of London; could rectify the opinions of her new friend in many articles of tasteful attire' (p. 18).

sweetest Creature . . . shocking and not fit to be seen: this is the young-lady jargon also of Isabella Thorpe, who describes 'a particular friend of mine, a Miss Andrews, a sweet girl, one of the sweetest girls in the world' (*Northanger Abbey*, 24).

Halifax Family: the name 'Halifax' suggests a thoroughly Whiggish family. George Savile, Marquis of Halifax, the 'Trimmer' of Charles II's Parliaments, chaired a deputation of peers who requested William of Orange to undertake the government; he was also the author of a blunt and condescending conduct book, *The Lady's New-Years Gift: Or, Advice to a Daughter* (1688), much reprinted in the eighteenth century. Charles Montagu, first Earl of Halifax, was a lord of the treasury under William and founded the National Debt; he became First Lord of the Treasury on George I's succession, and was created Earl of Halifax in 1714.

195   *in Public*: in places of public assembly or resort.

a blue hat: possibly of dyed straw, more likely a hat (or bonnet) of blue velvet or blue silk, or a hat trimmed with blue ribbon. See Cunnington, *Handbook*, 364–8. 'Gaily coloured silk hats were also worn, though less often [i.e. in the 1790s than in the 1780s]' (*ibid.*, 368).

Brook Street: see note to p. 39.

every Month during the Winter: giving a monthly ball during the London season would be a very expensive undertaking, justifiable only if the family had numerous daughters to be married. For the London season, see notes to pp. 15 and 191.

find her in Cloathes: supply her with clothes; this use of 'find' customarily refers to the upkeep of a servant.

Curacies: a clergyman could hold plural 'cures' or livings, often hiring at low wages other clergymen who in fact performed priestly functions. See notes to pp. 69 and 189. JA's eldest brother James had plural curacies; he was curate of Overton in Hampshire when he was inducted as vicar of Sherborne St John, Hampshire, in 1791; in 1792 he became vicar of Cubbington and curate of Hunningham, both in Warwickshire, where he never took up residence (Tucker, *Goodly Heritage*, 105).

196   *Cheltenham*: a spa in Gloucestershire, fashionable after George III's visit in 1788. JA's friend Eliza Fowle and her husband lived near Cheltenham, and JA and Cassandra were to visit it in 1816.

196 *School . . . in Wales*: Welsh boarding-schools were markedly less expensive than those in England, and presumably the boys, like the unfortunates sent to northern schools such as Dickens's Dotheboys Hall in *Nicholas Nickleby* (1838–9), would be unable to complain or run away, as the distance from their homes was so great.

197 *Ranelagh*: Ranelagh Gardens, a place of amusement in Chelsea, opened in 1742; in the late eighteenth century it offered a more expensive version of Vauxhall, with a high charge for admission (five shillings on a firework night).

frightful Cap: ladies were required to wear something on their heads at all times; the usual wear was an attractive 'cap' made of lace and ruffles.

But do you call it lucky . . . knows to the Contrary: Catharine's shocked reaction to the harsh marrying-off of women is reflected also in Emma Watson's protest: 'To be so bent on Marriage—to pursue a Man merely for the sake of situation—is a sort of thing that shocks me . . . Poverty is a great Evil, but to a woman of Education and feeling it . . . cannot be the greatest.' Camilla Stanley's flippantly optimistic view of the matter is reflected in the more prudent Elizabeth Watson's refusal to see an evil in husband-hunting or in an unreflecting marriage born out of financial panic: 'I should not like marrying a disagreable Man any more than yourself,—but I do not think there *are* many very disagreable Men;—I think I could like any good humoured Man with a comfortable Income' (*The Watsons*, 278).

198 *Barbadoes*: one of the southernmost islands of the West Indies, noted for sugar-cane production; it had nothing in common with Bengal (in the East Indies), apart from being a British colony.

nice: 'difficult to please or satisfy . . particular' (*OED*). See Henry Tilney's criticism of the new and inexact use of the word 'nice' in *Northanger Abbey* (pp. 83–4) and his insistence on the older and more proper use: 'Originally perhaps it was applied only to express neatness, propriety, delicacy, or refinement.'

Draws in Oils: is able to make sketches and paintings in oils rather than in water-colour or only with crayon.

199 *Cap . . . Gold Net*: Camilla's cap will be a dressy affair; the

gold net may act as an elaborate hair-net, catching part of the hair within a sparkling bag.

receipt book: household recipe books, both in print and in manuscript, contained many recipes for remedies of common ailments. Mary Delany includes the following remedy for toothache in a letter of 8 Aug. 1758: 'Little trefoil leaves, primrose leaves and yarrow pounded, made into a little pellet and put to the tooth or tied up, in muslin and held between the teeth' (*The Autobiography and Correspondence of Mary Granville, Mrs Delany*, 3 vols. [London, 1861–2], iii. 504).

200 *Mortality*: the human race, all subject to death and the ills of the flesh.

200–1 *She would herself . . . no greater vexation*: Catharine summons to her aid a philosophy presumably partly gained through reading Samuel Johnson. Unlike Mary Bennet, she is not pompous with her morality, but tries to use it as an antidote to self-pity.

201 *drawn*: extracted.

202 *John*: the use of the first name indicates that John is an indoor servant, presumably a footman; outdoor servants, such as gardeners, were generally called by their last names.

correspondence between Girls . . . bad Example: Mrs Percival here recalls the Harlowe family in Richardson's novel, who plan to confiscate Clarissa's paper and pens and thus stop her correspondence with Anna Howe.

203 *Regency*: the period in which the Prince of Wales reigned in the place of his incapacitated father, George III. The Regency was brought about by an Act of Parliament, the Regency Act, passed 5 Feb. 1811. Certain restrictions were placed on the Prince, but these were lifted one year later, as it was evident that his father was unlikely to recover, and in fact the Regency continued until the death of George III in 1820, when the Prince Regent became King as George IV.

Regency walking dress: a walking dress is a dress for day and street wear, with a shorter hem than a dress for evening or formal occasions. The *Lady's Magazine, or Entertaining Companion for the Fair Sex* of the period customarily published monthly, under the heading 'London Fashions', an example of 'Full Dress' and one of 'Walking Dress'. We have found no example of a 'Regency Walking dress', but the term

'Regency' did enter the discourse of fashion almost immediately. The *Lady's Magazine* of 1811 refers to plumes of three feathers 'universally worn for the Regent's fete' and the 'Supplement' for the year 1811 offers 'a new and elegant Pattern for Regency Borders &c'.

203 *Pelisse*: Mary Delany describes a 'pelisse' as 'a long cloak made of satin or velvet, black or any color; lined or trimmed with silk, satin, or fur . . . with slits for the arms to come out' (Letter to Mrs Dewes, 20 Jan. 1755; *Autobiography and Correspondence*, iii. 321).

hour of dressing: in *The Watsons*, JA describes preparing for a dance as 'the first Bliss of a Ball' (p. 283); there, Emma Watson and Mary Edwards dress before dinner and tea, rather than after dinner, as here.

203-4 *the Kingdom . . . prosperous a state*: Mr Stanley, a Member of Parliament, is obviously a supporter of William Pitt 'the Younger' (Prime Minister 1783, 1784–1801, 1804–6). Pitt's government inherited an England struggling to pay the £100,000,000 cost of the American War of Independence. At first, Pitt was a champion of reform, introducing measures to reduce the National Debt, regularize taxes, revise the civil service, and reform Parliament. But he opposed the republican principles of the French Revolution and his government received the support of conservative Whigs. War against France was declared in 1793.

204 *Scotch Steps*: Scottish reels, strathspeys, and quicksteps were popular in JA's period, as evidenced by the large number of publications about Scottish dance listed in James Johnson, *The Scots Musical Museum* (1853; repr. Hatboro, Pa., 1962), i, pp. lxi–lxxv, xcix–cxiii.

205 *Chaise and four*: a chaise is a light vehicle; Stanley's use of four horses demonstrates that he is dashing and extravagant.

now his hair is just done up: men's natural hair was often curled to look like a wig. James Stewart writes in *Plocacosmos* that 'it is certain gentlemen's hair cannot be curled and dressed in perfection without putting it in papers as carefully as the ladies' (p. 308). Tom, the footman, mimics the behaviour of the upper classes, like Fielding's Joseph Andrews, who upon moving to London cuts his hair 'after the newest Fashion' and goes 'abroad with it all the Morning in Papers' (*Joseph Andrews*, 22).

Apron: Nanny needs the protection of an apron, since she
has been powdering Kitty's hair. Powdered hair became less
fashionable as the century drew to its close, and, sometime
after 1792, JA dropped the clause explaining the apron and
emphasizing the powdering. See textual note.

206 *Livery*: the distinctive uniform of a servant; liveries indicated
the master's status and wealth.

hack horses: horses hired from a stables; this detail counters
Catharine's high expectations of the visitor.

handsome as a Prince . . . the look of one: this image derives from
the Cinderella story and from contemporary interest in
George, Prince of Wales, officially still unwed though
secretly and morganatically married to Mrs Fitzherbert.

perfect Ease and Vivacity: Mr Stanley is easy and self-assured
when he should be formal; in his vivacity, chatter, and
inattention, he omits proper introductions.

207 *Devonshire*: a large county in the south-west of England, a
great distance from the east of England, from which Mr
Stanley has come.

her to be so: i.e. surprised.

208 *Unreserve*: Catharine does not display coldness, distance,
silence to others; she is willing to be familiar.

go to the door when any one comes: the responsibility of a servant
(preferably male).

smart: fashionably dressed.

209 *extremely welcome . . . Ball*: a violation of etiquette by both
eighteenth- and twentieth-century standards.

travelling apparel: male travelling attire included overcoat
and boots; Stanley has no indoor shoes or pumps.

powder: see note to p. 6.

Lyons: a large commercial city in central eastern France.

linen: shirt and possibly undergarments.

pomatum: see note to p. 6.

the Clock had struck ten . . . the party had gone by eight: eight
o'clock was the normal announced time for evening parties
(see *The Watsons*, 286), though guests generally arrived late.

210 *Prudery*: extreme propriety, implying affectation.

210   *monthly Ball*: not a private party but a subscription ball, as
       had formerly been held at the Crown Inn in *Emma* (p. 177).
       Mr Stanley had not heard Catharine's description of the
       party as a private ball.

211   *the small vestibule . . . the Dignity of a Hall*: the small
       antechamber or lobby is being used as if it were the large
       hall of a manor house, the traditional place for balls and
       other large assemblies. JA suggests the Dudleys' pretension.

212   *Consequence*: 'importance in rank and position' (*OED*).

       Cards: older people were not expected to dance; card tables
       were provided for their entertainment. See Pope, 'Epistle to
       a Lady',

       See how the World its Veterans rewards!
       A Youth of frolicks, an old Age of Cards. (ll. 243–4)

213   *Hunter*: a horse on which he rode to hunt. Hunters were
       expensive horses.

       Brampton: a village in Cambridgeshire.

214   *coming in the same Carriage . . . entering the room with him*:
       Catharine's behaviour violates conservative standards of
       propriety and etiquette. An anonymous author describes the
       disaster which can come to the unchaperoned girl: 'Why
       some pert, forward, impudent young fellow comes up to you,
       and, by his gentle and artful address, insinuates himself into
       your company and conversation; and perhaps you are very
       well pleased with his politeness, and take a turn with him
       around the garden . . . yet do you know who this same young
       spark is? why possibly one of the most notorious and
       abandoned rakes about town . . .' (*The Polite Lady; Or, A
       Course of Female Education: In a Series of Letters, from A Mother to
       Her Daughter* [Philadelphia, 1798], 119).

       led her to the top of the room: to take the head of the line in the
       country dance; a place of great honour: the man of greatest
       consequence leads a woman to be honoured. Mrs Elton, as a
       bride, leads the ball at the Crown Inn, though Emma feels
       that she herself is the woman of greatest consequence
       (*Emma*, 292–3).

215   *tradesman*: see note to p. 153.

       Mr Pitt: the Prime Minister; see note to pp. 203–4.

       the Lord Chancellor: the Monarch's official secretary, the keeper of the Great Seal, the head of the judiciary; the Lord Chancellor ranks below the Monarch, the Princes of the blood, and the Archbishop of Canterbury, but well above the Prime Minister.

216 *I am come out*: young ladies who were 'out' attended evening parties and by mingling with adults announced their marriageability. See Mary Crawford's deliberations on Fanny Price: 'Does she go to balls? Does she dine out every where, as well as my sister's? . . . Oh! then the point is clear. Miss Price is *not* out' (*Mansfield Park*, 46).

218 *impudence*: blatant lack of modesty.

219 *romantic*: 'going beyond what is rational and practical'; 'influenced by the imagination' (*OED*).

221 *the character of Richard the 3^d*: see note to p. 136.

222 *Profligate*: abandoned to vice or vicious indulgence. See the hyperbolic use of the word in *Northanger Abbey* to describe Catherine Morland: she does not advance in music, drawing, writing, French, and accounts and thus displays 'symptoms of profligacy at ten years old' (p. 2).

Blair's Sermons: the sermons of Hugh Blair (1718–1800), Scottish divine, contain sentiments Mrs Percival wishes to inculcate in Catharine. In 'On the Duties of the Young', Blair writes, 'To piety, join modesty and docility, reverence of your parents, and submission to those who are your superiors in knowledge, in station, and in years. Dependence and obedience belong to youth' (*Sermons* [Boston, 1792], i. 187). Mary Crawford refers to Blair's *Sermons* (*Mansfield Park*, 83).

Cœlebs in Search of a Wife: originally JA had Mrs Percival allude to Archbishop Thomas Secker's *Lectures on the Catechism of the Church of England* (1769). See textual note. JA later deleted this title and substituted Hannah More's *Cœlebs in Search of a Wife* (1809). Perhaps JA had second thoughts about appearing to ridicule the Church of England's Catechism, but it seems more likely that the change arose from a desire to mock More's long moral tale about a bachelor (*cœlebs*, cf. celibate) who searches for the perfect wife and rejects young ladies on account of their moral flaws until he finds the perfect young woman. JA had ridiculed the book on its first appearance: see *Letters*, 256, 259.

222 *Library*: either a room or, more probably, a large locked cupboard or bookcase.

the welfare of every Nation . . . hastening it's ruin: Mrs Percival's argument was made repeatedly during the French Revolution and the Napoleonic Wars, when conservative moralists in England fearfully maintained the absolute necessity of enforcing female chastity, modesty, and propriety in order to preserve England against the onslaught of revolutionary ideas and consequent disintegration. For example, in 1802 John Bowles writes, in *Remarks on Modern Female Manners*: 'Of all the dangers to which this country is now exposed . . . not one, perhaps, has so destructive a tendency, as the disposition which manifests itself among the fair sex˙. . . to sacrifice decency at the shrine of fashion, and to lay aside that modesty, by which the British Fair have long been pre-eminently distinguished. . . . [Such lapses produce] a more formidable enemy than Buonoparte himself, with all his power, perfidy, and malice. Female modesty is the last barrier of civilized society' (London, 1802, pp. 11–12). Claudia Johnson discusses such views and their relation to JA's work in some detail, especially in her first chapter, 'The Novel of Crisis', which takes this passage in 'Catharine' as one of its epigraphs (*Jane Austen: Women, Politics and the Novel* [Chicago, 1988], 1).

223 *catching Cold!*: Mrs Percival's caution is outdone by that of Mr Woodhouse, who throughout *Emma* expresses constant fear of sickness. At the ball at the Crown, he will not allow couples to dance across the passage between rooms: 'it would be the extreme of imprudence. I could not bear it for Emma!—Emma is not strong. She would catch a dreadful cold' (p. 223).

224 *Sport*: cf. Henry Crawford's careless wish to make, in his own words, 'a small hole in Fanny Price's heart' (*Mansfield Park*, 206).

what a silly Thing is Woman! How vain, how unreasonable!: a recollection of Hamlet's words to Rosencrantz and Guilden-stern: 'What a piece of work is a man! How noble in reason, how infinite in faculty' (II. ii).

226 *governed by the whim of the moment . . . the love of doing anything oddly!*: here JA provides a sketch like that of Charles Bingley in *Pride and Prejudice*, who demonstrates, in Mr

Darcy's words, 'rapidity of thought and carelessness of execution' (p. 42). As Charles Bingley says of himself, 'if I should resolve to quit Netherfield, I should probably be off in five minutes' (p. 36).

227 *nice*: see note to p. 198.

228 *London as the hot house of Vice . . . gaining ground*: Mrs Percival's sentiments seem to parody those of William Cowper (JA's favourite poet); see his repeated lamentations over the passing of the good old days in *The Task* (1785), e.g.:

> . . . were England now
> What England was, plain, hospitable, kind,
> And undebauched. But we have bid farewell
> To all the virtues of those better days,
> And all their honest pleasures. (Bk. iii, ll. 742–5)

London is the abode of

> Ambition, avarice, penury incurred
> By endless riot, Vanity, the lust
> Of pleasure and variety . . . (ll. 811–13)

Cowper ends Book III with an apostrophe to wicked London:

> Oh thou, resort and mart of all the earth,
> Chequered with all complexions of mankind,
> And spotted with all crimes . . . (ll. 835–7)

(*The Poetical Works of William Cowper*, ed. John Bruce [London, 1896], ii. 91, 93, 94.)

vicious inclinations: i.e. inclinations towards vice, probably sexual; a shocking suggestion.

229 *Lascelles*: a name perhaps suggested by the Whig Thomas Lascelles (1670–1751), quartermaster-general and engineer for the Duke of Marlborough's campaign during the War of the Spanish Succession.

Exeter: chief city in Devon.

Quartered: lodged in private houses; the situation in *Pride and Prejudice* (p. 24). See Mrs Tow-wouse's objection to lodging Joseph Andrews: 'what the Devil have we to do with poor Wretches? The Law makes us provide for too many already. We shall have thirty or forty poor Wretches in red Coats shortly' (*Joseph Andrews*, 50).

Races: players put on their acts wherever people gathered, as at fairs and race meetings, which were rougher and more boisterous than today.

Plan of a Novel

230 *hints ... quarters*: As Southam and Chapman note, the 'immediate occasion' of this 'Plan' was Austen's correspondence (Nov. 1815–Apr. 1816) with the Revd James Stanier Clarke (*Minor Works*, 428). Clarke's commission was to inform the novelist that the Prince Regent would be graciously pleased to have her dedicate her next novel to himself (*Emma* was dedicated to the Prince Regent). But Clarke far exceeded his commission in chattily suggesting themes, topics, and characters to the novelist.

Mr. Gifford: reader for the publisher, John Murray, who read and criticized the MS of *Emma*. See Honan, *Life*, 370.

Fanny Knight: JA's niece; see note to p. 65.

Mary Cooke: JA's second cousin, daughter of Mrs Austen's cousin Cassandra and the Revd Samuel Cooke. JA went about London with her in 1811; see Le Faye, *Jane Austen: A Family Record*, 164.

dark eyes and plump cheeks: perhaps a jocular description of JA herself. See note to p. 16.

Father ... his Life: the clergyman as spiritual hero had repeatedly appeared in eighteenth-century literature, perhaps most notably and heretically in Rousseau's portrait of the Savoyard Vicar in *Émile* (1762). JA is probably thinking also of the good and unworldly father in Ann Radcliffe's *The Romance of the Forest* (1791), a novel heavily influenced by Rousseau. That her own beloved father (d. 1805) had been a clergyman of the Church of England may have made JA the more sensitive to the overdone romanticism of such portraits of clerics, and the more readily amused at Clarke's serious egotism. The imagined clergyman's narrative here jumbles together all the elements Clarke had suggested, often in his own phrases.

Mr. Clarke: see note to p. 231.

Tythes: see note to p. 189.

231 *nobody's Enemy but his own*: Clarke's self-admiring phrase which, as JA is surely aware, he has stolen from Henry Fielding's *Tom Jones*, in which it is a description of the hero (p. 124).

Mr. Sherer: the Revd J. G. Sherer, vicar of Godmersham. B. C. Southam suggests that JA 'was getting her own back on Sherer for his recent censure of *Emma*'; she notes he was 'Displeased with my pictures of Clergymen' (Southam, *Literary MSS*, 82).

Story . . . adventures: a number of novels seem to be drawn upon, including Regina Maria Roche's *The Children of the Abbey* (1798), Mary Brunton's *Self-Control* (1810), Frances Burney's *The Wanderer* (1814), and possibly Mary Hays's *The Victim of Prejudice* (1799).

Mrs. Pearse of Chilton-Lodge: nothing is known of this lady; cf. Southam, *Literary MSS*, 82.

232 *support herself . . . work for her Bread*: in Mary Brunton's *Self-Control*, Laura Montreville relieves her despondent father of financial care and determines to look after them both and pay his medical bills by her own exertions (chiefly artistic): 'Could she but hope to obtain a subsistence for her father, she would labour night and day, deprive herself of recreation, of rest, even of daily food, rather than wound his heart, by an acquaintance with poverty' (*Self-Control*, Pandora repr. [London 1986], 140). JA read Mary Brunton's novel and makes an amused reference to it in a letter of Oct. 1813: 'I am looking over Self Control, again, & my opinion is confirmed of its being an excellently-meant, elegantly-written Work, without anything of Nature or Probability in it. I declare I do not know whether Laura's passage down the American river, is not the most natural, possible, everyday thing she ever does' (*Letters*, 344).

Kamschatka: modern Kamchatka, peninsula at the extreme east of the Asian land mass, acquired by Russia in the eighteenth century. This extremely improbable and chilly location surpasses in Russian remoteness the setting of Mme 'Sophie' Cottin's *Elizabeth; Or Exiles of Siberia* (1806), translated into English in 1809. Mme Cottin's novel deals with the heroine's heroic journey undertaken to save her father. According to an extract from the *Edinburgh Review* printed at the front of the 1810 edition, 'The celebration of filial piety was the object of Madame Cottin. . . . She has contrived to make this noble species of passion so engaging . . that . . . a more romantic feeling is hardly required.'

expires   Enthusiasm: compare the death of the good

missionary and guide Father Paul, Elizabeth's companion, who dies in mid-journey in *Elizabeth*, 136–42.

232 *Mrs. Craven*: Mrs John Craven of Chilton House near Hungerford.

Mr. H. Sanford: Henry Sanford, a friend of Henry Austen.

Verses

THIS LITTLE BAG

234 *This little bag*: this poem accompanied a small bag containing a 'housewife' given by JA to her friend Mary Lloyd when the Lloyds had to move 15 miles away. A 'housewife' was a cloth container for needles, pins, thread, etc.; these were frequently homemade gifts. Joan Austen-Leigh describes JA's bag as 'made of white cotton with gold and black zigzag stripes' (*Country Life*, 28 Oct. 1982, p. 1323).

recollect your friend: not only the 'housewife' proper or needle-book (see note above) but also some accompanying ornamented container for it constituted an appropriate gift from one lady to another. Cf. *Sense and Sensibility* in which the ugly-tempered Mrs Dashwood gives each of the Steele sisters 'a needle book made by some emigrant' (i.e. some French *émigré* or prisoner-of-war, a victim of the French Revolution). Although this is not a sentimental gift, the greedy Steele girls prize the present and want to hang on to it even when they have fallen out with the donor; Anne Steele tells Elinor, 'I was all in a fright for fear your sister should ask us for the huswifes she had gave us a day or two before' (pp. 222, 240).

[THRO' THE ROUGH WAYS OF LIFE]

Thro' the rough ways of Life: in Chapman, *Minor Works*, entitled 'On Capt. Foote's Marriage with Miss Patton'. Captain Edward James Foote, a friend of the Austens, married Mary Patton in 1803.

patten: wooden sole mounted on an iron ring, raising the wearer above the ground and keeping shoes from mud, wet, and snow. JA's nephew J. E. Austen-Leigh informs us that Cassandra and Jane Austen 'took long walks in pattens', adding, 'mortal damsels have long ago discarded the clumsy implement. First it dropped its iron ring and became a clog; afterwards it was fined down into the pliant galoshe' (*Memoir*, 40).

Clog: a heavy wooden shoe; also an impediment, a block or thick piece of wood put on an animal to prevent its running about.

MISS LLOYD HAS NOW SENT TO MISS GREEN

Miss Lloyd: Martha Lloyd, the eldest daughter of the Revd Nowes Lloyd and his wife, was a close friend of the Austens. (In 1828 she was to become the second wife of JA's brother Francis.) Miss Lloyd's mother had died 16 April 1805. Cassandra had gone to help the family in Mrs Lloyd's last illness, and it was probably through Cassandra that JA and her mother heard of the trouble Martha was having in obtaining mourning. As Anna Lefroy's title for this verse ('Lines *supposed* to have been sent to an uncivil Dressmaker') indicates, the verse may not actually have been sent to Martha during her mourning, and was certainly not sent to the dressmaker, Miss Green.

Black Ploughman's Gauze: the adjectival 'ploughman's' indicates simplicity, so the 'gauze' (see note to p. 68) is simply woven without a pattern, and perhaps with a slightly coarse weave; it must be black for mourning.

made up directly: dressmakers made clothing from fabric provided by their customers and according to their instructions.

OH! M^R. BEST, YOU'RE VERY BAD

235 *M^r. Best*: Martha Lloyd had hoped that a Mr Best would escort her to Harrogate; nothing else is known of him.

Harrowgate: Harrogate; an inland watering place in central Yorkshire, north of Leeds. The northern rival of Bath, it had handsome hotels and a Royal Pump Room.

Posting: cost of travelling post, by a hired conveyance which changed horses at posting stations along the way, cf. p. 88 and note.

stouter: stronger, healthier (also perhaps in the sense 'fatter').

Richard's pills: we have no information on these.

Consort's care: care taken of you by your wife.

236 *Newb'ry to Speen Hill*: Newbury, a bustling town in Berkshire nearly 20 miles from Steventon, was a centre of the postal service. Speen is one mile outside Newbury on the Bath

road. Martha Lloyd's aunt, Mrs John Craven, lived at
Speen Hill. JA writes of another village that it 'stretches
itself out for the reception of everybody who does not wish
for a house on Speen Hill' (8 Jan. 1801, *Letters*, 107).

236   *Morton's wife*: unidentified.

Clifton: the Austen family spent part of the summer of 1806
in Clifton, a residential area west of Bristol. JA was pleased
to leave Bath for Clifton, as her letter to Cassandra of 30
June 1808 indicates: 'It will be two years tomorrow since we
left Bath for Clifton, with what happy feelings of Escape!'
(*Letters*, 208).

SEE THEY COME, POST HASTE FROM THANET

Thanet: the north-east corner of Kent is historically named
'the Isle of Thanet', although it is not an island. JA prefers
this dignified name to that of 'Ramsgate', the watering place
and resort town in whch Captain Francis Austen met,
courted, and married his bride, Mary Gibson. JA disliked
Ramsgate, referring contemptuously to the 'Bad taste!' of a
man who wished to reside there, and thought but little of
Mary Gibson and her family (Honan, *Life*, 199–200, 206–8).

Richard Kennet: unidentified.

Stamford-bridge: JA describes the route taken from Ramsgate
to Godmersham Park where the couple, after their wedding
(24 July 1806), were to spend their honeymoon. The
Stamford-bridge referred to here is outside Canterbury, not
the more famous Stamford Bridge in Humberside.

Chilham village: only 3 miles or so from Godmersham, a
beautiful village with timbered houses; the country seat of
Viscount Massereene and Ferrard at Chilham boasted
gardens by Capability Brown.

Pier gate: presumably the main gate of the estate, with gates
set in masonry pillars.

Uncle's Bride: the poem is in the voice of young Fanny
Knight, daughter of Edward, welcoming her uncle Francis
and his wife to Godmersham.

HAPPY THE LAB'RER

237   *Happy the lab'rer*: this comic exercise seems to have been part
of a family game; Lord Brabourne's edition of JA's *Letters*

prints four sets of verses rhyming with 'rose' including those by JA's mother, sister, and sister-in-law Elizabeth.

light-drab: of a dull light brown, made of undyed cloth.

cabbage rose: a double red rose, *rosa centifolia*.

rows: common seats in a church, such as are now called pews, as opposed to box seats for the higher classes.

OF A MINISTRY PITIFUL, ANGRY, MEAN

Ministry: Lord Portland became First Lord of the Treasury in 1807 at a very low point in the war with France. William Windham and the Ministry of all the Talents had hoped for great things from attacks on South America, not least the replenishing of the supply of British gold, but taking a continent was no simple matter, and the diversion from the European theatre was unhelpful. The ministers wanted someone to blame for the failure of their design.

gallant commander: this poem was written in support of Sir Home Riggs Popham (1762–1820), a naval commander who supported William Carr Beresford in 1806 at Buenos Aires, where Beresford and his force were defeated and captured by the Spanish. Popham was reprimanded by a court martial in 1807. He argued his own case, and won a good deal of sympathy; he soon resumed naval duties and, after the Napoleonic Wars, was made a Knight Commander of the Bath. As Chapman remarks in his note (*Minor Works*, 446), JA's interest 'might be personal' as Popham lived in Sonning, Berkshire, where the rector Dr Edward Cooper was the husband of JA's aunt Jane Leigh.

CAMBRICK! WITH GRATEFUL BLESSINGS

Cambrick! with grateful blessings: these verses were sent to Miss Catherine Bigg, fifth daughter of Lovelace Bigg-Wither of Marydown. In 1802 JA had been engaged for one night to her brother, Harris Bigg-Wither. Catherine Bigg married the Revd Herbert Hill in Oct. 1808.

Cambrick: fine white linen, originally made in Cambray in Flanders.

CAMBRICK! THOU'ST BEEN TO ME A GOOD

238 *Cambrick! thou'st been to me a good*: see textual note.

TO THE MEMORY OF Mʳˢ. LEFROY

238 *The day . . . natal day*: these verses form an elegy for Mrs Anne Lefroy, née Brydges (1749–1804), wife of Isaac Peter George Lefroy, rector of Ashe, near Steventon. Anne, a close friend of JA, was killed by a fall from her horse on 16 Dec. 1804; the Austen family heard the news in Bath, where they were living at the time. Dec. 16th was also JA's birthday (b. 1775).

Johnson's death: the celebrated Samuel Johnson, lexicographer, poet, essayist, and critic, also died during the month of December, on the 13th in 1784.

Hamilton: in one MS, JA attributes this remark to Burke. Honan believes JA consulted Boswell's *Life* and found Hamilton to be the real source (Honan, *Life*, 211). The Rt. Hon. William Gerrard Hamilton (d. 1796) was a good friend of Johnson.

'Seek we . . . the Man': the exact words uttered by Hamilton as recorded in James Boswell's *Life of Samuel Johnson* (1791) are as follows: 'He has made a chasm, which not only nothing can fill up, but which nothing has a tendency to fill up.—Johnson is dead.—Let us go to the next best:—there is nobody; no man can be said to put you in mind of Johnson' (*Life*, ed. George Birkbeck and L. F. Powell [Oxford, 1971], iv. 420–1)

'ALAS! POOR BRAG'

240 *'Alas! poor Brag'*: humorous recollection of 'Alas! poor Yorick' from *Hamlet* (v. i).

Brag: 'A game at cards, essentially = "poker"' (*OED*).

Spec: short for 'speculation', 'A round game of cards, the chief feature of which is the buying and selling of trump cards, the holder of the highest trump card in a round winning the pool' (*OED*). In *Mansfield Park*, Henry Crawford teaches Lady Bertram and Fanny Price to play Speculation (pp. 216–19).

MY DEAREST FRANK

Frank: JA's brother, Francis (see note to p. 11).

Mary's safety with a Boy: Francis William, son of Captain Francis Austen and Mary, was born in July 1809.

Mary Jane: first child of Captain and Mrs Francis Austen, born 1807.

'Bet, my be not come to bide': 'Bet, I haven't come to stay', the child's appeal to the nurserymaid (couched in rural language, an echo of the maid's), on his getting up or coming into the room without permission.

Fearless . . . pain: Francis Austen was attracted by hunting from an early age, and 'when seven years old, bought on his own account . . . a pony for a guinea and a half; and after riding him with great success for two seasons, sold him for a guinea more' (Austen-Leigh, *Memoir*, 39).

241 *Donkey's . . . Bray*: this verse is a chief source of information about Francis Austen's childhood; see Tucker, *Goodly Heritage*, 165.

Our Chawton home: JA, Cassandra Austen, and Mrs Austen had just arrived at Chawton on 19 July.

Charles and Fanny: the naval brother Charles and his wife Frances (née Palmer) did not in fact return to England from Bermuda, where Captain Charles Austen was stationed, until 1811.

over-right us: just across the way from us.

'I'VE A PAIN IN MY HEAD'

Beckford: Maria Beckford, the daughter of Francis Beckford of Basing Park, Hampshire, was a cousin of William Beckford, author of *Vathek*. Maria lived in Chawton 1808–12.

242 *Newnham*: Dr Newnham, a physician in Alton, a mile from Chawton.

calomel: mercurous chloride, used as a purgative.

'I AM IN A DILEMMA'

Emma: Emma Plumtre. JA introduces this couplet with the remark: 'Oh! yes, I remember Miss Emma Plumbtree's *Local* Consequence perfectly' (30 Apr. 1811, *Letters*, 278).

Henry Gipps: the Revd Mr Henry Gipps, who married Emma Plumtre in 1812. In a letter of 6 Nov. 1813, JA remarks, 'Oh! & I saw Mr. Gipps last night—the useful Mr. Gipps, whose attentions came in as acceptably to us in handing us to the Carriage, for want of a better Man, as they did to Emma Plumtre.—I thought him rather a good-looking little Man' (*Letters*, 372)

BETWEEN SESSION AND SESSION

242 *Session*: session of Parliament.

villainous Bill: a bill proposing the construction of a canal through the Weald of Kent, between the North and South Downs. In 1809 John Rennie had put forward a plan for uniting the Medway with the Rother, with ambitious extensions to convey timber to dockyards and chalk and lime to the heart of Kent. A more limited plan was sketched out in the Bill of 1811 'for making a navigable canal from the river Medway, near Brantbridges, in East Peckham, to extend to and unite with the Royal Military Canal near Appledore, at an estimated cost of £320,000. It received the Royal assent in the following session; but the project was eventually abandoned' (Robert Furley, *A History of the Weald of Kent*, 2 vols. [London: John Russell Smith, 1874], ii. 662).

Wicked Men's Will: JA introduces this piece by saying, 'I congratulate Edward on the Weald of Kent Canal-Bill being put off till another Session. . . . There is always something to be hoped from Delay' (30 Apr. 1811, *Letters*, 279). It is not clear why Edward Austen (later Knight) and JA were so heartily against the proposed canal, but perhaps Edward felt his own lands endangered, or thought the region would deteriorate under the pressure of such industrial improvements. JA assumes that the developers are looking only for gain at the expense of the country.

'AT EASTBOURNE MR. GELL'

Eastbourne: a fishing town in Sussex which became an army headquarters and a popular seaside resort during the late-century wars with France.

Mr. Gell . . . Miss Gill: we know nothing of these people, save that a newspaper account of their marriage inspired this verse. See textual note.

WHEN STRETCH'D ON ONE'S BED

243 *flounces or hearts*: recollection of 'or lose her Heart or Necklace at a Ball' (Pope, *The Rape of the Lock*, ii. 109).

Peels: or 'peals'; a 'peal of bells': a style of ringing bells in a set of mathematical patterns. Peals are rung to celebrate happy occasions, such as weddings.

Knells: ringing of bells for a death or funeral.

Corse: corpse.

MARIA, GOOD-HUMOURED, AND HANDSOME, AND TALL

244 *Maria*: originally Camilla, referring to Camilla Wallop, who married the Revd Henry Wake at Southampton, on 26 Mar. 1813. See textual note.

IN MEASURED VERSE I'LL NOW REHEARSE

lovely Anna: Anna Austen (1793–1872), the eldest daughter of JA's brother James; married Ben Lefroy in 1814.

Ontario's lake: at 193 miles long, this is the smallest and easternmost of the five Great Lakes. JA describes her young niece in terms of well-known if exotic points of the geography of North America, in the later eighteenth century a popular and even over-used setting: see Charlotte Smith's *The Old Manor House* (1793), Mary Brunton's *Self-Control* (1810), and Frances Brooke's *Emily Montague* (1769).

Niagara's Fall: for Europeans, Niagara Falls symbolized the wildness and sublimity of the new world. See Oliver Goldsmith's description of melancholy British emigrants in *The Traveller, or A Prospect of Society* (1764):

> Forc'd from their homes, a melancholy train,
> To traverse climes beyond the western main;
> Where wild Oswego spreads her swamp around,
> And Niagara stuns with thund'ring sound.

> (*Goldsmith: Selected Works*, 600–1).

transatlantic: 'Situated or resident in, or pertaining to a region beyond the Atlantic; chiefly in European use: = American 1782' (*OED*).

'CHARADES'

245 *Charades*: the Austen family was fond of charades. See textual note. See also 'The History of England', p. 142 and note. The solutions to these three charades are (1) hemlock, (2) an agent, and (3) a banknote. An agent was a steward (or manager of a country estate) or a business agent, both of whom could be expected to rook their employers.

WHEN WINCHESTER RACES

245 *When Winchester races*: Jane Austen, mortally ill, was moved
to Winchester on 24 May 1817, and died there on 18 July.
These verses, written three days before her death, were her
last work. See Henry Austen's 'Biographical Notice', published with *Northanger Abbey* and *Persuasion* (1818): 'She wrote
whilst she could hold a pen, and with a pencil when a pen
was become too laborious. The day preceding her death she
composed some stanzas replete with fancy and vigour'
(*Persuasion*, 2–3). Henry is slightly wrong about the date of
the verses, but is doubtless referring to this piece. See textual
note, and Introduction pp. xxi–xxiii.

races: 'On Monday, 14 July [1817], the *Hampshire Chronicle*
advertised the "WINCHESTER RACES" for horses, mares and
geldings' (Honan, *Life*, 401).

Saint Swithin: bishop of Winchester (d. 862), who did not
wish to be buried in a place of honour, but rather in the
open, where rain might fall. According to legend, Swithin's
body was transferred into the Cathedral on the day of his
canonization, 15 July 971. The saint expressed his dis-
approval of this removal by causing forty days of rainfall.
JA's poem was written on St Swithin's Day, 1817.

William of Wykeham's: William of Wykeham (1324–1404)
was bishop of Winchester and Lord Chancellor of England,
founder of Winchester College and instrumental in the
construction of the Perpendicular nave of Winchester
Cathedral.

Palace: Wolvesey Palace, the former episcopal residence,
destroyed by parliamentary troops during the English Civil
War, rebuilt after the Restoration, perhaps designed by
Wren, in 1684.

sadly in ruins: part of the Restoration building was pulled
down in 1781 (W. Lloyd Woodland, *The Story of Winchester*
[London: Dent, 1932], 258).

246 *Venta*: the Roman name for the camp and town on the site of
Winchester. R. W. Chapman used the word as his title for
this poem in *Minor Works*, 451, although both surviving MSS
are untitled.

command o'er July: legend has it that rain on St Swithin's Day
ensures forty days of precipitation. See the traditional
rhyme:

> St Swithin's Day, if thou dost rain,
> For forty days it will remain:
> St Swithin's Day, if thou be fair,
> For forty days 'twill rain na mair.

(In W. Carew Hazlitt, *Faiths and Folklore of the British Isles*, 2 vols. [London, 1905], ii. 577.) This legend was well known in the eighteenth century: John Gay writes in *Trivia: Or, the Art of Walking the Streets of London* (1716):

> How, if on *Swithin*'s Feast the Welkin lours,
> And ev'ry Penthouse streams with hasty show'rs,
> Twice twenty Days shall Clouds their Fleeces drain,
> And wash the Pavement with incessant Rain.

(*John Gay: Poetry and Prose*, ed. Vinton A. Dearing and Charles E. Beckwith, 2 vols. [Oxford, 1974], i, Bk. I, ll. 183–6; p. 140.)

Prayers

247 *Prayers*: the influence of the Church of England's Book of Common Prayer is everywhere apparent; as a clergyman's daughter and sister, JA attended church regularly, and the family may also have observed daily morning and evening prayers at home. We do not presume to give every allusion to prayer-book services and collects. We quote a Book of Common Prayer from 1771.

hearts . . . lips: cf. the General Thanksgiving: 'that we may shew forth thy praise not only with our lips, but in our lives'.

from . . . hid: cf. the collect which opens the Communion Service: 'Almighty God, unto whom all hearts be open . . . and from whom no secrets are hid . . .'.

Give . . . blessings: cf. the General Thanksgiving: 'And we beseech thee, give us that due sense of all thy mercies, that our hearts may be unfeignedly thankful'.

guard us . . . this night: cf. the Collect for Aid against all Perils, from the service of Evening Prayer: 'by thy great mercy, defend us from all perils and dangers of this night'.

May the sick . . . captives and prisoners: cf. the Great Litany: 'That it may please thee to preserve all that travel by land or by water, all women labouring of child, all sick persons and young children, and to shew thy pity upon all prisoners and captives. . . . That it may please thee to defend and provide for the fatherless children and widows, and all that are desolate and oppressed.'

248 *Fatherly goodness*: cf. a post-communion prayer: 'we thy humble servants entirely desire thy fatherly goodness . . .'.

Give them . . . affliction: cf. Collect or Prayer for all Conditions of Men: 'giving them Patience under their sufferings and a happy issue out of all their afflictions'.

249 *faith and fear*: see the Prayer for the whole state of Christ's Church Militant here in earth: 'And we also bless thy Holy name, for all thy servants departed this life in thy faith and fear'.

brought . . . this day: cf. the Collect for Grace in the service of Morning Prayer: 'O . . . heavenly Father . . . who hast safely brought us to the beginning of this day'.

250 *Keep . . . night*: cf. above, Collect for Aid against all Perils.

safety . . . day: cf. above, the Collect for Grace.

knowledge of thy truth: cf. the Prayer of St Chrysostom, at the conclusion of the service of Evening Prayer: 'granting us in this world knowledge of thy truth'.

JANE AUSTEN	**Emma**
	Persuasion
	Pride and Prejudice
	Sense and Sensibility
ANNE BRONTË	**The Tenant of Wildfell Hall**
CHARLOTTE BRONTË	**Jane Eyre**
EMILY BRONTË	**Wuthering Heights**
WILKIE COLLINS	**The Woman in White**
JOSEPH CONRAD	**Heart of Darkness**
	Nostromo
CHARLES DARWIN	**The Origin of Species**
CHARLES DICKENS	**Bleak House**
	David Copperfield
	Great Expectations
	Hard Times
GEORGE ELIOT	**Middlemarch**
	The Mill on the Floss
ELIZABETH GASKELL	**Cranford**
THOMAS HARDY	**Jude the Obscure**
WALTER SCOTT	**Ivanhoe**
MARY SHELLEY	**Frankenstein**
ROBERT LOUIS STEVENSON	**Treasure Island**
BRAM STOKER	**Dracula**
WILLIAM MAKEPEACE THACKERAY	**Vanity Fair**
OSCAR WILDE	**The Picture of Dorian Gray**

THE OXFORD SHERLOCK HOLMES

American Literature

British and Irish Literature

Children's Literature

Classics and Ancient Literature

Colonial Literature

Eastern Literature

European Literature

History

Medieval Literature

Oxford English Drama

Poetry

Philosophy

Politics

Religion

The Oxford Shakespeare

A complete list of Oxford Paperbacks, including Oxford World's Classics, OPUS, Past Masters, Oxford Authors, Oxford Shakespeare, Oxford Drama, and Oxford Paperback Reference, is available in the UK from the Academic Division Publicity Department, Oxford University Press, Great Clarendon Street, Oxford OX2 6DP.

In the USA, complete lists are available from the Paperbacks Marketing Manager, Oxford University Press, 198 Madison Avenue, New York, NY 10016.

Oxford Paperbacks are available from all good bookshops. In case of difficulty, customers in the UK can order direct from Oxford University Press Bookshop, Freepost, 116 High Street, Oxford OX1 4BR, enclosing full payment. Please add 10 per cent of published price for postage and packing.